Eagle Eyes Trilogy:
Book 1: Violence in Vegas
Book 2: Rescue in Reno
Book 3: Danger in Dallas

By Julie C. Gilbert

Aletheia Pyralis Publishers

http://www.juliecgilbert.com/
https://sites.google.com/view/juliecgilbert-writer/

Love Science Fiction, Fantasy, or Mystery?

Choose your adventure!

Visit: **http://www.juliecgilbert.com/**

For details on getting free ebooks.

Eagle Eyes Book 1: Violence in Vegas

By Julie C. Gilbert

Dedications:

Violence in Vegas:

To Jane L. and the rest of the people attempting National Novel Writing Month in 2016.

And to the Tunnel People of Las Vegas, whose stories may never be heard but whose lives still matter.

Rescue in Reno:

To friends old and new, sharing life together is precious.

Thank you, Erin F. for lending me your amazing eagle eyes.

Danger in Dallas:

For Alycia M.

Do **<u>NOT</u>** try any of the escape methods described in this book.

Note: A variant of each story was previously published as a Kindle Worlds novella.

Table of Contents:

Prologue:
A Simple Assignment

"So, you want something retrieved from this tech guy, but you're not sure what it is, what it does, or where he keeps it." Derrick Belmont paused a beat to let the other man interject as needed. He kept his voice low even though the restaurant was quiet at this early afternoon hour. "How does this qualify as a 'simple assignment'?"

"It's simple for you because all you need to do is turn the job over to one of your little lady friends and let her handle it." Lou Sands—probably not his real name—otherwise known as Steel spoke with exaggerated patience. He sucked down half of his scalding black coffee at once. "Look D, I've got lots of people I can ask. I'm doing you a solid bringing it to you first."

"I get that," Derrick said, trying to keep the snap out of his tone. "But there's got to be more. Since when does the Club care about this sort of thing?"

"Since it's worth a lot of money." Steel shrugged casually.

Derrick perked up at those words.

"How much?"

Technology fell far outside their usual areas of interest. Normal Club business revolved around drugs, women, and games of chance. The mob had never truly abandoned Las Vegas. It had simply slimmed down and changed forms. Even so, things had been changing more since the new leader took over, but Derrick thought the subtle shifts in business policies made sense for the most part. He was hardly in a position to critique. His two business ventures had potential but were going nowhere fast. Besides, he wasn't high enough up the ladder to know the new leader's identity.

"Enough that your Club accounts would be square." Steel gave Derrick a look that had earned him the nickname, and his tone shifted to match the warning glare. "It's got the sort of worth that makes people stupid, but don't let the temptation get to you, man. Like I said, I got other people, but their methods are a little more … direct, if you know what I mean."

Nodding, Derrick held out his hand for Steel to shake. The simple gesture signaled his formal acceptance of the assignment. He really had no choice but to accept, but it was nice that the Club bothered asking. The slow returns from his investments plus his fondness for gambling left him deep in debt.

Steel finished off his coffee and handed over the plain, manila envelope containing the assignment details.

"You need something for the job, you call me, and I'll make it happen."

Accepting the thin envelope, Derrick acknowledged the statement with a tight smile. He knew how things worked. Club jobs always came with plenty of support that doubled as oversight. They would be watching, and if they saw anything they didn't like, they'd step in. The consequences of that weren't pleasant to ponder.

Clearing his account with the Club would be great, but Derrick couldn't shake the feeling this job could be so much more. The restaurant was barely making enough to keep the lights on, and his other business had been recently plagued with every kind of problem imaginable. For a second, he missed the simplicity of his old life.

Should have stayed a college computer technician.

He didn't mean it. That life had bored him.

Except for the women.

College girls were so naïve. It was adorable.

Resting his fingers on the envelope, Derrick waited until the door shut behind Steel before snatching it up and ripping it open. His eyes drank in the details instantly. Unfortunately, the information didn't amount to much more than Steel had used in his pitch.

The target would be Jeffrey Gatton, Founder and Chief Executive Officer of Gatton Technologies. The item of interest was simply known as Eagle Eyes. Derrick knew the name could refer to anything from a new app to sensitive software to a new gadget. He doubted it was an app. The things were so common, the Club would hardly care. As a betting man, he'd place money on it being a gadget.

Software, no matter how powerful, tended not to get people as excited as a good gadget.

About the only new thing in the envelope was a picture that had been ripped from the front cover of a magazine. It featured an average-looking guy in an expensive suit standing between two high-end models.

Habit made Derrick compare himself to the young man.

Money must be attractive.

The kid wasn't much to look at. He had dark, scruffy hair that hung over his forehead and into his eyes. With a bit of styling, the hair could be corralled into subtle waves like Derrick's hair. Young Jeffrey's smooth face looked like it had never needed to meet a razor. The eyes were attractive. Derrick had to admit the pale blue contrasted nicely with the hair. Women would dig that. Dark, smoldering eyes worked for Derrick, but pretty and bright had its charms too. The kid's face looked ridiculously young. In different attire, he'd pass for a high school dropout.

While troubleshooting tech problems for Rutgers University, Derrick had seen many young people just like this one.

Only this one runs a billion-dollar company.

The thought brought on a jealous pang. For a moment, Derrick pictured himself in the kid's place. That kind of money could do so much more for the kid. Whoever he hired to handle his public image ought to be fired.

At his signal, Charlene rushed over to refresh Derrick's coffee. He rewarded her with a small smile then waved her away. He needed to think and research. After fixing his coffee with some milk and sugar, Derrick pulled out his phone and started researching his target. The cup went cold while he immersed himself in one article and blog after another. Interviews were rare, but Derrick attributed that to the reclusive nature of super-rich types. The media loved Gatton.

"That must be *very* interesting for you to ignore me almost a whole minute," said a sultry voice from across the table. "Care to share?"

Derrick's heart seized and his shoulders tensed.

Without waiting for an invitation, Lillian Marquez sat down across from Derrick.

"What are you doing here?" The question sounded more defensive than he'd meant it to.

"I came to see my boyfriend, of course." The woman's tone sharpened.

As he opened his mouth to brush her off, a new idea struck

Derrick. He sat up straighter.

"Oooh, what's that look mean?" asked Lillian.

He hesitated.

She could do it. In fact, she'd probably be the best choice, but Derrick didn't want to share her with anybody, even for a short job like this.

Spotting the picture he'd left on the table, Lillian snatched it up and glanced at the job description below.

"Club business?" Her right eyebrow jumped to emphasize the question. "Do tell." She picked up his ice-cold coffee, took a sip, and grimaced. "Gah! How do you drink that swill? It's a wonder your teeth don't rot right out. It's like drinking a coffee flavored sugar packet."

"It's a retrieval job," Derrick said.

Normally, Derrick wouldn't discuss a job with one of the girls before thoroughly thinking through the choices. Ava or Mallory might be able to handle the job, but they were far less experienced than Lillian. Besides, Lil's position was somewhat unique. She occasionally deigned to run errands for the restaurant or the escort service, but Derrick wouldn't put her in the same category as the working girls.

They'd only been dating a few weeks, though they'd met several months ago, but Derrick knew if he wasn't careful, he might actually fall for this one. That was unacceptable. Giving Lil this job would give him some distance and have her answering direct orders from him. He liked that idea.

Lillian had been the one to introduce him to Steel. He didn't often discuss Club matters with her, but she had a sharp mind and knew an awful lot about how the organization worked. He couldn't pin down her role, but he'd also never found a way to bring it up with Steel.

"I'm guessing Junior here's the lucky guy in the crosshairs," said Lillian. She turned the picture so she could see it right side up. "Who is he?"

Derrick fought down a surge of irritation.

"The target."

"Fine. Don't tell me." Lillian tossed the picture back onto the job description and stood.

The abrupt shift threw Derrick off balance a moment.

"Wait! I think you should do it. The job, I mean."

"Me?" Lillian's expression showed both shock and interest. "Why me?"

"You've got some acting experience. You're gorgeous. And

you're his type," Derrick explained. He pointed to the picture where two models hung on the rich kid. "Steel said we need to pick up something called Eagle Eyes, but we don't know what that is."

"And you think Junior's just going to tell me what his toy is?"

"If you ask nicely," said Derrick, matching her playful tone.

"Steel gave you the job, so you'll probably get credit towards a Club debt, but what do I get out of the deal?"

"I'll be really grateful." He gave her a suggestive grin.

Lillian walked around the table and kissed him full on the lips. It lasted so long that his brain skidded for a few seconds. He hated that she had that effect on him.

"You're going to have to do better than that," she whispered.

"What do you want?" he asked, trying to breathe slowly.

"I expect to be well paid."

"I'll see what Steel can do," Derrick promised.

"Great. Now let's return to a previous part of our conversation," said Lillian.

"Which part?"

"The part where you said I was gorgeous."

"As you wish." Derrick stood and gallantly held a hand out to Lillian. "If you'd like to adjourn to my office, I can find more nice things to say about you."

Chapter 1:
Welcome to Sin City

Grateful to be off the plane and finally have her luggage, Megan Luchek stretched and turned her attention to the issue of finding her ride. Her friend had said somebody would meet her near the luggage claim area for her flight from Honolulu to McCarran International Airport. She'd never had the pleasure of being in this particular airport before, but she wasn't a stranger to traveling.

"There she is!" The loud cry shot through the crowd surrounding Megan and snagged her attention.

Every head whipped toward a kid jumping up and down and pointing frantically.

"I see her. Calm down. We're in public," hissed the lovely lady standing behind the child.

Megan couldn't hear the words so much as read them on the woman's lips. Amusement and relief rushed through her as she recognized the tall, dark-skinned woman. Gathering up her giant suitcase, Megan started to press toward the woman and child.

"Wait, Jaden, you don't—"

The woman cut herself off as the child darted through the crowd and stepped directly into Megan's path.

"Hi! I'm Jaden." The boy glanced back at his mother before facing Megan again. "I'm supposed to ask you how you'd like to be addressed." He thrust out a hand for her to shake.

Amused, Megan released the luggage handle and met the firm handshake.

"Hello, Jaden. I'm Megan." She shrugged. "That works well

enough for me."

"Can I call you 'Agent M.'? Please. Please. Please." The kid beamed her a thousand-watt smile to seal the deal. "That'd sound so much cooler!"

"Sure." Megan thought the title sounded more like an MI-6 title than Federal Bureau of Investigation, but if it made the kid happy, she could live with it for a few days. She leaned away to avoid the boy's wildly swinging arms. The boy did more *hand talking* than her Great Aunt Celia.

"Jaden, quit bothering the lady. She just got off an airplane." Angela Melkin-Pierce gently nudged the boy a step left and leaned down to wrap Megan in a huge hug.

When the embrace ended, Megan grasped her friend's hands and took a half-step back to look her up and down. Angela had always been taller than Megan and had a lot of energy, but now, instead of overflowing, the energy brimmed from somewhere deep inside her.

"You look good," Megan commented.

And she did. Angela's jet-black hair barely brushed her shoulders. Neatly trimmed eyebrows nicely emphasized long black lashes which framed coal-colored eyes that glittered with mischief. High, broad cheekbones balanced the nose and wide smile. A simple, silver necklace hung around her neck.

"So do you!"

Formal introductions went around. The fact that Jaden still had the last name Melkin surprised Megan because she thought Anthony Pierce was going to adopt the boy.

"We'll talk later," Angela promised, seeing the surprise on Megan's face.

Just then, Megan's fingers brushed the ring on her friend's hands, so she flipped the left hand around to inspect the goods.

"I must see this ring." She forced more cheer into her voice than she felt. The tension in her friend's short statement tugged at her heart.

"You already saw it," Angela said. "Remember the zillion pictures I sent you?"

"I do," Megan replied, "but it's so much nicer to see in person."

The thin, white-gold band was studded with tiny diamonds leading up to a large stone in the center. Megan would have studied the ring closer if she wasn't acutely aware of the child bouncing on the balls of his feet next to them.

Letting Angela retrieve her hands, Megan waited, sure the boy was dying to ask something. She suppressed a comment about the apple landing directly at the foot of the tree.

"All right. You can ask her now." Angela shot Megan a half-apologetic grin.

"Can I see your badge? Do you have your gun?" The questions flew out so close together they almost merged.

"I don't have my gun," Megan admitted. It truly felt weird to not have a weapon, but she'd left it behind to solidify her self-promise to relax at least a little on this vacation. "But you can see the badge." Reaching into her purse, Megan pulled out her ID wallet and flipped it open to display the badge.

Angela had warned Megan her son would probably bombard her with questions. Since learning of her visit, Jaden had changed his life goal from becoming a firefighter to joining the FBI.

"We should get on the road. We've got a half-hour drive ahead of us," said Angela.

Jaden didn't react to the words. He stood transfixed, gently tracing the badge with his fingers.

"I think you just became his hero," Angela whispered.

Megan nodded. The glow of working for the FBI had slowly worn off, but she understood the awe the agency could inspire in young hearts and minds.

The moment stretched almost to an awkward point. Angela suggested Jaden give the badge back, and he bargained for a few more minutes. Megan didn't particularly like leaving the badge in another's hands for more than five seconds, but since Jaden was practically glued to her side, she doubted he'd lose the badge between the luggage area and the car.

As promised, he had prepared dozens of questions. Megan felt like she was being interviewed by a crack investigative reporter. After fielding most of the standard questions, they finally reached the one she'd anticipated first.

"Have you ever shot anybody?"

"No comment." She had, but Megan wasn't about to give a ten-year-old boy the details. Her mama had taught her better than that.

"Aww, man!" Jaden said.

"I think that's enough questions for now," said Angela. She leveled a look that turned the suggestion into an order.

They had reached the car. As Megan prepared to wrestle her suitcase into the trunk, her friend reached down and hauled it up and into the space with ease.

The ride from Paradise to Las Vegas, Nevada passed swiftly. The sun had set long before Megan's plane landed. As they neared the outskirts, many bright lights gave the city a magical glow.

"Welcome to Sin City," said Angela.

"What happens here, stays here!" pipped up Jaden. "I wonder what that means."

The women were spared the need to answer because Jaden launched into a dozen other topics over the course of the next ten minutes. Megan half-listened to the chatter and silently wondered where the boy found that many words to fill the air.

Finally, they pulled up in front of a modest-sized building fashioned to look like a Greek palace. A uniformed valet and a bellboy rushed over to help them. Angela greeted both by name, but Megan missed the information because Jaden asked yet another question.

"What made you want to become an FBI agent?"

"I wanted to do some good in the world," Megan answered, falling back on the reflex answer. In truth, she'd escaped a dark time in her life by fleeing to the far side of the world for a short stint in a CIA training program. There, a series of fateful meetings showed her a better path, which led to the FBI.

"Jaden, help George take Megan's bag up to her room, please," said Angela.

"Do I get a tip?" asked Jaden.

The question made everybody laugh.

"George gets a tip," said Angela. "I'll slip it into your locker," she added.

"Thank you, ma'am," said the bellboy. He hustled around behind the car and dug out Megan's bag.

"What about me?" asked Jaden.

"How about a piece of chocolate after dinner?" Angela countered.

"Two pieces," said Jaden.

Megan looked to her friend to see how she would respond.

"He drives a hard bargain," she commented.

"Two pieces, if you clear the plate of everything green." Angela held her hand out to her son. "Deal?"

The boy contemplated the hand before shaking it.

"Deal." He didn't sound very enthusiastic, but he rushed to open the door for the bellboy bearing the luggage.

"I almost forgot. An Amazon package came for you, ma'am,"

said the bellboy, pausing outside the hotel door.

"Thanks, George. That's probably for Jaden."

The boy cheered.

"He wanted some flashlights," Angela explained in response to Megan's questioning glance. "I swear the boy goes through those things like toilet paper."

The valet cleared his throat nervously, capturing both Megan's and Angela's attention. His body language said he had an urgent message and that Angela probably wouldn't like it.

Angela gazed at the door to make sure her son and the bellboy had gone before turning back to the valet. Her shoulders slumped a little.

"Say what you need to say, Phil."

The man's gaze flickered over to Megan.

"She's here to help," said Angela.

Megan didn't think it wise to go announcing that around. She made a mental note to clarify that with her friend later, but the statement put the valet at ease enough to deliver the bad news.

"It happened again."

Angela groaned.

"Room or tires? And to whom?"

"Tires. And it's the Ellisons in room 605."

"Do they know?" asked Angela.

"Not yet. Mr. O'Brien said to keep a lid on it until you could handle it," replied the valet.

Anger caused Angela's posture to stiffen, but she merely gritted her teeth and nodded curtly.

"All right. Have Nancy comp their room for their two-night stay and go with you when you tell the Ellisons about their car," Angela instructed. "Give them vouchers for the restaurant and get written permission to have the car taken to Killian's Autocare to get the tires changed. Assure them we'll pay for the tires."

"Are you sure that's wise?" inquired a new male voice. "We oughtn't admit guilt here. It'll open us up to legal problems later."

"If we take care of it now, they won't have reason to sue us later," Angela argued. Her tone implied that the debate was a rehash of older exchanges. Wearily, she waved from Megan to the newcomer. "Megan, this is our General Manager, Ardan O'Brien. Ardan, this is my good friend Megan Luchek. She'll be a guest here for a week or so."

The portly man gave Megan a minute nod of acknowledgement before opening his mouth to resume his arguments.

Angela held up a hand to stop him.

"Get the details sorted first. Run it by legal if it'll make you feel better. I'll stop by the Ellisons' room in an hour, and I expect to hear good things from them."

The General Manager bristled but spun away to carry out the orders.

"What should I do?" wondered the valet.

"Park the car, then see if Mr. O'Brien needs help," said Angela.

When they were finally alone, Megan let silence reign. Angela took the time to rub her temples wearily.

"This is why I called you," said Angela.

"What's going on?" Megan was too tired for anything but the direct approach right now.

"I honestly don't know," Angela admitted. "Somebody's been causing trouble for about two weeks now."

"What kind of trouble?" Megan pressed.

"At first, it was just odd phone calls—hang ups and the like. But yesterday and today, people's tires have been slashed and a room was ransacked last week."

Megan fired off the usual questions about motive, but she could tell her friend was too upset to give the matter much genuine thought. She halted the interview when tears pooled in Angela's eyes.

"Go throw some cold water on your face. I'll crash in your office until you're ready to talk about it," said Megan.

Her friend was too dazed to argue much. Megan couldn't imagine being able to do much in a case like this, but if her presence helped comfort Angela, she'd count the effort worth it.

Why would somebody sabotage a hotel?

The screech of tires drove the thought from Megan's head. She whirled in time to see a black-clad figure light something and raise his arm to throw the thing.

"Down!" she ordered Angela.

Ignoring her own advice, Megan spared a split-second to regret not having her gun with her. Then, she charged the motorcyclist, screaming her head off like a maniac.

Chapter 2:
Escalation

The mad charge worked as expected. The rider slammed the Molotov cocktail to the ground about ten feet from his bike, directly in Megan's path. A wall of flames eight feet wide and five feet high sprang up in front of her. She skidded to a halt and stared as the motorcycle rider threw a mock salute, revved the engine, and drove off.

Though ticked he'd escaped, Megan silently admitted she had no idea what she would have done with the guy had she caught him. He looked small enough but tackling somebody off a 500-pound bike wasn't exactly a healthy habit.

The flames died out almost instantly as the fire consumed the fuel, but a line of glass shards and scorched asphalt marked where the weapon had struck.

"Are you all right?" Angela asked, squeezing Megan's left arm hard. "What were you thinking? You could've been killed!"

"Not likely," said Megan. She stepped back, not wanting Angela to get too near the glass. "He probably couldn't have hit us from that distance. Molotov cocktails aren't the most aerodynamic weapons."

"What was that?" asked Jaden. Excitement and curiosity rang clear through his question.

Fear entered Angela's eyes. She let go of Megan's arm and ran to intercept her son.

"Stay back," she called.

"Why?" Jaden sounded disappointed.

"Because there's glass everywhere out here, and we don't want you getting hurt," Megan reasoned. She pulled out her cell phone and snapped a few pictures of the debris. One of the glass shards held part of a label. She took three pictures of the partial logo. It didn't tell her much, but somebody would recognize it.

"What are you doing?" Angela's question held all her weariness and a fair amount of alarm.

As Megan briefly explained the odd behavior, she became aware of the growing crowd. People started firing standard questions, but she ignored them in favor of focusing. Kneeling near the bulk of the glass shards, Megan closed her eyes and pictured the scene in her mind. The figure lit the item in his hands and cocked his arm back to throw. When she'd started running at him, he hesitated. He'd waited for her to approach within range, and then launched his weapon.

This was a warning, but against what?

Police sirens told Megan that she'd have official company soon. Wondering what had been used as a fuse, she scanned the ground until she spotted the remains of a white cloth. Not much of it remained, but she thought it might be a cloth napkin like one would find in a fancy restaurant. She had no jurisdiction here. The locals had no reason to share information, and since nobody had been hurt in the incident, Megan seriously doubted much of an investigation would be launched. With her final moments of alone time at the crime scene, Megan turned the cloth napkin several ways and snapped half a dozen pictures. She thought part of a logo might be hidden among the char marks, but that could also be wishful thinking.

"Who called the cops?" Angela's question didn't really have a target, but a male voice answered anyway.

"I did." Ardan O'Brien's bold tone held more than a hint of challenge.

Sensing her friend could use some backup right about now, Megan pocketed her phone and slipped up beside Angela.

"Ask anybody who saw the incident to stay. The police are going to want to speak with them but get the general onlookers back inside. They're only going to get in the way."

Angela looked ready to cry, but she gathered her courage, raised her arms for attention, and addressed the crowd.

"If you witnessed what just happened, please stay for a moment. Otherwise, return to the hotel."

"Is it safe?" asked an old woman.

"I'm not staying here another night!" cried a young woman.

The declaration sparked a debate that quickly rose in volume and tempo.

"Don't be ridiculous," chided a different young woman.

"At least at the Hilton we won't be firebombed," argued the first young woman.

"*You* weren't firebombed," Megan pointed out. "An empty patch of pavement was hit. There's no immediate danger. Go back to your rooms."

"Who are you? You can't order us around," said the hyper woman.

"Please, Ms. Stewart. It's not an order," said Angela. "It's a request. Please retire to your room, the bar, or the gaming tables. We need to make room so the police can do their job and leave as quickly as possible. Then, my people can deal with the broken glass."

"Do we get free drinks?" asked a young man.

The question angered Megan, but Angela responded coolly.

"Mr. O'Brien will sign soda vouchers for anybody who returns to his office right now."

Mr. O'Brien looked like he'd swallowed a rather potent lemon.

"Aw, I was hoping for a real drink," complained the young man.

"I think there's been enough alcohol out here recently," Megan commented.

"Lame," muttered the man.

"Free is free, man," consoled the guy's friend. "It's kinda early to start drinking anyway. There's plenty of time to get wasted later."

Megan thought they both looked young enough that the bartenders would have to card them before serving *real* drinks.

As the police arrived, the crowd slowly dispersed. Angela made sure Jaden went with one of the staff. Soon, only Angela, Megan, and a little old lady were left in the parking lot.

"Did you need something, Mrs. Ellison?" asked Angela.

"No. No, dearie," said the white-haired, bespectacled lady. "I wanted to thank you for the lovely gifts and assure you we don't hold you responsible for what some hoodlums did to our car."

The woman's speech gave the police officers time to approach, but they politely waited for her to finish speaking before introducing themselves and asking for details. Mrs. Ellison took her leave and shuffled off, leaving Megan and Angela to deal with Officer Eric Wentworth and Sergeant Nigel Vickers.

Megan let Angela handle most of the description of events. She considered not telling them her occupation, but decided to work it into the conversation so they'd give her observations more credence.

"The perp's on the small side, but he—or she—knows their way around a motorcycle. They're also right-handed if judging solely on how they handled the Molotov cocktail. I'm not sure what the perp's initial intentions were, but when I rushed him, he settled for this statement."

"You're lucky he didn't want to take you out," noted Sergeant Vickers.

"A device that size couldn't do much damage," said Megan. She shrugged to downplay the danger.

"Maybe not to a structure," agreed Sergeant Vickers, "but it could have done a lot of damage if it broke on you. You ought to be more careful, Agent Luchek."

The man was starting to sound like her boss, but Megan knew he meant well.

"Has anybody made any threats?" inquired Officer Wentworth.

"No," Angela answered.

"Have there been any other incidents?"

Angela hesitated but nodded.

Both officers grew still like drug dogs alerting on a big find.

"How many incidents have there been? And what was the nature of them?" asked Officer Wentworth. He looked ready to fling a few more questions, but a look from the sergeant calmed him enough so Angela could answer.

"There have been two—maybe three—odd phone calls within the last month. Two customer cars have had their tires slashed, a room was ransacked, and now this." She waved to the glass fragments glittering under the streetlights.

"Do you have any enemies?" Sergeant Vickers voiced the question, but Megan wanted it answered too.

"Not that I know of," said Angela. She drew a breath, held it a moment, then released it slowly in a bid for time. "We turned down an offer to buy the hotel six months ago, but other than that, we haven't had any issues with anybody."

The officers put forth a few more probing questions, but Angela had little more information to add to the conversation. When they finally left, she had Phil Douglas—the valet—fetch some maintenance people to clean up the mess.

Angela probably would have borrowed a broom to help if Megan didn't convince her to retreat to her office to recap. In minutes, they both had glasses of ice water in hand and were seated on the comfortable couch in Angela's spacious office.

With great effort, Megan concentrated on her drink, holding questions in to give her friend time to process and organize her thoughts. The effort finally paid off.

"What will we do, Maggie?" Angela's question barely qualified as a whisper. Now that they were safely locked in the office, her emotional guards started slipping.

Megan didn't particularly enjoy the nickname "Maggie," but she could tolerate it from exactly three sets of non-family people: Special Agent Ophelia Pitman, Angela, and Dan Cooper's family. Ophelia could get away with calling people whatever she wanted because of her uncanny ability to obtain nearly anything an agent could ever want. Angela and Megan's friendship was old enough to get a pass on the issue, and Dan's kids were excused on cuteness. Dan knew better than to try it, but his wife could use it in the interest of not confusing the children. Even then, Megan wasn't simply *Maggie*, she was *Aunt Maggie*.

"What do you mean?" Megan pressed.

Silent tears worked their way down Angela's face. She grabbed a wad of tissues and sopped up what she could before attempting more words.

"Anthony's away in Reno trying to sooth skittish investors, and meanwhile, everything's falling apart."

"What's the financial situation?" Megan wondered. She suspected she knew the answer, but the fact needed to be aired.

The question made Angela wince.

"We're so far in the red, it'll take a miracle to come within miles of the black again," she reported.

"Why didn't you sell a few months back?" Megan tried to ask the question delicately, but it still felt like lobbing a sledgehammer at her friend.

"We weren't technically the owners then. Anthony's grandparents wanted the business to go to him since his father had died relatively young without other heirs." Angela wiped more tears from her cheeks. "We didn't really have the money to buy the hotel from them, but they've were kind enough to help us work with the bank to get reasonable terms on a loan." She attempted a half-smile that fell flat. "We're all in here. If this business fails, we'll be broke, and worse, Anthony's grandparents will have nothing to retire with."

"Can you think of any other reason somebody would cause this sort of trouble?" Megan felt like she was running on a hamster wheel, but she wanted Angela's mind off the financial issues for the moment.

"No."

"Phone calls to tire slashing to messing with rooms to tossing Molotov cocktails is a serious escalation," Megan noted. "What's going on at the hotel this weekend? Could the perp be trying to disrupt one of the meetings you're hosting?" She was throwing random ideas around at this point, but the possibility of a new motive intrigued her.

"I'm too tired to pull the files right now, but I'll get them to you tomorrow," said Angela.

Megan wanted to dive into the investigation right now, but Angela looked like she needed some distracting girl-talk instead of further case discussion.

"Fair enough, but I expect a thorough tour to follow this file feast on the morrow." Before relaxing, Megan had one more serious question to ask. "What's your security set up here?"

"What do you mean?"

"I saw several cameras. Who monitors them? Do you have live guards too? Are they armed?"

"We have a few dozen guards on staff," said Angela. "They watch the cameras from the control room at the end of this hallway. They're mostly retired police officers, except for Henry. He's more of a relic. Anthony's grandparents sort of took him in when his parents died in a car accident. That's how the Alley got started. They gave him a job and let him stay. When hauling bags got to be too much for him, they moved him over to security. Monitoring the cameras was a whole lot less stressful."

Megan thought that was a terribly stupid way to pick your security guards, but since most establishments were more interested in catching cheaters than criminals, it made sense to invest heavily in monitoring equipment. When the current crisis ended, she'd have a word with Angela about updating the hotel's security.

Kicking off her shoes, Megan spun and tucked her feet beneath her legs so she could face her friend.

"I'm tired of shop talk. It's only been eleven or so years since we've had a heart-to-heart. Tell me about this hot man I've never met."

Chapter 3:
Only You

Derrick Belmont frowned down at his phone. He'd been with Lillian Marquez not more than two hours ago. She could be needy sometimes, but a call now could only be about business and probably wasn't good.

"What's up?" he asked, going for casual. "Did you settle in at the hotel?" He'd decided she should take up a post at the hotel and linger until a chance encounter could be arranged with the target.

"Do you know who I just saw?" The tension in Lillian's voice executed any sense of casualness he might have been feeling.

"Look, Lil, I don't have time to play games. Tell me."

"Megan Luchek."

"How do you know that name?" The question came out by reflex. The word *stunned* failed to adequately describe Derrick's feelings at hearing the name.

"That doesn't matter. Why is she here?" Lillian's tone entered a frosty state.

"How should I know?" he responded.

"You keep tabs on her." The statement flew out like an accusation.

How do you know that? Derrick narrowly held that question in, but it showed that Lillian knew way more about him than he was comfortable with.

"She's led an interesting life." He winced at the defensive—and quite pathetic—response.

"If I find out she's here with you, we're through," said Lillian.

"There's nothing between us, Lil. Whatever we had ended years ago." Despite his words, the thought of Megan brought a strange rush of feelings that tightened his chest.

"Good. Because when I say 'we're through,' I mean you and me *and* you and the Club. Got it?"

"There's only you, baby," Derrick said in a soothing tone. "Concentrate on the job at hand. The target will arrive tonight or tomorrow."

She grunted and ended the call.

Derrick stared down at his phone. The short conversation gave him a lot to think about. It might be time to move on from Lillian and the Club, but he'd have to settle his accounts with the Club first if he wanted the exit to be peaceful.

He went over to the liquor cabinet and poured a few fingers of whiskey. Sitting at his desk was depressing. Besides the usual junk, it seemed to be dominated by bills. Derrick took the drink over to the large leather reading chair situated on the far side of the room. This office was much more impressive than the one he kept at the restaurant. He kept it for appearances sake for the few occasions when he had to entertain a potential investor or some other VIP.

Before the liquor even had a chance to relax him, Derrick's thoughts wandered to Megan Luchek. She'd been the most beautiful mistake he'd ever made, and the only woman who had ever walked away from him.

Fled.

Their affair had been brief but intense. He'd left his old job because of the rumors swirling around after her abrupt departure. Much as he hated to admit it, she'd come to mean a lot to him during those months. The knives, the control issues, and the mental games were merely tools meant to break down barriers, allowing their souls to merge.

She hadn't exactly bought in to the lessons.

If he closed his eyes, a mental image of Megan immediately filled his mind. She'd been nineteen the day she walked into the computer help center to get a jammed USB out of her laptop. At the start, she'd been a vibrant, happy young woman, little more than a child really. Her long brown hair, wide eyes, broad smile, and beautiful body still had the power to stir him up from the inside out. By the end, she'd been moody and withdrawn.

He could have fixed that if she'd let him.

Thoughts of Lil intruded on his memories. He'd never let a woman think she had any control over him, even the few times in his life where it was true. Lil was different. She knew she had the advantage. He needed to break free in a big way.

She had to go.

The simple conclusion hit his gut the same time as the whiskey, lending him a glowing warmth. The feeling was both relaxing and empowering. He swallowed a large gulp that made his eyes water then finished it off with a more cautious series of sips. Normally, Derrick would walk away. He'd left lots of women in his wake. The trick would be in ending it and remaining on good terms with the Club. Like it or not, he needed them to keep his businesses afloat. He couldn't let Lillian ruin a good thing.

But she had threatened him.

That kind of behavior could not be tolerated. Still, he had to make it look like part of the job gone wrong without actually derailing the job. He couldn't afford to not complete the contract.

Am I really trying to think of ways to kill my girlfriend?

It struck him that Megan wasn't the only one who'd changed dramatically in the eight or so intervening years. She'd gone from aimless college kid to CIA recruit to world traveler to FBI agent in that timespan. He'd gone from lowly computer technician to semi-successful businessman to part time retrieval expert for the reimagined mob in Las Vegas.

Who can I trust?

Derrick spun the empty whiskey glass in his hands as he thought. Unfortunately, Lil had way more Club contacts than he did. It couldn't be anybody remotely connected to Club business. That presented another problem since the majority of the contractors he used for the shadier side of the escort business came to him through the Club.

He couldn't afford an official assassin, which meant he'd likely end up doing the job himself. He really didn't want to do the job himself because that would require going to the hotel. Lil would get suspicious if she saw him there. He could excuse his presence as keeping tabs on the job. She wouldn't like the explanation, but she'd buy it. Then again, going to the hotel would run the risk of seeing Megan.

His heartbeats quickened at the possibility.

No woman should ever have that effect on his head. A surge of anger nearly had him throwing the whiskey glass across the room.

Maybe Dante would help.

Derrick paused to consider. Dante's boys ran a small but profitable strip of the Vegas drug trade. Derrick had heard rumors that for the right price they'd take on other odd jobs too. He didn't trust drug dealers as a general rule, but most of them were businessmen too. Lil never did drugs. If she did, that would make this so much easier. Maybe it could be that easy. He could get some of Dante's boys to give Lil an overdose of heroin or cocaine.

Cocaine. Might as well go with the cheaper stuff.

Derrick kept modest quantities of the drugs on hand for special customer requests, but he wasn't going to deliver it anyway. The boys would have to bring proper paraphernalia to make the overdose scene stick.

On the other hand, Dante's boys might stick out approaching a respectable hotel like The Grand Game. Maybe Derrick was better off getting one of his girls to deliver the goods. That he could arrange easily enough as long as he timed it right so Lil and the girl never crossed paths. Derrick discarded the idea with a frustrated grunt. A girl could get the drugs to Lil safely enough, but that brought him back to the problem of getting Lil to use the drugs. He could throw some sleeping pills into her coffee then inject her with the drug, but that would require him meeting her in the hotel room.

That's the best you can come up with?

Derrick's mind worked itself through a few circles of why Lil needed to go, how the deed could be done, and what other details needed sorting before he could break away from the Club. Knowing his mind worked best when allowed to wander, Derrick spent some time fantasizing about where he'd go next and what he would do when he got there. He'd started life on the East Coast and spent much of the last decade in Nevada.

Continental U.S. life bored him. Maybe he'd spend some time abroad or visit the Hawaiian Islands. He had decent sums of cash stored up if he cut all ties with the restaurant and the escort business. A lot of people would be disappointed, but as long as the Club was satisfied, nobody would come after him. The bank would sell the restaurant space, and the Club would probably be more than happy to distribute any product left behind.

Hawaii made him think of Megan again. The repeated tendency to dwell on her was disturbing. Maybe she'd have to go too.

He dismissed the thought almost immediately. He'd read enough of her recent exploits to know he wanted nothing to do with tangling with the FBI Special Agent version of Megan Luchek. In the interest of avoiding her, he needed to know more about her presence at the hotel.

He'd have to check the payroll to see who among the hotel staff would be suitably loose of lip to tell him about her.

Are you here officially or unofficially?

A memory of his lips on hers intruded. Derrick forced himself to his feet. He had a lot of phone calls to make. He couldn't waste time dwelling on the past.

Chapter 4:
Scraping for Suspects

Megan had never faced a case quite like this. For one thing, nobody was shooting at her. That made identifying suspects a little harder. As much as she didn't enjoy the *getting shot at* part, she had to admit straightforward cases were easier on the head.

"Your suspect pool stinks," Megan complained.

Angela Melkin-Pierce smiled sympathetically.

"I really don't think the problem's with anybody staying at the hotel."

She topped off Megan's glass of ice water from the carafe sitting on the coffee table next to them.

"I know, but we're assuming that the target for the harassment is the hotel," Megan gently argued.

"We are the target, aren't we?" Angela asked.

"Probably, but we can't be certain of anything yet." Megan idly wiped sweat from the side of her water glass. "All right, let's go over the groups one more time then we can choose a strategy for actively waiting for the bad guys to make their move." Angela's confused expression prompted Megan to explain further. "It means we wait but not while sitting on our hands, so that when they make a move we can respond."

She waved for Angela to take her cue. The files scattered around them told her each major group, but Megan had always been a fan of hearing things aloud.

"The hotel has three hundred and eighteen rooms, two hundred and fifty-three of which are currently booked. That's lower than I like, but we have a small convention of birdwatchers coming in today that should fill in some of the gap."

Seeing the relevant file sitting on the stack right next to her, Megan picked it up and flipped it open.

"Reno Birdwatchers Society," she murmured.

"Yes. They're regulars," said Angela. "They hold their annual conference here. The timing varies a little, but it's usually sometime in the first quarter."

Megan skimmed the booking information for the group before tossing the file aside.

"Next."

"The other three organizations holding conferences here this week are the Paradise Quilting Club, West Coast Writers, and Gatton Technologies."

The first two of that list were obvious as to what the conferences would focus on, but the third was a mystery.

"Tell me more about Gatton Technologies," Megan prompted. "What's on their agenda?"

Angela shot Megan a puzzled look.

"I'm not sure. We don't demand to know what they're doing when they rent the event space."

"They must have special requests," Megan pressed. "Number of chairs, types of refreshments, access to electrical outlets. Stuff like that." When Angela didn't immediately fill the air, Megan asked another question. "Do you know who's on their guest list?" Once again, she had to elaborate. "Shareholders, all employees, officers only?"

"I don't know off the top of my head, but I can find out for you," said Angela. "I think they're the ones who wanted a projector, sparkling water, and only green olives, not black ones. The past few weeks have scrambled my brains though so I could be crossing them with a different group."

"It'll be good information to get," said Megan, "but let's move on for now. Who else stays at the hotel?"

Angela relaxed visibly at moving into familiar conversational territory.

"Vegas runs on tourism. We don't really have an off season, though weekends are always more expensive. Over the years, Sin City's built up a reputation that sort of speaks for itself. At any given time, one can count on a steady stream of honeymooners, wedding parties, college kids, general tourists, and gamblers, of course. Convention attendees are probably the biggest bulk group, but smaller operations like ours can't always attract the major convention players. We simply don't have the necessary space." Angela paused to take a drink of her water and give Megan an apologetic smile. "Sorry, didn't mean to sound like a tour guide."

"How many conventions are in town at any given time?" That question served more to satisfy Megan's curiosity than anything else.

"There's a full list on the Las Vegas Tourism website, but if I remember correctly, it's well over a hundred a month. They range from a couple of dozen attendees to over 10,000. That's what I meant when I said we didn't have the space to handle large conventions, but we still benefit sometimes."

"Meaning …?" Megan tried to wrap her mind around a convention that big.

"Some of the regular convention goers book their room here even though we're not an official sponsoring hotel for their event. They like the relative quiet, and we have a modest rewards program that keeps some of them coming back."

"Do you handle all the event booking?"

"Yes, it's been my job for the last three years," Angela blushed. "That's how I met Anthony."

Megan nodded. Angela had told her that story the previous evening.

"What's the easiest job for me to take on that will get me into these conventions?"

"You want to go undercover?" Angela sounded alarmed by the notion.

"It'll be the easiest way to investigate," Megan said, confirming her intentions with a nod.

"You don't have to investigate. Really. We'll be fine." Angela's protests were half-hearted at best.

Reaching out, Megan placed a hand on her friend's knee.

"Your tone tells me you need my help," she said gently. "Besides, I did not fly over 2500 miles to play card games and drink cocktails, though there might be time for that later in the week."

"Thanks for coming, Maggie."

"Uh-uh. None of that until we figure out this mess." Megan wanted to return to the question of motive. "Now, if the hotel is the target, then what's your best guess at a motive?"

"The sale that was turned down," Angela answered immediately. "The Grand Game Hotel might not be the biggest or the flashiest hotel, but we're located on prime real estate. Somebody less attached to the sentimentality of the place might tear it down and build something three times as tall and pocket millions later."

"That's a heck of a motive," Megan admitted. "But is the harassment you're experiencing the brand of pressure needed to get you to sell? Wouldn't the potential buyer be the first suspect?"

"It's rapidly headed that way," said Angela. "But we can probably hold out another few months as long as Anthony can shore up the investors' nerves. If any of the key backers withdraw, we'll be in trouble." She drained the rest of her water then toyed with the glass for a few seconds. "As for the buyer being a suspect, we'd probably never meet the real buyer. They'd come at us through a lawyer and probably a shell company or two." She offered a one-shoulder shrug. "That's how most buyouts work in this city."

Megan pondered the problem. In her very limited experience with this sort of thing, the harassment seemed mild. Somebody motivated by millions to get a company to sell could probably come up with a better plan than cold calls, wrecking tires, and making a mess with a Molotov cocktail.

"If the hotel's not the target, who or what is?" Megan wondered, not really expecting Angela to have an answer.

"Of the official guests we have, I'd say the tech company," said Angela.

"Why?" Megan sat up straighter and stared hard at her friend.

"On the whole, they probably have more money than the birdwatchers and quilters," Angela pointed out. "The CEO's a billionaire, I think."

"Is he coming?" Megan asked.

"He's coming," Angela confirmed. "I only know that because he's the one who called about the olive stipulation."

"Why didn't you mention that first?"

"Money has different meaning here," said Angela. "If you run down Main Street, you'd probably run into a dozen celebrities and a half-dozen millionaires trying to be seen without being seen."

Megan had no trouble working through the logic. She'd visited New York City enough times to understand the mentality.

"Tech company; got it. So, what's my job?"

"I guess you could be a waitress, if you want." Angela grimaced. "I'm going to have to make you sign some papers to officially hire you though or Ardan's going to have a coronary on me."

"Not a problem, but I can't accept any money. My tax guy will throw coconuts if I need to report alternate income. I mean that literally. He's got a good arm and decent aim. My poor baby car still has a dent from his last hissy fit."

"That's an interesting way to deal with frustration."

"What can I say? Hawaii attracts all kinds of eccentric people."

A man walked by the window on stilts.

"This place has some interesting people too," Megan noted, staring out the window.

Angela followed her gaze.

"Oh, that's Donny Lira. He handles light maintenance duties. He used to work for one of the circuses until a training accident put him out of commission for a few months. After that, companies were reluctant to hire him again. He doubles as a clown and comedian as necessary."

"You get requests for clowns?" Megan asked. She'd always assumed society as a whole had come to its senses and concluded clowns were creepy and should be best left to horror movies.

"Maggie, we get requests for everything," said Angela. "Most requests are odd, but some are illegal and others would make Sister Mary Ellen turn beet red. It's the price of doing business in Vegas."

Getting up, Angela went to her desk and rummaged through some papers in the bottom left drawer.

"Let's get the paperwork signed," she said, pulling out a clipboard and a pen. "For my tax purposes, I have to pay you something, but you can donate it to a charity if you wish. We can deal with that later. Hopefully, you won't be working here long."

"Gee, thanks, boss," said Megan, taking the clipboard and starting to fill in the job application. "Do I at least get a uniform?"

"Only if you end up working in the casino," replied Angela. "There's a Roaring 20's theme in the game room. So staff uniforms are era appropriate."

"You want me to dress like a flapper?" Megan asked, both intrigued and horrified by the idea. She stopped filling in papers long enough to level a questioning look at Angela.

"We have an entire room of impressive costumes that are close enough to pacify most of the clientele. We only have to be careful about what is worn when the historical society holds their convention here. Most other people wouldn't know fashion from the 1920's vs. the 1930's or any other decade for that matter. The only problem I can see is footwear."

"I'm sure I have something," said Megan honestly. She resumed her paperwork duties. Shoes were the one area of her wardrobe never lacking since her mother's obsession for shoes often translated into random gifts. Megan counted it one of the perks of being the baby. Her older sister, Tara, had been very up front about having zero interest in their mother's taste in shoes. Megan felt much the same but didn't have the heart to burst their mother's bubble. The lady needed something to obsess over besides the current lack of grandchildren. Presumably Tara and Jason were working on that, but Megan wasn't going to hold her breath. The end result was spare shoes for Megan. Even on a quick trip like this, she had brought a good supply of evening and casual wear.

"Oh, that's right. I forgot about your mother's collection. How are your folks?" asked Angela.

"Dad's enjoying his retirement," Megan said. She'd last seen her folks around Christmas, but she was overdue for a long, quality conversation with them. "Mom's slowed down on the shoe front, but now, she's experimenting with hobbies and that's driving him crazy. I guess that means things are normal with them."

After dealing with the legal side, Megan followed Angela on a tour of the hotel. They agreed that only a select few should know of Megan's true purpose here. Angela promised that the few who already knew would be sworn to secrecy posthaste.

The costume room lived up to its reputation. Megan signed out two evening gowns, one in the flapper style and another more modern dress. Angela promised that several nights they hosted all-era mixers where the staff chose outfits from any decade, including projections of future fashions. Next, Angela handed responsibility for Megan's orientation off to Lisa McAdams. Megan had insisted on that step since it wouldn't look right for her to be getting preferential treatment.

"Welcome aboard, Ms. Luchek. We're glad to have you with us," Angela's greeting doubled as a farewell in this instance, but the warm handshake conveyed her gratitude.

Megan hoped she wouldn't let her friend down.

Chapter 5:
Proxy

"Been waiting here a while," Steel complained. "Where you been?"

"I had some business to take care of," Derrick replied coolly. He shut his office door, trying hard not to slam it. This wasn't the first time he'd returned to the restaurant and found Steel in his chair. "Needed to check on the girls. What do you want?" He eyed Steel's boots balefully. Checking on his girls had only been part of his nightly errands, but he couldn't trust Steel with his plans for Lil. Steel would likely side with Lil over him, which was a shame because Derrick liked the man.

Taking the hint, Steel removed his boots from the top of the desk.

"Got a new angle for this retrieval job. Thought you might wanna hear about it."

"I'm listening." Derrick leaned back against his closed door and folded his arms. He refused to sit in his own guest chairs.

"We got lucky and intercepted the proxy on his way to the hotel. I've got people sitting on him, but I don't think he knows much about the product. It's very hush-hush, but that's not unusual with stuff like this."

"If he doesn't know much, how did we get lucky?" asked Derrick.

"You can pass for him."

It took Derrick an extra beat to absorb that information.

"Me?"

"Yeah, the tech kid doesn't know what the buyer's proxy looks like, only what he'll be wearing. You're about the same build as the guy,

29

so you can take his place. Once you find out what you're looking for either take it or send Lil in to get it."

"Can I talk to the real proxy?" Derrick figured it would be easier to impersonate the guy if he knew more about him.

Steel shrugged and stood up.

"You can if you want, but I can also have one of my guys get you a file with details tomorrow. You're going to need to know what the buyer's cap was and what kind of contact he's supposed to have with the real buyer. He's being very cooperative. Do you still want to see him?"

Curious about the inner workings of the Club anyway, Derrick agreed.

"You're going to have to go blind," Steel warned as they threaded their way through the empty restaurant.

Derrick felt a thrill of excitement. He didn't see the point in the cloak-and-dagger part, but it made him feel important to be taken to a secret lair.

Steel led the way out to a black SUV with tinted windows and opened the back door. Derrick climbed in, knowing the tinted windows would be painted over on the inside. A small screen showed him Steel's face a moment later as the man climbed into the driver's seat. A moment later, the screen died as Steel turned it off.

Hoping the screen worked as a TV, Derrick pressed a few buttons along the bottom. Nothing happened. He settled in, not knowing how long the ride would take. Two minutes into the ride he got bored, so he tried to roll down the window, forgetting that he couldn't. It would have been nice to be able to see the city go by. He didn't often get a chance to be chauffeured around, and Las Vegas at night still had the power to impress him.

Pulling out his phone, Derrick pressed the power button.

"That's not going to work in here," said Steel through an intercom built into the passenger seat.

"Why not?" asked Derrick.

"The vehicle's equipped with a jammer. I let you keep your phone as a courtesy, but I'm going to have to ask you to put it away."

Steel neglected to give an *or else* scenario, but Derrick understood that one lingered in the air anyway. The excitement for the trip faded quite a bit at the phone announcement, but Derrick endured without complaint. He guessed they didn't want him checking the location on Google maps or something. It annoyed him, but at least, the policy made sense.

Without being able to check his phone, Derrick had a hard time keeping track of the passing time. He guessed the ride lasted less than a half-hour, but without knowing a direction, that meant very little to him. He could be almost anywhere in the city at this hour. Vegas had a livelier night scene than most cities, but it still had quiet hours where traffic wasn't the bear it could be at civilized hours.

Finally, the SUV stopped, and Steel let Derrick out. As expected, they were in an underground parking garage. To Derrick's great surprise, the place had an abandoned feel to it. With space at a premium, an abandoned parking lot was a foreign concept. A second surprise followed a few seconds later when Steel led Derrick to an old maintenance door instead of an elevator. After tapping gently, Steel waited until a man opened the door for him. Derrick didn't recognize him. The stranger didn't look armed, but he wore a nice suit that could easily conceal a handgun. With an earwig and appropriate shades, the guy could impersonate a secret service agent.

The path beyond the door led downward. Soon, the path broadened from a normal, hallway width to a larger tunnel. Even though the ceiling was higher here, Derrick fought a sense of claustrophobia. The ground was cement with puddles of water pooling here and there. The smell of mold and mildew made Derrick stick to the center of each tunnel. Somebody had installed lights at regular intervals, but they merely outlined the path without really providing enough illumination to see much of the surroundings. He suspected there wasn't much to see down here.

"Where are we?" Derrick didn't expect an answer, but he needed to ask anyway.

"Doesn't matter," said Steel. "We're almost there."

Their journey continued through a maze of tunnels. Derrick tried to memorize the twists and turns, but quickly gave up. He stuck close to his guide, knowing he could easily get turned around and lost down here. A vague recollection of tunnels beneath Las Vegas came to mind, but Derrick pointedly held questions in. He didn't want to sound needy.

Eventually, Steel stopped in front of a wooden door. The finish looked too new and unblemished to have spent long down in the dank atmosphere. Once again, Steel's gentle knock obtained an immediate response.

Derrick's eyes widened at the scene that met his eyes. The room beyond the door was probably twenty feet by twenty feet, but it seemed crowded. A bare mattress had been shoved up against the back wall with a bucket and a sink in the far left corner. The far right corner held a serious-looking hose. The floor sloped inward toward the center where a bloodstained drain sat in front of a wooden chair.

On the chair sat an exhausted, terrified man. He had a split bottom lip and a black eye, but otherwise, he seemed intact. Although not bound to the chair, the man looked quite content to continue sitting there.

The man who'd answered the door appeared annoyed at the interruption, but he adjusted his attitude upon seeing Steel.

"What'd you learn?" asked Steel.

"Lots of nothing," replied the guy. He tilted his head back to acknowledge Derrick's presence.

"Derrick, this is Holder. He's our temporary jail keeper," said Steel.

"Please. Just let me go," whispered the guy in the chair. "I've told you everything."

"This ain't personal, and you're gonna get out alive if you cooperate," Steel assured the prisoner. "But unfortunately, you gotta stay here until the job's done. My colleague's gonna need to know enough to be you, so start talking."

The prisoner made a noise that had the essence of a growl and a grunt.

"I don't know much." Genuine frustration came through clearly. "I was asked to go to The Grand Game Hotel and meet Jeff Gatton about a huge, secret deal."

"Who's your employer?" Steel questioned.

"I don't know," replied the prisoner. His expression conveyed exasperation and resignation. "That's not as unusual as it sounds. I run errands like this to supplement my income. It's good money."

"How does that work?" Derrick had a tough time buying the guy's ignorance.

"I run a few internet ads that lead to my website, people call the number, they pitch their needs, and if I take the job they pay a setup fee and fifty percent of the total cost. When I fulfill their requirements, I get the rest of my money."

"What did this buyer want?" asked Steel. "Was the buyer a man or a woman?"

"Everything was handled online, so I'm not sure if it was a man or woman. I don't ask if they don't offer that info." The prisoner shifted in his chair causing it to creak. "The buyer said the CEO of Gatton

Technologies would have a prototype called Eagle Eyes for sale. I was to meet him and work out a deal to buy it. Negotiations like this are kind of my specialty."

"And Gatton knows to meet you?" Derrick pressed.

The prisoner shook his head.

"He only knows that my employer is sending somebody from my company."

"How is he supposed to recognize you as the potential buyer's associate?" Derrick voiced the question, but he sensed Steel would have raised it soon anyway.

"The company's called Desert Gophers. I have T-shirts and polos with a suitable logo."

Holder pointed to the right corner behind Derrick where a suitcase leaned against the wall.

"That part checks out."

"There's gotta be more," said Steel. "Dangerous deal or not, nobody would trust something that vital based on recognizing a T-shirt."

The man kept a fairly decent poker face, but Derrick saw him wince a little.

Holder must have seen it too because he crossed over to the chair and placed a large hand on the prisoner's right shoulder. He didn't say anything, but he put enough pressure into the grip to make the guy whimper.

"All right! All right! I'll tell you." When Holder let go, the prisoner muttered, "Geez. No job is worth this." He huffed indignantly. "I'm supposed to wait at the bar from six to eight tomorrow night. If nobody shows, I'm supposed to go down to the gaming room from eight to ten. If anybody approaches at the bar, I'm supposed to ask about a drink called Lucky Number Nine. If anybody approaches down in the gaming room, they're supposed to ask about whatever gaming table I'm at. I'm supposed to tell them to forget whatever I'm playing and try the craps tables. Obviously, I'm not supposed to play craps."

Derrick could hardly believe his ears. The whole thing sounded like something out of a kids' spy novel.

"How does Gatton know what to look for and what to say?"

The prisoner looked at Derrick curiously.

"Did you establish that or did he? How was initial contact made?" Questions crowded Derrick's mind. "And why do they even need you?"

"I set up the codes with one of his assistants." The prisoner spoke in a slightly wounded tone. "I've been to that hotel before, and I've wanted to try that drink for a while."

"And the thing with the craps table?" asked Derrick.

"I suck at the game," said the prisoner. "Seriously, it was a favorite in college because I won the first time I tried it. Ever since then, I've done nothing but lose money on it."

The interrogation continued for another half-hour, but they didn't learn much new. The return trip to Derrick's restaurant flew by because his mind was occupied with details of impersonating the prisoner. He wondered why they didn't ask the prisoner's name. Given the stupid company name, he could probably find out easily enough. He pulled out his phone to look it up.

"No," said Steel.

Derrick muttered an apology and tucked the phone away again. To take his mind off not using his phone, he placed mental odds on the prisoner's chances of surviving. They hadn't blindfolded the guy, but he didn't strike Derrick as the sort to seek justice. If he made it out alive, he'd probably lay low. Still, the only true way to silence somebody was permanently. Derrick tended not to have anything to do with that side of the business, but he knew it existed.

Chapter 6:
Code Blue

Megan Luchek spent the rest of the morning with Lisa McAdams learning the ins and outs of working for The Grand Game Hotel. She finally got that thorough tour of the building thanks to Mr. Radcliff, one of those regulars Angela had mentioned. He demanded all hands on deck to help haul his baggage to his third floor room. When asked what was in the cases, he shot the inquirer a dirty look and yelled at another kid hauling bags. Megan helped where she could, but mostly, she tried to stay out of the way while Lisa organized the small baggage handling crew into an efficient team. Megan meant to ask Lisa what the cases held, but the opportunity never arose.

Normally, orientation would last a few days, but the roster was thin enough to make McAdams not question Angela's order to waive the usual processing procedures. After all, Megan did have legitimate experience as a waitress. Drunks in bar settings were the same the world over.

As part of the cover story, Angela had Megan's luggage moved down to the Alley, a string of rooms on the first floor that the hotel rented out to certain struggling workers. In the privacy of Angela's office, the woman apologized a dozen times, but Megan insisted on full immersion. She needed to get the other employees to trust her as quickly as possible. The room might not be as nice as the other one, but she'd come to work a case, not sit in a pretty room. To that end, she'd talked her friend into giving her a skeleton key. They'd waged quite a discussion over that point. Electronic locks weren't supposed to have such a thing as skeleton keys, but if technology can create something it can break it too.

After a light lunch in the café, Megan started her first shift as a waitress. Her waitressing experience was sorely out of date, but she knew enough to get by. Lisa had wanted to start her down in the gaming room, but upon request from Angela, she made room on the rotation for Megan to work the Gatton Technologies welcome meeting. The CEO was a no-show, but the General Manager rolled with it. Megan got the feeling the man was well-practiced at handling his boss's eccentric behavior. There could be a legitimate reason for Jeffrey Gatton missing his own welcome party, but she doubted it.

Standard fare speeches and intriguing chatter flowed around the room but told Megan precious little real information. She quickly determined that the sixty-two employees present were excited to be a part of something big, but they had no idea what the big announcement would be about. The company struck Megan more as a think tank than a company that turned out a particular type of product. The boss man was generally revered and respected but not really understood.

As Megan handed out drinks and appetizers, she observed the conference attendees. She didn't possess the people-reading skills her partner—Daniel Cooper—did, but she had learned a few tricks by hanging around him. She spotted two pairs of people likely having affairs with each other, three guys playing video games on iPads, six people texting, and about two dozen people checking their social media pages. Although the conference attendees mostly knew each other, they wore helpful nametags. To pass the time, Megan tried to think of a reason somebody would go after the hotel to somehow hurt the tech company. She came up blank.

The meeting didn't really *end* as much as *relocate* to the bar and game room. Megan took a brief break to eat something and change into her night uniform. She chose one of the flapper dresses she'd picked up from the costume room. It was black with inch-wide blue, metallic stripes running down the front and the back. A four-inch black section of lace ran around her waist right at the hips. More metallic blue stripes flowed down the skirt. She paired the outfit with a pair of Walter Steiger pumps that matched. Despite the height to them, they were surprisingly easy to wear for long periods of time. Even though the FBI insisted its agents dress formally, the practicalities of the job precluded most of Megan's shoe collection.

Since these were mostly the same people she'd served in the conference room, Megan had a little fun by affecting a New York accent as she took people's orders. Her memory skills were stretched by the sheer volume of information, but she did well and was rewarded accordingly with decent tips.

Throughout the evening, Megan milled about handling small odd jobs as needed. Serving drinks, picking up empty glasses, fetching small plates of food, cleaning tables, and directing people to and from various gaming opportunities occupied her time. She got very familiar with the gaming room, which basically ran the length and width of the hotel's basement.

Certain games like poker had private rooms along the sides. Most of the gaming tables were grouped by type with mini-bars strategically set up near them. Each drinking station had a few high tables where people could stand and have a snack if they wished. The slot machines were grouped near the main entrance. Thick, velvety curtains divided the room to help confine the noise of each type of game to its section. Soft beams of light from antique lamps created a refined, elegant atmosphere for people to spend their money in peace. A more extensive bar and restaurant were located on the first floor, but a well-stocked offshoot was located in the first private room on the gaming floor.

Megan wasn't officially assigned to the bar in the gaming room, but she did visit often to pick up and drop off orders. Aware of her surroundings, she noticed one woman in particular giving her dirty looks. She tried to imagine why, but when no answers came, she contented herself with watching from afar. Generally, Megan could care less what people thought of her. The job of FBI agent came with enough nutcase encounters to give one a high tolerance for hostility. Still, this woman's irritation seemed personal. Megan searched her brain hard for past run-ins, but she was positive she'd never met the lady. That could mean Megan reminded the woman of someone or they had a mutual acquaintance.

The young blonde sat in a corner by herself nursing a vodka cranberry. Whenever she spotted Megan, she'd stiffen ever so slightly, but otherwise, the lady seemed to be enjoying her own company. From time to time, single men would stroll by her table and try to strike up a conversation. The woman would flirt for a few minutes before gently sending the guy packing, usually with a dumb grin on his face.

Finally, the woman got up to leave. She didn't ask for a bill, so Megan assumed she had an open tab connected to her room. Curious, Megan slipped over to the computer and glanced around. Finding nobody near, she swiped her brand new employee card to access the console. It took a few seconds for Lisa's quick lesson on working the machine to kick in, but eventually, Megan fumbled her way through the recent entries until she found the correct table and noted the room number.

I'm due for a break anyway.

It was approaching 11:30. A new wave of people would storm the casino around midnight. Megan figured she should take her break while a natural lull existed. Finding the nearest punch clock took her a minute, but then, she hustled up to room 414. Since the stairwell was far closer than the elevators and probably less traveled, Megan chose to take the labor-intensive way. She removed her shoes before attempting the ascent. The climb gave her a few minutes to ponder her next move. She wasn't sure what she'd do when she reached room 414, but curiosity drove her forward.

Upon reaching the correct floor, Megan put her shoes back on, straightened her dress, and caught her breath. She'd missed her morning workout due to her meeting with Angela and felt a shot of guilt along with the slight burn.

Walk with confidence.

The miniature pep talk was enough to get Megan to exit the stairwell and start toward her target room. As she tried to act casual, a figure tore out of a room at the end of the hallway and darted toward the far stairwell. Megan paused and mentally replayed the two-second look. Her pulse quickened. Judging by height and shoulder width, the figure was likely a man. His speed indicated he was in a heck of a hurry. However, the distance was too great to know much more than that.

A quick glance at the door numbers combined with a brief calculation and gut instinct, told Megan that the man had come from the room she wanted to visit. Her footsteps quickened accordingly. Six hundred-dollar shoes or not, Megan needed to be in that room immediately.

The door was closed with a Do Not Disturb sign hanging from the handle.

Megan hesitated. She wasn't certain she wanted to blow her cover this quickly. Taking off her earrings, Megan figured she could give the woman a story about finding the earrings and thinking they might be hers. It was lame, but she lacked the time to spin quality fiction. Holding her breath, she knocked firmly.

No response.

She knocked louder.

Still nothing.

Praying Angela would forgive her, Megan unlocked the door with the skeleton key and cautiously swung it open. The place looked like somebody had let a drunken monkey have a party in there. A bottle of champagne had tipped over on the end table and slowly dribbled its contents to the ground. The coffee table was askew with white powder lines arranged at one end. Small plastic bags holding more white powder littered the floor near the couch. A heavy leather chair had tipped over. The bedsheets were half on the floor, and the pillows had been tossed near the TV.

A body lay at the foot of the bed.

Recognizing the woman from the bar, Megan raced forward and dropped to her knees. Visual assessment showed a needle sticking out of the woman's upper right arm. The state of the victim's clothes said there had been a knock-down brawl before it got to that point. That explained some of the furniture rearrangements.

Emergency training asserted itself. Carefully, Megan removed the needle to prevent any more of whatever was inside it from getting into the lady. After confirming there was a pulse, Megan administered CPR for a minute then called 911 and the front office from the room phone. As instructed, she resumed CPR.

Angela arrived well before the emergency medical technicians, but Megan persuaded her to return to the ground floor to guide the EMTs to the correct room. Once help arrived, Megan gratefully turned over the responsibility. They used an AED to jump start the lady's heart before stabilizing her and packing her up to take to the hospital.

A responding police officer grilled Megan and Angela on how the woman got in her current condition. He wasn't pleased that Megan had removed the needle, but he grudgingly accepted it needed doing.

"You've had quite an eventful few days," Officer Kain noted.

Angela nodded miserably.

"So it seems," she murmured.

When the officer finished taking pictures and finally left, Angela collapsed onto the couch and cradled her head in her hands.

"I don't know how much more of this I can take," she said.

"Do you think it's related?" Megan wondered. The thought hadn't occurred to her until Angela's despairing cry. After considering the woman's actions and replaying the man's abrupt exit, Megan shook her head. "It's a big, fat coincidence, but I don't think it's related to your troubles."

"You don't?" Angela's question sounded hopeful. A moment later, her expression turned worried. "Does that mean I have two sets of problems?" She looked ready to faint at the prospect.

"I'm not sure," Megan admitted. She wished she could encourage her friend, but she refused to sugarcoat anything.

"It's a good thing you were here to save her. It would have been awful if she had died at the hotel." Angela blushed. "I mean, her dying would be bad on its own, but ...."

"You don't have to explain," said Megan. She understood her friend's meaning perfectly. "What I don't get is this." She waved to the room around them. "We were probably meant to think she would die of an overdose of some sort. It seems ... elaborate and expensive, yet sloppy."

The impressions didn't jive very well with each other. Megan hadn't worked many homicides in her career, but crime of any stripe required means and opportunity, both of which cost something. Perpetrators didn't bother unless they had weighty grievances with somebody.

How could somebody that young and beautiful make such a motivated enemy?

Although Megan believed her assurances to Angela about the incident not being hotel related, she couldn't shake the odd sensation that it had something to do with whatever had the woman casting dirty looks all evening.

That meant a personal connection to Megan.

Chapter 7:
Dilemma

Dante's report filled Derrick with rage and fear. His mind raced. His first instinct was to drink the Scotch straight from the bottle until it was gone. He resisted the temptation because he needed a clear head. Self-preservation instincts kicked into overdrive.

"You're fired," he said. The words felt great coming out.

"You can't do that, man!" whined Dante. "We had a deal."

"Yeah, we did, and your guy screwed up the job."

"He wants to finish it," said Dante. "Just say the word and it's done."

"If it was that simple, it would already be done. What does he want?" Derrick could guess, but he wanted Dante to say the words. He knew Dante was waiting for the invitation. Verbal dances struck him as stupid, but they were a part of his life.

"Chick's in the hospital. She gonna be harder to finish there. He wants an extra two grand above the final payment."

"No deal. The contract terms were clear. One thousand down and four more upon proof of completion. He either finishes the job or I report it to the Club as an incomplete assignment."

Dante cursed then chuckled, calling Derrick's bluff.

"Man, you suck at lying. This ain't no Club contract. I don't do those. My boy says he can finish and dispose of the body in the hospital, no questions asked. He's just gotta pay the maintenance guy a fee for letting him down with the furnace for a while."

Derrick wanted to turn the offer down, but it would take care of the body issue. The less the Club had to work with, the more they'd have to take Derrick's word for.

"I need to think about it for a few minutes. I'll call you back when I've made a decision." Without waiting for a response, Derrick disconnected the call.

Tossing his phone onto the couch, he stood and stretched then rubbed his temples.

Either move was risky.

Going with this modified plan would essentially be doubling down. If he followed this path, Derrick would pay the extra money and have to hope that the man who couldn't do the job correctly the first time would come through on a promise. The amount of required trust was worrisome, but the promise was indeed tempting. The Club might suspect foul play in Lil's demise, but they shouldn't be able to connect it to him. The longer the messy business dragged out, the more chances it had to unravel. Lil might be higher up the food chain than Derrick, but neither of them was high enough for much of an investigation to be launched.

Something had to be done quickly. Dante's report of Lil being unconscious was already old news. She would eventually wake up. The hotel insider said one of the new cocktail waitresses had stumbled upon Lillian minutes after the attack. Derrick silently cursed the meddlesome do-gooder.

If Lil woke up, she'd figure out what had happened. Derrick could pretend nothing happened. He'd have to call her cell phone a few times to place messages. Then, he could claim to have gone to the hotel, heard what happened, and tracked her down at the hospital. The scenario would get him to her bedside where he could do some damage control or take her out himself. He had far more control over this plan, but which was a better option?

He could brush off her suspicion, placing blame on the trauma. If he played the hand right, Derrick might even come out looking like a hero to her. Then again, letting her live at this point would be more dangerous than if he'd made no move.

If he couldn't allay Lil's suspicions, he could expect trouble with the Club. They wouldn't simply forget the debts he owed them. If they stopped sending him jobs to slowly work off the tremendous debt, they would expect repayment in full, including their ridiculous interest and fees. His businesses might about cover the debt in terms of sheer monetary value, but they'd kill him and put their own people in place.

Personally, killing Lil in the hospital would be doable, but it left the problem of many witnesses. Derrick didn't know enough to arrange for something subtle. Getting in would be easy. Getting out without being traced to the murder, would be nearly impossible.

Derrick had always hated relying on other people, but he wasn't a huge fan of doing dirty work. Murder definitely fell under that category.

Do I really need Lil dead?

Part of him still sort of liked her. Getting rid of her in a furnace that handled medical waste would be thorough, but it would be such a waste of a great body.

Could I sell her?

The tiny thought sailed in out of nowhere. Derrick sank down onto the couch as it took root and spread in his mind. He'd had a similar thought a few days earlier and dismissed it because most of his people suppliers worked Club contracts too. He'd worked hard to keep his operation independent of Club business, but they'd been there to help him set up. Naturally, most of their recommendations came through previous experience rather than reputation.

Most of his suppliers hated surprises, but Yves might jump at the chance. If memory served Derrick, Yves too had once owed the Club big time for his business. He might welcome the chance to get back for the hard times they'd put him through. Lil's father likely even had a hand in that deal if he was a Club man during the right decade. She'd never told Derrick much about her father, but his reputation preceded him.

Snapping up his phone, Derrick unlocked it and navigated over to the keypad. He hesitated. Yves wasn't exactly the nicest guy and trying to predict his mood was impossible. If Derrick caught him at the wrong time, he could turn around and alert the Club to the proposal.

All life's a gamble.

Derrick placed the call.

"Derrick! Salut! Quoi de neuf?"

Hi. What's up?

It took a second for Derrick's brain to accomplish the French translation. His maternal grandmother had refused to speak any other language but French, so he'd once had a solid grasp on the language. Decades of disuse made him rusty, but he quickly settled into the conversation. Simply being able to speak French competently had given Derrick an advantage when dealing with Yves.

"I have a job to discuss with you. Can you stop by or would you prefer to discuss the matter over the phone?"

"My end is secure. How is your end?"

"Let me call you back on a burner phone." Derrick wasn't sure why that hadn't occurred to him first. He was getting sloppy.

Two minutes later, Derrick had re-established phone contact with Yves on a disposable phone. They picked right up where they'd left off.

"What are your thoughts on Lillian Marquez?" asked Derrick.

"Your lady friend?" Yves question was cautious.

"I'm thinking of moving on, but she doesn't seem to be on the same page as me. And that's a problem because a lot of my business contacts would side with her if she asked them."

"Women. Always trouble," commented Yves.

"I need to know what you think of Lil because my job offer has to do with her."

"Ah, you want me to take her off your hands, don't you, my friend?"

"It would be a tremendous help," said Derrick.

"I would like to help, but you'd have to understand and appreciate the risks involved," Yves began.

"How much?" asked Derrick. Normally, he enjoyed the negotiation phase, but he'd wasted a lot of time and needed to get back to Dante soon. Thoughts of receiving a payment vanished. He'd be lucky to get by paying the rest of Dante's fee. The diversifying drug lord would not be happy to be outbid, but he couldn't exactly complain to anybody who mattered. The Club would kill him for taking a contract on one of their own, and the police tended to frown upon murder-for-hire jobs.

"Fifty thousand."

"One thousand."

"Forty thousand, but only because you are a friend."

"Five thousand. You can make a tidy profit by selling her overseas anyway." Derrick was prepared to go to ten thousand, but he held hopes Yves would have mercy on him. "You did say blondes move well over in Asia."

"That I did. Okay, my friend, you have a deal, but you have to deliver the product."

"Ten thousand and you do the retrieval yourself," Derrick countered.

"Retrievals can cost way more than five thousand dollars," Yves complained.

"She's at the hospital. I know you've moved people from there before."

Yves sighed theatrically.

"I may have a way to do this," he admitted.

"You've seen Lil. You know how much she's worth on the open market. I don't have time to get multiple bids to make this happen, but don't pretend you're being cheated here. My only demands are that it's done tonight, and it never comes back to me. She becomes a random woman who disappears into the abyss."

"I can make her disappear," Yves promised, "but not tonight. I have previous obligations and it is almost morning. There's a shipment leaving the continent Friday. I'm moving some cargo for the Club. I can have my people slip her into the mix."

"I don't want the Club anywhere near this," Derrick protested.

"They won't be," Yves assured. "I have access to some of their holding cells, but the staff guarding them is on my payroll, not the Club's. They're allowing me use of the space in exchange for a discount on my services."

Derrick didn't like the idea, but he wasn't really in a position to negotiate the point. As long as no Club members got anywhere near Lil, it should be fine.

"Either keep her unconscious or keep her quiet," Derrick instructed. "She can't be allowed to talk to the other women."

"They're not all women, but your point is noted, my friend. You will not regret hiring us."

"I expect standard commission for a premium referral," said Derrick, deciding to press his luck. "A target like this is rare."

A referral of this magnitude would usually be worth 5% of the sale price. Slave markets didn't exist like they did in ages past. But the right connections could still mean excellent sale prices. Bored princes, millionaires with fetishes, and many other categories of men—and a few women—paid dearly for their living toys. Connected women like Lil didn't often fall into the types of situations Derrick and Yves were talking about. Aside from her father, who was in a nursing home, Lil didn't have much in the way of family who'd care if she fell off the face of the Earth. Her work associates were all Club members who knew the risks in the business. They would wonder and perhaps mourn her loss, but they wouldn't seek justice for her.

"If the sale goes well, I will give you half a standard commission rate for a premium referral," said Yves.

Derrick's heart leapt at the news. He might not be able to retire on the money, but if they won the buyer lottery, he'd get a couple of thousand dollars. He'd honestly expected Yves to tell him he'd get nothing.

Business done, Derrick endured a few minutes of small talk before closing the conversation. He wanted nothing more than to sit back and fall asleep on his comfortable office couch. But his night wasn't over yet. Dante still needed to be called to get his guy to back off. Having too many people on the job would increase the risk of problems arising.

As expected, Dante hated Derrick's decision. His ruffled feathers were soothed a little by the news that Derrick would pay a thousand dollars severance directly to Dante if he could control his attack dog.

A check of the safe told Derrick he couldn't afford many more nights like tonight, but at this point, he couldn't afford to let the plan fail either.

It would be best for everybody. Lil would live, Yves would make money, and Derrick would be clear with the Club.

As he moved to put down his phone, Derrick received a text message from Steel saying they had a new plan. Somebody would pick him up in an hour and take him to the debriefing location.

Chapter 8:
Uninvited Guests

Billionaires. They're like spoiled toddlers.

Despite deep reservations about billionaires, Megan Luchek had to admit they knew how to throw parties. If she ever wanted to retire from the FBI, she could always work for Angela. Who knew event planning could be so darn complicated?

On the way to the hotel from the airport, Jeffrey Gatton decided he wanted to host a masquerade party that evening. Upon arrival in a stretch limousine, he informed Angela of his grand idea and turned over a credit card for them to use while making the arrangements.

Angela Melkin-Pierce cleared her whole schedule to get on the phone and start planning. Lisa too dropped her normal plans. Her to-do list involved mustering the necessary staff for the party and preparing the space.

"I want only the most competent and best-looking people working my event tonight," Gatton insisted.

"We only hire competent people, Mr. Gatton," said Lisa.

"Yes, yes. That's all well and good. But if they're ugly or over forty, keep them out of the room," said Gatton.

"I'll see what I can do," Lisa promised.

"That's not good enough. I want to see pictures before the party opens. Oh, and invite all the pretty women staying here tonight."

"I'll arrange for an invitation to be printed, but for legal reasons, I can't hand out staff information," said Lisa.

Megan happened to be heading to Angela's office at that moment, which is how she overheard the conversation.

Gatton grumbled, but Lisa handled him with practiced patience.

"I will personally handle the staff list," she assured him.

"Fine, but if any ugly people slip by, I reserve the right to kick them out. The same goes for the additional female guests."

Megan missed the rest of the conversation as it moved into Lisa's office. She didn't envy the woman's job this morning.

"Is he always like this?" Megan asked, once she'd firmly closed the door to Angela's office behind her.

Angela held up a finger and shot Megan a harried smile. She rolled her eyes and nodded yes, but she couldn't respond verbally because she was on the phone. Mouthing an apology, Megan flopped down onto the couch to wait. A large arrangement of irises took over the coffee table. Although a bit much, Megan admitted that they went well with the tasteful oil paintings of similar flower arrangements strategically placed around the room. From Angela's side of the conversation, Megan gathered her friend was hashing through details with the caterer.

"Mr. Gatton's never been a customer here before, but from the three conversations I've had with him, I'd say 'yes,' he's always like that." Angela placed her phone on her desk with care. "It's going to be a long day."

"That's why I'm here," said Megan. "I saw his grand entrance. What can I do to help?"

"Say you'll work the party tonight," answered Lisa, entering the room briskly. She checked that the door had shut tightly behind her. "Once Mr. Gatton learned you were our newest cocktail waitress, he demanded you work the event tonight. Would you mind?"

"Of course, I want to learn more about the man anyway," said Megan. She imagined that his attitude could generate some enemies, but she wouldn't know more unless she got close to him.

"He's insufferable," Lisa declared. She went on to explain exactly what Gatton wanted in terms of guests at his masquerade party.

"If you get tired of dealing with him, send him my way," said Angela. "I'll do the same. Maybe we'll both finish the evening with at least a shred of sanity."

"I hate to ask it, but can you work tonight too?" asked Lisa. "He's insisting only young and beautiful people work at the party, and you're the only one besides Aliana who knows the house specials. Jack and Benny can help, but they're new at bartending."

"I'll be there," Angela promised.

Megan marveled at her friend's fortitude. Arranging the party meant getting black masks, ordering extra cases of Dom Perignon champagne, obtaining blue and silver balloons, finding an outside caterer, a DJ, a photographer, a florist, and a videographer. If she was lucky, things would come together by late afternoon. The party wouldn't kick off officially until 10:30, but if she planned on working there, she'd need time to dress the part.

Showering them both with thanks, Lisa left to continue her duties.

The party wasn't the only thing going on at the hotel, just the largest and most pressing event. Megan reiterated her desire to be given work to do and was assigned the task of wording the invitation. She whipped up a reasonable invitation in forty minutes, but it took another two hours of tweaks before the twit was happy with it. Then, she had to go to a print store to get three hundred and fifty color copies made. They had to be done manually because the print company needed three days' notice on jobs of that magnitude. By the time she finished giving the fliers to the bellboys who would distribute them room to room and post them around the game room, exhaustion crept over Megan.

She took a brief nap and ate a quick meal. Her scheduled shift in the game room was canceled so she could rest before the party. Instead of relaxing, she spent the time with Angela and Jaden prepping for the party. He wanted to attend, so with his mother's permission, he brought the matter up with Mr. Gatton. Megan expected the young man to pitch a fit, but he took a shine to Jaden and magnanimously granted the request.

Angela found a tuxedo in the costume room for Jaden to wear. He was given permission to attend the party for an hour, but then, he had to go to bed since it was a school night. After fixing the boy's hair, she sent him down to the game room with a few extra fliers to drum up some interest in the event. It felt a bit like a sleepover. Despite the slight age gap between them, Megan and Angela had been close in middle school and high school. They helped each other into fancy evening gowns borrowed from the costume room.

After much debate and several different outfits, Angela settled on a royal blue gown that flowed down to the floor, hugging her body until it reached her knees. Silver jewels decorated the straps an inch above the bust. Although long enough to hide the shoes, she wore a pair of silver pumps borrowed from Megan.

In a daring move, Megan went with a deep red, sleeveless gown that had quite a bit of flow to it. A small section at the center of the bust was more gray than red. It fit her form nicely through the torso down to the waist before flaring ever so slightly. She'd considered a few dresses with straps but decided the greater range of motion would be appreciated, especially if she had to haul trays around all evening. She chose her shoes for comfort rather than looks since she would likely be on her feet until the early morning hours.

The last major preparation feat was fixing their hair. After attending to her hair needs, Angela expertly braided, twisted, and finally pinned the bulk of Megan's hair in a fancy updo. It took thirty-two pins to accomplish, but the results were stunning.

Things started off beautifully. The ballroom had been decked out in silver and blue balloons. Tables alternated blue cloths with white napkins and white cloths with blue napkins. A tall champagne flute already sat at each place. The centerpiece was an arrangement of white and blue roses with a single black rose rising above the others. A person looking closely might notice they were slightly different from one another as they came from eight different florist shops. The silverware and plates looked expensive. The head table was covered in blue table cloths with red and white bunting arranged on the sides.

A mask marked each seat. The sheer number and variety of different masks was impressive. Certain ones covered the whole face, but most only obscured half of one's face. Megan detected an animal theme to the masks.

The tables were soon occupied by most of the people from Gatton Technologies, although Megan noted a few conspicuous absences, namely the members who were over fifty. She felt a surge of resentment on their behalf, but she guessed this appalling behavior was normal for their boss.

The only slight hitch in seating guests came when Gatton took exception to Mr. Radcliff's presence.

"Sir, I must ask you to leave. You're too old to be here."

"Son, I may not have the kind of money you do, but you invited my daughter," said Mr. Radcliff. His Southern accent drew the sentence out. He waved to his right where a pretty young woman stood wearing a purple dress. "She has no other escort this evening, so if you want her to stay, you'd best get used to the sight of me."

"Dad, maybe we should go," said the girl.

"You'll hardly know the difference once everybody's masks are in place," said Megan. "It would be a shame for such a lovely young lady to be denied entry. I can find an unobtrusive spot for them if you wish."

Gatton considered Megan's logic before granting permission for the Radcliffs to stay.

"Fine. But I want the young lady at my table."

Megan waited for both the girl and her father to agree before escorting them to their respective places.

The DJ filled the air with soft, classical themes that created a relaxed atmosphere. Megan didn't have much down time, but she made a game of trying to guess who was beneath each mask. The company officers sat at the head table with Gatton and Heather Radcliff. The rest of Gatton's employees were spread evenly throughout the room. Female guests of the hotel filled most of the gaps between employees. It struck Megan like a bizarre matchmaking ritual.

Soon after dinner, Gatton made a fine speech then instructed the DJ to put some life into the party. The serene atmosphere quickly died, kicked aside by pulsing, modern dance music. Megan arranged to be as far from the speakers as possible to preserve her eardrums, but a moment later it didn't matter.

The music cut off abruptly.

People on the dance floor stood and stared at each other awkwardly. Nervous chuckles rose from the crowd along with a few curses and many confused questions. Those staring down at their phones frowned in dismay. Megan glanced at a nearby woman's screen and saw the thing blink off. Nothing happened when she frantically poked at the power button. Confusion quickly turned to annoyance. Angela moved toward the microphone but halted when the two sets of doors leading to the room burst open.

Two masked men entered through the main doors, and two more slipped through the staff entrance. In each case, one man stopped near the door and waited while the other moved toward the front of the room.

Megan's danger sense kicked into high gear. She moved instinctively to Gatton's table. Whatever trouble was rolling their way would definitely hit him, so she needed to be there.

A fifth man—the one responsible for killing the music—moved through the crowd, making a beeline for the head table.

"Gun!"

Megan couldn't tell which man shouted the word first, but it was echoed a dozen more times in a matter of seconds. The crowd instinctively dove for the ground. Megan took a knee, no easy feat in the dress she wore. She wanted to continue forward, but sense told her to stay in the background for now. She kept her head up and scanned the room.

Angela stood in front of the head table looking like an angry goddess in her blue evening gown.

"How dare you!" shouted Gatton, rushing forward. "This is a private party! Nobody gets in without my express permission."

"Come with us and nobody gets hurt," said the lead party crasher. He held a gun in his right hand, but it was pointed at the ground. Megan thought his voice had a familiar quality to it, but she couldn't be sure of anything. It could be that the guy had a generic voice.

"Is there a problem?" Angela asked. She shifted left, placing her body between the man and Gatton. "You can't—"

The man lifted his gun and pointed it in Angela's face.

"I can," the man countered. "The quicker I get what I want, the sooner we leave, so keep shut a few minutes and this'll be over."

"What do you want?" Gatton asked. The man looked pale, but he held his ground admirably.

"You're coming with me."

The man's statement made Megan flinch, but her heart froze when she heard one more desperate cry above the other rumblings in the room.

"Mom!"

Chapter 9:
Tricky Exit

Angela must have heard it too because she looked stricken.

"Please. I can't have you threatening my guests." She spoke softly and raised her hands in front of her body in a calming gesture.

The two men who'd been striding toward the head table moved to either side of Gatton and each seized an arm. Shaking off the hold on his right arm, Gatton wheeled around and punched the other man in the gut. He grunted but merely tightened his grip. The first guy recaptured Gatton's arm and wrenched it around behind his back.

Megan watched the proceedings with horror, wanting to make a move but not daring. The leader still had his gun pointed at Angela. Although his attention was on his men, he could still kill Megan's friend in the time it took her to take two steps.

Nobody moved or breathed throughout the next several seconds.

Megan took that time to check the position of the five party crashers. The ones by the staff entrance and the main entrance hadn't moved. The leader stood in front of the head table, and the final two goons held tightly to Jeffrey Gatton.

"We're going to leave now," said the leader. He raised his voice even though the dead silence in the room made that unnecessary. "If everybody stays still, everybody lives."

In Megan's opinion, the plan was sound. Letting a billionaire get kidnapped from the hotel wouldn't be good for publicity but having a couple of guests die in a shootout would definitely be worse. The exit would be tricky. The odds of this many people keeping their cool for the extra minute it would take the bad guys to leave with Gatton were terrible.

Her fears sprang to life when the main entrance banged open, hitting the guy guarding it in the back. He stumbled a step but caught his balance a split-second later. Pulling out a gun, the man pointed it at the door, but it was too late.

A man about the same age as Megan's father rushed in. Seeing the door open, people started scuttling toward freedom.

A gun went off somewhere, kicking the crowd into panic mode. The bad guy brushed past the guard and slammed both doors shut again. Slipping a zip tie around the door handles, he took up his position again. Megan didn't have the time to wonder why he hadn't done that in the first place. People shrank away from him as he waved a handgun in an arc from left to right.

Shouts, cries, and curses punctuated the situation.

The leader pulled Angela close and used her as a shield. The area around the head table immediately cleared as everybody but the assailants, the prisoners, and the leader moved away from it at top speed.

Megan fixed on Jaden's position. As expected, the boy wanted to go to his mother. Running in heels slowed Megan down, but she managed to halt Jaden's progress around the time a second gunshot rang out. Since nearly everybody else was occupied with ducking, screaming, shooting, or not being trampled, Megan had a clear path to the bar area. The hiding spot wasn't ideal, but it would have to do. Thankfully, Jaden was too upset to fight her much. Pushing the boy down behind the bar area, Megan cautiously peered around the side to get a new handle on the situation.

She caught a glimpse of royal blue disappearing into the space beyond the staff entrance. Gatton and most of the assailants were gone. The last one sprinted through the room away from the main entrance which he'd zip-tied shut. The security guard tottered after at a much slower pace.

People cried, prayed, huddled on the floor, clung to each other, or some combination thereof. The cell phones still wouldn't work. Small conversations ignited all over the room, but Megan ignored most of them. Her attention fixed on a weeping young woman near the head table.

"Stay here," Megan ordered Jaden.

Slipping off her shoes, Megan crossed the room as quickly as possible until she reached Heather Radcliff and her father. Mr. Radcliff lay on the ground with blood-soaked napkins pressed to his right shoulder. Tear streaks ran down the young woman's face, but she quickly folded two more napkins to replace the soaked ones.

"Leave the other ones in place," Megan instructed. "Press the new ones over it. The pressure will help stop the bleeding." She wished they had one of the devices that would seal the wound with tiny sponges, but XSTATs weren't exactly stocked in general First Aid Kits. Spotting a small gun next to Mr. Radcliff, Megan scooped it up and checked to see if it was loaded. Unfortunately, both shots had been fired.

When she looked up, she found Heather's eyes boring into her.

"You're not a cocktail waitress." Anger strengthened the young woman's voice. "Who are you?"

Megan didn't see much point in clinging to her undercover identity.

"I'm an FBI agent."

"Are you going after them? Because if so, I want to help."

Megan shook her head then nodded.

"Yes, I'm going after them, but you should stay with your father," she said, misinterpreting the woman's offer of help.

"I will, but you won't get far without weapons." Heather's gaze took in the sight of Megan's bare feet. "And shoes. I can help with both."

"I can help too," said a soft-spoken male voice.

The newcomer knelt next to Megan and handed her a watch.

"This has a GPS device that will let you follow Mr. Gatton," said Milton Jennings, Vice President of Gatton Technologies. "He insisted every top company officer wear one, but it only works well within a couple of miles. If you're underground or in areas with a lot of concrete, you'll have to be closer."

"All right. Stay with Mr. Radcliff and keep pressure on his wound until help arrives," said Megan. As she strapped on the oversized watch, she noticed that most of the room had emptied out as people realized the danger was over. The emergency hotline was likely receiving quite a few calls about now, assuming the jammer quit or people got far enough away to get their cell phones to work. Megan quickly showed Mr. Jennings how to hold the cloth down properly then climbed to her feet and faced Ms. Radcliff.

"Show me what you've got."

The girl dashed away a few more tears, grabbed her tiny purse, and bolted from the room with Megan on her heels. They reached the main entrance doors before remembering that the one guy had thrown a zip-tie over the handles. Megan was about to switch directions and head to the staff doors when Heather whipped out a giant pocketknife and cut away the piece of plastic.

"How did you get that through customs?" Megan wondered.

"We didn't have to. We drove up from Texas. My father's a salesman for a gun shop down there," Heather explained. "You remember all those cases he was shouting about when we moved in?"

Megan nodded.

"They're filled with guns."

The last four words of the young woman's speech were music to Megan's ears. Since the party had been in the fifth-floor ballroom, they had to go down two floors to reach the Radcliffs' rooms. Heather unlocked her room and let Megan through the connecting door into her father's room.

Megan stood in the threshold and stared. Large and small cases were stacked everywhere. It would take ages to sort through them. Luckily, as her father's assistant, Heather knew right where to go. Stopping next to a small case located at the foot of the bed, she popped the latches and stepped back to let Megan see the contents. It held fifteen handguns of various make and models.

I officially love Texans and their obsession with guns.

"What would you like?" asked Heather.

"I usually carry a Glock 23, but I'm not going to be picky right now," said Megan, aware of how much time had passed. She needed to start her pursuit pronto.

"I'll get it ready for you," Heather offered. "Go take a look at my shoes and see what fits. Socks are in the upper compartment of my suitcase."

"Do you have a knife?" Megan asked.

"What do you need a knife for?"

"This dress is going to slow me down, and I don't have time to change completely," said Megan.

"Ah, I'll see what I can do," said Heather.

By the time Megan returned with a comfortable pair of cowboy boots, Heather had a gun belt and vest prepped for her. The boots were a little snug, but they were a much better option than the heels.

"There are four spare gun clips in the tactical bag and another two strapped to the belt itself." Heather helped Megan into the gear then used a pair of hunting shears to deal with the flowing fabric of the red dress. Somehow, she managed to cut everything free without stabbing

Megan's legs. "I've tucked my cell phone in the other half of the tactical bag just in case. Good luck."

Megan thanked the young woman for her help and dashed out of the room. She had no idea where to go. A glance at the watch told her approximately which direction, but other than that, she was lost. She decided her first move would be to exit the building.

Upon reaching the lobby, Megan nearly ran over Jaden who had been standing in front of the elevators. In cowboy boots, a vest, a gun belt, and a ripped red dress, Megan figured she made a frightful sight, but Jaden didn't care. The kid looked agitated. He'd obviously been waiting for her. In another moment, he tackled her with a tight hug. Megan winced, hoping he didn't hurt his head against the bulky bulletproof vest.

"I know where they went!" Jaden cried, when he finally let go. "We have to go after them! They have my mom!"

"Slow down," said Megan. She gripped Jaden's shoulders and willed the kid to take some deep breaths. "Tell me what you know."

"I overheard one of the men tell the others to take them to the tunnels," said Jaden, bouncing on the balls of his feet.

"Tunnels?" Megan searched her mind for mention of tunnels.

"There are lots of them beneath the city," Jaden explained impatiently. "There are miles of them. Lots of people live down there. We need to go now!"

Even with the GPS watch, Megan didn't think charging down into unknown tunnels would be wise.

"We need a guide," she muttered to nobody in particular.

"I know one! I can show you!"

Megan liked neither option. On the one hand, she could wait for the police to arrive and conduct a proper investigation into these tunnels. Sirens told her she didn't have long before that option would be her only one. The other option—letting Jaden take her there himself—had a slightly better chance of success and a way higher risk factor. Angela would probably slug her for endangering her son, but if they waited for the police, they'd likely never see Angela again.

"You can lead me to the tunnel guide, but then, you stay put, got it? I mean it. You stay back."

Jaden nodded vigorously.

Megan would probably have to handcuff the boy to a pipe to keep him from following, but she had no other way to find a guide.

Chapter 10:
Tunnel People

Megan followed Jaden Melkin through The Grand Game Hotel and out one of the back exits that led to an alley. The boy picked up a black backpack and strapped it on as he headed for the parking garage that served six nearby hotels.

They took the elevator to the bottom floor and trekked over to a door marked: RESTRICTED. Graffiti also covered the door. The clearest message consisted of a skull and crossbones symbol.

"Here. Take this." Jaden handed Megan a flashlight.

"How many times have you been down to the tunnels?" Megan wondered. She tried to keep her tone casual, but it wasn't working.

"A couple of times," Jaden mumbled. The way he avoided eye contact—combined with his obvious expertise—told Megan to add a few dozen to that estimate.

"Does your mother know?"

"No way. She'd never let me come here." Jaden opened the door, took a step inside, and shook a jar filled with bottle caps, loose coins, and other small debris.

"What's that for?" Megan asked, impatient to be moving on.

"We have to ask permission to enter," said Jaden.

"Jay-dog. My little Light Man, how you been?" called a cheerful voice from deeper in the tunnel. "Come in. Come in. Happy to have company. Who's with ya, boy?"

Jaden and Megan proceeded about thirty feet down a tunnel until they came to an area that had been walled off with blankets and curtains. A flickering flashlight struggled to light the dim area. One side of the tunnel featured a grungy mattress elevated on some wooden pallets. An overturned bucket served as a seat for a man wearing only a pair of ripped jeans. From the looks of things, he was playing a card game with about half a deck gathered from several different casinos. The glow from Megan and Jaden's flashlights revealed glazed, bloodshot eyes.

Jaden handled quick introductions.

"Mel, this is Agent M.; she's here looking for some people who took my mom!"

The man nodded his head rhythmically.

"Tough break. Tough break. Say, you wouldn't happen to have another light in there, would ya? Mine's gonna die soon."

"Mel, this is important! Have you seen anybody come this way?" asked Jaden.

"Get him a flashlight, Jaden," said Megan. She doubted the man had any useful information, but the sooner they determined one way or another if the man knew anything, the sooner they could move on.

The boy set his backpack on the ground and started rummaging. Finding another flashlight, Jaden handed it to Mel.

That explains the mystery of the disappearing flashlights.

"You the best, Jay-dog, but naw, I ain't seen nobody this way. The Coons might know something though. They been collecting strays again."

"Who are the Coons?" asked Megan when they were a few steps beyond Mel's hovel.

"Jake and Rena Coon are the couple who live down here a little farther on," said Jaden. "They kind of take care of kids who end up in the tunnels."

The idea of people living beneath Las Vegas fascinated Megan, but she needed to find her friend and the missing billionaire before thinking too hard on the subject.

When they reached the next inhabited section, Jaden whistled sharply. The curtain flew back and a small blond-haired blur flew out and rammed into Jaden.

"Hi, Sarah," greeted Jaden, carefully extricating his arms.

"Jaden! What's going on? Rena said she saw some people with your mom. She never comes down here."

"Where is Rena?" asked Megan.

Once again, Jaden performed introductions.

"Is Rena still here? We need to talk to her." Jaden's anxiety showed up on his face and in his voice.

The girl let go and retreated inside the curtain. Compared to the camp they'd just seen, this one was palatial. A queen-sized bed had been mounted on pallets which were raised up on plastic cartons. A worn but clean looking flower quilt lay atop the bed. Shelves made of more plastic crates held everything from folded clothes to shoes to books, games, and food. Strategically placed camping lamps provided gentle lighting for the space. It almost looked cozy, if one could ignore the pool of water in the middle of the floor.

"Rena!" called the girl.

A large black woman looked up from a worn out book she was reading.

"Hush, Sarah. People be sleeping at this hour." The woman eyed Megan's outfit curiously. "I take it you're interested in the folks that came through the tunnel near here not long ago."

"I'm an FBI agent in pursuit of possible kidnapping victims," said Megan.

Anger flared in the woman's eyes.

"I been telling upside folks there's trouble down here for months. Why you care now?"

"Please, Rena," begged Sarah. "You said you saw Jaden's mother with the men. She's in trouble. We have to help."

The woman's eyes softened.

"You're right, baby. You're right," said the woman. "A few tunnels over that way, there be some bad things going down." She pointed to her left in the opposite direction of where Megan and Jaden had entered.

"What kind of bad things?" asked Megan.

"Don't know, but tough men be moving through there a lot. Sometimes they're armed, sometimes not, and sometimes they have people who don't look like they want to be with them, if you know what I mean."

Megan nodded.

"Are the people being moved men or women?"

"Mostly women."

"Can you tell me how to find these people?" Hot anger blossomed within Megan's chest. She could overlook a lot of things that might take place in Sin City, but kidnapping, abuse, and human trafficking struck all of her injustice nerves.

"I can take you there," offered the woman.

"Rena, your ankle," said Sarah.

For the first time, Megan noticed the dirty wraps swaddling Rena's left ankle.

"I'll be fine, sweets," Rena assured.

"I can find it myself if you tell me the way," said Megan. She did not want an injured civilian limping into a dangerous situation with her.

"You'll get lost," said Rena matter-of-factly.

"I can show her," said Sarah.

"No." The answer came from Rena and Megan with equal force.

"It's too dangerous," Megan added.

"Where's Jaden?" Sarah's next question chilled Megan.

Two seconds of frantic looking about confirmed the sinking feeling in her gut.

He was gone.

"Do you know where he went?" Megan asked, spearing the small blond girl with a pointed stare.

"I think so," replied the girl. She looked at Rena guiltily. "We sometimes spy on the men."

Rena looked furious.

"Child, how many times do I have to tell you those folks is dangerous?"

Megan racked her mind for a solution. Morally and legally she was on shaky ground. Rena wasn't exactly up to sneaking around the tunnels, but Megan couldn't ask a minor to guide her into a den of dangerous men either. She checked the watch and received a weak, spotty signal. It would have to do.

"Thank you for your time. I'll make do with the tracking signal," said Megan. "Meanwhile, send somebody up to the surface to call the police and the FBI."

"They won't do anything," said Rena. "They don't trust folks like us."

Megan more than half agreed with her. The rebellious look in Sarah's eyes said she'd follow Megan in a heartbeat.

"Sarah, do you want to help?"

The girl nodded. Rena shot Megan an alarmed look. The agent put her hand up to calm the woman.

Taking her room key out of the cowboy boot where she'd tucked it, Megan handed it over to the girl.

"Do you know where The Grand Game Hotel is?"

Another nod confirmed that the girl knew.

"Good. Go to room 103 and use this key to get in. Find my

badge in the nightstand and call the police. Ask to be transferred to the FBI's Las Vegas Field Office. When they ask, read them the badge number. Tell them Agent Megan Luchek is investigating a kidnapping in progress in the tunnels then direct them here. Can you do that? I need to go after Jaden and his mother, and I can't be in two places at once, but this is very important."

The girl wore a dazed expression, but she nodded yet again. Taking a deep breath, she took the key and sprinted away.

Megan felt like she'd just placed a dozen lives in a pair of tiny, untested hands.

"She's a good girl. She'll get it done," Rena assured Megan, reading her expression perfectly. "You best be on your way. That little boy is gonna need you soon. I'll be here praying for ya." Rena picked up the book she'd been reading and clutched it to her chest. "If you get lost and desperate, call out for help, somebody will find you, but wait until you're truly desperate. You may not want some people to find you."

"That's good advice," said Megan. "Where should I start my search?"

Rena described a confusing series of lefts and rights to follow. Most of the markers she mentioned were various pieces of graffiti.

Megan's brain felt scrambled, but she tried to keep everything straight. At the very least, if she kept moving away from this camp, she should run into the bad guys. The trick would be finding them before they found her.

From time to time, the GPS tracker would have mercy on her and give a faint green glow and a tantalizing piece of information like 825 meters. She didn't trust it because the next second it would tell her 220 meters, but since the bearing was the same, she concluded her target must be somewhere in that general direction.

She kept the flashlight on until she heard faint echoes of voices. Megan traded the flashlight for the Glock 23, and took a second to absorb the flood of adrenaline that raced through her. The heels of the cowboy boots could be like canon shots down here, so she moved forward carefully, keeping her weight on the balls of her feet. The black vest would help, but Megan really wished she'd taken the time to change out of the bright red dress. The loose dress ends flapped against her knees.

"Kill him," said one male voice.

"Let him go," said another. "He's just a tunnel rat."

"But he knows we're here," protested the first man.

"Yeah, so do the other hundreds of tunnel people. Nobody listens to them," argued the second man.

"He's no tunnel rat," said a third male voice. This one sounded familiar again.

Megan would bet this man was the head party crasher.

"Smell his hair. Look at his clothes. It's too clean. He's too clean," continued the third man.

The reference to Jaden's hair stirred up a memory within Megan. Fingers running down her hair and pulling it close to smell.

Disgust and alarm collided within her. The familiar sense crept in and surrounded her senses, threatening to overwhelm her.

Derrick.

She'd pushed the name out of her head for years, but this time, she let it linger. He'd been a mistake that almost proved fatal. At first, Derrick Belmont was charming, courteous, and amusing, but slowly, over the course of their three-month affair, Megan had seen a darker side of him. His need to control people manifested in big and little ways. In the end, it turned to psychological and physical *games* he liked to play. Her body still bore scars from their last encounter, the one that finally convinced her to break free.

He can't hurt you. He can't hurt you.

The prospect of facing the man again both relieved and terrified her, for though she'd come a long way in life, she'd always been on the run. An emotional beast haunted her dreams and drove her forward from place to place.

Finding Derrick embroiled in dark dealings didn't surprise her. Megan always knew he was capable of such things, but she didn't know where he was in the hierarchy. He probably wasn't top tier, but the little she knew, told her there were people who answered to him or at least listened to him.

Who are you now, Derrick?

Chapter 11:
Cold Storage

Megan tip-toed closer to the voices. She needed to be near in case an opportunity presented itself to help Jaden.

As she passed a side tunnel, the unmistakable scent of sweat, urine, and fouler things tugged her attention that way. The argument concerning Jaden continued in a circle. She should press on, but curiosity wouldn't release her. Straining her ears, Megan heard soft sobs coming from farther along in the side tunnel. A dozen swift, soft steps brought her to a thick partition rigged from sleeping bags.

Everything in her wanted to fling the partition aside and face these people, but wisdom prevailed. She couldn't help them now anyway, and if the bad guys had some way to monitor their human cargo, that system would alert them to her presence. Judging by the amount of voices, she was sorely outgunned. Surprise was about the only effective weapon she had left.

Megan made a mental note of her position and moved on. Spotting another side tunnel off the other side, Megan ducked in and leaned against the wall.

The voices had gone silent.

"Where did she go?" asked a man. The voice belonged to the nice guy who'd wanted to release Jaden.

"I don't know," grumbled another man. This was the man with the deeper voice who'd wanted to kill the boy. "She was headed to the cold storage area, but the baby monitor's still squawking the usual gibberish."

"Where's my mom?" demanded Jaden.

"Shut up, kid," barked the grumpy guy.

"Agent M. will save us. She'll throw you all in jail," Jaden boasted.

The boy's faith almost made Megan cry, especially because she wasn't sure if she could come through for him.

"She's close," murmured Derrick. "Perhaps close enough. Go ahead and kill the boy if she doesn't surrender in three minutes."

"What if she's not close enough to hear the threat?" asked the reasonable guy.

"She'll hear the gunshot," replied Derrick.

Megan couldn't believe her ears. Several precious seconds slipped by while her mind picked apart and rearranged Derrick's statements. Was he talking about her? Probably. Would he really have Jaden killed? Yes, he was that kind of crazy. How was she supposed to surrender? She didn't even know which tunnel they were in. The acoustics down here were strange.

Cold storage.

The other man's earlier statement about *usual squawking* finally unstuck Megan's feet. Throwing caution aside, she sprinted back to the side tunnel where she'd resisted moving the curtain. This time, she didn't hesitate. She grabbed a handful of sleeping bag and threw it left.

The sight beyond made her freeze again.

Light from a few dozen glowsticks showed ten figures crammed into space probably once occupied by one person. The glowsticks had been arranged like a little campfire with a baby monitor settled on top. The people—mostly young women—stared blankly at Megan. Many of them had their hands and feet caught in prisoner transfer cuffs which linked the ankles to the hands around mid-waist. The stench turned Megan's stomach, but she fought off the instinct to run.

Instead, she panned the flashlight beam over everybody in the small, makeshift room. Most of the women had dark hair and desperate eyes. As she met the nearest woman's eyes, she saw anger there and a plan formed. On par with Megan's usual plans, it was nuts, but it offered a slim chance of success, which beat the heck out of no chance. Some of the women started to stir, but Megan frantically motioned for quiet. A few of the prisoners wept quietly, and a few were either sleeping or otherwise unconscious. The figure stretched out on a mattress to Megan's right was notable for two reasons: one, she had blond hair and two, Megan knew her. It was the woman she'd saved from room 414 yesterday.

How do you fit in? she silently asked the woman. She wanted to help her, but that problem would have to wait.

Moving over to the angry woman, Megan gently shook her shoulder and got no response.

Returning to the woman nearest the glowsticks, she snatched up the baby monitor and turned it upside down. Then, she leaned close and whispered in the woman's ear. She wasn't sure how much of three minutes she'd already used, but she didn't want to push it.

"Do you understand English? Nod if you do."

The woman nodded.

"We haven't much time. I'm going to release you and anybody else I can. Go left out of this tunnel and keep running. You'll have to make some turns but keep going. Find a woman named Rena and tell her your story." As she spoke, Megan took one of the thirty-two bobby pins Angela had stuffed into her hair earlier in the evening and used it to pick the lock on the handcuffs. It was slow going because she didn't have time to strip the end properly. She made do by biting off some of the plastic at the end.

"I can," said the woman quietly. She waved for Megan to give her the modified pin then went to work on the leg shackles. The latch popped in less time than it'd taken Megan. This woman wasn't a stranger to captivity.

The success gave Megan a new facet to her plan. She quickly explained what she wanted and then picked up the baby monitor.

"I'm here, and you have my attention," she said softly. Megan held the monitor's pickup part close and moved away from the prisoners. A sense of déjà vu hit her as she remembered uttering something similar to a different madman. She briefly considered turning over the handgun to one of the women, but her faith in people didn't extend that far. Desperate people like these women were even more of a gamble, but in some ways, her life was now linked to their fate. "Let the boy go."

"Maggie. It's good to hear your voice. As soon as I saw Angela, I knew you'd come."

"What's this about, Derrick?"

"I'm afraid you've stepped into quite a mess this time, my dear. I need your unconditional surrender or the boy dies."

"I believe you," replied Megan, "but there are always conditions. The first being, Jaden gets to live or there's no incentive for me to follow through with the surrender."

Derrick chuckled.

"You always were good at debating. Fine. The boy gets to live for now."

"Where do you want me to go?" asked Megan.

"Stay there. We'll come to you."

"Who are these people I'm standing with?"

"They're just passing through. Don't worry about them," said Derrick.

"You don't know." Megan picked up that much from his tone. If he knew about them, he'd be more than happy to rub it in her face. The information told her a lot. The operation was much bigger than these women or the hotel incident. They might be related, but Derrick's ignorance said they were probably separate missions. "Okay, what about the woman I saved yesterday. What's she doing here?"

"I might have known that was you," Derrick muttered. "No matter. She's being kept unconscious so she can't interfere with anything. That's what happens when people interfere."

"You can share more of your twisted logic when you get here," said Megan. "We're done for now." She flipped off the baby monitor.

Once given a bit of hope, the women rallied. Eight of them picked up the blanket holding the unconscious woman. Megan turned over the flashlight and the baby monitor to the first woman she'd freed.

"Hurry," Megan urged. "They'll be right behind you. Remember the lefts and rights, but if you get lost, get to the surface."

"Gracias," said the woman.

"De nada." Despite the lack of time, the small ritual of giving and receiving thanks solidified a bond between them.

Megan hoped they would get far enough away. In the meantime, she picked up a few of the glowsticks and tucked them into a pocket in the tactical gear bag holding most of the ammunition. After arranging the sleeping bag over the back section again, Megan tossed the glowsticks midway down the tunnel toward the entrance to give the area a little light. Finally, she drew the handgun and waited.

Normally, she hated waiting, but this time, she knew that every second it took Derrick and his goons to get here was another the women had to get away. She passed the time by counting the heartbeats pounding through her head, willing her heart to slow so she could think.

Three flashlights appeared at the end of the tunnel roughly twenty feet away. One beam flashed in her face, but she shut her eyes in time to avoid too much damage.

"You're terrible at this surrendering thing, Maggie," Derrick observed. "Put the gun down."

One of the men stepped to his left, pulling Jaden along with him. The man had a firm grip on the boy's left shoulder. His other hand held a gun next to Jaden's ear. If it went off, the boy would probably go deaf in that ear.

"Let Jaden go, and I'm all yours." The last part of her statement made Megan's skin crawl.

The man holding Jaden's shoulder released his grip.

"Get out of here, Jaden," Megan said.

To her surprise, the boy just stood there and shook his head, looking miserable.

"Your bargain is for his life," said Derrick. "He made his own deal. Now, put the gun down."

Megan wanted to kick herself. Of course, Jaden would stay if he thought they still had his mother.

"Where is Angela?" she wondered.

"We'll see her in a moment," Derrick promised, "but do hurry up. I'm running out of patience."

She wasn't fond of this part of her plan. Surrender would probably lead to her premature death as surely as a shootout here, but at least it delayed that possibility.

Stooping, Megan gently placed the handgun on the ground. When she stood, the men with Derrick moved in and each grabbed an arm. Her heart climbed up her chest and lodged in her throat. She wanted to throw off their hands and break them for good measure, but instead, she allowed herself to be dragged away from the odd little prison cell. They abandoned her in the midst of the glowsticks she'd scattered. Derrick picked up the gun.

Please don't check.

The thought was a hope and a prayer.

"Stand still," Derrick ordered.

He circled her once like a beast studying prey. Megan's fear magnified when she realized he held a knife in addition to the handgun. Tucking the gun in his belt, Derrick went to work on the bulletproof vest straps. In less than a minute, he lifted the vest over her head and dropped it to the ground. A moment later, the belt with the extra ammo and the gun holster joined the vest groundside.

A chill gripped Megan, and the lack of straps on the dress made her self-conscious. One of the men with Derrick whistled.

"I call dibs when you're done with that, D-man," called the man who'd been threatening Jaden.

"Shut up, Nico," Derrick muttered. The words lacked conviction though because most of his attention stayed on Megan. Stepping up behind her, he leaned close and whispered in her left ear. "He's right though. You look great."

Megan stiffened. Either these guys were completely off their heads on something or they weren't factoring in her attire. She figured it was the latter option and felt like busting their noses for being pigheaded, never mind the evil part.

"Take me to Angela," she said.

"As you wish." Derrick executed a mock bow, stepped away, and waved his minions forward.

Nico pulled Megan's arms behind her back and handcuffed the wrists together. The other guy pushed her until she started walking. Jaden fell into step next to her. He looked frightened yet determined to be brave.

Chapter 12:
Eagle Eyes

Megan quickly lost track of the tunnel paths. This section was relatively devoid of graffiti marks she could use as reference points. On the positive side, as they moved deeper into tunnels controlled by the bad guys, the paths started to be better lit. While she walked, her mind kept busy trying to fit Derrick into the big picture. Thankfully, she didn't need to tell Jaden to stay close. The kid was practically her shadow throughout the trip. At last, they arrived in an area that widened out more than usual. It had been blocked off with thick tarps, creating a cave-like atmosphere. Although they could hear muffled voices upon approach, the words eluded them until the tarps were brushed aside.

The scene that greeted them was unexpected.

Four men, likely the original party-crasher crew, stood along the perimeter watching Angela and Jeffrey Gatton face off. She looked livid while he appeared apologetic yet defiant.

"How dare you risk my business, my livelihood, and my life for a stupid test?" Angela's declaration was a quarter question and three quarters righteous indignation.

"The risk analysts said the hotel's reputation would recover, and you'll be compensated accordingly," said Gatton. His tone wavered between defense and plea with a hint of whine thrown in.

"What's going on here?" Derrick demanded.

"D-man, you're right on time," said one of men cheerfully. "We're gonna be rich."

The other three didn't say much, but all four men straightened subtly.

Derrick glared at everybody, uncertain who to wring answers from.

Gatton spoke before the silence that fell could grow too uncomfortable.

"We've been negotiating," he said. "These gentlemen have agreed to let me and the lady go in exchange for an exorbitant ransom fee."

"Just like that?" Derrick asked, directing the question to the four turncoats. "You think the Club's going to let you walk out?"

"It's not a bad idea," said Nico. He walked over to stand beside the nearest of the men ready to step out on their employers. "Alec, you in, man?"

"Yeah, I'm in." He too moved away from Megan, Derrick, and Jaden.

Their side of the tunnel room was getting kind of sparse. Megan watched the proceedings with interest. She gathered this could be good, but her gut also said it could turn ugly in a heartbeat. The unease made her stomach do some weird flips.

Angela gasped upon seeing Jaden.

"What's he doing here?" she demanded.

"He's here to ensure everybody behaves," said Derrick. As he spoke, he put his hands on Jaden's shoulders and pulled him close.

"Come on, D-man. You should come with. Gatton's got enough money to get us away from Vegas." The cheerful man continued with his spokesman duties.

The other four nodded in a gesture of solidarity.

"You're crazy," Derrick muttered, "and you'll never make it."

"Who's going to stop us?" asked the man standing left of the spokesman.

"Sorry. If you're not with us, you can't be trusted," said the spokesman.

The four men plus Nico each pulled out a handgun, and Megan's bad feeling intensified.

"There's no need for violence," said Gatton. He sounded oddly calm for a man surrounded by people holding handguns. "Gents, I trust you know the way out? Lead on and we'll follow."

"I'm not leaving my son," Angela declared. "Or my friend."

It was nice not to be forgotten.

Gatton shrugged.

"Suit yourself."

"Wait, does that mean we get paid less?" asked the cheerful guy. He looked less enthused now.

"It would make sense," said Gatton. "But I'm not going to argue about price now. The time for negotiations is growing thin."

"How do you know that?" wondered Derrick.

"Because I called the police and GT security teams."

"If you called them, you can get them to back off," said Derrick.

"I'm not taking any chances," declared the chatty one. "Sorry, lady. You're coming with us."

Two of the other men moved to Angela and took hold of her arms.

She screamed.

"Let go!"

Jaden tried to go to his mother, but Derrick held him in place.

Angela stilled when one of the escorts shoved his gun in the tender spot under her chin, tilting her head up.

Everybody started shouting at once.

Gatton kept chanting, "We've got to go."

The men who wanted to whisk him and Angela away demanded everybody shut up.

Derrick tried to reason with them.

Finally, Megan had to let out the Irish-Italian in her and shout everybody down.

"Hey! This isn't helping!" Once certain she had everybody's attention, Megan continued at a more reasonable volume. "If you want to leave, get going. Angela, go with them. It'll be all right. We won't stop you."

"But—" Derrick began.

"What do you care if they get themselves killed?" Megan asked Derrick.

"Gatton's my payday too," he replied.

"If you're after Eagle Eyes, you'll be disappointed," said Gatton.

Megan wanted to smack the guy. Now was not the time to be disappointing any of the men holding guns.

"Why?" demanded Derrick.

"Because it's not really for sale." Knowing he might have overstepped his bounds, Gatton started babbling at a faster rate. "There's exactly one copy of them in play here, and I'm wearing them. If they come out of my eyes, you have a minute to enter the correct password or they'll self-destruct."

"You're not really Jeffrey Gatton." Jaden lobbed that bombshell into their midst, causing dead silence to fall.

Everybody stared at the boy.

Gatton broke into a cold sweat. The reaction told Megan that Jaden had hit upon the truth. All eyes shifted slowly from Jaden to the man they'd been calling Gatton for hours.

"He's right! My name is David Stanley. I'm an actor. I just work for Gatton. He hired me to test drive his new toy. That's all."

"So, the ransom's a lie," said Nico.

"No! That's real. I can get the money from Gatton. Promise. He'll want the prototype for Eagle Eyes back."

"What is Eagle Eyes?" asked Derrick. "If it's worth so much to him, then it'll be worth more to us."

"It's basically a computer," said David Stanley. "It's unique in the sense that it works like a pair of contacts."

"That's it?" Derrick sounded disappointed.

"I've heard enough," said Nico. "Ricky, get them out of here. We can work the ransom details later when we're away from here." He pointed his gun at David. "And don't even think about talking to the police again."

"The only one I'm in contact with right now is my boss. I swear," said David.

"You're talking to him now?" asked Nico. "Tell him the price went up. He's got more people to pay for."

"He can hear everything I hear." David paused and nodded like he was acknowledging new orders.

"What'd he say?" Nico's voice oozed eagerness.

"He wants the FBI agent instead of the hotel woman."

"What?" The reflex question came out of most of the people present.

"How do you know she's FBI?" Derrick sounded confused.

David smiled smugly.

"This is the wave of the future. 24/7 access to the internet, though to be fair my boss has much better facial recognition programs than most governments."

"Megan stays here," said Derrick stubbornly.

She didn't have to look to sense his gun shifting her way.

David turned to his guards turned guardians.

"That's the new deal, guys. And he's willing to pay double the original offer for the hotel woman's safe passage out of here."

Something didn't seem right to Megan. Stanley had no motivation to call the police then walk this fine line between death and life. Calling the cops should be enough. If he'd kept his mouth shut, they would be found and probably rescued after a long hostage negotiation. Why the extra drama? If they were going to escort two people to a new location, they could easily adjust for a few more tagalongs.

The rest of the handguns drew a new bead on Derrick and Jaden since the boy was standing directly in front of him. Instinctively, Megan stepped right. Her arms hurt and her shoulders tingled from being cuffed. Being the center of attention never felt so tense before.

"Take us all to safety," Megan said. She directed her words to David Stanley since he clearly held the others' leashes.

"Not happening," said David. "I offered my boss that option, and he turned it down." The man had the grace to look ashamed.

"Derrick, you should join them." Megan couldn't believe the words coming from her mouth.

"He missed the boat, Agent," said Stanley. "You won the who-gets-to-live-lottery, so let's go."

Nico motioned and the men holding Angela shoved her toward him. He caught her and put the gun to her head.

"What's it gonna be, lady?" The message was crude but clear.

Megan watched her friend close her eyes and wait. She thought her heart might crumble to dust soon. Hoping Derrick didn't shoot her in the back, Megan stepped forward cautiously. When she didn't die, she took another step and another. She tried to walk with dignity, but the handcuffs threw off her natural gait.

"Fair's fair, D-man. We get two. You get two," said Nico.

"Better head to the south tunnels," said David. "Cops were told to approach from the north. If you can successfully elude the police, my boss will wire twenty-five thousand dollars to your account. And if your phone rings, answer it."

Megan turned and watched helplessly as Derrick dragged Jaden away. Angela followed, needing to be near her son.

"Let's go," said Nico impatiently.

"No," countered David. "We wait here."

"No cops?" Megan asked, eyeing David. She wouldn't put such a lie past this slippery sucker.

"Oh, the cops are coming," David assured her. "They're just not that close, and we're safe enough here for the moment."

"Man, you better not be lying," Nico muttered darkly.

"What are we waiting for?" Megan wondered.

Instead of answering, David ordered the men to release Megan from the handcuffs. Rubbing some feeling back into her wrists, Megan studied the nerdy young man. A few of the puzzle pieces clicked together for her.

"What does he want me to do?" she asked softly.

"Nico, give the lady your gun," said David.

"No way, man. This already be some weird—"

"Check your bank account," David interrupted.

Nico looked at him like he'd gone insane.

"Man, phones don't work down here."

"They do if I want them to. The computer in Eagle Eyes can boost the signal," said David. "Go ahead and check."

The young man did so and whooped for joy.

"You'll get another bonus if you get out right now," David promised.

In another second, Nico shoved his gun at Megan.

"Peace out." With that farewell, he took off, practically skipping.

One by one, David showed the men their newfound wealth and sent them on their way. Finally, only David and Megan stood in the brightly lit tunnel room.

Drawing his hands out of his pockets, David held a small box out to Megan.

She stared at it without moving to take it.

"This is a second prototype of Eagle Eyes. Each of the phones I touched had the GPS activated remotely. If you can successfully track two of the fugitives before they exit the tunnels, your friend and her son will live."

"That doesn't make any sense. Derrick—"

"Is addicted to money, which my boss has plenty of. He's receiving a phone call with his instructions now. He'll see reason, but your time to track the thugs is disappearing."

"And if I can't catch two of them in time? What then?"

"They die."

Megan really wanted to punch the man in front of her, but he wasn't the sadistic psycho who really needed it. He was just the messenger.

"This was the plan all along," she muttered. She had about a million questions about how things had gotten this far, but she had no time to ask them.

"With some slight modifications," David confirmed.

"Show me what to do." Megan's teeth clenched so hard her jaw hurt, but she managed to get the words out. Angela and Jaden needed her to keep her cool for now.

Chapter 13:
Test Run

Despite deep reservations, Megan let David Stanley talk her through the process of putting the miniature computer into her eyes. She'd never had to wear contacts, so the prospect of putting a thin film over her eyes terrified her. Only the memory of Jaden and Angela disappearing with Derrick forced her to go through with it.

"Close your eyes for about ten seconds," David instructed. "The program will prompt you for a username and password. Look at the line where you're supposed to type in a response for username and think 'GT614355.' It's your new employee number."

"What's the password?" Megan asked.

"Jeffsslavegirl. No spaces." David winced and took a small step back. "It wasn't my idea!" He held up both hands as if to ward off a blow.

Megan added a mental tick to the *reasons-to-punch-the-real-Gatton* list, and followed the instructions.

"Your boss better hope one of these punks kills me," Megan said darkly. As soon as she entered the password, her mind flooded with information.

"Kneel down for a few seconds. It can be disorienting at first." David eased her down to the ground.

Bracing herself with her hands, Megan stayed on one knee as the information flood slowed to something her mind could keep up with.

"Good help is so hard to find, Agent Luchek," said a voice inside her head. "You'll have to speak your responses or think them and move them to the text box in the bottom left corner if you want to have a proper conversation. The program can deliver my voice, but sadly, I've not been able to teach it to spontaneously read thoughts yet. I've taken the liberty of prioritizing your targets in order of probable success."

"Next time, consider asking for help nicely," Megan said, forcing herself to her feet. Though she spoke mildly, she channeled her anger into sprinting.

The first few steps were more like staggers, but she quickly got used to the odd sensation of seeing everything through Eagle Eyes. The edges of her view held information like a video game display. The health status indicators were clear enough even though she couldn't tell what every number meant. Six colored arrows blinked at her. Each had a number on top which kept changing as she moved. Megan mentally selected the blue arrow and watched the others disappear. A dotted blue line with occasional arrows led her through a maze of tunnels.

When the blue arrow was twenty meters and one turn away, Megan slowed to a jog and caught her breath, wondering why the blue arrow had stopped moving.

"He's checking his phone," informed Gatton. "I sent him some more money to slow him down. You've done well so far. Shoot him and move on to the next target."

"I'm not killing them for you. The deal was to capture them, so that's all you get," said Megan.

"These are not nice men, Agent Luchek," argued Gatton. "Statistically, they'll die in a gang-related shooting in a year or two. They deserve their fate. Do the world a favor and help me cleanse it."

"If you hand-picked me for this job, then you know how I'm going to answer that. So shut up and help or keep out of it."

Gatton sighed theatrically.

"Fine. Subdue them then. It'll be less satisfying and cost the city of Las Vegas more to prosecute, but a deal's a deal."

Rounding the corner, Megan saw Nico up ahead, attention fixed on his phone. Since she wasn't going to shoot him anyway, Megan ran forward. Instinct made her want to utter a warning, even though she wasn't exactly on the official clock right now.

Trading stealth for speed, Megan dashed the last few feet separating them. Gripping the gun's barrel, she used the butt end as a battering ram, plowing it into Nico's gut. The young man went down instantly. Having little time for finesse, Megan followed the strike with a sharp downward rap on the back of his neck.

"Don't move," Megan said. The belated warning soothed her

conscience.

Gatton chuckled.

"One down, one to go. Better hurry."

Megan brought back the little arrows. Only the yellow and red one showed up, and those were blinking rapidly. The distances seemed impossibly high.

"Mmm. You might lose here." Gatton sounded mildly disappointed at the prospect.

"Get me a ride," said Megan.

"No, but I like the way you think."

"Then, show me Derrick."

"He wasn't one of the options."

"But he could be. I was only instructed to track two fugitives. He's on the run; therefore, he qualifies."

"You should have become a lawyer," Gatton commented.

Megan feared he might not agree, but soon, a yellow arrow blinked and a dotted line indicated that she should turn around.

"Show me the fastest route," Megan demanded.

The dotted line blinked then solidified as the program grew more certain of the chosen route. Megan tossed a prayer heavenward and took off. She settled for a swift pace short of a sprint to conserve energy. Much as she loathed the program's creator, Eagle Eyes was growing on her. The ability to track a target and calculate distances could be invaluable. It had limitations certainly, but the potential applications were staggering.

The sound of a gunshot prompted Megan to concentrate on the current task instead of speculating about the future. She also slowed down. The Eagle Eyes program flashed a warning. The words **THREAT ASSESSMENT ...** appeared then disappeared. Soon after, Megan received a succinct report about the direction and speed of the shot fired. The threat level soon adjusted as the program decided that the bullet was headed away from the user. The information begged a question.

Who is he shooting at?

Needing the answer to that question, Megan trotted to the next bend, knelt, and peered around the corner. To her surprise, she recognized the tunnel they were in. It was inhabited by Rena, her husband, and at least one child. Derrick stood in the middle of the tunnel with Angela planted firmly in front of him. He fired another warning shot toward the far end of the tunnel, which Megan now saw had been

79

blocked off with pieces of plywood and other debris.

"Move that stuff or they're dead!" Derrick shouted.

Aware she didn't have much time, Megan nevertheless forced herself to wait and think. Eagle Eyes told her two people stood behind the barricade, one adult and one child if she read the information correctly. If she boxed Derrick in, would he give up or crack? Giving up would mean Jaden and Angela get to live, but if he cracked, he'd kill them. Her heart beats came faster due to her nervous tension. She had to handle this right, but that required predicting a man who'd scarred her in so many ways.

"Let them go and the stuff gets moved," Rena replied. "We don't want no trouble, but we do want our folks back."

Megan wondered if she could sneak up on Derrick. She noticed a text box in the lower left hand corner of her vision and mentally typed the question in.

What are the odds of a peaceful outcome if I sneak up on Derrick?
12.25%

Megan winced. The program hadn't even hesitated before spitting the number back.

Negotiation success?

The program didn't understand the question, so she reworded it as a formal question.

25.15%

She liked the chances better, but they were still dismal.

Drawing a deep breath, Megan stepped far enough into the tunnel entrance to draw a bead on Derrick with her borrowed handgun.

"Don't do this, Derrick," Megan called. She kept her tone even, relying on work experience to remove emotion from the equation.

Derrick reacted by pulling Angela over to the right wall, if one judged lefts and rights from Megan's perspective. The move left Jaden standing in the middle of the tunnel.

"Jaden, get to that barricade," Megan instructed.

The boy looked to his mother.

"It's okay, baby. Go ahead," said Angela.

Jaden cast one more desperate look at Angela and Megan before doing as bid. Megan breathed a little easier when somebody slid a piece of plywood aside and pulled Jaden inside the safe zone. The wood probably wouldn't stop a bullet, but it still provided psychological comfort.

"Give up if you want to live, Derrick," said Megan.

Since she was the bigger threat, Derrick moved Angela into Megan's line of fire.

Can I offer him a way out?

Megan thought the question directly into the text box so the program would carry the message to Gatton.

"No."

His answer didn't surprise Megan, though it did frustrate her.

"I'm cutting my losses and leaving," said Derrick. "Your friend's going to make sure I have safe passage."

"The police are never going to let you waltz through with a hostage," Megan reasoned. "But if you stay down here, there are miles and miles of tunnels to lose them in."

"Thanks, but I'll take my chances with the cops," said Derrick.

"Don't let this happen, Maggie," said Angela.

"Quiet," snapped Derrick.

"Please. Remember my wishes." Angela shifted more of her weight to her right leg, subtly moving her left leg in a manner that freed the lower half from the loose fabric of the dress.

Angela's hard tone made Megan take notice. She thought back to their childhood sleepovers where they'd spent hours talking about randomness. Somewhere along the way, they'd played a few rounds of "would you rather." When the question was would you rather be shot or stabbed, Angela had given a rather long lecture on why and where she'd rather be shot.

The reminder gave Megan a new plan. She instantly hated it, but Angela's expression told her to get it over with.

"I said—" Derrick began.

Without warning, Megan adjusted her aim and shot her friend in the left calf.

Chapter 14:
Negotiator

Several people screamed. The bullet's impact threw Angela off balance and she promptly collapsed. Derrick lost his grip on her. The best he could do was point his gun at Megan.

They settled into a standoff. Megan's heart lifted. She needed to end this soon, but at least she'd tipped the odds in her favor. She adjusted her posture to a more classic shooter stance to relieve some of the pressure on her aching arms.

Angela's soft sobs filled the tunnel.

"It's over, Derrick," said Megan. "Put the gun down."

"You're not going to kill me." Derrick's voice held bitterness and contempt.

"I do a lot of unexpected things when I have a gun in my face," Megan replied. "And I'm a better shot than you are. It's crazy-hard to hit anything when you're nervous."

"Kill him," said Gatton.

Megan asked the program to mute Gatton until the end of her negotiation phase. After analyzing the request, Eagle Eyes concluded that the user's chances of survival improved with this temporary change, so it blocked Gatton's administrator privileges. The last thing Megan heard was the start to what she assumed would be a long string of curses.

"You've changed," said Derrick. "I remember—"

"Good observation," Megan interrupted. "That happens. People grow up. They get less stupid. At least some of us. Now drop the gun."

"Get out of my way, and I'll disappear," said Derrick.

"Twenty minutes ago, I would have taken that deal, but I've got a voice in my head telling me not to do that."

"Do you always listen to the voices in your head?" inquired Derrick.

"This one's rather persistent, and you're lucky I'm not listening to everything it wants me to do," Megan answered. "These are the best terms you're going to get. Gun down, hands up, and life goes on."

"I'm not going to jail," Derrick declared.

"You'd prefer a morgue?" Megan used the time Derrick took to think about that question to ease a step closer. "I can arrange that, though I'd rather not. The paperwork stinks."

Megan saw Derrick's decision in his eyes while she was still a few feet away. As he started to turn the gun on himself, she planted her feet and dove forward, tackling him over Angela. Having no way to brace himself, Derrick fell backwards and hit his head hard on the tunnel floor. His gun went flying toward the barricade. Megan barely hung on to her gun. She rolled to her left off of Derrick and came up on a knee with her gun once again pointed his way. He looked at her, dazed.

Two seconds passed, convincing Megan the crisis might truly be at an end. As she climbed to her feet, Gatton's voice sounded in her head.

"Congratulations. Thank you for your time. I think this was a successful mission. I'll be—"

"Let me wrap this up, and I'll deal with you," Megan murmured.

Once Derrick was subdued, the barricade opened and several homeless people shuffled forward to help. A skinny guy wearing a dirty T-shirt gave Megan a belt to bind Derrick's hands with. She directed him to use it as a tourniquet for Angela's leg. By this time, Rena had lumbered out and took over the supervising duties.

Megan went to Angela and checked on the wound. Since Angela was wearing a dress, Megan simply swept the fabric aside. She wasn't really sure where to start apologizing for shooting her friend in the leg. The other woman's eyes were clenched shut against the pain.

"Well, it worked," said Megan.

"Here, honey, get that covered," said Rena.

Megan accepted a clean rag and pressed it over the bleeding wound. Angela moaned at the new pain.

"Mom!" Jaden plopped down next to Angela, looking horrified.

"Gentle," Megan cautioned. "She's had a rough night."

"What happened?" Jaden asked.

A raised eyebrow from Megan threw the answering duties over

to Angela.

"Don't worry about it, baby," whispered Angela.

After a few minutes of reassuring and cajoling, Rena managed to lead Jaden back to the inhabited tunnel section.

"Know how I said being shot wouldn't be so bad?" asked Angela.

"Yeah?" Megan gently tied a second clean rag around the one already on Angela's wound.

"I lied. Hurts like a demon."

Chuckling, Megan leaned down and kissed her friend's sweaty forehead.

"It's better than being dead," she whispered.

Angela uttered a noncommittal grunt.

"Are you done yet?" asked Gatton. He sounded grumpy at being made to wait.

Sitting up, Megan sighed.

"What's that noise for?" wondered Angela.

"Excuse me. I need to go deal with the voice in my head. Will you be all right?"

Angela's tired nod was worrisome, but Megan figured she could spare a moment to square things with Gatton. The man needed a serious talking to about his people skills.

To minimize the chances of being seen talking to herself, Megan retreated around the corner she'd been crouched behind mere moments ago.

A phone icon in the upper right hand corner let Megan know she had an incoming call. Bracing for a verbal duel, she accepted and started speaking at the same time to be sure she was heard.

"I'm sure you're eager for my report, so here it is. Eagle Eyes is a remarkable invention with a lot of potentially useful applications. It's also dangerously intrusive and probably illegal. That said, your methods are definitely illegal. You may think you can control me but think again. You do not want me as your enemy."

"No, indeed," said Gatton, finally managing to speak. "I think we could have a mutually beneficial working relationship. My lawyers have assured me the legal ramifications are minimal, given our sponsors. Please take a look at the terms I'm offering. I'm sure you'll find them more than generous."

Megan had anticipated such a pompous offer and come to a decision. She deleted his terms without even looking at them.

"I'm willing to consider certain jobs you offer, but only on my terms. First, you fix The Grand Game Hotel's public image which you tarnished over the last few weeks and square their accounts. Second, you start—or at least pay somebody to start—a program to help the homeless people living in the tunnels under Las Vegas. Third, you stay far away from me, my family, my friends, and random people I meet on the street. That goes for your minions too. In fact, condition four is that my contact with them is minimal. If you want something, you call and ask like a normal person."

"That's quite a list," Gatton commented.

"I'm not even done yet," said Megan.

"This is the part where you tell me you don't want my money, you can't be bought, or some other noble drivel."

"Oh, I want your money," Megan corrected him. "Condition five, any legitimate earnings I make through contract work for you goes into accounts I'll specify later. The first three will need to be set up. They'll be trust funds for Jaden and my partner's kids to go to college. Six, every job has a contract. Seven, I reserve the right to turn down any job. And eight, I'm not at your beck and call. I'm keeping my day job. Any questions?"

"What makes you think I'll agree to hire you with all those conditions?" asked Gatton.

"One, it's probably cheaper than what you initially offered." Megan started counting the reasons with her fingers. "Two, I already know a little about your fancy toy. Three, I'm probably one of a handful of people the government vetted to accept your contracts. You can correct me if I'm wrong about them holding your leash. Four, although it hurts my ego to think it, I'm probably not the first person you've tried to work with. I'm guessing the others turned you down flat after your eloquent initial overture. And five, we're still having this conversation, which means you really want this to work."

"Are you always this … abrasive?"

"I get a little worked up when psychopaths have my friends kidnapped to get me to test prototypes. If this is the way you treat everybody, I'm shocked you're still alive."

"Why do you want to work for me? You obviously don't think highly of me."

The question made Megan pause.

"I respect your invention. I think it's a powerful tool, and I'm not eager for it to fall into the wrong hands."

"When it progresses beyond the prototype stage, what's to prevent me from selling to the highest bidder?"

"Self-preservation," Megan answered. "For all your lack of people skills, you're probably surrounded by advisers, who would suggest not double-crossing the government. If we have a deal, I'm taking these out now. I'll check in tomorrow to learn how best to care for them. Since you can probably get my cell phone number, I'll give it to you." She mentally typed the digits into the text box at the bottom left of her vision. "Anything else?"

"No, I believe that covers everything for now. Welcome aboard, Agent Luchek."

After signing off, Megan realized that she couldn't take the Eagle Eyes interfaces out since she no longer had the fluid-filled box to put them in. She'd use the program to locate David Stanley later or find something else to store them in. Even though she needed to keep them in, she wanted them off, so she had the program go into a sleep mode.

A few seconds later, she was back by Angela's side. The bleeding had stopped, and somebody had brought Angela several blankets to lay on. The woman still looked miserable, but at least she was still conscious.

"Hey, how's the leg?" Megan asked softly.

"Sore," Angela replied. "Did you settle things with the voice in your head?"

"Oddly, yes, and I even got Jaden a college fund in the process."

"Do I want to know how?" The question barely qualified as a whisper.

"Nope. Ignorance is bliss," said Megan. "But I will say that the voice should be fixing the mess he made with the hotel's reputation. You let me know if he doesn't follow through."

"Thank you."

Megan picked up Angela's left hand and patted it.

"That's the first time anybody's ever thanked me a few minutes after I shot them."

"Homemade painkiller," said Angela.

"I'm not going to ask about that because I'd probably have to lie about it later," said Megan. "Get some rest. I'll go get some EMTs moving, if they haven't been dispatched already."

"They're on the way," said a male voice.

Megan glanced up and saw a tall, suited man walking their way. He had a *federal agent* vibe coming out every pore. With brown hair, intense eyes, and scruff on his face, the agent reminded Megan of

Derrick, minus the creeper aura. He could have modeled the phrase tall, dark, and handsome.

"Do I give off that agent vibe?" Megan wondered.

Angela looked from Megan to the newcomer and back again.

"Not in that outfit," she replied.

Megan started to feel self-conscious then decided it wasn't worth the mental effort. Standing to meet the man, she waited for him to approach.

"Agent Luchek, I presume," said the man cheerfully. He held out a hand for her to shake. "Luke Kramer, Las Vegas FBI. It's nice to meet you." His brown eyes absorbed her appearance. "I've heard you had quite an evening."

"Get me some decent coffee, and I'll give you the gory details," Megan promised. "But I want to wait for the EMTs to get here first."

"Don't worry about me," said Angela. "Just take me to the hotel."

"You're probably short a few pints of blood. You don't get a vote on the matter," said Megan. "You're going to the hospital."

"My partner will be here with them soon," said Agent Kramer. The way he said *partner* brought out a subtle Southern accent. "Is there anything else I can do to help?"

"Ask her out," said Angela.

Megan rolled her eyes.

"Sorry. She's delirious." Despite the words, she subtly checked for a wedding ring.

She didn't find one.

"I do have a task for you though," Megan continued after only a slight pause.

"What's that?" Kramer asked, puppy-dog eager.

"Derrick and his ilk, had some women held captive down here. I set some of them loose, but I don't know if there are more. Somebody needs to organize a sweep of the tunnels."

Kramer whistled low.

"That could take a while," he commented. "Will you be around to help?"

"I'll see what my boss says," Megan answered, deciding she was okay sticking around Sin City at least a few more days.

Eagle Eyes Book 2: Rescue in Reno

By Julie C. Gilbert

Table of Contents:

Prologue:
Could be Trouble

Lillian Marquez looked at the three men around her. She trusted only one of them implicitly. The other two tolerated her because they had to, but she understood that they'd turn on her in a hot second if they thought it would help them advance in the Club. Any betrayal would likely get them killed, so they at least pretended to defer to her authority. Part of her sympathized with their frustration. Although she had worked very hard to advance up through the ranks fairly, the influence of her grandfather and father played a large part of that success. She couldn't help that. The Club was steeped in its own bloody traditions, complete with dynasties.

"Give me your reports, gentleman. Where do we stand after last night's ... festivities?" asked Lillian. She had mixed feelings about those *festivities*. Her wrists still bore the marks where a betrayal had almost gotten her killed, but Megan Luchek's actions had saved her. That complicated the issue at hand.

"Only one shipment was compromised," said Steel. Lou Sands—a.k.a. Steel—was the only trustworthy soul present. Pure old-school mobster, Steel kept to the code and expected everybody else to do the same. He treated his people well and kept his public nose clean.

"Good. What about the personnel side?" Lillian really wanted to move past the compromised shipment part. Having been among those who escaped captivity at the time was a huge embarrassment. Holding this meeting in the restaurant owned by the vanquished foe helped offset the insult, but she had to assert control quickly or face a different rebellion. She kept her hands wrapped around the coffee cup to prove she wasn't self-conscious about the raw spots where the handcuffs cut her.

It was a lie. She could barely think of anything else. The meeting had gone on long enough that the men had each finished two or three cups of coffee.

"Nico and Derrick were handed over to the cops," said Garrett Falco. Little G-man had picked up his nickname by defecting from the local FBI office ages ago, practically before Lillian was born.

Lillian knew flipping officials was a professional sport among her people, but traitors made her nervous on principle. A lot of the business hinged on trust.

"We should retire them," William Barr commented. BB managed the local enforcer talent. "I got a few candidates who can do the hits and be relocated in a few days."

"Killing them sends a message, but it'll also stir up trouble," Steel noted. "Do we wanna risk it?"

"Before I make a decision on that, how are we doing with our inside FBI guy?" Lillian asked. She directed the question to Little G-man, since he maintained assets in certain government offices. "Can he suppress the investigation?"

"He's not as senior as I'd like, but he stands a good chance of being assigned to the investigation. I'll check in with him again and get you an update later tonight." Little G-man took out his phone and tapped in a reminder for himself.

"Thank you. I'd like to meet him sometime. Can you arrange that?" Lillian's father had always emphasized the importance of niceties. She also needed to buy a few seconds to think. Ordering a hit was never something to do lightly. From a business standpoint, hits were like highly controversial political advertisements. They declared the Club's presence and position on a matter, but they also drew a lot of attention. The wrong sort of publicity could be disastrous.

Little G-man nodded. He understood her request to be an order.

If they stayed true to form, Steel would urge caution while the other two endorsed firm action. Lillian usually leaned toward caution, but she couldn't afford to dismiss the others' opinions outright. They would take it personally. Technically, her word was law here, but the Club members notoriously kept mental score of getting their way. If she slapped Little G-man and BB down here, she'd pay for it in some other way.

There was also the small matter of face. Derrick Belmont had tried to kill her. Despite the fact that he definitely deserved to die, Lillian's heart hurt at the thought of ordering it. Part of her still loved him. She had no strong feelings about Nico's fate. He was a foot soldier. His crime of betrayal affected the Club as a whole more than Lillian herself.

While on the subject of deserved punishments, Branson, Arnold, Antonio, and Caleb had earned spots on her agenda through action or inaction last night. The latter four's only saving grace was the good fortune of not being caught.

Sensing the silence stretch uncomfortably, Lillian cleared her throat and met each of her lieutenants' eyes.

"I want Branson, Arnold, Antonio, and Caleb on probation for three months. Don't dock their pay but make them very aware of how closely their actions will be monitored. If you even think they're likely to have a disloyal thought, you can deal with them accordingly."

The three men nodded, though Steel's response was far less enthusiastic than Little G-man or BB.

"What about D-man and Nico?" BB pressed. His dark eyes narrowed, showing his eagerness to debate.

Lillian met the challenging gaze with a cool, indulgent smile.

"Your people have one chance to take them out, if and only if it can be done quietly," said Lillian. "You may want to wait until they're in prison and let some of our guests of the state take care of them rather than burn an important asset now, but I'll leave that decision up to you." By placing the responsibility in BB's hands, Lillian earned plausible deniability should anything go wrong. It also distanced her from the situation more than outright ordering their termination.

Steel's expression didn't change much, but Lillian sensed his reservations about the decision.

"The next matter is that of Megan Luchek," said Lillian. "How much of a problem is she going to be?" She let her tone stay soft and curious.

"I can remove her along with Nico and Derrick," BB offered.

"That's not a good idea," argued Steel. "She's not from Vegas, but she saved Lil. People are gonna know that. We need to find a different way of controlling her that doesn't involve killing her. It sends the wrong message."

"She's built quite a reputation within the FBI," Little G-man noted. He ran a hand through his graying light brown hair. "She's a bit of a maverick, but she gets most jobs done. And, worse, rumor has it she may join the investigation into the tunnel business. That could be trouble."

"My people can sit on the key players underground," said BB. "We can afford to divert shipments to alternate locations for a short while, but eventually, we're going to need to reset our tunnel operation."

"Get on that as soon as possible," Lillian instructed. "Do we have any informants among the homeless population?"

"Not really," BB admitted.

"See if we can develop some assets there," said Lillian. "They're probably relatively cheap and easy to keep happy. Find their vice and feed it."

"Do you want me to fully recruit anybody?" asked BB. His tone conveyed skepticism about the wisdom of such a plan.

"No. Give them small incentives to spread our messages throughout the underground network," said Lillian. "Keeping people away from our operation is for the best and keeping them quiet is even more important. We need to make nice with the locals where possible. We can't have a body count drawing undue attention to the operation."

"And the Luchek issue?" asked Little G-man, calling Lillian on the delaying tactic.

Lillian sighed, weighing the pros and cons for the umpteenth time. Not killing Agent Luchek would run the risk of having her interfere, but it would also show that the Club rewarded those who treated its members right. Killing her would nip the interference bit in the bud, but it would also send mixed messages about doing good to Club members.

"Quietly spread the word among those that matter. Agent Luchek gets a pass this round because of what she did for me," said Lillian. She spoke slowly to let the words sink in and gauge their reactions. "If she becomes a problem, rescind the immunity."

The men bobbed their heads briefly in acknowledgement. A hint of a smile indicated Steel's approval of her plan.

"Send scouts into the underground after the investigation team," Lillian continued. "I want to know how bad the damage is before making a final decision about how to handle the tunnel people. I want to avoid bodies, but if we need to make a statement, we do it."

"I've already sent a few of my guys around to remind the locals to keep their mouths shut," said BB.

"Do they know enough to damage the operation?" Lillian

wondered.

"Hard to say," said Little G-man.

"I'll question the boys involved again to get a feel for which locals would make the best statement should it come to that," BB offered. "Based on the territory, my guess is Jake and Rena Coon or one of the brats staying with them."

"No kids," said Steel.

"We don't have to kill the brat," argued BB. "A trip on the Circuit would be just as effective to those left behind. I bet that would shut down loose lips faster than any verbal threat."

"Nobody but the tunnel people are gonna care what happens to one of the Lost Ones," said Little G-man with a shrug. "As long as the kid's body doesn't surface here, the cops won't care."

"No kids," Steel repeated. His tone had a quiet, deadly edge that made even Lillian sit up straighter.

"No kids for now," Lillian agreed, wanting to keep the peace. "Where are you diverting the shipments?" The shift wasn't subtle, but she needed the information anyway.

"North to Reno," Little G-man answered. "It's not ideal, but the safe houses there have been idle for a while. From there, the shipments can be split to head west into California or north again into Oregon or Idaho."

"What's wrong with Reno?" Lillian inquired. "Could the reroute be permanent?" She didn't like showing such ignorance of the operation supposedly under her command, but these systems had been in place way longer than she'd been in control.

"Nothing's wrong with the city itself," BB explained, "but the Las Vegas stop was the major sorting hub. The drivers are going to be pulling much longer shifts to get up to Reno to rest. We might have to put two drivers per truck. That's going to eat up profits."

"Can we run a modified operation here?" asked Lillian. "I know the tunnels should be avoided for now until the FBI finishes their initial sweep, but we have other safe houses here."

"It's risky," Steel commented. "We don't have the privacy the underground affords."

"What about the parking garages?" Lillian knew the Club owned several throughout Las Vegas.

"We're going to be using some of them in cases of emergency," Little G-man reported, "but we can't change too much about their operation without tipping off the cops. Each garage has its regulars as well as tourist overflow. They're profitable in their own right, but it's nothing compared to the Circuit."

"The best option is to make the tunnels safe for business again," BB concluded.

"Then that will be my priority," Lillian promised. "I need to meet with the lawyers later today to sort the legal mess surrounding this place, but you know how to reach me if you think I should know something. Does anybody have anything else they'd like to talk about before we close?" She sort of hoped nothing else came up. Meetings with lawyers could be soul-sucking. She needed to rest before heading into that storm.

"The business at The Grand Game Hotel might still be on the table," said Steel. "My read on the reports is that Agent Luchek ended up with the tech prototype. Since she's still staying at the hotel, we could toss her room for it. I think the owners are both away at the moment."

"Find out for sure," Lillian cautioned. "If you think you can get it, you have my blessing to do so." She sipped at her cold coffee to keep from giving Steel further instructions. He knew the business better than she did. Micromanaging him would be insulting. Taking point on that job had been foolish, but she knew better now. The satisfaction of having that job completed would be good for her sense of closure.

"The woman was wounded last night," said BB. "She's probably in the hospital, and I believe the husband's been away for a few weeks."

"Find them both," Lillian instructed. "If the room search yields nothing, perhaps we can ask Agent Luchek where she put it. I want to know where all the moving pieces are when we make our approach."

"I'll have a word with my hotel people," said Little G-man. "The manager should know where his boss went."

"The woman is in Sunrise Hospital," said Steel. "One of my guys heard that much from the scanner chatter last night."

"Who's taking care of the boy?" Lillian wondered. She'd done enough background research while prepping to get the mystery technology to know Angela Melkin-Pierce had one son before marrying Anthony Pierce.

Everybody shrugged.

"These people are important to Agent Luchek and key to the hotel," Lillian reminded her men. "Do we know where Gatton's man went?"

"He disappeared, but most of the employees of Gatton Technologies are still at the hotel," said Little G-man. "I'll get somebody to trace the proxy. Somebody will know how to track the head honcho down."

Signaling Charlene to bring the check, Lillian subtly closed the meeting. She couldn't shake the nagging feeling that they should cut their losses and forget the GT job. Nobody liked admitting defeat, but the job had been one disaster after another so far. Obtaining the prototype known as Eagle Eyes would do wonders for her little slice of Club paradise, but it could also ruin them. She wasn't even clear on what Eagle Eyes did exactly, but the bounty on the prototype meant it would be a technological game changer. A word from her could halt everything right now. That would be the safe move. But Lillian couldn't bring herself to quit just yet.

Let it ride.

Chapter 1:
Code of Silence

Standing outside a flood tunnel entrance near The Grand Game Hotel, Megan Luchek reflected on how much a few hours of sleep—and a change into fresh clothes—could fix. Sunlight lent her a sense of hope and optimism.

She didn't consider herself a workaholic, but at the same time, she couldn't deny how nice it felt to officially *unofficially* be wearing her FBI Special Agent hat again. Technically, vacation would go through Saturday, which was still three days away, when she'd fly back to Honolulu. However, Megan had obtained clearance from Special Agent in Charge Bryan Maddox to help a Las Vegas agent interview some homeless people. The short stay in Sin City had thus far been very eventful, allowing her to butt heads with a billionaire's flunky and human traffickers.

What more could a girl want?

"Did you sleep well?" asked a polite male voice, pulling Megan out of her reverie.

"Yes," she answered by reflex. "The late night wore me out quite well. Thank you."

Twisting her head around, Megan saw a lovely sight. Special Agent Luke Kramer approached holding two large, steaming Styrofoam cups. The young agent had a lean face, brown eyes, dark hair, and even more scruff than he'd had early this morning upon their first meeting.

"Care to risk a local brew?" he asked, holding out one of the two cups.

"Sure. You've caught me in an adventurous mood," said Megan, turning to accept the coffee with two hands. She smiled her thanks and brought the cup close to smell. The warmth felt good against her hands. Although not particularly cold this morning for Vegas January standards, the years in Hawaii had spoiled her. The shock to her system wasn't as bad as December in Philadelphia, Pennsylvania had been, but she enjoyed the brief brush of steam across her face. "What's the game plan?"

Getting underground quickly would stave off the cold issue.

"I want to start with the folks we met last night, the couple with the kids." Kramer's use of the word *folks* emphasized his slight Southern accent. "I had people on most entrances last night, but I think some of your runners slipped through. The city boys and girls picked up three young ladies and are holding them until proper interviews can be conducted. Care to join me later for that? Even if we miss the actual interviews, I've been assured we can see the recordings at our convenience."

"I'd like that," Megan said, acutely aware how much it sounded like she'd just accepted a date.

Business. Stick to business.

"Great. As soon as we finish with these, we can head on in." Agent Kramer held up his coffee cup to illustrate his point.

Despite the scalding nature of the liquid, both agents downed the coffee as quickly as humanly possible. Kramer gallantly took the empty cup from Megan and jogged over to a conveniently placed garbage can. At first, the location had struck Megan as odd, but she figured it was the city's quiet nod to the homeless population. She wasn't sure of the legalities surrounding homelessness in Las Vegas. Generally, people frowned upon the homeless for one reason or another, but nobody had offered a great solution for getting everybody affordable shelter. So the city, like any other, had learned to cope with its unwanted inhabitants.

As they prepared to enter, Megan saw they weren't alone.

"Hello, Sarah. Have you come to guide us?"

Jaden Melkin's young friend took a tentative step into the sunlight and waved to Megan.

"Rena said you'd want to see us today." The girl's voice was wary. "Did you bring any social workers with you?" The tone slipped from caution to mild contempt.

"No social workers," Agent Kramer promised. He held his hands up in a disarming gesture. "It's only us. Some of my colleagues will be visiting other locations, but we're the only ones here." Catching

Megan's puzzled look, Kramer explained, "They don't trust a lot of social workers."

"They're always trying to make me go to school," said Sarah. "Don't need school. Got lots of books at home. Rena tells me stuff too."

The girl's heartbreaking reference to the section of flood tunnel as *home* hit Megan hard, but she managed to keep emotions locked inside. The girl should be in school, but now wasn't the time to fight that battle. They followed Sarah through the convoluted series of tunnels to the section chosen by Jake and Rena Coon.

"I wonder why they chose this particular tunnel," Megan mused.

"It doesn't flood much," said Sarah. "And it's safer. Most of the drug addicts like to stay near the Strip."

No child should ever have to worry about avoiding drug addicts, but once again, Megan kept the opinion deep inside where it wouldn't show up in her expression. Her mind started working the problem. Pride prevented a lot of people from accepting the help they needed, but maybe Sarah was young enough to still see a future in life above ground. Perhaps Jeffrey Gatton could help Megan change the girl's fortunes. It was worth consideration anyway. He wasn't a vending machine, but the billionaire still owed Megan for the massively stupid plan that blew up in their faces yesterday.

After escorting them to Rena, Sarah ran off in the opposite direction from where they came in. Rena sat on the raised queen-sized bed in almost the same position as Megan had found her in the previous night. This time, she had her right ankle perched atop a stack of books. Megan was pleased to note that the bandages looked fresh.

"The EMT folks wouldn't stop nagging until I let 'em take a look," said Rena, noticing Megan's attention to her injury. "Had to promise to mind their instructions to avoid getting swept off to the hospital. Can't afford to land in a place like that." Her tone asked for no pity.

"Is there anything we can do to help, ma'am?" asked Agent Kramer. His gaze swept around the makeshift room.

If it were up to Megan, she'd have Kramer start by getting somebody to deal with the pool of stagnant water dominating the room's center.

Rena waved them over and leveled a long, serious gaze at each of them.

"Been doing some thinking over the last few hours," she began, lowering her voice a little. "Gonna have to ask you folks to leave." She raised a hand to halt their protests. "Ain't trying to be rude, but y'all can't do much unless you've got an army with ya. Rumors already be starting."

"What kind of rumors?" Megan asked, inching as close to the bed as she could without crowding the woman. She wondered how Rena heard anything in this isolated place, but then she remembered how efficiently Sarah made her way around the flood tunnels. The thought of the girl wandering these lonely corridors gave Megan a chill.

"Oh, the usual," Rena said wearily. "Reminders to keep to the Code or suffer the consequences. The Code—of course—being silence."

The news didn't surprise Megan, but the speed did. It didn't bode well that threats had already circulated throughout the underground. Not even twelve hours had passed since the chaos that was last night's adventures. The bad guys were highly organized. She supposed they'd have to be to coordinate effective use of the tunnel system for their trafficking purposes, but she didn't like the demonstration of clear communication.

"I know you've left some messages with the police department over the last few months," said Kramer. "And I apologize for the delay in getting a response, but we're here now. If you help us, we can clear out whatever's going on down here."

"These people be like rats," said Rena. "You can scatter 'em for a time, but they be back, only angrier, next time."

"Human trafficking's a federal crime," said Agent Kramer. "I've got enough evidence to launch an investigation with or without help, but it'll go much faster and be more effective if you help us."

"Please. What I saw last night didn't look like an isolated incident," Megan said. "A lot of lives could be saved if we understood the organization better. We're not asking you to actually show us, but if you can help us make a map or describe where you think the bad things are going down, we'll take it from there."

"A lot of lives could be lost if I say something that gets back to the wrong ears," Rena replied. "The underground be a small world. The only difference be which lives get lost, and I ain't gonna put Sarah, Josh, and Reggie at risk for strangers."

"I understand," said Megan. "I don't agree, but I respect the tough position you're in." She took a small step back to signal acceptance. "If you change your mind, have Sarah come find me at the hotel. She knows where my room is." The girl had retrieved something from Megan's room mere hours before. "If she can't find me, have her leave a message with Jaden. I'm only in town a few more days, but if you need something, ask at The Grand Game Hotel. They're good people."

"How is your friend?" asked Rena.

"I don't know," Megan admitted. "I'm going to visit her at the hospital later this afternoon."

"Tell her I be praying for her recovery," said Rena.

"I will," Megan promised.

Agent Kramer cleared his throat softly.

"If you're sure there's nothing we can do for you, ma'am, we'll take our leave," he said.

"I know I can't stop you, and most of me don't even wanna try. But it be for the best if you left well enough alone. Folks ain't gonna talk to you. These men be bad news for everybody."

"How long has this been going on?" Megan asked.

"Don't know, but not more than a few months in the tunnels near here." Rena's expression turned frightened. "There I go saying too much." She pressed her lips firmly together to prevent more damaging information from slipping out.

Waving farewell, Megan ushered Agent Kramer out the back exit. The next three hours slipped by in a frustrating combination of getting lost, doubling back, looking over the crime scene, and occasionally conducting a fruitless interview with a tunnel inhabitant. Most of the conversations ran along similar lines. Either people genuinely had no clue or they clammed up soon after the pleasantries.

One man screamed bloody murder when he saw their suits, but between the hail of curses, they gathered it was a case of mistaken identity. Once they finally assured him they weren't there to kidnap him for the aliens, he calmed down.

"I wish we could speak with Sarah," Megan mused, as they headed back toward the entrance nearest the hotel. She wasn't sold on the idea, but the girl probably knew more about these tunnels than the men who designed the place.

"Looks like we might get that chance," Luke Kramer commented. He nodded briefly ahead where the girl peered at them around a corner.

"No," said Megan. She stopped abruptly and lowered her voice to a whisper. "We're not asking that girl a single question."

"Why not?" Luke asked, taken aback by her firm tone. "She's probably got a better handle on what goes on than any of the adults."

"Agreed, but if we know that, so do the bad guys," Megan

argued. "I don't want to be the reason they go after her, do you?"

"Of course not, but how would they even know?"

Kramer had a point, but Megan firmly believed in Murphy's Law. The last few months of her life were proof that anything and everything could go wrong in a heartbeat. If she didn't find taking down corrupt and evil people so satisfying, Megan would consider running away from society altogether. She didn't answer Kramer until they stepped out into the sunshine.

"Bad guys have a knack for finding out stuff they're not supposed to, but let's focus on what we can do," said Megan. "As you said to Rena, we can make do without the homeless people's help. It'll just take longer and require more agents. Do you think you can round up the necessary manpower?"

"I'll have to," said Luke. The troubled look in his eyes told Megan he was recalling some of the places they'd seen today. The tunnel sections used as prisons had a lingering air of misery, as if the captives' anguish soaked into the concrete. "That can't go on."

"No, it can't," Megan agreed. She considered asking Maddox for permission to stick it out through the rest of the investigation. Although she didn't think he'd go for it, she'd have Luke start the paperwork from this end.

Chapter 2:
Damage Control

Anthony Pierce thought the day couldn't get worse. He'd been awakened at the crack of dawn by two cops and a nervous hotel manager and informed that his wife was in the hospital. He would have canceled his meetings and driven the seven and a half hours from Reno to Las Vegas if a very long conversation with Angela hadn't convinced him she would be fine.

The emergency room doctor had cleaned the bullet wound on her lower left leg and patched it up. They wanted to keep her for a few hours to make sure an infection didn't spring up and to give her time for the painkillers to work through her system. She might even be home—or at her home away from home—by now. He'd bet good money she went to her office instead of the house. Since the hotel was in walking distance of Jaden's school, Angela liked to wait in her office for his arrival.

The meetings earlier in the week had gone okay, but today's meeting could have gone better. Three key investors were getting nervous, and no matter how many times Anthony reminded them of The Grand Game Hotel's long history and good reputation, they couldn't see much beyond the last few months of low occupancy numbers. If things didn't turn around soon, they'd lose the hotel. Even selling wasn't really a profitable option anymore.

The only slightly good news was Angela's claim that the sabotage issue had been settled. He'd told the investors the news, but they didn't seem to care. The damage had already been done. Several scathing reviews had already been posted at various travel sites. Numbers weren't likely to improve much if people feared having their tires slashed or their rooms broken into. They could revamp the electronic lock system. It was slightly outdated after all. But a new system would cost money they didn't have.

On par with his lousy day, the grim skies decided to release torrents of rain as he prepared to leave the bank where his meeting marathon had finally concluded for the day. Rain meant fewer cabs. He could hire a car, but he didn't want to deal with the foul weather surcharge those companies tacked on.

To his surprise, he stepped out and saw a man exiting a taxi van. Splashing through giant puddles that had formed on the sidewalk, Anthony practically dove into the van. Before he could rattle off his hotel's address, the man who'd gotten out slammed the door shut and hopped into the front passenger seat.

The locks clicked with a dull shutting noise.

Automatically, Anthony's hand flew to the handle and pulled.

Nothing happened.

"What's—"

"Keep quiet and you don't get hurt," said the man in the passenger seat. He had twisted around to face Anthony.

The driver pulled out into the late afternoon traffic.

"Man, we are in so much trouble," muttered the driver.

"Just drive," growled the passenger.

"Here's my wallet," said Anthony, pulling out his wallet and holding it near the tiny slot used to pay fares in cash. "There's not much in it, but it's yours. Let me out at the next corner. I don't want any trouble."

"It's not about money, Mr. Pierce," said the passenger.

Anthony squinted at the man and racked his brain for a motive besides money. Fear and anger fought for supremacy within him. Since fear was closer to the helplessness he'd been feeling all day, Anthony indulged the anger.

"Let me out!" he snapped. "You've got no right to hold me—"

"He's right," said the driver. His hand hovered near the unlock button.

For a second, Anthony thought reason would prevail and the driver would release him. Whatever discord lay between the driver and the passenger, he was rooting for the driver.

"You touch that lock, and I'll kill you," said the passenger.

The driver's left hand returned to the wheel.

"Man, this is insane!" he complained. "We were supposed to watch the dude, not snatch him."

"You want to join the Club or not?" asked the passenger. His tone hardened with annoyance. A moment later, his voice turned conciliatory. "Quit worrying. We do them a few favors and we're in. Easy. No problem. We'll be on our way to bigger jobs and serious money in no time."

The driver sulked in silence for a while.

Anthony considered trying to reason with them again, but he also wanted to hear more about their plans. The fact that they seemed not to have a plan gave him mixed feelings. They knew his name, so it probably wasn't a random mistake that the cab was waiting for him. The driver's last comment mentioned being hired to watch him. Who would bother? He was nobody. He couldn't even manage a hotel he'd mostly inherited from his grandparents. With effort, he yanked his mind back to the present problem of being kidnapped. It really was insane.

"Call and ask for instructions," said the driver, "and hope the boss-man is in a good mood."

***

"Your timing tells me I'm not going to enjoy this conversation," said Lillian Marquez. She'd excused herself and stepped into the tiny, airless office off the main conference room in the Law Offices of Wolfe, Crane, and Paterson.

"Got a problem with some freelancers looking to impress us," said BB.

"What kind of problem?" Lillian's patience levels were already scraping rock bottom from dealing with Brant Paterson and his paralegal minions most of the afternoon.

"The kind where the idiots kidnap the guy they're supposed to keep tabs on," BB reported. His tight tone indicated his simmering anger.

"They grabbed Pierce," Lillian muttered, needing to voice the problem.

"That's about the sum of it," said BB. "What do you want me to tell them?"

Lillian hated making snap decisions, but this kind of problem would only fester if given time. Shoving her anger aside, she let the possibilities scroll through her mind. Option one: they could release Pierce and pretend it never happened. He'd probably go running to the police even if they warned him not to. Option two: they could kill him. It seemed extreme and unfair, but the option was arguably the safest from her point of view. Option three: they could keep him. Though merely a delaying tactic, the move would keep the most options open.

Releasing Pierce would make him harder to grab if they decided they needed him later. Killing him would remove him from all equations, but Lillian wasn't sure she wanted to upset the delicate balance that way. The move would get a strong reaction from the wife, but Lillian couldn't guarantee the turmoil would carry over to Agent Luchek. Therefore, it made little sense.

"Have them deliver Pierce to somebody you trust," she instructed.

"Do I pay them?" BB inquired.

Tough question.

Their actions were both reckless and bold. The Club needed men with guts and intuition, but it also needed men who followed orders.

"Pay them in advice," Lillian suggested. "In the future, they follow orders to the letter. They're not paid to think. I'm assuming they wanted to join the Club. Pass it off as an initiation. Give them another errand of your choosing and see how they do." An idea blazed to life. "In fact, bring them here."

"Shouldn't we keep them far away from important business?" BB asked cautiously.

"Yes, but we also have quite a few homeless people to intimidate over the next few weeks," said Lillian. "I don't think they can mess up that task. Plus, if they get themselves lost down there, you'll know they weren't worth your time."

"You've got it," said BB. "Do you want Pierce brought back to Vegas or should we leave him up in Reno?"

"Do you have a trustworthy soul up there?"

"I do," BB confirmed, "but it's going to require bringing Pierce to one of the safe houses we're using as a holding tank right now. Do you want to take that risk?"

"Do it," said Lillian, after only a brief hesitation. "Have the newcomers meet your guy in a neutral zone. He can take proper precautions and move Pierce to the safe house. Blindfold, ear plugs, the works. Drug him if you have to. I don't want the man to know so much as the state he's in."

BB acknowledged the orders and signed off.

Not quite ready to go back and deal with the lawyer again, Lillian called Steel.

He answered on the third ring.

"We're going to have an unexpected guest up in one of the Reno houses soon," said Lillian. "I need you to do some damage control." She explained the situation as swiftly as possible. "What do you suggest?"

Steel had long been her most trusted adviser. If anybody could turn this situation around, it was him.

"It's risky, but we can work with this," said Steel. "I think the agent's friend is going to be released from the hospital soon. I'll have somebody drop off a phone. Have BB's boys get me pictures when they can. If the agent's with the woman, all the better. We won't have to wait for the message to be delivered."

"What message are you sending the agent?" Lillian could think of half a dozen things she wanted to say, but they mostly boiled down to: **drop the human trafficking investigation.**

"I'll suggest she end her Vegas trip early," said Steel.

Lillian doubted that would work. She bit her bottom lip to keep from telling him to use a burner phone. The days of delivering threats in person were long since expired.

"She's not going to, but that's the way the game goes," Steel continued. "It's the equivalent of firing across the bow."

A few beats of silence passed while Lillian considered the wisdom of sticking to ancient unspoken rules of engagement. The world had changed in the last couple of hundred years. Becoming predictable would ruin them.

"Am I making a mistake?" Lillian surprised herself with that question. "Should we release Pierce and ride out the investigation? What's there to find in the tunnels anyway? We could move the operation out of the Vegas underground altogether."

"Moving the operation completely will take a lot of effort and cost the Club a lot of money," said Steel. "You know how they feel about that."

Lillian's thoughts flashed back to her childhood where she'd witnessed her father's heated conversations with his lieutenants over money matters. There had been times when outright violence happened right in their living room. Her father had once caught a truck driver who'd been skimming profits. He'd spent three hours trying to reason with the young man. When that had failed, he'd washed his hands of the man. Lillian didn't know the guy's fate for certain, but she could guess. The Club definitely did not like losing money.

"I think keeping Pierce is the right move. If we want the tunnel investigation to go our way, we've got to deal with the outsider influence soon," Steel explained. "Little G-man's insider can kill it as soon as the catalyst is gone. Luchek won't bow to a lone threat, but when it becomes clear Pierce could die, her friend will provide added pressure."

"Isn't she leaving soon anyway?" asked Lillian.

"Not according to Little G-man," said Steel. "She probably asked to be assigned to this investigation. They could grant her a temporary transfer to the Vegas office. Then, she'd really be a thorn in our sides."

"When does killing her become an option?" Lillian didn't want to ask that, but it would come up eventually anyway.

"Killing's always an option," Steel reminded her. "But we've got to consider the pros and cons. Feds get riled when their people go down. For now, it's better to get her to voluntarily bow out of the investigation."

Lillian couldn't argue with his logic.

"Let me know what happens."

Before Lillian could disconnect the call, Steel asked one more question.

"Are you prepared to order Luchek's death if it comes to that?"

Normally, Lillian would be offended, but she understood where Steel was coming from. He'd come up through the ranks while she was still learning to crawl. He'd seen the best and worst of her throughout the years.

"I'll do my job," Lillian replied. Going with the principle that less is more, she left it at that, but for some reason, her throat suddenly felt very dry.

Chapter 3:
Get on the Plane

Time marched steadily toward 5:00 p.m. by the time Megan picked up flowers, a stuffed bear, and a card from the hospital's version of a tourist trap.

Convenience is expensive.

When she compared the cost to the size of the apology she owed Angela, it didn't seem so bad. A kindly nurse gave Megan directions up to her friend's third-floor room.

The décor reminded Megan of a sparsely furnished dorm room. The entryway struck a fine balance between cramped and bare. She guessed they didn't want anything to inhibit movement of beds and gurneys, but the designers had stuck a tiny bathroom in between adjacent rooms. A chair vying for the title of ugliest monstrosity ever took up most of the far corner beyond the bed. Cheap wooden cabinets blended in with the beige walls, both of which contrasted starkly with the blindingly white bedsheets. A faint antiseptic aroma filled the air, and a soft, steady beep provided the perfect soundtrack to going insane.

"Hey, are you conscious?" Megan asked, stepping cautiously into the room.

Angela's eyes popped open and honed in on her.

"Get me out of here!" she demanded. "I need to go someplace with decent food and good TV."

"There's never anything good on TV, but I can sympathize with you on the food thing." Megan walked around the bed to the end table where she could lay her pricey burdens down before presenting them properly. She spotted a white bag on the floor. "I see you've been cheating on the food thing anyway."

Angela followed her gaze and waved dismissively.

"That was chicken soup from the hotel's kitchen. I had to bribe Phil to bring me lunch so I wouldn't starve, but that was hours ago. Help a girl out here."

"Did the doctor say you're well enough to leave yet?" asked Megan.

"This is a city hospital, honey. Spotting a doctor is like winning the lottery," said Angela. "Sadly, it comes down to 'he who makes the biggest stink gets helped first around here.' I was drugged most of the morning, so I'm behind on my stink-making."

"I can help with that," Megan promised. "If you're truly well enough." She leaned down and gave her friend an awkward half-hug then handed over the teddy bear wearing a Get Well Soon T-shirt. Angela looked like she needed to cuddle something.

"The bandage is on the wrong leg," Angela teased, smiling her thanks. She turned the bear around and folded her arms around it, so that the thing stared up at Megan with big, glassy black eyes. The bear's right leg was swaddled in white bandages, and it had a soft, plushy crutch tucked up under its right arm.

"Sorry, they were out of left-leg bandages," said Megan.

"At least you got the flowers right," Angela noted with a wink. "I'm touched that you remembered I love irises."

"Anybody who's ever stepped foot in your office would remember you like them," Megan commented. "I think—"

Two sharp raps at the door interrupted her. Something slid across the floor.

Megan dashed around the bed to get a better look at the thing.

It was a cell phone.

"What is it?" asked Angela.

Without answering, Megan raced to the door and looked both ways. Seeing nothing unusual, she hesitated. She couldn't be everywhere at once. There were dozens of places to duck inside and hide. Whoever had knocked and slid the phone in could be in the next room over for all she knew. If she checked along the right hallway and guessed wrong, she'd never have time to check the left hallway. In any case, leaving Angela alone didn't seem wise. The sound of a ringing phone drew Megan back into the room.

"Talk to me," said Angela. "What's wrong?"

"I'm not sure," Megan admitted. She knelt down next to the

phone. It kept on ringing.

"Are you going to answer it?" Angela inquired.

Unease tightened Megan's stomach. She really didn't want to answer the phone, but she had a feeling ignoring it would only compound the problem. Picking up the cell phone, Megan turned it over and examined it for signs of tampering. With the kind of week she'd been having, she wouldn't put it past karma to send an exploding phone her way. A glance at Angela's frightened expression threw a shot of guilt into the mix.

Sliding the bar over to accept the call, Megan tapped the speaker button and waited. Jogging over to the door, she closed it firmly before returning to Angela's side and holding the phone between them. After a quick internal debate, she decided on the formal and direct approach.

"I assume you know whom you're addressing. What can I do for you?"

"Put Angela Melkin-Pierce on the line." The male speaker's tone came across as business-like.

Angela's eyes widened in confusion, but she managed to whisper a response.

"This is Angela."

"Find the photos on this phone," instructed the man.

It seemed a reasonably harmless request, but Megan tilted the screen in her direction so she could view the images first. If she could shield Angela from what was to come, she would. Her fingers flew over the touch screen until she found the Photos app. Six tiny images popped up. She hoped for a location tag, but she wasn't that lucky. Tapping the first photo showed her a man she'd never met but instantly recognized from the pictures in Angela's office. A time stamp in the corner told her the photo had been taken about an hour ago.

Each picture showed Anthony Pierce having a really bad day. In the first picture, he was bound hand and foot and staring up with haunted eyes from a large trunk. The second picture featured a close up of his face. Thin glasses perched at a strange angle on his nose. His left eye looked slightly swollen. With a broad forehead and short, spikey brown hair, Anthony was handsome in a nerdy sort of way. The lower half of his face was a mask of duct tape. The third, fourth, and fifth pictures chronicled his transfer from the car trunk to a dark room with a sturdy wooden chair. The last image showed him bound to the chair, shooting eye daggers at his captors.

Megan's teeth clenched as she dealt with the surge of anger rising from deep within.

"Show me," Angela pleaded, reading enough in Megan's expression.

"Show her," echoed the man. His unyielding tone made it an order.

"She doesn't need to see the pictures," Megan argued.

"You will show her them or we'll hurt him."

Silently cursing the heartlessness of that, Megan turned the phone so Angela could see the pictures and scrolled through them quickly. Angela gasped and tears sprang to her eyes.

"She's seen them," Megan reported tightly. "Now, what do you want?"

"I'm going to put Mr. Pierce on the line for a moment so you believe the promises to come."

In a few seconds, a new male voice joined the conversation.

"Angela? Are you okay?"

"Anthony! Where are you?"

"I don't know. I—"

Anthony's voice cut off abruptly, but the sound of his voice had a marked effect upon Angela. Tears flowed steadily now. Her eyes searched Megan's face, desperate for answers.

"Are you convinced?" asked the stranger with the cold voice.

"Yes, we believe you have Mr. Pierce," said Megan.

"Good. Go home, Agent."

The man's simple order shocked Megan.

"Drop the tunnel investigation and catch the next available flight back to Hawaii," continued the man. "Mr. Pierce will be returned safely once I receive confirmation that you've obeyed these instructions."

Megan's mind raced. Threatening Anthony to obtain compliance from her made little to no sense. She barely knew the man and hadn't so much as shaken his hand in real life. A look at Angela showed her where most of the threat's damage was being done. By telling Megan they wanted her out of the tunnel investigation, they'd revealed how much they valued whatever had gone on down there.

"I have no jurisdiction up here," Megan pointed out. "The investigation doesn't hinge on my approval or participation, so why take the risk of kidnapping Mr. Pierce?"

The more laws you break, the more attention you draw to yourself.

She decided not to share that thought.

"There must be more than you're telling me," Megan pressed.

She didn't want to upset the man, but the longer he talked, the more likely it was he'd let something slip.

"If Mr. Pierce is of no use to me, shall I have him killed?"

"No!" The emphatic answer came from Megan and Angela.

Gripping the phone hard, Megan reached out to her friend. She seriously hated giving the evil guy what he wanted in terms of a reaction, but she couldn't help it. Angela seized her hand and squeezed hard. Megan thought it high time to wrap up this little heart-to-heart.

"Give me 48 hours to make my plans," said Megan.

"There's a plane leaving from McCarran International in six hours. Be on it, or I send him back in pieces."

The call ended.

Shortly thereafter a text message came through.

It read: **No cops. No feds. Get on the plane.**

Megan let her eyes linger on the screen as it faded to black.

"What will you do?" Angela's question conveyed her fear. "You have to go." The firm grip she maintained on Megan's right hand demonstrated the conflict within her.

"I have a plane to catch," said Megan. She gave her friend a tight, unconvincing smile.

She did not tell Angela what she intended to do beyond getting on the plane. As of this second, she had no idea what she was going to do, but she was not going back to Hawaii. They'd kill Anthony before the plane landed in Honolulu International Airport.

The tight timeline told her that he probably had about 24 hours to live.

Angela opened her mouth to speak, but Megan held up a finger to warn her to keep quiet. She wouldn't put it past the bad guys to slip a bug into the phone. Six months ago, Megan would never have dreamt of being so paranoid, but her brushes with the Shadow Council had altered her perceptions. She also marveled how power could corrupt even the most ordinary people. A small part of her wondered what the manipulative shadow organization was up to these days.

No good, probably.

After extricating her hand from her friend's grip, Megan headed to the bathroom. She locked the door to the adjacent hospital room, flushed the toilet, and turned on the sink. Next, she set the phone carefully on the sink's edge. Since the water was running anyway, Megan splashed her face a few times with cold water. A fluffy white hand towel waited to be put to good use. After drying her face thoroughly, Megan studied her reflection in the mirror above the sink. The move didn't give her a lot of time, but at least she could have a private word with Angela.

When she reentered the main room, Megan found her friend struggling to stand and reaching for the old-fashioned desk phone.

"We've got to call the police!" Angela cried. Fresh tear streaks marked her face.

Racing over to the bed, Megan gently pried the phone away. She set the phone back where it belonged and knelt before her friend.

"We can't call the police," Megan said, speaking swiftly and softly. She squeezed Angela's knee to grab her attention. "Whoever these people are, they have a lot of connections and power. They will know if we turn to the police or the FBI."

"They're going to kill him," Angela said in a choked whisper. "Don't let them kill him! Please! I can't lose him!" She started weeping quietly.

Standing, Megan pulled Angela into a hug. Because the other woman was still sitting on the hospital bed, the heights were right for Megan to briefly rest her chin on top of Angela's head.

"I don't know how, but I will get him back." Megan resisted the urge to elaborate. She needed to retrieve the phone soon or arouse the bad guys' suspicions.

Chapter 4:
The Game Plan

Megan would have stayed to help Angela with the checkout details, but her friend kicked her out of the room.

"Go make your plans," Angela ordered. "The less I know the better for everybody."

Despite agreeing completely, Megan still felt like she was abandoning her friend. With one last firm hand-squeeze, she retrieved the phone from the bathroom and exited the hospital room at a jog. She caught a cab back to The Grand Game Hotel, intending to lock the phone in her room and slip out to Angela's office to have a few private conversations.

The second she stepped foot in her hotel room, Megan got a funny feeling somebody had searched the room. Nothing looked overtly disturbed, but the stuff on her end table looked out of place. The Chapstick was located to the right of the alarm clock. Megan distinctly remembered it being on the left because she'd used it upon waking from her long mid-morning nap. A visit from the cleaning crew might explain the movement, but she decided it more likely the bad guys were in there looking for something. If that somebody looked into the single drawer on the end table, they might have closed it too hard and knocked the Chapstick over. A part of her admitted the recent threats could be making her needlessly paranoid, but hypersensitivity to these sorts of things had saved her life before.

One crisis at a time.

She needed a game plan to deal with the Anthony-Pierce-kidnapping thing first. On the way out the door, Megan dug through her purse for the black card that had mysteriously shown up in her mail one day.

Before utilizing the black card, Megan awakened Eagle Eyes. She'd tracked down Jeffrey Gatton's main henchman and questioned him long enough to receive a few boxes of specialized cleanser to care for the fancy computer contact lenses. The brief encounter had been long enough to cover basic care and answer some of Megan's burning questions about contact protocols. He'd assured her the things could safely be worn for a week without eye damage. Though not ready to completely trust the man or his boss, Megan concluded it was safe enough to leave them in for the day. Given the new developments, she was glad she'd done so.

The bad guys probably didn't know she had something as valuable as Eagle Eyes or they would have demanded she hand the prototype over. Then again, they did break into her room. She had no solid evidence of that, but the court of gut instinct had rendered a clear conclusion. What they wanted still eluded her, but Megan decided she could worry about that point later.

For her sanity, she'd shut down all of the display options. When she tried to access them, the program asked for her username and password. Gritting her teeth, Megan focused on the entry boxes and thought her answers. The username—GT614355—didn't bother her, but the password—Jeffsslavegirl—really irked her. She'd have to speak with him about resetting the darn password immediately. The young man might be a genius, but his way of handling people was dangerously callous.

After about a minute of fumbling around, Megan managed to get the program to call Gatton.

"To what do I owe the pleasure?" asked Jeffrey Gatton. His promptness told Megan he'd anticipated it, and the tone said he welcomed the call. "I would have thought you'd be out with the intrepid agent trying to solve the mystery of tunnel traffickers."

"Tell me this isn't your doing," said Megan. She didn't bother with pleasantries. Time wasn't on her side right now. She needed somebody's help, but if he was part of the problem, she wanted to know that up front.

"You shut down most of my access," Gatton reminded her, "but I gather from your tone something's wrong."

The surprise sounded genuine. Gatton might be arrogant,

foolish, and narcissistic, but Megan couldn't picture him taking orders from human traffickers.

"Angela's husband was kidnapped, and then, I got a call ordering me off the tunnel case," Megan explained. "I'm supposed to catch the red-eye flight back to Hawaii tonight."

"And you don't want to go," Gatton concluded.

"I can't," Megan said flatly. "As soon as I give in, the safest thing for them to do is kill him."

"Why are you calling me?" To his credit, the question sounded serious.

"Because I think you're a man with the connections I need, and I intend to use your invention to get Anthony back," said Megan. "I may not like you, but I need your help. And I think you'll benefit from having Eagle Eyes tested this way."

"It's not going to help much if you get yourself killed and lose the prototype," Gatton pointed out.

"Then you'll have to work very hard at making sure I live through this," Megan replied. "It's going to require a lot of coordination and cooperation."

"What did you have in mind?"

Megan had been working the problem since the moment it materialized for her. Most of the half-baked plans struck her as risky, stupid, foolish, doomed, or some combination thereof. Maybe talking some of it through with Gatton would help.

"I need to switch places with somebody at the airport," Megan began. "I will call a different contact who should know somebody who can help with that part, but once the switch happens, I'll need a ride up to Reno."

"What's in Reno?"

"That's where Anthony's supposed to be," Megan replied. "I haven't the slightest idea where to start looking for him up there, but if you can get me access to the traffic cameras for the right timeframe, I'll have a starting place."

"Ask Eagle Eyes to do the search for you," said Gatton. "It might take a while, but there's a program that can remotely hack the proper servers for you."

The news both thrilled and slightly horrified Megan, but desperation knocked her off the moral high horse before she could mount it.

"I'm not sure I want to know the full extent of illegal tracking programs you've got in here," she admitted. "But I would be happy to use that program in this instance. Tell me how to work it."

Gatton's instructions were oddly patient and thorough. At least the man knew his business. Within five minutes, Megan had entered the series of commands to have Eagle Eyes search for Anthony Pierce's kidnappers. First, she had to teach the program its target. Second, she had to input the proper timeframe. Third, she needed to give it a starting point. Since Megan didn't know much about Mr. Pierce or his schedule, she worked through Angela. Social media links gave Megan and the nosy program plenty of pictures of Anthony to work with. A peek into Angela's public calendar gave her the name of his hotel in Reno.

"Be patient with it," Gatton advised.

I can't afford patience.

"Of course, if you had his phone number, you could try tracking it through GPS," Gatton continued. "Most people never turn that off. They like having their phones link to mapping apps and automatically mark their photo locations. That's how I knew you were back at the hotel."

Megan made a mental note to disconnect all that junk immediately if not sooner. Pulling out her phone, she checked to see if she had Anthony's phone number. To her relief, she found it. She'd forgotten he'd called her once for advice on arranging a surprise party for Angela. Once again, she followed Gatton's instructions on setting Eagle Eyes to work.

"Hang on," said Gatton. "Let me try something from here. I've got a better program than the one Eagle Eyes will use. The prototype needs a software update, but I don't want to do it now because the amount of info I need to send it could shut it down for several hours."

"Will the update help?" Megan inquired.

"Well, yeah," Gatton said like that much should have been obvious. "It should beef up the hacking protocols and give it more security options so people can't remotely interfere with the user. I'm also testing some new tracking options and other programs."

Megan wanted to know more about the updates, but she also had other plans to start.

"Give me the full rundown later," she said. "I have another call to make but I'll check in to see where you're at with my transportation details after that." Megan fiddled with the black card in her hand. The conversation had almost convinced her Gatton had a softer side. "And Jeff?"

He grunted, probably shocked by use of his first name.

"Thanks," said Megan. "I mean it."

"I expect good data from this little exercise," Gatton responded. He tried to sound stern, but his concern bled through. "And don't turn off the tracking functions on your phone or Eagle Eyes just yet. I'll walk you through that later, but right now, I think knowing where you are will do us both good."

Arguing with the logic would take too much effort, and she mostly agreed with him. After suitable promises to remain trackable, Megan closed out that call and used Eagle Eyes to call the black card number. The talk with Gatton had moved Megan past the weird factor of making a phone call without an actual phone.

Two rings in, a woman answered.

"Agent," she greeted.

"Assassin," Megan replied.

The exchange had become a strange inside joke during the course of their sporadic contact the last few months.

"Retired assassin," the woman corrected, "but what can I do for you? I assume there's a new crisis."

Megan winced. She wasn't sure what she considered Cassandra Mirren, but she liked to think she checked in more than just during times of need. Nevertheless, she couldn't afford to waste time with small talk. They'd been through too much both in Pennsylvania and Hawaii to need the social niceties. This woman was one of the deadliest Megan had ever come across in her career, yet somehow, she also exuded a sense of trustworthiness. Megan idly wondered if that assumption would come back to bite her one day.

One crisis at a time ...

"Somebody got kidnapped, and I'm going after the people responsible." Upon second thought, Megan considered the statement misleading, so she took a quick breath and started over, sketching the whole scenario as best she could in a minute. She finished up by telling the lady what she needed and what would likely be handled by others.

"Let's start with the appearance alterations," Cassandra said, quickly settling down to business. "If you've never cut your own hair, don't. Ideally, changing the color is best, but it doesn't sound like you have time for that. Are you being watched?"

"I don't know, but it's possible," Megan answered.

"Okay, then don't change anything until we meet at the airport."

"You're coming?" Megan couldn't keep the surprise out of her tone. "I thought you'd send a contact."

"It might be tight timing, but I'll make it," Cassandra promised. "We're close enough in height. Most people can't judge that accurately anyway. And I don't trust anybody else. If these people are confident enough to play kidnapping games, they're a lot more organized than I'd want my people tangling with. Besides, I've wanted to see Oahu again."

"Will you be safe there?" Megan asked. She wasn't about to let one friend endanger herself to protect another. The notion of Cassandra being a friend still felt strange, but she couldn't deny that their complicated relationship had formed an oddly strong bond between them.

"For the amount of time I plan to linger there, yes," said Cassandra. "Take a picture of yourself and send it to me. I'll do what I can to match it. Do you know your way around McCarran International Airport?"

"Not really, I've only been there on the way in," Megan admitted.

"Do you have a clean phone?"

"Sort of." Megan wasn't sure what to think about Eagle Eyes in terms of being a secure line. Gatton was probably monitoring the call. For now, she was okay with that.

Cassandra chuckled.

"I'll have somebody drop a kit off for you within the hour. It'll at least have a clean phone so I can text you the exact meeting location. Turn off the ringer and leave it on vibrate. I'll send instructions when I know more. Wait until my kit comes before taking the pictures in case they're monitoring what your phone does."

"Clearly, you've done this before."

"I'll see you later, Agent," said Cassandra, ignoring Megan's comment. "Go make a show of packing."

Chapter 5:
Agent G.

The second call to Gatton was mercifully short. Megan assured him she'd secured a way out of the airport. He promised to have a car waiting for her in one of the public parking lots. The next major hurdle to face was preparing for the journey. Megan's packing got interrupted by a series of excited knocks.

"Agent M.! Are you in there? Guess what! You're not going to believe who I met today!" Jaden Melkin's voice floated to Megan through the door.

She froze. Fresh off the conversations with Jeffrey Gatton and Cassandra Mirren, Megan didn't think she was up to dealing with Jaden right now. But if she didn't speak to him, he'd run off and blab his exciting news to the rest of the world. Besides, the kid had orders to check in with her and the current craziness made her want to keep a close eye on him until his mother could take over those duties. Assuming the paperwork went smoothly, Angela should return soon to pick him up. At least Megan hoped that would be the case. They'd agreed early this morning that Jaden's day should proceed as close to normal as possible. Sworn to secrecy on the previous evening's excitement, he probably needed to talk to somebody or risk an excitement-induced hernia.

Tossing a recently folded shirt onto the bed, Megan jogged to the door, dealt with the safety latch, and let the kid in.

"Look what I've got!" Jaden held up a Junior Special Agent badge. "Sarah got one too. When I grow up, I'm going to get a real one like yours."

"That's great," said Megan, struggling to rally the proper amount of enthusiasm. "Where did you get that?" She'd seen the badges before. Her partner, Special Agent Daniel Cooper, had done a short stint in charge of that program last year. During the graduation, he'd roped her into helping him haul fifty-three such badges to the elementary school and present them to the kiddos. "Did you enjoy the program?"

The question earned a curious look from Jaden.

"What program?" He tucked the badge into his pocket and bounced on the balls of his feet while awaiting her answer.

"Never mind. It's not important," said Megan. "Who did you meet?"

"Do you have anything to eat?" asked Jaden. "I'm starving. Mom usually has cookies." The boy dashed over to the counter and spotted the complimentary pack of fresh cookies that appeared every day. "There they are! Can I have them? Please."

"Go for it," said Megan, happy to give him the chance to stuff his face. It gave her a few precious seconds to think.

She wasn't about to tell him of the situation with Anthony. It would only worry him. But she had maybe half a minute before he started asking questions about the obvious signs of packing. Lying to him would make her feel lousy and not work for long anyway since she'd not had time to concoct a believable story with Angela. Being a curious kid, Jaden would certainly check the story with his mother.

"Hey. Where you going?" The question was garbled due to the partially chewed cookie in Jaden's mouth, but Megan got the gist. The boy fixed her with wide, wounded eyes. "You're leaving us? What if something bad happens?"

Taking Jaden by the shoulders, Megan led him over to the couch and sat him down. Her mind scrambled for the right words.

Stall! Stall!

"Tell me your story first. Then, I'll tell you mine," said Megan. "Who gave you the badge?"

"Agent G. did." The boy straightened his shoulders and puffed out his chest. "I spotted his car right away. It was junkier than the rest of the cars, and it didn't move forward to pick up kids like the others."

"Slow down," Megan pleaded. She sat on the coffee table to face Jaden directly. "And start over. Who is Agent G., and how did you spot his car?"

"He's the man assigned to protect me while I'm at school," Jaden declared.

The news alarmed Megan because she was certain somebody would have told her if the bureau planned such a move. She worked hard to keep her expression neutral, wanting the boy's impressions to be untainted.

"Did he show you a badge?" Megan asked carefully.

"Of course! I made him show me that first," said Jaden. His tone asked what kind of a fool she took him for.

"How did you meet him? And what did he look like?" Megan wasn't sure which question she wanted answered first.

Jaden's expression turned curious, but he launched into the tale.

"Sometimes Sarah meets me after school, and we talk for a while as we watch the other kids get picked up. We bet each other packs of gum to guess the right order of who gets picked up first, second, third, and so on. It's usually the same order, and sometimes, I let her win because I can get gum easier than she can. Doug Satler's mom usually beats everybody there. She's got a red Mercedes-Benz AMG S65! Those things cost a quarter million dollars!"

"So, you noticed the agent's car because it wasn't that nice," said Megan, needing to focus her interviewee.

"Sarah noticed it first," said Jaden. "She said it didn't belong. I said it might be an au pair or some other servant doing the pickup run. That's not unusual, but we know most of those cars. We argued about it some before deciding to ask. I won the race to the stop sign next to the car, so I was going to knock on his window, but he got out."

"Was he tall? Can you describe him?"

"Why do you want to know?" Jaden asked.

"I'm testing your observation skills," said Megan. "Agents need to have great observation skills."

The suspicion in the boy's eyes lingered, but he closed his eyes to facilitate recalling the agent.

"He's tall. Like a foot taller than me," Jaden reported. "He's got short, dark hair and really bad breath." He opened his eyes and wrinkled his nose at the memory.

Megan had to smile at that. She shuddered to think how the kid described her. Brutal honesty wasn't pretty. Since he was a few inches shorter than her, though tall for his age, Megan guessed the man might be 6' 2" or 6' 3" tall.

"What's his name?" she inquired, silently scolding herself for neglecting that important question.

"Special Agent Ryan Galloway."

Bringing up a search box, Megan threw the name into Gatton's nosy machine and bid it to find everything possible on the agent. To keep from being too distracted, she forced the search to happen in the background. A sense of relief stole over her at learning it probably wasn't Luke Kramer using a false name. His concern for the trafficking victims had seemed genuine. She would hate to find out he served other masters besides the US government.

"What's wrong?" Jaden stared at Megan hard. "Do you think he wasn't a real agent? His badge looked like yours."

"I'm sure he was a real agent," Megan assured the boy.

I'm just not sure he was there on official business.

"I told you my news. Now, it's your turn," said Jaden. He shoved the second cookie into his mouth and chewed noisily.

Megan found his lack of manners disturbing, but she couldn't spare the effort to correct him. No perfect answers had come to her in the intervening minutes. Lacking a better plan, Megan decided to level with the kid as best she could.

"Jaden, something came up. I need to go away for a little while to sort a personal matter." Reaching out, she placed a hand on the boy's left knee. "I'll be back quick as I can. I promise."

"Who's going to protect my mom when you're gone?"

"I think your mom can take care of herself," Megan said. With great effort, she stood to return to her packing.

"She got hurt yesterday," Jaden argued.

The simple statement was a gut shot, but thankfully, Megan had her back to the boy so he couldn't see her reaction. Turning to face the kid, she plopped down on the bed. They hadn't told him how Angela had received her leg wound. The temptation to tell him weighed upon Megan, but Jaden's next question blindsided her.

"Are you scared the bad guys will come back?"

The bad guys never went away.

"I'm going to make sure that doesn't happen," Megan promised, hoping she wasn't lying to the kid. The urge to say more rose up and burned her throat. She swallowed the lump that was forming. "Being scared isn't bad, Jaden. It's natural. It's how you react to being scared that makes a difference."

"Then why are you running away?" The boy's eyes accused her of abandoning them.

What could she tell him that wouldn't reveal too much?

"I'm not running away." The protest sounded weak to her.

"But you're leaving! That's the same thing!" His jaw trembled with the effort to not cry.

The boy's reaction seemed disproportionate to the event. Megan had only met him a few days earlier. He had an obsession for joining the FBI someday, but that wouldn't explain why her leaving now would upend his world.

"Did Agent G. ask you to do anything for him?" Megan asked carefully. "You said he was supposed to protect you. What did he say exactly? What is he protecting you from?"

Jaden flushed.

"He didn't say. He said I should watch you carefully so I could learn a lot."

Megan nodded absently. If Jaden and his young friend had startled the man watching the boy, he'd probably had to conjure a story on the spot. Holes and inconsistencies were to be expected in that case, but why would the bad guys bother tailing a ten-year-old boy anyway? Was this dubious agent supposed to snatch Jaden? Did Sarah's presence prevent a second kidnapping?

"When's Mom coming home?" asked Jaden, interrupting the flow of questions.

"Soon." Megan answered by reflex.

"I'm hungry. Let's go get something to eat."

Eating didn't sound appealing, but Megan couldn't think of a better way to occupy the boy. News of a mysterious observer convinced her she needed to stop this mess at its source before more harm found her friends.

"Sounds like a good plan," Megan commented. "Do you have any recommendations?"

She half-listened to Jaden rattle off the hotel's specialties. The packing wouldn't take too much longer, but Megan's mind kept wrestling with the other details. Getting to Reno would only be the start. If Gatton's miracle machine couldn't cough up an address for her, she'd need to do some lightning-quick detective work without being seen and without adequate backup. Relying on others for information was nerve-racking.

As they crossed the lobby, Jaden spotted his mother being ushered through the front doors by one of the bellboys.

"Mom!" Jaden dashed across the room and threw his arms around Angela.

Megan watched from a distance. The way her friend's face lit up with joy renewed her conviction to help these people. Whoever was messing with the family must really have big secrets to hide. A profitable human trafficking network might be motivation enough to go to desperate lengths to shut down an investigation. If Jaden's Agent G. was a conspirator inside the FBI, that might explain the need to move Megan away from the case.

Does Eagle Eyes factor in?

She couldn't forget the fact that she'd likely had an unwanted guest recently. Gatton's stupidity could be blamed for much of last night's trouble, but the men after the prototype seemed authentic in their efforts to steal it and cut ties with their employers. What had they called it? The name skimmed her thoughts and slipped away several times before firmly snapping into place.

Club.

Derrick, Nico, and the other men had argued about walking out on the Club. The organization also seemed responsible for the human trafficking victims in the tunnels. Megan couldn't believe that connection hadn't reared up and bit her in full before. She added *Club* to her Eagle Eyes search items and returned to her room to finish that packing. Angela and Jaden needed time together, and Megan didn't feel like eating. There was too much work to do.

Chapter 6:
Bait

Jeffrey Gatton stared at the readouts. He didn't enjoy playing games where real people could die, but he loved his job because it offered genuine challenges. He knew he wasn't normal, and so did his parents. They'd figured that out after the third private tutor quit after only one week with him when he was in elementary school. Formal learning had never been his strong suit, but once he'd hit his preteen years and gotten into computers, nothing could stop him. He'd built Gatton Technologies from the ground up, despite his father's insistence that he take over the family's chain of hardware stores.

Government agents had approached one of his online avatars about some freelance hacking work when he was fourteen. Since then, he'd always made time for their jobs. Standard government contracts were almost too painful to even entertain given the unholy amount of stupid paperwork that came with it. However, these private contracts came from the secret organization that really ran national security. The FBI, CIA, and Department of Homeland Security might be the public face of protection provided to the American people, but the stuff Jeff knew could fulfill every conspiracy theorist's wildest dreams.

The conundrum facing him now was different than many others he'd faced because he bore some responsibility for the situation. His plan to get Agent Luchek to test Eagle Eyes had backfired big time. He'd not heard from the fake buyer he'd sent to The Grand Game Hotel three days ago, and the people he'd contacted to act as "muscle" got greedy and turned on his other representative, David Stanley. The FBI agent had saved Stanley's hide last night, but the human trafficking ring they'd stumbled across was very real, hence his problem.

The entire day from dawn until dusk had been spent researching the Club. Such an investigation would have taken months or years through legal channels, but he'd been given permission years ago to operate outside the law. The more he learned, the more he considered them a threat worth removing. Like a good little citizen, Jeff had informed his handler of the Club's existence. Their reply had been the electronic equivalent of a pat-on-the-head-and-here's-a-cookie routine.

The government's lack of enthusiasm told him much. First, they would not go out of their way to rescue anybody he sent in. Second, if he truly wanted to take down the Club's Nevada traffickers he would need to draw out the leader on his own. That required bait. Stanley would soon be taking Megan Luchek up to Reno to find her friend's husband. She would make good bait, but the Club really wasn't a fan of hers. Getting caught would probably be fatal. Jeff could order Stanley to play the part of a new investor and demand to see the man in charge, but that approach also offered a 50-50 chance of disaster. Third, his temporary help acquisition practices still had some flaws, as demonstrated by accidentally hiring Club goons. So, he couldn't simply whistle up a team of ex-special forces, though that would be awesome. He'd have to investigate that for the future.

The option to buy out the business would only move the problem to somebody else's patch. Having grown up on unhealthy portions of TV and internet news, Jeff had developed a keen dislike for certain kinds of criminals. Those who enslaved people earned a top spot on his personal hit list.

Jeff knew his reputation as a wild, eccentric, genius could intimidate some people. He'd worked very hard to build up that reputation. His publicist had insisted on the free-spirit ladies' man aspect to boost his image, but he found most women tedious. Megan Luchek had the potential to be different. Despite her low opinion of him, he was starting to genuinely like the lady. Before even considering her as a contact, he'd done a thorough background check, probably even more extensive than the FBI had conducted during the hiring process. Given some of the crazy things in her past, Jeff had been surprised she passed the psychological tests. She never held back.

He needed to weigh the idea of ending this human trafficking ring against the idea of permanently damaging Agent Luchek's trust and endangering her life.

Tell her the truth.

The idea held a lot of appeal, but he needed to get the balls rolling soon. Some of them would take quite a while to build up momentum. Timing would be rather important.

He spent the next two hours trying to set up a meeting with somebody high up in the Club. Finally, he accepted that posing as a buyer would never work. He needed to offer them something they wanted. They seemed very interested in Eagle Eyes, but that wasn't really his to bargain with. Besides, giving them that would be like giving a toddler missile launch codes. For all he knew, their interest could be due to a competitor looking to score the tech. Most likely, they'd simply try to sell it.

What bait would work?

The Club's cyber security was Swiss cheese. His company could help them fortify their lines of communication. Maybe he needed to activate Lester Malik. The identity was nearly six years old but should still be clean. Upon starting Gatton Technologies, Jeff had padded the personnel databank with a dozen or so non-existent employees. The idea was that if he ever needed a back door into any of GT's systems, he'd have several identities he could burn through before anybody came looking for him.

Lester Malik worked in the cyber security division as an integrity analyst, which was a polite term for a hacker who tried to break into systems to find the holes. He was also a disgruntled employee: overworked, underpaid, and very unappreciated. Jeff had planted a nanny program to leave enough of a digital footprint around in case anybody Googled the guy. Lester had most of the common social media profiles, though he wasn't overly active on them. Another program had created a series of family photos by combining pixels from thousands of other photos.

Jeff's mind raced. Lester was perfect. After this, the identity would need to be scrubbed from the internet, but he existed solely for an operation like this. David Stanley could pass for the guy because he could now pass for Jeff. Most of the male ghosts had facial structures similar to Jeff, in case he needed to use them if things got too hot. That had been the original plan anyway when it'd popped into his fifteen-year-old brain. The current, twenty-one-year-old Jeff might scoff at the paranoia, but this might actually work. Poor Stanley had needed some plastic surgery to really pull off the role, but the man couldn't complain about his salary or benefits.

The plan formed rapidly. Posing as Lester, Jeff would call one of the restaurants he'd been able to link to the Club and reveal a small fraction of the vulnerabilities he'd found. He'd demand a lot of money for fixing the system and insist on meeting somebody in management, whoever was above Derrick Belmont. He knew that name from the events that went down early this morning. Then, he'd send Stanley to the meeting, hopefully with Agent Luchek as backup.

The meet would have to be in Reno since Stanley and Luchek would be up there for Anthony Pierce anyway. Maybe Jeff could demand Anthony's life as part of his payment? It didn't really fit with a disgruntled security hacker image, but Agent Luchek's priorities wouldn't shift until she had Mr. Pierce safely away from the bad guys. If he wanted her help with Stanley's meet and greet with the upper echelons of the Club, he'd need to help her find Pierce fast.

That wasn't a problem. He'd already discovered three possible locations based on tracking the kidnappers' car. The problem was firepower. Stanley could drive like an Indy-500 racer, but he'd be useless in a shootout. Agent Luchek could handle a gun, but she'd be seriously outnumbered at any of these locations. They might even need to search multiple locations because the Club didn't keep people in one place very long.

Jeff's sweep had turned up five likely Club safe houses, but only three of those had hosted the kidnappers' car in the last twelve hours. What he really needed was a way to track the human trafficking ring organically. Maybe Lester the ghost, played by Stanley, could demand a tour. The point could be considered later. Jeff first needed the Club to take the bait, which meant he had to offer it.

Agent Kramer came to mind as possible help. Jeff hadn't been able to do a full workup on the man, but the initial sweep had come through squeaky clean. Kramer had already picked up the flag on this human trafficking thing, he'd want in. Agent Galloway, the other name Agent Luchek wanted run, was definitely dirty. Could Jeff move Kramer without alerting Galloway? Despite their difference in rank, Kramer and Galloway were often paired up on assignments. After a small internal debate, Jeff put on a headset and moved to make some secure phone calls.

***

"How do you want me to respond?" asked Steel.

Lillian Marquez tapped her fingers on the large desk crammed into Derrick's restaurant office. She mulled over Steel's news and thought of several décor changes to make if she planned on keeping this office. Apparently, some idiot hacker had broken into one of their systems and now wanted to be paid to shore up their security. If true, an overhaul would be warranted, but it could be an elaborate trap.

"Did he give you proof?" she pressed.

"I didn't understand it, but one of my guys says the problems mentioned are legit," answered Steel. His large form filled the single guest chair. "I don't want to work with the fool, but he seems to know what he's talking about."

"Do we have any known entities who can deal with the problems he's talking about?" Lillian wondered.

"Yes, but he's hinting there are more problems he's not telling us about," said Steel. A flash in his gray eyes told her what he'd like to do to the punk.

"Okay, set up the meet and take him in," Lillian said. "Give him the full captivity experience, minus too much pain. I want him scared and willing to deal with us on our terms. When he's properly softened, take him to a bunker and have the tech boys watch him like a hawk as he works. We'll go with the simple rewards system: he does good work and we let him live and eat."

"I can't meet him until the day after tomorrow," Steel said apologetically. "I'm scheduled to get a detailed update from my cooperative fed in the middle of the morning here. The tech guy insists he won't meet anywhere else than Reno."

"Why Reno?" Lillian wasn't really directing the question to Steel, but she did want to hear his thoughts.

"Guess it's convenient for him," replied Steel. "He works for Gatton Technologies. They have a small office there. I didn't talk to him long, but he didn't seem to like his employers too much."

"Could he help with retrieving Eagle Eyes?" Lillian asked.

"Don't think so, but I'll ask him once I arrange the meet," said Steel.

"I can ask him just as well as you can," Lillian noted, realizing it was a decent idea. "I should check in with the Reno people anyway. I don't like having to rely on so many others without proper oversight. I'm going to have to make a decision on the Anthony Pierce matter anyway. To do that, I need to speak with the man to see if he'll be a problem should we let him go. Who's currently hosting him?"

"House Fourteen," Steel answered. "I'll tell him you're coming. Should I direct this Lester guy there too?"

"Only if it's secure," said Lillian. "That's Hugh Cormac's place, right? Does he have enough people to handle two separate transactions?"

"Three transactions," Steel corrected. "He's got one of the diverted shipments and Pierce currently. This guy would make three, but yeah, he can handle it. The place is located in a new housing development a little south of Reno. I'll give you the address when you get close."

"How many men does he have?" Lillian wondered. She liked to know as much information as possible. The modular way the Club was organized argued against asking too many questions, but if these people technically answered to her, she wanted to know her facts.

"He's only got two or three at the house at any given time, but the electronic security's top-notch. That's another reason to send the hacker there. Have him test the house's system and see what can be improved."

Lillian loved technology, but she questioned the wisdom of automating certain parts of their business, like guarding captives. Sure, real guards could get lazy, fall asleep, be bought off, and have a whole host of other flaws, but at least one could deal with them. People understood risks and rewards. Machines couldn't be threatened into compliance.

The plan solidified for her. She'd go to Reno and see the place for herself. Her bosses wanted to change every safe house over to one of these new, overly wired deals. Fewer men meant more profits and less loose lips, which could be great for business, but Lillian needed to be convinced of their effectiveness first.

"Get me that meeting," said Lillian, knowing Steel awaited a firm order.

Chapter 7:
Switch

Cassandra's promised survival kit arrived soon after Megan retreated to her room. It contained a burner phone, a note promising a gun at a later time, a baggy green, long-sleeved shirt, a pilot's license, and a driver's license. Both fake IDs were in the name of Gabrielle Reese. The quality was decent enough that Megan guessed Cassandra had ordered them made quite some time ago. Although tempted to puzzle over why the former assassin would bother having fake ID's made for her, Megan chose to accept the blessing and moved to the bathroom to take a picture in the mirror for Cassandra. She'd come to expect a fair amount of paranoia from her and concluded it must be an occupational hazard.

Must be a stressful life.

The thought struck Megan as ridiculous given the last six months of her life. Within that span, she'd been shot, kidnapped, and forced to deal with so many brands of crazy people she was starting to lose track. Despite the useless factor, she wished things were as straightforward as some of those other adventures. At the very least, most of the time the enemy had a face and a real name instead of an innocuous title that hid untold numbers of foes. The hamster wheel of thoughts occupied her so thoroughly that a half-hour slipped by between time checks.

Shaking her shoulders, Megan ran through the list of things that needed doing soon. Obviously, she needed to be at the airport as soon as possible so she could get familiar with the layout. Even if she tried the fake identification documents, she'd run into some security. She should check in with Angela and arrange a ride to the airport. Although she really didn't want to upset her friend, Jaden's excitement over Agent G.'s interest in him warranted a few warnings.

Grabbing her iPhone, Megan used an app to hire a car to the airport.

As she finished, a text message came through on the burner phone.

It read: Eat and move. Instructions coming.

Accepting the plan, Megan hurried to the hotel's restaurant, hoping to catch Angela and Jaden. She found them tucked into a corner booth, lingering over dessert. Thankfully, the restaurant was empty at this hour. Megan dispatched Jaden to the kitchen to request one of the specials. She told him he could choose for her, thinking that might buy her a few extra seconds of alone time with Angela.

"Did he tell you about his visitor?" Megan asked quietly.

The worry in Angela's eyes told her the news had definitely been delivered.

"What does it mean?" Angela demanded in a fierce whisper. "Are they after my son too?"

Lie to her!

"It's possible," Megan said, "but it's not likely."

Internally, she admitted: *They're probably keeping their options open for later moves.*

"I told them I don't know anything!" Angela blurted.

"They called?" The idea shouldn't surprise Megan, but it did.

"They want something called 'Eagle Eyes.' They said Jeffrey Gatton had tried to sell it from the hotel." Angela's gaze darted about the room as if the whole place was bugged. "I explained what little I know and told them honestly I'd never heard of it. When I asked to speak to Anthony, they hung up. Do you know anything about it?"

Megan thought about the new development.

Is this about Eagle Eyes or hiding human trafficking?

The two threads seemed too different to be related.

After a lengthy pause, Angela nodded curtly as anger replaced the fear.

"I see that you do." She held up a hand to forestall a response. "Don't tell me if you don't want them to know because I will tell them everything."

"Do you have a phone number for contacting them?" Megan asked. She didn't know if the information would be helpful or not, but she could add it to the long list of things to throw at Gatton's miniature computer.

Jaden showed up with Megan's dinner as Angela searched for the number. Megan thanked the boy and eyed the mountain of spaghetti sitting under a meatball the size of a softball. The sight brought a faint smile to Angela's lips.

"That's one of Jaden's favorites. It's off the kids menu," said Angela.

"I didn't know Vegas restaurants had a kids menu," Megan commented.

"Many don't, but we're a little more family friendly than some places," Angela explained. Her smile wavered as she struggled to keep a light tone for her son. "Honey, why don't you go see if Mark or Tanya will help you grab your spare clothes from the south closet?"

The kid whooped with joy and sprinted away.

"I think we should stay near people ... until this is finished." Angela's eyes were shiny with unshed tears.

Megan stood.

"I think I'll go do some of that 'finishing,'" she said. "Add the meal to my room's tab."

"Don't worry about it," said Angela. She waved to a plain white bag Megan hadn't noticed. "And don't forget your burger."

Opening the bag released a lovely wave of steamy air carrying the scent of juicy hamburger.

"I figured you'd be in a hurry," Angela explained.

"Why did you let me order something else if you'd already taken care of it?"

"Same reason you had Jaden order for you," Angela replied.

Resealing the bag, Megan set it down and moved to give her friend a hug.

"Thank you," she said.

Angela's return hug was fierce enough to hurt.

"I really need this over with soon but promise me you'll be careful!"

"I've got good people watching out for me," Megan assured her friend. The mental jury was still out on Gatton being *good people*, but Megan had trusted Cassandra Mirren with her life before. She could do so again.

The farewell with Angela was more emotionally complicated than Megan wanted it to be, but eventually, she pulled away and gathered her luggage. She had just enough time to inhale the large burger before the hired car pulled up.

In less than forty minutes, Megan sat in a crowded waiting area holding a lukewarm coffee and an airport map. Unsure of what to wear, she'd gone with jeans and the long-sleeved shirt included in Cassandra's kit. In case she had observers, Megan waited near the correct terminal for Hawaiian airlines. The fake IDs were stored deep in her purse. They'd slipped past security the first time, but she didn't want to tempt fate by moving around too much.

While waiting for Cassandra's next text message, Megan checked on her Eagle Eyes queries. Only the report on Galloway was ready for her. She pulled out her normal phone and stared at the screen. Since most other people were doing the same, she blended right in. The guilt over utilizing such intrusive technology lasted about four seconds.

FBI Special Agent Ryan David Galloway was indeed legitimate—and likely corrupt. He'd joined the bureau when he was thirty-two and worked his way up to Senior Special Agent. His application to move up to Supervisory Special Agent had gone nowhere. Megan had never looked at her file—or anybody's for that matter—but Agent Galloway's seemed thin. While it didn't hold much in the way of disciplinary notes, it also didn't burst with commendations.

Bank records showed a typical agent income and expenses until Megan searched a tab simply marked *other*. A short list of accounts with possible connections with the party of interest appeared. The top six were 100% likely to be the same man's accounts. Megan ignored these since they were normal retirement, checking, and savings accounts. The probabilities of ownership went down from there, but the accounts grew more intriguing. She skimmed the details of how the program had drawn its conclusions, but soon gave that up in favor of wondering why a corrupt agent and his mystery handlers would bother with Jaden Melkin.

The kid was too young to have made many connections. They could certainly use him to get to Angela, but what did she have that they'd be after? Thinking they'd work through Angela to weasel information about Eagle Eyes from Megan relied on the gigantic assumption that the bad guys knew she had it. Taking Anthony also seemed illogical. What did the bad guys know that Megan didn't? The sad answer was a whole heck of a lot.

She hesitated before checking Luke Kramer's personnel files and financial records. Having such easy access to things that should be behind the most robust cyber security out there disturbed her, but she needed answers now. Obtaining the information through proper channels would take months. Megan breathed a little easier once she saw the large college debt and mortgage. His finances also revealed alimony and child support payments. That removed him from the list of people she'd ever consider dating but made her see him in a new, more favorable light.

Her mother would be the first to tell her she needed a man, but one without too much baggage was a must for her. She had enough to cover three lifetimes let alone deal with somebody else's.

One of the burner phones buzzed in Megan's left pocket, interrupting her research and life musings. Whipping it out, she read over the lengthy message describing where she should go next and what to do once there. Finding the nearest garbage can, she ditched the lousy coffee and prepared to move on. The public restroom described wasn't far, but it was a little out of the way. Ignoring the "Closed for Cleaning" sign, Megan rolled her suitcase around the large cart filled with cleaning supplies that partially blocked the doorway. She felt odd dragging her suitcase past several open stalls to the large handicap one on the end.

As promised, Megan found a dark navy-blue suit waiting for her inside the stall. She changed swiftly and dug around in her purse for the pilot's license. A gentle double-tap on the door caught her attention as she donned the comfortable flats.

"How is the transformation coming?" inquired Cassandra.

"Almost done," said Megan. She unlocked the door and stepped aside to let the taller woman enter.

She didn't get a good look at Cassandra as she breezed past, but when she turned, Megan felt like she was looking in a mirror that had decided to change her hair and clothes.

"Sit," Cassandra ordered, waving to the only available seat. "I need to fix your hair."

Megan reluctantly sat on the toilet.

"Thanks for coming," she said, not sure of the etiquette details that applied here.

"You keep life interesting," Cassandra commented.

Over the next five minutes, Cassandra combed, pulled, twisted, and pinned Megan's hair into a tight arrangement at the back of her head. As she worked, Cassandra explained the rest of her plan, which sounded surprisingly simple, and gave Megan pointers on how to walk. Then, she spent several minutes making sure their makeups matched.

The procedure reminded Megan of the previous evening's preparations for the masquerade party. She fervently hoped tonight would run smoother. By the end, Megan and Cassandra had effectively switched identities.

The former assassin wore blue jeans and the green shirt Megan had come in. It was slightly shorter than it had been on Megan due to the difference in their heights. The suit Cassandra had arrived in was stuffed into her suitcase.

"There's a gun for you in the main compartment along with two extra magazines," Cassandra announced.

"I can't afford to get caught with a gun."

"It's inside a box that looks like a copy of *Modern Case Law*," said Cassandra. "It will allow you to get the weapon through metal detectors. I'd like the box back if possible."

Megan wanted to dive in and examine the container, but she didn't want to spend the time.

"I owe you big time," said Megan.

"Don't worry. I'm keeping score," Cassandra said with a wry smile.

"Oh? And where do we stand?" Megan inquired.

"This puts me up by one," Cassandra answered. "Pennsylvania and that latest business in Honolulu cancel each other out, and I'm not counting anything before that since we weren't exactly on the same side."

"Fair enough," said Megan. She gave the taller woman a careful hug to avoid messing up her hair. "You know how to reach me when it comes time to even up."

"Hopefully that's a time far in the future," said Cassandra. "Just worry about getting to tomorrow." She stepped back. "You should leave first. Move the cart aside and take off the cleaning sign. I'll wait for some people to fill in the gaps before exiting." Pulling out a set of car keys, she held them out to Megan. "If your ride falls through, take the black Ford Focus that answers to this. It's in the closest parking lot to this terminal."

Nodding thanks one more time, Megan gripped the handle of Cassandra's suitcase and left the cramped stall. It had seemed a lot roomier with only one person and one set of luggage. Her first few steps were tentative, but she quickly settled into a good rhythm. Having access to a gun greatly comforted her.

Will I need to use it?

She hoped not, but the odds of getting Anthony Pierce back without a fight were absolutely dismal.

Chapter 8:
Updates

When Megan finally found David Stanley's car, she wrestled Cassandra's suitcase into the back seat and climbed in after it.

"You can sit up front," David offered, craning his neck around to see her. "I have some things to discuss with you."

That sounds ominous.

"No, thanks. I'm fine. I'm probably going to nap most of the way," said Megan.

"The front seat reclines. You'd be more comfortable, but suit yourself." David started the car and pulled out of the parking space. "Give me ten minutes before you sleep though. My boss set something in motion you should know about."

The last statement fired a spike of alarm into Megan's gut.

"What'd he do now?" she demanded. The last plan had almost gotten them killed.

"Before I tell you, please remember I'm only the messenger. This is not my doing."

"With that much prefacing this must be good," Megan muttered. The long day was catching up with her. "Should we wait until after I'm rested or get it out of the way?"

"It's a couple of different things," said David.

"Straight answer. Now," Megan prompted. "What did he do?" Each word in the repeated question came out like a fully charged sentence.

"He wants to draw out the Club's leaders, so he broke through some of their crappy cyber security and offered to fix it for them,"

David began.

Megan listened carefully as David outlined Jeffrey Gatton's plan. The idea of creating ghost identities that could be used for purposes such as theirs confirmed Megan's suspicions that Gatton had a twisted mind. A check of the Eagle Eyes queries gave them a map to each of the three possible locations where Anthony Pierce could be held and an address where *Mr. Malik* was supposed to meet his new best buddies. Since that address happened to be near one of the three possibilities where Pierce might be, Megan knew they'd be checking that location first.

When David finished, Megan leaned back and tried to get comfortable. She closed her eyes to facilitate processing.

"Let me think about this for a minute," she said.

David hadn't gotten around to asking for a response yet, but he was obviously in need of one. If Megan let him wander into the meeting blind, he'd be caught, questioned, and killed in a matter of hours. If he had any sense at all, he'd refuse to go through with the job. On the other hand, the daft plan might bring down the wrath of the US government upon a whole ring of those who richly deserved it. Unlike Gatton and Stanley, Megan wasn't naïve enough to believe it would dismantle the Club completely, but she agreed the blow would be significant.

"While you're thinking, the other matter you should consider is letting Eagle Eyes update itself," said David. His tone warned her there might be pros and cons to that idea.

"Why wouldn't I let it update?" asked Megan, opening her eyes. She tried to recall what Gatton had said about the changes, but the previous conversation was a blur to her at this point.

"It can take anywhere from two hours to eleven or twelve hours, and since the interfaces need to stay in during that time, you'll probably want to be asleep for that time," David explained. "Live updates are possible, but they can be disorienting."

Two hours would be fine, but eleven or twelve hours would be way too long.

"Okay. What are the benefits?" Megan asked.

"He didn't tell me everything, but this version should have the advanced target tracking system, night vision, and a better communications suite." David's tone sounded like a kid explaining the wonders of a new video game.

Each of those benefits sounded very helpful considering what she needed to do once she got to Reno.

Julie C. Gilbert

"What could go wrong?" Megan inquired. There was no levity in her voice.

"Well, the program could sense you need to be asleep for the updates to proceed smoothly," David admitted. "In that case, it'll work to keep you asleep until it's finished." He hastened to state the mitigating factors. "It's not dangerous, but that could mean you're out of it for the full update time. It's only happened to one subject, and I think it was a fluke."

"So I go in with the old version of Eagle Eyes or risk getting the bigger, better, faster version," Megan summarized. She considered what they would be up against. "We need more help."

"You'll do it?" David asked hopefully.

"You'll die if I don't," Megan reminded him.

"Good point," David said, sobering immediately.

"I need to make a phone call," she said, taking out the clean phone Cassandra had given her.

"Calls with Eagle Eyes are secure," David offered, trying to be helpful.

"I need the normalness," Megan explained, not caring either way if David understood her.

Despite this claim, she used the computer program to find Luke Kramer's phone number. He answered on the third ring, stating his title and inquiring as to what he could do. Megan yanked the conversation past pleasantries quickly and launched into the heart of the matter.

"I've got a lead that could bust up some of that human trafficking ring we were looking into today," Megan announced.

"That's great! What's the catch?" Luke asked, inferring there must be a catch from her inflection.

"The 'catch' is two-fold. Part one is that it takes us up to the Reno area, and part two is that you can't tell anybody," Megan answered.

"Not even my partner?" Luke sounded shocked. "He was very helpful with the case this afternoon."

I'll bet he was, Megan thought darkly.

"Especially not him," Megan confirmed. She didn't want to break the news to Luke over the phone like this. It seemed wrong, but she also didn't have time to play coy games with him. If he didn't take her seriously, they'd be in big trouble. One phone call to the wrong person would alert the bad guys. Surprise was their best weapon. Ruining it could give them time to kill Anthony and move their operation before David and Megan even arrived in the correct part of Nevada. "He's

144

dirty."

Silence fell between them.

"I don't believe it," Luke declared. "Prove it." His challenge crackled with anger.

"Look, I could email you proof, but that would probably tip him off," said Megan, trying not to take the anger personally. She also tried to put herself in his place. If a stranger had told her Daniel Cooper was corrupt, Megan's first instinct would be to laugh in their faces. Her second instinct would be to punch them. Luke had simply skipped the laughing part.

"Then make me believe you."

"I can set up a secure email for him and get him proof," Jeff Gatton offered. "He's online now."

Megan had forgotten that keeping Eagle Eyes active meant an open invitation to having Gatton loose in her head. On the other hand, if he could convince Kramer to help, she might forgive him for the intrusion.

"A … friend of mine can get you the proof, but you'll have to access a secure email my friend can set up," said Megan. "It might take a while—"

"Done," Jeff chirped, sounding smug. He rattled off the new email address and its password. "The goods should be there in a few seconds."

"Never mind. Go here." Megan walked the other agent through the process of finding the proof of his partner's corruption.

"Hang on. I'm going to put you on speaker so I can check," Luke said.

"I'm going to let you see what he's seeing," said Gatton. "Close your eyes. It'll go easier on your head."

Before Megan could respond, an alert appeared in the bottom right corner of her vision. A second later, she saw a typical email display. The inbox was bare. Aside from the few welcome emails, only one email had come in from an unknown sender. Megan had seen blocked phone numbers before, but she'd never heard of the ability to block email addresses.

The cursor moved seemingly on its own, showing Megan that this wasn't really her screen. The email opened and nine attachments appeared. The cursor moved again, opening the first attachment. A series of bank statements filled the space.

What am I looking at?

She typed the question into the text box that would let Gatton see the thought.

"It's an overview of Agent Galloway's finances," said Gatton.

"These could be fake," argued Luke, unaware of Megan's side conversation.

"What are you seeing?" Megan asked. She didn't want Luke to know she already saw what he saw. That would require an explanation she wasn't ready to give.

"Bank statements," Luke said tersely. "And phone records. A lot of phone records."

As he talked, Luke opened several more attachments, each of which held several months' worth of phone records and text message threads. From what Megan could see, they must be burner phones because they'd only be active for one to two months. She held that observation in because he hadn't said anything that would reveal that information.

"You're going to have to do better than that," Luke announced.

"Tell him to check the last two attachments," Gatton suggested.

Megan relayed the message. He did so and grunted like somebody had hit him.

Both attachments were jpg files that took a moment to load once clicked on, but once revealed the pictures were conclusive. The first image showed Agent Galloway meeting with a large, muscular older man wearing an expensive suit. When the mouse cursor hovered over the picture a text box popped up and explained the meeting was between Galloway and somebody called Steel. A time and date stamp already declared other pertinent information. The second image thoroughly confused Megan. It showed Galloway meeting a woman earlier that morning. The explanation identified the woman as Lillian Marquez, a known Club member, rank unknown.

Megan had to concentrate not to react aloud. She'd seen this woman before. It was the same woman Derrick and his cronies had tried to hide along with some other captives down in the tunnels.

"I believe you," said Luke. "What do you want me to do?"

His wounded tone made Megan want to reach through the phone and hold the man's hand. Once again, she imagined how she'd react to news that Dan Cooper had gone rogue. Dan would never do such a thing, but that's why the news would be shocking. Nobody wanted to hear their partner—somebody they trusted with their life— could be a bad guy.

"Meet me a few blocks from the address I'm sending you. We'll compare notes and form a better plan when we're there," said Megan. She used the message box to tell Gatton to send along the correct address.

"On it," Gatton assured her, "and tell him to step on it. His apartment's south of Vegas. He'll be at least a half-hour behind you."

"It's a long way," Megan commented. "Please hurry." She thought about telling him about Anthony, but she didn't want to complicate matters. He'd probably insist they call out additional agents.

"Are you sure I shouldn't rustle up some more help?" Luke wondered, as if reading her mind.

"I can give you a list of the solid people," Gatton offered.

If you can get such a list, then get them on the road yourself. Check the Reno resident agency and Sacramento field office first.

This time, Megan let the thought form then instructed it to appear in the box instead of typing it out. Right now, she didn't care about turf wars. She cared about not getting killed by walking into a situation with a dozen aggrieved bad guys.

"Will do," Gatton promised. "Playing it close to the vest. I feel ya."

"I don't know what we'll be facing," Megan said honestly. "We can regroup when you get up here."

After thanking Kramer, Megan had Gatton present the whole update story, complete with a detailed look at the risks. Deciding she needed the added edge, Megan authorized the updates.

"Don't worry. I'll end it early if you run out of time," said Gatton. "In theory, it should keep whatever set it completes before the interruption."

"This better work, Gatton."

"It will," he promised.

Chapter 9:
Go Now

Something shook Megan. Returning to consciousness felt like fighting uphill through fog with creeper vines wrapped around her ankles. When she forced her eyes open, David Stanley's concerned face filled her vision. She flinched. He yelped and recoiled, smacking his head on the doorway.

"Ouch," Megan said sympathetically. "Where are we?" Fully alert now, she looked around and noted they were parked in a gas station.

"We're near Virginia City," said David, clutching the back of his head and grimacing. "Boss said to wake you. We need to refuel and refresh. The restroom's not pretty but it's functional. The coffee's so-so, but it'll be waiting here for you when you're done. I didn't grab you anything to eat because I didn't know what you'd want. The guy still has my credit card though. We're less than thirty minutes from the destination."

Unbuckling the seat belt, Megan carefully climbed out. She didn't want to suffer David's fate, and she also wanted to check out the new updates.

"Move slowly," Gatton advised.

"How do you know I'm awake?" Megan asked, keeping her voice low so nearby patrons wouldn't see her talking to nothing.

His voice was not the first thing she wanted running through her head, but until this mess ended, she'd have to deal with the inconvenience. Nevertheless, she accepted the advice. The six plus hours without moving also left her stiff.

"If I'm in a certain mode, I can see what you see," said Gatton.

"And the program's tracking your vital signs. Brain activity shifts when people are conscious."

"Now is a very good time to tell me how to turn off some of those fun little displays," said Megan.

"What? Why?"

Megan pointedly stared at the restroom's sign until it sank through Gatton's thick skull.

"Ohhh." The young man quickly explained what she needed to know and how to recover those displays and lines of communication later.

Ten minutes later, Megan carried a few packages of trail mix, a bag of chips, an apple pie with more preservatives in it than apples, two power bars, a bottle of water, and a package of beef jerky out to the car. Her mother would pitch a fit if she knew the way Megan normally ate, but this was particularly low by any standards. The convenience store hadn't counted on needing to prepare people for armed conflicts.

David examined her choices with a critical eye.

"We'll stop by a restaurant if we have time," he said, accepting the credit card she'd retrieved from the attendant.

"We should get there quickly," Megan argued. Her thoughts went to Anthony Pierce whose time in captivity was approaching its one-day anniversary.

"We have to wait for the other agent anyway," David reminded her.

Megan didn't force the issue. On the way to a small restaurant with decent reviews, David filled her in on the last few hours. His meeting was scheduled for 3:00 p.m. at a house fifteen minutes away from their first destination. Slowly, Megan restored Gatton's ability to remotely access the Eagle Eyes displays.

Midway through their delicious breakfast of giant pancakes, an alert appeared in the bottom corner of Megan's vision. At the same moment, David's phone rang. He snapped it up and listened. Megan accessed the alert and stood abruptly.

PIERCE MOVING. GO NOW.

The other patrons eyed them curiously, but nobody moved to stop them as David threw some cash down to cover their bill. They raced each other to the car.

As she dove into the back seat, Megan put a call through to Gatton.

"Why would they move him?" she demanded.

"I don't know!" Gatton cried like the question was a personal accusation. He spoke faster than she'd ever heard him speak. "I hacked their security system and programed it to alert me if something significant happened. When there started to be a lot of activity, I turned on the receivers of every phone accessing the Wi-Fi. Someone said the house was compromised and put in a call for confirmation, but I blocked it. That might keep them there a little longer, but eventually, somebody's going to move far enough away to get a call out."

"Are there any cops stationed near here?" asked Megan.

"Yes, but I'll move them away from you," Gatton promised. "Tell David he's got a clear path until he nears Virginia City."

After relaying the message, Megan made Gatton recite everything he knew about what they would face. They traded ideas for dealing with the guards. Although prepared to use deadly force, Megan needed that to be a last-ditch option. Finally, Gatton said he could draw most guards away from the three areas of the house he'd identified as good places to keep prisoners. A schematic for the house appeared in Megan's mind. The program plotted a few approaches and gave its best recommendation for safely entering the house. Electronic security would be easy to bypass as long as Gatton remained in control of the system. If they got suspicious, they could lock him out by shutting off the Wi-Fi.

"There are only three men in the house right this second, but that could change," Gatton reported.

On the way, Megan opened Cassandra's suitcase and retrieved the loaded Glock 23 and its two spare magazines. The case it came in was ingenious. It looked like a large legal manuscript, but she could see the heavy-duty lining that surrounded the weapon compartment. Megan wished there'd been a way to store more ammunition, but she was lucky to have a weapon at all.

"We'd better not get stopped," Megan mumbled.

"Actually, if it comes to that, keep the gun in plain sight," said Gatton. "Nevada doesn't have a law against loaded handguns in vehicles, but if you want it out of sight, you need to hold it in a bag of some sort. An ankle holster would require a concealed carry permit."

"You sound like a dictionary page."

"Sorry, I had to look it up," Gatton explained.

Megan considered how to keep the weapon holstered without a belt and quickly concluded that the thing could safely be left behind. The suit jacket suddenly felt confining. Shedding the jacket, Megan arranged the spare magazines in the back left pocket since that seemed less likely to let them get knocked out.

Twenty minutes later when they arrived at the gigantic, isolated house, Megan asked Gatton about the best approach.

"Drive right up to the front door," he said. "I'm going to draw them to the back, but you'll have about six minutes tops to get in and get out."

"How will I find him in time?" Megan tried not to let the desperation enter her tone.

"Use the tracker," said Gatton. "It's been updated to give you heat signatures upon request. It's not perfect, but it should help."

Megan turned the feature on and felt like she'd donned glasses that make you see an alternate reality. Objects still appeared, but the color scheme was reduced to a mass of deep blue punctuated by brilliant patches of yellow, orange, and red. A glance at David in the front seat, dazzled Megan's eyes. She switched over to normal view.

"You might want to use that sparingly," Gatton noted.

"No kidding." Megan checked the gun one last time.

As David slammed on the brakes, Megan jumped out of the car and dashed to the door. A helpful timer started counting down from six minutes in the upper left side of her vision. Since subtlety wasn't really something she could afford, she sent a bullet into the doorjamb and gave the thing a solid kick. She winced at the unholy racket that made. Next, she dove inside and sidestepped to get out of the doorway, pressing her back against the wall near the front door. Ideally, a second person would be covering her, but her backup was late.

Turning on the heat signature reader, Megan swept her eyes around the room.

"Look up and down too," Gatton instructed.

Megan complied. Straight ahead, three small yellow-orange figures glowed in the distance. Below, three separate sections showed patches of glowing heat. Above and to her right, a single figure blazed like a lighthouse.

"That must be him," Gatton commented.

Flipping off the disorienting view, Megan held the handgun at the ready and cautiously moved through the room toward the area where she remembered there being stairs. The timer read 4:53 as her foot hit the bottom step. Once clearing the hallway, Megan turned right and sprinted to the last room on the left. The lock on this door made her pause.

"Any idea how to beat an electronic lock?" Megan questioned. Unlike the front door, this setup looked more likely to break her foot than yield if she tried to kick it.

"Switch to heat signatures again and give me a close look at the keypad," said Gatton.

The top five numbers showed up bright yellow.

"Amateurs," Gatton said scornfully. "The code's 1-2-3-4-5."

Megan jabbed her right index finger into the correct sequence and listened as the keypad emitted a friendly beep of acceptance before disabling the lock.

The timer now read 4:01.

Bursting into the room, Megan swept her gun over the whole space even though the heat readout had told her the room only held one person. Her heart leapt then crashed into the pit of her stomach when she realized Anthony Pierce was barely conscious. His face looked like someone had worked off some serious frustration there. Droplets of blood decorated his shirt. A bloody rag showed somebody's paltry efforts to clean him up, but several streaks still marked Anthony's face. Cold anger spread through Megan like ice water.

"Get David up here," Megan said grimly.

The clock read 3:12 by the time David barreled into the room.

"They're coming back," Gatton warned.

"Cut him loose and carry him out," said Megan. "Can you handle him?"

"I can handle him," David said, nodding. "Can you hold them off?"

"That's the plan," Megan replied. "Get going."

Without waiting to watch the struggle, Megan sent a bullet through one of the windows facing the back yard. A man shouted a warning to his companions, and a return shot slammed into the roof slightly left of her position. Sunlight blazed everywhere, making visibility difficult, so Megan ducked down and flipped the view over to heat signatures again. Lifting only her gun hand above the sill, Megan rained down bullets at the three men. She made sure to direct an equal number of shots at each man to keep them pinned in place.

Her hand ached as the gun clicked.

"Get out," Gatton ordered.

"There are still people here," Megan said stubbornly. She ejected the spent magazine and loaded one of the two spares. When one of the heat signatures made a cautious move forward, Megan sent another

152

bullet in his general direction.

"You don't understand!" Gatton cried. "They've got backup coming! You don't!"

"What do you mean I don't have backup coming?" Megan fired the question and another three bullets.

"The Reno guys are dragging their heels, and I was wrong about Kramer," Gatton said, after an uncomfortable pause.

"How wrong?" Megan ran Gatton's sentence back and forth across her mind, trying to make it compute. She hugged the floor as a hail of return fire peppered the window frame. One bullet slipped through the open window and lodged in the wall on the far side.

"He's theirs," said Gatton.

"I get that part," Megan snapped. She vented the anger by firing off the rest of the second magazine. "How did we miss that? And what does it mean?" Hours of range practice kicked in as Megan loaded the last gun clip without really thinking about it.

"It means he probably poisoned the well against you, and when he arrives, it won't be as your friend," said Gatton.

Leaning her head back against the wall, Megan thought. Oddly, parts of her life flashed through her mind's eye like scattered dream highlights. She saw her parents at her high school graduation and her sister's wedding. Dan Cooper, Bethany Cooper and the girls, Jaden, Cassandra Mirren, and Angela flashed into and out of Megan's head.

Hauling her weary body off the floor, Megan went over to the door and slammed it shut.

Chapter 10:
Start of a Plan

"What are you doing?" Gatton hissed the question.

"Quiet. I'm thinking," said Megan, returning to the semi-safe spot below and left of the window. Leaving with Anthony would only postpone the problem. In fact, it would probably make things worse. Once the Club figured out their hostage was gone, they'd know Megan had never returned to Hawaii. They'd be highly motivated to strike back, and the easiest way to do that was to go through Angela and Jaden.

"Think in the car!"

"Tell David to leave." Megan knew she couldn't hold up the bad guys long with only one magazine left. "I'll give him as much time as possible." She watched with the heat signature view until she saw significant movement.

When one of the bad guys got too bold, she'd discourage him with a bullet or two. A tense minute passed in this fashion.

"Do I have one bullet left or two?" Megan wondered.

A moment later, the place that used to hold a timer read: 2 Bullets.

"Thanks. Is David gone yet?"

"He's still waiting for you," Gatton grumbled.

"Patch me through to him," Megan ordered.

"I thought at least one of you would have the sense given to squirrels," Gatton complained. Nevertheless, he pulled David into the conversation.

"I can't wait much longer!" David cried.

"Don't wait," said Megan. "Go into Reno and get Anthony

154

somewhere safe. Drive around at random if you have to. I'll signal if and when it's safe to come get me."

"What about you?" David demanded. "I'm not—"

"I'm down to two bullets," Megan broke in. "That means the three guys in back are going to come charging your way shortly. You need to be as far away as possible."

"Won't they just follow me?" asked David.

"Gatton? Can you give him a head start?" Megan asked.

"I can kill the power to the garage doors, but it won't help for long," Gatton replied.

"Boss? What do you want me to do?" David inquired. "She's crazy!"

"I'm reasonably sure they won't kill me right away, but I can't say what they'll do if they catch the two of you here," said Megan. "Anthony can't get caught again. He barely survived the first round."

"Go," said Gatton. He clicked something on his end and David dropped out of the conference call.

A small map of the house appeared. Parts were highlighted as Gatton fiddled around, messing with the electricity.

"Tell me you have a plan." Gatton sounded both annoyed and worried.

"I have the start of a plan," Megan said, "and I'll need your help with it."

She jumped up and fired one of the last two bullets out the window before diving for the floor again. Megan had to fight the urge to unlock the door and sprint for freedom. Right now, that would probably be the most dangerous thing she could do.

"You know you're not just risking your life here," said Gatton. "You tick them off too badly, and they'll go after people you like for sport."

"I'm aware," Megan replied. Oddly, the brutal reminder had a focusing effect on her. "So, if this goes wrong, I need you to get Angela, Anthony, and Jaden moved somewhere beyond the Club's reach."

"What are you going to do to keep it from going wrong?" asked Gatton. "I don't want my tech falling into their hands."

"It won't," Megan assured him. "I'm sure you have a self-destruct mode on these things."

"In theory, yes, but we've never tried it," said Gatton. His mounting frustration was clear. "We didn't exactly have a hundred volunteers wanting to risk getting their eyes burned out."

"Can't I remove them and crush them between my fingers?" Megan inquired.

"If you're conscious and if you can reach them and if the Club grunts don't see you trying ... then maybe," said Gatton. "I don't know about you but I'm not a big fan of 'ifs,' especially that many of them. What's this 'start' of a plan you have?"

"I'll get there," said Megan.

"Lady, you're going to have three angry dudes knocking on that door in about thirty seconds. Two seconds beyond that, they'll be breathing down your neck! They know the code!"

"So change the code," Megan responded.

Jeffrey Gatton said nothing, but Megan noticed that the control panel from this side blinked a few times.

"They'll override that in a matter of minutes," Gatton pointed out.

"It'll be enough time for me to explain, but first, how good is your ability to track your precious Eagle Eyes?" Megan asked.

"Depends on the signal strength and the amount of interference," Gatton explained. "Eagle Eyes can boost the signal to remain traceable but they're going to feel that because it'll affect all nearby electronics. Why?"

"Because the easiest way to bust this trafficking ring is to take a tour."

"*That's* your plan?" Gatton's tone implied: worst plan ever! "You expect a bunch of traffickers to find you, pat your hand, and send you on a merry trip down their product pipeline?"

"Not exactly like that," said Megan. "You're going to sell me out."

"That's exactly what I'd like to do," Gatton growled. His tone flipped from frustrated to confused. "How is that going to help?"

"Call them in your guise of Lester the disgruntled hacker," said Megan. "Tell them you've reconsidered meeting them in person but arranged for a demonstration. They get the door code when you get confirmation that Lillian Marquez is ready to meet your terms."

"And what are those terms?" Gatton's question held a lot of caution.

"One, they can't kill me. Two, you want a quarter million dollars wired to an account you give them. Three, you want a steady stream of work from them or you turn everything you have over to the FBI Headquarters in Washington, D.C.. Think of it as a job interview. By the way, how's that list of clean agents coming?"

"Slow," said Gatton. "After Kramer slipped through, I had to tweak the algorithm to account for non-monetary incentives."

"How are they paying him?" Megan asked, curious.

"They're not. They're threatening him," said Gatton. "That's the part that slipped through the system. I was looking for a money trail."

Megan suddenly remembered bits from her research into Kramer. He had an ex-wife and a daughter somewhere nearby.

"Are they safe?" Megan asked. "I mean Kramer's wife and daughter."

"As far as I know, they're fine," Gatton answered. "He's been very good at following his orders."

"Find out for sure," Megan insisted.

"Why? They're not exactly tops of the target list."

"Because if you can assure Kramer of their safety, you can probably flip him to our side," Megan explained with a surprising amount of patience.

Angry pounding on the door told her the men had arrived. Megan moved to the corner right of the door. She didn't want to get shot accidentally if they were a little too enthusiastic about getting the door open.

The control panel made a sad noise and blinked red, telling her their code was wrong. Muffled angry voices came through the door, but she couldn't make out words.

"Make the call, Jeff," said Megan.

"I will, but first, you tell me who Lillian Marquez is and why you think she's the one to deal with."

"She's the woman in that last picture you sent Kramer when we were trying to convince him to come and help us." Megan pictured the beautiful woman in her mind. She had a lot of questions for the lady. With luck, Lillian would be amenable to a new deal. "She was meeting with Galloway. I don't know where exactly she fits in, but you said she was affiliated with the Club. I'm hoping she has enough sway to get these guys to follow the plan you lay out to them."

"Calling them now," said Gatton.

Megan listened to Jeff's end of the discussion. The electronic voice he chose chilled her, but it also scared some manners into the toughs darkening her doorway. They cursed and ranted until Gatton backed up his words with actions, but at least they didn't jump straight to shooting. For a moment, every light in the house blazed on, flickered three times, and died. Megan would have found the display unnerving if she didn't know Gatton was playing. She made a mental note to never rent or buy a smart house that had everything controlled by a central hub. The world held too many creepy hackers to ever trust a system completely.

The grunts talked over each other and argued in circles. Two wanted to flee the haunted house, while the other told them it was a trick.

Tell them to call their boss and make the arrangements or you'll lock them in the house.

Megan transferred the thought to a text box that Gatton could read.

In another ten minutes, everything was settled. A quick check with heat signatures confirmed that two of the men flanked the door to Megan's temporary prison.

"I hope you know what you're doing," Gatton commented. "This Lillian Marquez lady doesn't have much of a digital footprint, but I think your guess about her having some sway was right."

"What did you find out?" Megan prompted. If she was going to spend untold hours waiting to talk to the lady, she might as well have story time and get some background information.

"Lillian's dad and granddad were mobsters. They got out right before the mob families took a big hit from your people in the 1980's. Rumors say they caused that collapse to weed out some competition, but whatever happened a decade after the mob disappeared, the Club appeared."

"Any guess on how high up the ladder she climbed?" asked Megan.

"No, but the gentlemen I was negotiating with seemed perfectly happy to take orders from her."

"Great. Gather as much evidence as you can against her. I might find a use for it later. I think Lillian's going to be our biggest supporter soon."

"If she doesn't kill you for meddling," Gatton muttered.

"You did make that a condition, right?"

"I did," Gatton confirmed, "but you're still relying on way too many things to run smoothly. Lillian's got to agree to meet you, she's got to not kill you on sight, and she has to believe the evidence I'm gathering. How do you want that delivered anyway?"

"Same way we convinced Kramer," Megan answered. "I'll give

her a similar email address to check. You make sure the evidence is there and that she knows that's not the only copy you have."

"Anything else?"

"Yeah, hurry up with vetting the good guys," said Megan. "I want them mobile as soon as possible. I'm not taking this tour for my health. I expect each location to be carefully documented and placed on a warrant list. If 'my people' continue having trust issues, find some other law enforcement personnel who will play ball. If that fails, find somebody else. This is an open carry state. There's got to be some do-gooder with an itchy trigger finger who's got a problem with human traffickers. Find me some backup."

"Yes, ma'am," said Gatton. "I really hope this works. I've got to meet you someday."

Megan chuckled. Gatton was the proverbial annoying little brother she'd never had. Being the annoying sibling had always been a job she cherished growing up.

"Get me out of this and we'll talk," said Megan.

Chapter 11:
Desperate Deal

Megan Luchek had waited for many things in her life, but this was a first. Despite being too late to change much, her thoughts kept turning over the case and trying to determine whether this plan qualified as clever or crazy. Without Gatton and his high-tech toy the plan would be impossible. To pass the time, Megan ran scenarios of what she would have done if Eagle Eyes wasn't an option. She kept hitting the inconvenient thought that she'd probably be dead by now.

Once the fear of being shot through the wall faded, Megan took stock of the room she'd locked herself in. The moderately spacious room sported three windows. Megan had moved to the left of the door because the right corner was directly in front of the window she'd shot out. Since she'd left her suit jacket in the car, the air entering through the broken window chilled her. At first, it seemed like too much space, but once one factored in anything bigger than a twin bed, the room's dimensions made more sense. The furniture consisted of the chair Anthony had been tied to. Fragments of rough rope and droplets of blood still lay near the chair as an unpleasant reminder of what the future might hold if Megan couldn't sweet talk Lillian into some kind of deal.

Habit made her consider every option for fight or flight. Without bullets, the gun couldn't help her much, but she held on to it anyway. It comforted her to know Cassandra had gone to great lengths to get that gun to her. The weapon might give her a slight edge as a blunt force object. The window glass was useless to her since it shattered into a hundred thousand little round pieces so the manufacturer wouldn't get sued if somebody got cut.

The chair looked like it could damage somebody if one could wield it properly. Megan tentatively lifted it with one hand to see how much effort would be needed to turn it into a weapon. She concluded it would do better as a door blocker if she wedged it under the handle.

Flight was the best option and even that held considerable hazards. The logical place to exit the room—besides the door—was the window she'd shot out. The drop didn't look too far, but it was likely a good fifteen feet. If she got a decent grip on the sill and slowly lowered herself down until she hung from both arms, she might get away with sore ankles instead of broken legs. The backyard didn't offer much cover, so she would want working legs to make good on any escape.

Megan sighed. She might as well have locked herself in the Tower of London.

"How are you doing?" Jeffrey Gatton's gentle question broke into her thoughts.

"I'm a little cold," Megan admitted. She knew that wasn't what he meant.

"I can fix that. Go sit by the vent. I'll turn up the heat."

Not having a good reason to ignore his help, Megan found the heating vent at the bottom of the left wall and sat down directly in front of it. In a few seconds, a blast of warm air moved across her back. After thanking him, she leaned her head back against the wall and closed her eyes to rest. Soft classical music filled her head, making her smile.

"How did you know I like classical music?" Megan wondered.

"Part of the updates involved a program I'm beta testing," said Gatton. "It analyzes brain patterns and predicts preferences for things like music and food. It's terrible at guessing favorite foods, but it's usually 80% accurate with music."

"Why would you want something like that?" Megan wasn't certain she wanted to know the inner workings of Gatton's mind, but chatting seemed more productive than letting worry gnaw her guts in silence.

"We're still a long way off from reading minds but analyzing and predicting preferences should eventually unlock the way for learning more."

"Jeff, you have a scary mind," Megan commented.

"So I've been told," he said.

Before he could elaborate, the murmurs from outside the door changed.

"I think Lillian might have arrived," Gatton noted. "She's earlier than expected. She must have been well on her way when we spoke. I'm not sure what that means."

"Open the door!" Lillian's command sailed through the door quite clearly.

One of the men replied but his voice was too low to be heard.

"That's my cue," said Gatton. "I'll let you listen, but I'm muting you so she doesn't learn about Eagle Eyes. I suggest you sit in the chair and look as non-threatening as possible. The woman seems high-strung."

"Then break it open if you have to!" shrieked Lillian.

Megan wandered over to the chair but couldn't bring herself to sit down yet. Wooden chairs reminded her of the brief encounter she'd had with Keith in Pennsylvania. Shaking off the thought, Megan focused on what she needed to tell Lillian. Somehow, she needed to convince the woman that her deal was the only way out of a long prison term.

An eternally long minute passed while Megan listened to Gatton prepare Lillian for the pitch. Even though she heard the conversation, not much of it sank in.

"Get ready," Gatton warned. "I've calmed her down some, and I'm about to unlock the door."

Sitting on the chair's edge, Megan placed the gun on the ground between her feet and held her hands out to the sides in a non-threatening position. The door swung inward. Lillian Marquez stood framed by the doorway, flanked by three men. The lady was lucky Megan only wanted to talk. An entrance like that would have gotten her killed otherwise.

Thug One and Thug Two were basic mid-level foot soldiers. The third man wore more expensive clothing and looked less likely to get his hands dirty. Thug One and Thug Two stepped around Lillian and the third man and rushed at Megan like professional football players. Instinctively, she lifted her arms and spread her fingers wide to emphasize the lack of a weapon. The grunts each snagged an arm and yanked hard, bringing Megan to a standing position. Thug One let go so Thug Two could get a better grip and hold her arms in place behind her back. The awkward position made her back arch, which brought her head up. Thug One took kicked her left knee forward so Thug Two could guide her to a kneeling position.

"Get her in the chair," Lillian ordered.

Thug One and Thug Two obeyed without question or comment. They simply picked Megan up by the arms, dragged her back to the correct spot, and forced her to sit down on the wooden chair. She worked very hard not to fight them. Punching either would feel great but ultimately be counterproductive.

The third man produced a handful of long zip ties and tossed them near the chair. Thug One retrieved them and put them to good use securing Megan's wrists together and connecting her elbows to the slats forming the chair's back. She adjusted her position to relieve some of the pressure on her arms. Her shoulders ached. She noticed that the thugs neglected to secure her ankles to the chair. She only wished she was skilled enough to make them pay for the mistake.

Lillian held a phone in her left hand, but her expression was tough to read.

"Yes, I have her, but what I don't get is why you're giving her to me," said Lillian, presumably still speaking to Gatton.

Since she'd not been able to concentrate on it, Megan had muted their conversation.

"I have a proposal for you," said Megan, speaking as slowly and clearly as possible.

The thugs snickered at the announcement, but the third man regarded her more carefully. She didn't like the calculating way he eyed her.

"Kill her." The third man's Irish accent lent a musical air to the suggestion.

Next instant, both thugs had whipped out handguns. Thug One's gun nestled hard into the back of her neck. If he fired, he'd probably kill Lillian or his boss in the process. Thug Two stepped a few feet away and adjusted his aim so that his bullet would impact center mass. Given the range, his bullet would probably take out Thug One when it was finished with Megan.

Get rid of him!

Megan hoped Gatton could draw that conclusion without the prompt. She drew very shallow breaths, not wanting to disturb anybody's concentration. Studiously ignoring the thugs with guns, Megan locked eyes with Lillian.

"We need to speak in private," Megan said. Her voice wasn't loud, but the words filled the small space anyway.

"She's trouble, she is," insisted the third guy, turning to face Lillian. "Kill her now."

Demand was the wrong approach with Lillian, but since it worked in Megan's favor, she kept quiet. The woman broke eye contact with her long enough to glare at the third man.

"I'll call you when I need you," Lillian said coldly.

The third man shook his head in frustration but jerked his head toward the door. The thugs obediently holstered their guns and followed their boss out.

"Give me your gun," Lillian ordered Thug Two as he passed her.

He hesitated, shrugged, and handed over the gun. Megan sort of hoped Lillian knew how to use it because having her armed and clueless about gun safety would likely get her shot.

When the men exited, Lillian slammed the door shut and turned to face Megan.

"You have thirty seconds to convince me of this proposal or I let Hugh and his boys kill you," Lillian said. Thankfully, she kept the gun pointed at the ground by her side.

"Can you access an email account from your phone?" asked Megan. Assured that she could, Megan walked Lillian through the process until the other woman found the report Gatton had prepared.

More than thirty seconds passed while Lillian quietly read. Megan could see what she was reading because Gatton used Eagle Eyes to show her the account as Lillian scrolled. Blood slowly drained from Lillian's deeply tanned cheeks.

"In the attachments, you'll find enough evidence to link you to quite a few crimes," Megan explained, knowing from the woman's reaction that reality was sinking in.

"How did you find this?" Lillian demanded. "It'll never stand up in court."

"Maybe it will. Maybe it won't," Megan said. "But it will give the FBI enough reasons to scrutinize your businesses with a magnifying glass. How much do you trust your record keeping people? My tech guy found all that in a few hours."

Gatton sniffed at being demoted to Megan's *tech guy*.

"Your 'tech guy'? I thought he worked for Gatton Technologies?" Suspicion flared in Lillian's eyes.

"He does," said Megan, scrambling to piece things together in a way that would allay the suspicions.

"What put him on to me?" asked Lillian.

"I did." Megan silently thanked the woman for adding that follow up question. She was much more comfortable answering it. "I remembered you from the bar in The Grand Game Hotel, so I ran your image from the security cameras through some FBI software. One thing led to another, and I reached out to some freelancers we use. This guy's name popped up. I had him run a lot of images and yours got the most interesting results."

"You've been busy for somebody who supposedly boarded a plane to Hawaii late last night," Lillian commented. "How did you pull that off?"

"I can't reveal my sources," said Megan.

"Try very hard," said Lillian. She backed up the words by shoving the gun in Megan's face.

The awkward way she held the gun made Megan nervous.

"It doesn't matter right now," Megan soothed. She suddenly saw the appeal of being able to pull mind tricks. If she lived through this, she'd sic Gatton on the idea. "The important thing is that you let me tell you the one way you can escape prosecution and prison."

"Let me guess," Lillian mocked. "I turn myself in and testify against certain people and poof, my problems go away."

"Not exactly." Megan tried to move her head away from the gun, but the zip ties around her elbows limited her range. "Help me gather the right kind of evidence against the Club and you might not need to testify."

The other woman's eyes narrowed at mention of the Club, but she failed to deny it.

"No deal. They'll kill me," said Lillian.

"If my tech guy releases the evidence we have on you, they'll probably kill you anyway," Megan pointed out. She hated resorting to blackmail, but these negotiations were much trickier than the ones with Gatton yesterday.

The gun lowered a fraction of an inch.

"You're saying there's a chance you'd not file this?"

"That's what I'm saying," Megan confirmed. She felt like she'd just shaken hands with the devil.

"How can I trust you?" The sincere desperation in Lillian's tone encouraged Megan.

"Fidelity. Bravery. Integrity," said Megan, surprised the FBI's motto popped into mind and out of her mouth.

Lillian scoffed.

"You feds can be bought. You'd be surprised at how many the Club has on staff," said Lillian. Her tone turned mocking again. "I don't know them all, of course, so I can't reveal them. Sorry, I can't be more helpful."

"I know Kramer's dirty," said Megan. She watched Lillian's eyes for clues to the latest revelation. "I also know he's not working for money. They threatened his family. If given the same choice, I'd probably do the same. We all fight for different things. If nothing else, fight for your own future."

Megan stopped speaking. Anything else she added would be redundant. She'd presented Lillian with her desperate deal.

Now, she could only wait for an answer.

Chapter 12:
The Grand Tour

The internal struggle within Lillian strained Megan's nerves because she honestly couldn't predict which way the woman would go.

"I want full immunity and a ticket anywhere I want to go," said Lillian. "Otherwise, I let you die and take my chances."

"Take the deal!" Gatton's voice boomed inside Megan's head. He'd been silent so long she forgot he was monitoring everything.

"The matter may not be in my hands," Megan said carefully, "but if it does, I'll do my best to see that you escape the fallout."

"That's it? Your life hangs by a thread and you'll 'do your best'?" Gatton said. He sounded one second off of jumping up and down and waving his arms. "Lie to her!"

Megan ignored the man ranting in her head. It was like having a really contrary conscience to deal with. She met Lillian's intense gaze.

"Let me clarify that a lot of things have to happen before either of us get to think about the future," said Megan. "One, we need to gather enough evidence to cripple the Club's operations. That means aside from sending me on the grand tour of the Club's facilities you also have an active role to play. Two, we both need to survive the next twenty-four hours. That means keeping your cool and going about business as usual."

"What are you doing?" Gatton hissed.

I'm going to give her my cell phone. Track it.

Megan fired the plan off to Gatton as it formed in her head. It made sense to her gut, but a few hours to ponder the possible things that could go wrong would be nice.

"Why didn't you say you wanted to track her phone?" Gatton

asked. "Hang on. Let me see if that part of the update finished."

"If I die along the way, the deal's void," said Megan, "so make sure your people know to treat the cargo with care."

"They're professionals," Lillian said, sounding offended on behalf of her people. "And let's get back to this deal. What do I get for risking my neck for you?"

"You get to start over if you can get cleanly away," Megan pointed out.

"I want clean documents and twenty-five thousand dollars in cash." Lillian's eyes took on a distant look. She glanced down and seemed confused that she still held a gun pointed in the general direction of Megan's head. Lowering the weapon to her side, she added, "It's going to take me at least that much to get away."

"Do I look like I can access any money right now?" Megan demanded.

"Talk to your tech guy. He must be able to—" Lillian broke off abruptly and snapped the gun back up. This time, she pressed the barrel up under the soft part of Megan's chin. Her features twisted with pure rage.

Gatton cursed softly.

Megan felt like echoing the sentiment, but she couldn't spare the brain power.

"It's funny." Lillian's steely tone contradicted the phrase at first before shifting to something between mocking and sickly sweet. "I've been in this business more than eight years and I've never had the trouble I've had today with technology people. What are the odds of that?"

"Deny! Deny!" Gatton chanted.

"What are you talking about?" Megan spoke slowly so as not to further unbalance the woman. Keeping up with both conversations was proving to be dangerously distracting.

"A hacker broke into our network today then demanded money and a job. Tell me what you know about that." Lillian paused a few seconds to give Megan a chance to answer. "What are the odds this little freak show and your 'tech guy' are one and the same problem?"

A hundred percent, Megan answered silently.

"I had nothing to do with that." Megan spoke the denial aloud, though she admitted she probably bore some guilt by association.

"That's a lie," Lillian snarled. She dug the serious end of the gun deeper into Megan's chin. "Keep it up and I'll end this right here and now."

"Let me speak to her," said Gatton.

"That's not a good idea," Megan said, speaking equally to Gatton and Lillian. After muting Gatton temporarily, she continued addressing Lillian. "You need me. I don't know what games the tech guy's been pulling, but my offer is very straightforward. You help me beat the Club, and I let you walk away."

"I'm sure she finds the offer tempting, but we'll have to pass on it," said an Irish accented voice from near the door.

Lillian stiffened like she'd been struck with a brand and whirled, pulling the gun in toward her chest defensively.

With the gun gone from under her chin, Megan could lower her head enough to see the trio they'd sent packing a few minutes earlier. Thug One and Thug Two stood shoulder to shoulder, blocking the doorway. The third man stood in front of them looking very pleased.

"I came up here to tell ya the sound was malfunctioning on the camera in here, but it looks like we arrived just in time," said the third man.

"This isn't your concern, Cormac," Lillian said. She didn't move the gun but her grip on the weapon tightened.

A blinking yellow exclamation mark in the lower right side of Megan's vision indicated Gatton's desire to speak. Since the conversation focus had shifted away from her, Megan unmuted him.

"Oh, but it is," Cormac insisted. "It sounds like you were close to some sort of deal."

"I've cloned the scary lady's phone and will do the same to the gentlemen as soon as they get in range—that's three feet or so." Gatton spoke with considerable speed, as if he expected Megan to mute him again any second. "I've also had a passive virus prepared, disguised as an update. When they install it, I'll have full access to every record on their phones. Plus, it'll leap from phone to phone if the calls go to somebody flagged as a Club member."

"Everyone tries to cut deals," Lillian said scornfully.

"Let me speak with them," Gatton begged.

Fine. Call them.

Megan really didn't have a better plan unless Lillian and company would do their parts.

Lillian's phone buzzed in her pocket, but she ignored it. Then, one by one, each of the men received phone calls as well. The quality and volume of each buzz differed, but the combination of all four phones being tried in succession had an interesting effect upon Megan's captors. Thug One and Thug Two stared down at their phones like dumbfounded twin statues. Cormac's expression tried to burn his phone to ashes in his hands. Lillian looked torn between fainting and throwing her phone out the busted window. The intrigue almost made Megan forget her aching shoulders and cramped arms.

"Somebody should answer their phone," Megan suggested as the phones started on a second round of calls, starting with Lillian.

On the fourth ring, Lillian slid her thumb across the phone to accept the call.

"Who are you?" she demanded, stabbing a finger at the speaker button.

Megan didn't recognize Gatton's voice through the electronic distortion, but she recognized the attitude.

"I am your new master," Gatton intoned. "The woman you hold is my servant."

Megan raised a figurative eyebrow at that statement, but she let him ramble.

"Do as she says, and it will go well with you," said Gatton. "See that no harm comes to her. If you interfere with her mission, I will systematically ruin each of your lives."

"You're bluffing," blustered Cormac.

"I do as I please, Hugh Cormac," Gatton said, putting extra emphasis on the name.

"Why would you care what happens to one woman?" Cormac asked, genuinely baffled.

"I'm not here to answer your questions!" Gatton shouted. "The Club has earned my anger, and I will destroy it with or without you!" Gatton left that rant in the air for three seconds before continuing in a more reasonable tone. "Should you choose to join this endeavor, I will consider letting you flee like ants from a hill I intend to kick."

"Maybe he has a point," mumbled Thug One.

"People die when they walk away from the Club," Cormac declared, turning around far enough to glare at Thug One.

"Nobody's walking away," Lillian said slowly. She moved to a position behind Megan's chair. "He's talking about collapsing everything."

Cormac now had his gun in hand. He pointed it at Megan.

"Step aside, Lil," said Cormac. "The lady's a bad influence."

Megan could no longer see Lillian, but she saw the gun the woman held over her right shoulder. Consciously or subconsciously,

Lillian had turned her into an honorary human shield.

"The Club is finished," said Gatton, still doing a stellar impression of irate deity. "You have very few options. You help or you die. I have overwhelming evidence of your crimes, and I will let any Club members who survive the sweep know of your thorough cooperation, whether I have it or not."

Cormac started shaking like a tea kettle left on the stove too long. His face flushed bright red, but he lowered the gun as Gatton's words sank in.

"What do you want?" Cormac's question came out very reluctantly.

"My servant will explain," Gatton said haughtily, "but please remember. I'm watching."

He cut the connection and interrupted the heat flow to prove his point.

Every eye focused on Megan.

Taking a deep breath, she ran down the list of things she needed them to do and had Lillian show the gentlemen the sample evidence gathered against her. By this time, Gatton had also provided beginning files on Thug One, Thug Two, and Hugh Cormac. Once truly convinced that helping Megan was their best option, Cormac stepped out of the room to make the arrangements. Gatton assured her he was monitoring Cormac's moves and would warn her if he attempted a double-cross.

Megan pushed the worry aside though being aware of a betrayal wouldn't exactly save her hide. She didn't like having to trust Hugh and his boys in addition to Lillian. More people inevitably meant more problems even if the four could be convinced to do their parts.

I've never worked so hard to get sold into slavery.

The amount of details that went into the business concerned her. Gatton kept her up to date on the negotiations Cormac was running. He made contact with some of the higher ups to ask for advice, as they would expect him to do.

Two hours and fourteen phone calls later, a dirty black Subaru Legacy pulled up and whisked Megan off to her next stopping point on the Highway to Hell. She gave the trip that name when she was transferred to an eighteen wheeler on a lonely patch of I-80 East. For the first leg of the trip, her accommodations had consisted of the sedan's spacious trunk, but the truck was far worse. In addition to the multiple zip ties interfering with her circulation, Megan was gagged with duct tape and forced to sit in a cardboard box. Only Gatton's constant chatter kept her somewhat sane. When he put his mind to it, the guy made a decent cheerleader.

"You can get out of this any time," Gatton encouraged. "Say the word, and I'll have every law enforcement officer in that county on your tail."

No. I need to do this.

Megan couldn't have spoken the words if she wanted to, but she threw them into the box for Gatton to read.

Please tell me you're tracking the movement and cataloging the people involved.

"Plan's working like a charm," said Gatton. The good cheer in his voice faded by the end of the statement.

What is it?

"The trip might last longer than we initially guessed," Gatton said, speaking gently. "Are you certain you want to travel the whole road? It could be days until you get wherever they're sending you."

What Megan really wanted was a good stretch, a soft bed, and a cold drink, but she'd already come this far.

I'll be fine, Gatton. Make sure the data gets into reliable hands. I want to be the last person taking this particular trip.

Chapter 13:
Full Circle

Over the next week, Megan endured several kinds of deprivation and many hours of loneliness. Lillian's strict handling instructions made her a pariah even during the few times she was thrown into a cramped compartment with others for temporary storage. Most of the genuine human trafficking victims spoke a foreign language. Megan counted five different languages and estimated that two to three more were represented. Not everybody spoke, though both hugs and tears were plentiful among the captives.

Upon request, Gatton installed a language program for Megan so she could listen to the chatter happening around her, but she didn't interact with the others. She had no valid reason for possessing great language skills, and she didn't want to risk the operation by giving their captors reasons to watch her more closely than the others.

To pass some time, Gatton shared multiple operational updates and even read her children's stories. Initially, Megan thought the simplistic stories an odd choice, but as the days dragged on, she cherished the wholesome innocence permeating each short story.

Megan appreciated the young billionaire's efforts to keep her company, but the constant travel put her on a very strange sleeping cycle. Many hours of stillness passed. Part of her found it peaceful. Sometimes Megan would access the stories and spend a long time studying the beautiful, hand-drawn illustrations. The art involved gave her hope for humanity.

She kept her mind strong by helping with the massive coordination efforts. Since Megan wanted to start with people she trusted implicitly, she had Gatton contact Dan Cooper, Ophelia Pitman, and Samuel Chang from the FBI's Honolulu Field Office. She debated herself over involving Bryan Maddox, but the Special Agent in Charge would probably disapprove of the entire mission. Although Gatton offered, Megan argued successfully against bringing Angela and Anthony into the small circle of people who knew the truth about Megan's disappearance. Cooper and Chang covered for her with Maddox while Pitman quietly utilized some of her contacts to prep agents all over the continental United States.

On the whole, the men who participated in the transportation weren't especially evil. Some didn't even know what illicit thing they were smuggling. The few exceptions generally kept their abuses confined to words and intimidation rather than actions. There was a general hands-off policy except where necessary so the Club could claim that *fresh product* reached its customers. Supposedly, most of the women were destined for specific massage parlors or brothels, but a few—like Megan—had been chosen to go to a specific buyer.

If Eagle Eyes didn't keep her apprised of the date and time, Megan would have lost track long ago. At 3:07 a.m. on the seventh day of her tour of America, she was startled awake by an internal alarm from Gatton.

"Sorry to bother you, but I've got the final word from relevant parties. The raid on the Club's headquarters is scheduled for tomorrow—today rather—at noon. Three of the bigwigs are having a private discussion. Do you want in?"

"Absolutely," Megan replied, snapping to full alertness. "Where is it?"

Gatton hesitated.

"Downtown Reno. It's under a restaurant right in the heart of the city."

The announcement surprised Megan, but she also found it fitting.

"Have you warned Lillian?" Megan found the question distasteful, but her word meant a lot to her.

"Ms. Marquez will be mysteriously absent today," said Gatton. "I've warned her that the authorities will put things together and likely come knocking, but as per our latest agreement, she has her head start."

"Thanks, and what was decided about Agent Kramer's case?" Megan inquired. She'd initially recused herself from that decision because she was torn on the issue.

"After thorough discussion with the Council, the vote was one for 'prosecution,' 'one for second chance,' and two for 'abstain.' So, the final decision falls to you."

Council was Gatton's pet name for the key players supporting this mission. Megan guessed Samuel went for prosecution, Dan chose second chance, and Jeff and Ophelia abstained.

"I'll make that decision later," Megan said, really not wanting to face it now. Needing to change topics, she asked, "Where am I?" She'd gotten used to ignoring the maps. For the first two days, she'd been obsessed with checking their location every fifteen minutes, but since then, she had refrained because knowing was driving her batty.

"You're forty minutes from Philadelphia International Airport," Gatton reported. "When you reach the next stop, some boys in blue are going to come crashing in. They've got orders to do the takedown as quietly as possible, and there's a drug trafficking cover story in place if needed. A local fed will drive you under police escort to the airport. Once there, you'll catch a ride on one of my private planes to the Reno-Tahoe International Airport."

"You're sending me on a private plane?" Megan asked, stunned. Her sleepy brain tried to do finances for a flight like that. "Isn't that a little ... extravagant?"

"The normal flights would involve a lot more security. Besides, the private jet will have better food, a place to shower, and a bed for you to rest before the raid," Gatton explained.

Megan couldn't argue about a private jet being worlds better, but the question of motive mattered. She really wanted to participate in the raid on the Club's beating heart, but she trusted the people behind the plan.

"Jeff." Megan let his name linger a few seconds before asking, "Why are you doing this?"

"Because you deserve it," he answered quietly. It was his turn to pause. "I've never met anybody willing to go through what you did to save strangers. It's ... humbling." He sounded like the word hardly ever crossed his lips.

"You still haven't met me," Megan pointed out, trying to deflect the praise.

"True, but I hope to fix that soon," Gatton said.

"You're going to be on the plane?" Megan couldn't keep the note of alarm out of her voice. She couldn't explain it, but keeping Gatton as an enigmatic voice in her head seemed important. Her mind jumped to the next logical conclusion. "You're not coming on the raid."

"So I've been told multiple times, both by feds and my own lawyers," Gatton said, exasperated. "Don't worry; I wouldn't dare cross your Special Agent Pitman. That woman is aptly named, though 'Pitbull' might have been better."

Megan wondered what Ophelia had said to Gatton to get that reaction, but she understood his meaning perfectly. Ophelia had a reputation for being fiercely protective of her *children*, which included every FBI agent within a ten-mile radius of the Prince Kuhio Federal Building in Honolulu.

"Oh. Speaking of Pitman, your accommodations will include a fresh suit and a Glock 23 courtesy of the Philadelphia feds," said Gatton. "By the way, they want their gun back, so take good care of it or it's my neck on the chopping block."

"I will," Megan promised.

In the wee morning hours, police officers from three municipalities around Chester Springs, Pennsylvania busted into a small home. Armed with full tactical gear, assault rifles, and a warrant, the officers liberated four captives, including Megan. They didn't know much about her except that she was their primary objective and had worked very hard to make the day possible. They asked few questions besides basic health inquiries once they'd confirmed her identity.

The rest of the morning proceeded as Jeffrey Gatton had described. Special Agent Asa Osler drove Megan to the airport where she met the boy wonder who'd spent an inordinate amount of time in her head this past week. He had short, messy brown hair, brown eyes, and enough scruff on his face to declare him a man with odd sleeping habits. His prominent eyebrows and large nose worked well with each other. He was handsome enough as tech geniuses go. The hands-in-pocket attitude and half-smile also suited him.

After meeting Gatton, Megan boarded a large, private jet, and immediately made a beeline for the shower. Once cleansed of the dirt, if not the bad memories, Megan ate the surprisingly light fare provided. Gatton promised a proper meal later, once it was determined Megan's stomach wouldn't reject real food. The week of power bars, beef jerky, and bottled water had not been kind to her. Speaking to Gatton in person was awkward at first. Megan had never met a billionaire before, let alone one who admired her bravery. Once one got past the bluster, he seemed like a decent guy.

Shortly before noon, Megan crouched behind Special Agent Jacob Sample. Her involvement in this raid was purely as a backup to the backup. Nobody knew what condition she'd be in when it came time to breach the building. Still, Megan fully appreciated the massive effort it took to get her there. She'd been warned against letting the bad guys catch sight of her. Personally, she didn't care who knew about her involvement, but the wisdom of not inviting more crazy people to target her made sense.

We've come full circle.

The gun and gear made her feel safe, though Megan knew the sentiment was an illusion. In a span of twelve hours, she'd experienced extremes of helplessness and power. The rush of preparations and adrenaline consumed her completely. By the time agents led the last protesting prisoner away, Megan felt weak with relief. She wandered into the main conference room in the basement to see the walls where so much evil had been plotted.

"Guess this is the end for me," said Luke Kramer.

Alarm spiked through Megan as she realized the two of them had the room to themselves. Her gun felt heavy in her hands.

Kramer also had his gun out, but it was pointed at the floor.

"Don't do something you'll regret." Megan kept her voice soft.

Kramer looked up at her with anguish in his eyes.

"What would you do if you threw away everything you believed in?"

"Did you?" Megan challenged.

"You know what I did," Kramer said.

Megan bobbed her head once in agreement.

"Yes, I'm aware," she said, "but I also know the why and that matters a great deal to me."

A noise that encompassed both grunt and scoff escaped Kramer.

"Tell that to the prosecutor."

"I will, if it comes to that," said Megan.

"What do you mean?" Kramer's eyes snapped up and focused on her.

"I mean I believe in second chances." The amount of conviction with which Megan said that surprised her. "I've done things that will haunt me forever, and I cope with the knowledge in my own ways. You'll have to do the same. I think justice was served today." As she watched Kramer's face shift from despair to disbelief to cautious to hopeful to relieved, Megan felt compelled to add, "Just remember second chances aren't third or fourth."

Holstering his gun, Agent Kramer approached Megan slowly

with an outstretched palm.

They shook over the unspoken deal.

"Understood," said Kramer. "Thank you for everything. If you're ever back in Vegas, you can count on me." With one last nod, Kramer strode out of the room.

As silence fell, Megan remembered that nobody had updated Angela. Pulling out her phone, she called her friend.

"Maggie! Is that you? Are you all right?"

Angela's desperation sent a jolt of guilt through Megan, but she didn't know where to begin.

"I'm alive," Megan said. "Is Anthony safe?"

"Yes. Yes. He's here. Mr. Stanley brought him back to the hotel with an armed escort! They've hardly let us breathe on our own since! How did you get free? Will things be normal now? Can I send Jaden back to school?" The comments and questions flowed rapidly out of Angela.

Megan laughed, enjoying the sound of her friend's voice.

"It's a long story. Give me a few hours, and I'll be back in Vegas to tell you some of it."

Eagle Eyes Book 3: Danger in Dallas

By Julie C. Gilbert

Table of Contents:

Prologue:
Customer Service

"I understand your concerns and disappointment, Mr. Carmichael, but that product is no longer available." With great effort, Lillian Marquez managed to keep her voice even. She wanted to scream at this pig-headed man. How many different ways could she state *unavailable*? If she had more time, she would paste Arthur Carmichael's picture onto this burner phone and take a mallet to it, but she had a lot of work to do if she wanted to keep her head. Unfortunately, that involved fielding customer service calls from loaded imbeciles. She rolled her eyes at Steel to express her exasperation at entering Round Five of this conversation. Nevertheless, she forced sweetness into her tone as she continued, "But because you're such a faithful, longtime customer, we're prepared to deliver two replacement products immediately."

"I want what's mine."

Carmichael's voice had a petulant note that reminded Lillian of her three-year-old nephew. At least Andres had the cute factor on his side. Arthur L. Carmichael's main redeeming quality was money.

Lou Sands—Steel—nodded encouragement. His phone buzzed in his pocket, so he discreetly stepped away to answer it.

"The replacements are much better ranked than the one you chose," Lillian explained. "You're getting an incredible deal."

"No substitutions," Carmichael replied flatly. "If you don't deliver the exact product described, I'll be forced to express my displeasure to your superiors."

I want to see you try. Good luck finding them.

Drawing a slow, deep breath to keep her head from exploding,

183

Lillian let her gaze wander to Steel who was busy scribbling something on a piece of scrap paper.

"Don't threaten me," Lillian said, letting her voice dip into deadly-calm territory.

"It's not a threat. It's a—"

"Mr. Carmichael, you hired us to find a particular product for you," Lillian cut in. "We did so, but things in this business are never certain. Circumstances have placed …." Lillian let the sentence trail off as Steel shoved the scrap paper across her desk.

O says agree if AC pays for specialist.

You've got to be kidding me.

Swallowing the instinct to utter a curse, Lillian straightened and stared at Steel.

He shrugged in answer to her unspoken question and withdrew the paper to write something else. It was a figure: $250,000.

Lillian cleared her throat.

"I can see you're passionate about this. Would you be willing to pay a retrieval specialist to complete the original contract?"

"Why should I pay more for something I already bought?" Carmichael complained.

"Page nineteen of the contract addresses your options in these unlikely circumstances," said Lillian, trying not to sound too smug. "You've already rejected the easiest option of accepting a substitute. That leaves the most expensive options on the table, and it sounds like you're already leaning toward the specialist option anyway."

"How much will that cost me?" Carmichael asked.

"Half a million," Lillian answered. Her mind started tackling the issue of who to hire.

As expected, Carmichael balked at the price. Fifteen minutes and a massive headache later, Lillian finally closed the deal for $255,000. If all went well, she'd transfer the extra five thousand to Steel to cover for the favor she'd have to ask of him. A shot of guilt stabbed her in the chest at the same time as a cold wave of déjà vu swept over her. Carefully, she placed the burner phone in the center of her desk, not sure if the deal would fix the problem or make it worse.

Lillian enjoyed gambling but not with her life. The Eagle Eyes disaster combined with the heightened FBI interest in the Club's Las Vegas and Reno businesses threatened everything she had worked years to build. Many of her superiors had been swept up in the latest raid. Technically, Lillian didn't owe Special Agent Megan Luchek anything.

They'd cut a deal which boiled down to Megan got to live and Lillian got a head's up before the feds crashed in on the Club. She couldn't shake the feeling that tangling with Luchek again would be bad news for everybody involved. Still, standard risk versus rewards calculations said this might be the time to make significant strides in her personal career advancement.

"We're on a sinking ship," Steel commented. His gray eyes watched her carefully.

"Do we get out or get on a new ship?" Lillian wondered. She checked that the audio interference program was running so the conversation would stay between her and Steel.

"Do you have a plan?" Steel wondered. His tone indicated mild curiosity, but his gaze remained intense.

"I have the beginning of a plan," Lillian admitted, "but I need your help." She spent the next ten minutes outlining her thoughts. By every measuring system, her words were downright treasonous to the powerful organization that had run in her family line for four generations. She ended by saying, "You could get a new job in a heartbeat. I'm the one who has to prove relevancy. I won't hold it against you if you decide to strike out on your own or stay with the Club."

The fact that Steel didn't respond right away made Lillian nervous, but she forced herself to wait. Saying more would emphasize the weakness of her position further.

"I'm in," Steel said at last.

"Thank you." Relief flooded Lillian. She wanted to leap across the desk and hug this wonderful man, but pride helped her refocus her mind. Maybe things would work out. "I'll handle things from this side. Get to Texas and lay the groundwork for the trap. The window for this opportunity won't last long."

"Who do you want to handle the product retrieval?" asked Steel.

"Curtis," Lillian replied. "He's a little more level-headed than some of the other specialists. His handling of the last two contracts we gave him was exemplary."

"I'll see if he's available," said Steel with a brief nod of approval. He checked his phone. "The additional money's in place." His eyes held a query, which he conveyed to her with a raised eyebrow.

"I'm not running," Lillian said softly. She wondered if she should be disturbed by Steel's ability to read her. Things crystalized in her mind, exchanging her nervous uncertainty for the peace of resolve. "I'm going to create an opening in the Shadow Council and show them how valuable we can be."

Since there wasn't much more to say, Steel took his leave.

Lillian made some strong black coffee and settled into the decrepit office chair. She missed her old chair. She missed a lot of things thanks to Derrick Belmont—the traitor—and Megan Luchek. The more she thought, the less sympathy she felt for the agent. She truly had no idea why Arthur Carmichael had fixated on the woman, but if handing her over gave them the excuse to get inside Carmichael's mansion, so be it.

Chapter 1:
Big Favor

Megan Luchek looked down from her penthouse suite in the Sky High Hotel and admired the view of downtown Dallas. This was only her fourth time in the state of Texas and two of the trips didn't really count since she'd never left the airport during those layovers. She considered stepping out onto the balcony but rejected the idea when her phone informed her that it was forty-eight degrees Fahrenheit outside. Even the week in Las Vegas and another being hauled around much of the country hadn't been enough to prepare her for such frigid temperatures. She shivered at the thought of the weather in her home state of New Jersey. Guilt stabbed her briefly over not spending her last few days in the continental states with extended family, but the doctor had ordered her to rest and she intended to obey. Visiting the Falco and Luchek clans would never qualify as *relaxing*.

Tossing her phone onto the king-size bed, Megan stretched and peeked at the view again. Her sleep patterns still hadn't reset to normal, hence her state of wakefulness at 6:35 a.m. while on vacation. As she considered the pros and cons of diving into the room's mini-kitchen or ordering something from the gourmet coffee menu, her phone rang. Her phone had settled in the center of the bed near the pillows, so she had to dive across the bed to reach it. Sweeping the device up, Megan rolled onto her back to see who was calling so early.

A jolt of alarm sailed through her as she saw the caller's name: Dan. Last Megan knew, Special Agent Daniel Cooper hadn't left Hawaii. She did the time zone math while sliding her finger across the phone to accept his call.

"What's wrong?" Megan demanded without preamble. They had worked enough cases together to allow her to skip over formalities. "It must be 2:30 there."

"I have a huge favor to ask of you," Dan admitted.

Megan's curiosity was thoroughly piqued. Aside from the demands of the job, Dan wasn't the sort to pull crazy hours. His wife, Bethany, made sure of that.

"Shoot."

"Are you sure? I know you're on vacation, but I need to ask you for a big favor."

"Out with it, Cooper," Megan ordered. When he didn't continue right away, she filled some of the silence. "It's been almost a full week since I got kidnapped or shot at. I'm bored here. Give me something interesting to do." The words were truer than Megan was comfortable admitting.

"I need you to visit my great-aunt in the hospital. She's dying."

"Oh, geez, Dan. I'm sorry," said Megan. She sat up and mentally kicked herself for taking this so lightly at first.

"It's not your fault," Dan assured her. "I just need you to deliver some flowers and stay with my mom a few hours. She's kind of a wreck right now, and I have to appear in court tomorrow. I can't exactly hop on a plane and swoop in to stay with her." His frustrated tone said he would like to enact that very plan.

"Of course, I'll do it. What are their favorite flowers?"

"I don't know," Dan admitted.

Megan thought she heard a voice in the background.

"White orchids for mom and purple tulips for Aunt Edith," Dan reported. "Hang on, Beth wants to say something."

Two seconds passed before Beth spoke.

"Hi, Megan. Beth here. If you can't find orchids or tulips in those colors, go for yellow roses or a mixed bouquet of Peruvian lilies. Let me get you a credit card number for those."

"Don't worry about it right now." Megan had no intention of letting Beth and Dan foot the entire bill. Two kids, a car, a truck, and a house bled their finances regularly. She switched the call over to speaker mode so she could open up notes and type in the flower names. "We can square up later."

"I want to see the receipt," said Beth.

"Why? You don't trust me?" The questions were out before Megan could decide if she should be offended or not. Thankfully, she managed to keep her tone light.

"I know how your mind works, and I wouldn't put it past you to underreport to help us out." Beth's statement was dead on, stunning Megan into momentary silence. "We love you for that quality, but this is something we need to do as a family."

"You got it." Megan marveled at Beth's deep understanding. They had only met a few times, albeit several of those times involved the sort of circumstances where you either band together or perish. "Text me the hospital address and the names I should seek out. I'll handle the rest."

"Thank you. This means a lot to us," said Beth. "Sorry to intrude on your vacation."

"There's nothing to apologize for," Megan protested. "I'm happy I can help. Really, I don't have grand plans to be interrupted. I'm scoping out a hotel for some friends."

"What does that involve?" Beth inquired.

"Checking out the amenities and visiting the restaurants," Megan said. "You know, strenuous stuff."

Beth chuckled.

"I'll let you get back to it then. Thanks again."

Megan swallowed the reflex reply as Dan re-entered the conversation.

"I'll buy you coffee for a month when you get back," Dan promised.

"As I told Beth, I'm happy to be able to help. What's your mom's name again? You told me, but I'm blanking at the moment."

"Virginia, but most people call her 'Gina.'"

Megan added to her flower notes so she'd know who to ask for when she reached the hospital. Recalling that Dan mentioned his great-aunt's name before, Megan added it to her list.

A text message came through with the hospital's name and address. Inwardly, Megan winced at the thought of stepping foot in a hospital. She had a general aversion to such places yet life seemed bent on throwing her there several times a year.

"What's your great-aunt's last name?"

"Shipley," Dan answered. "Edith Shipley, with an 'ey' at the end. She ends everybody's name with 'ey,' so expect to answer to a new name for a time."

Megan corrected her note.

"Got it. Is there anything else I should know?"

"Aunt Edith is my mother's father's twin sister, so the families were close. She practically raised my mom, so don't be surprised if they're both coping poorly with the liver failure," Dan explained. "The doctors don't want to do a transplant because she's eighty-one and probably doesn't have much time left anyway." Frustration hardened Dan's tone.

While Megan understood the logic, she sympathized with Dan and his family.

"Thanks for the info. I'll report back after the visit," Megan promised, opting for a business-like tone to level her partner's emotions.

"What's the rest of your day look like?" asked Dan.

"Haven't given it much thought," Megan said. "I'm sure I can find a fancy mall or something. I haven't been shopping in months. There's really no substitute for the selection one can get on the mainland."

Dan participated in the small talk a few more minutes before Megan noted the time again and wound the conversation to a close. After fending off a few more enthusiastic rounds of thanks, Megan managed to convince Dan to get off the phone and grab a few hours of sleep.

Flopping onto her back again, Megan enjoyed the soft feel of the bed. She lay there a few minutes, letting her eyes drift shut until a thought intruded. She had no idea when the hospital had visiting hours. A few quick internet searches answered her questions. She might have to fib a bit since the ward she intended to go to only let family and clergy through the doors on a regular basis. Since she wasn't ready to impersonate a religious leader, she'd have to go with the *adopted* route if challenged. That one steered closest to the truth as Dan's mother had greeted her like a daughter in the thank you letter following the incident where Dan and his family almost died in a deadly game aimed at Megan.

The thought sent her mind to a number of close calls she had experienced over the last couple of years. The pleasantly drowsy state also made her thoughts run to random things like guardian angels. If she had one, the poor being probably deserved hazard pay.

Since she had two hours until the hospital's normal visiting hours, Megan indulged in a long, hot shower and a big breakfast down in one of the hotel's three restaurants. Her meals were comped as this was a semi-business trip for the Grand Game Hotel in Las Vegas. For the next two days, Megan would be Angela and Anthony Pierce's proxy. Thoughts of the job conjured thoughts of her friends. She fervently hoped they were recovering from their recent terrors. Both had been kidnapped for separate reasons, and by some miracle, Megan had been able to rescue them.

I wonder how Angela's feeling.

That rescue could have gone smoother.

Wincing at the memory, Megan yanked her thoughts back to the task at hand. Her main job was to evaluate the hotel's viability and prospects as her friends considered a mutually beneficial merger with the Coalsteins, the couple who owned the Sky High Hotel. The plan had been in the works since before the Grand Game Hotel's problems, and now that those were vanishing, the deal was back on the table.

So far, Megan had good things to report. The western omelet with a side of French toast turned out amazing, though if she had to foot the bill herself, she would have been limited to plain white bread toast and tap water. Sparkling water cost $6.95. Prices aside, the hotel provided everything one would need to feel comfortable. She'd even read in the pamphlet that they would have their staff change the mattress for you if the original wasn't to your liking.

Midway through breakfast, Megan got that creeped-out feeling of being watched. As casually as possible, she scanned her surroundings. No red flags sprang up. A young couple sat tucked away in the far left corner nursing coffees. Three men in varying shades of gray suits sat at random tables around the room. And a family with three kids confined their chaos to the far right corner from Megan's perspective.

She cautiously checked the *I'm being paranoid* box in her head, but her senses remained on high alert. The last few incidents preceded by the feeling currently twisting her guts about ended up with drawn guns and shots fired. Despite her earlier complaints of boredom, Megan relished the normality of today's plan: hospital visit and shopping. Still, common sense and healthy paranoia dictated she at least take her gun with her. She'd have to think twice if this was New Jersey, but Texans loved their guns and wrote concealed carry laws accordingly.

The strange feeling faded.

Megan silently begged any unseen foes to wait until the end of the day to start something with her. Nothing prepared a woman to take on the world quite like a pair of killer shoes and a handgun. She would have preferred the handgun be hers, but the borrowed one from the Pennsylvanian agents would have to do. For that matter, she would have loved to have skipped meeting the PA agents, but since that win came with the knowledge of sticking a major monkey wrench into the Club's human trafficking ring, she'd take it.

Projecting her thoughts into the future, Megan wondered what flavor of crazy would flow her way next. Corrupt politicians, assassins, mobsters, and human traffickers had entered her crosshairs recently. For the briefest second, she longed for a few white-collar months, but the honest part of her confessed a love for the action. Her mother would definitely disapprove, but Mom didn't have to know everything. According to her mother, Megan worked in an office building, talked to people all day long, and needed a man.

The thought of men caused Megan to take stock of the other hungry patrons. Only two of the businessmen remained and they both looked thoroughly engrossed in their phones. Since the nearest one had his back to her, she could see the football game he played on his phone. She tried not to judge him for it, even if he was playing as the Cowboys.

The creepy feeling returned stronger than before. Shaking it off, Megan decided she'd had enough breakfast. It was time to head out and face the day.

As she passed his table, the man playing football glanced up, gave the neutral, stranger nod of greeting, and resumed his game. He had a clean cut, baby-faced look about him that made her smile. Blond wasn't typically her type, but she could still appreciate a pretty face.

Chapter 2:
Pricey Revenge

"I don't care about the cost, Maria," whispered Arthur Carmichael. "I will make them pay for what they did to you, to us, to our family." Taking the well-worn photograph off the end table, he tucked it into his wife's hands and reached for the rag to dab at the drool pooling near the corner of her mouth. "Hang on to this. We're closer than ever before."

Her eyes moved downward to stare at the picture of Leo at his eighth birthday party. Two tears slipped out, so Arthur rubbed them away with his thumbs. They had bought Leo a pony and a cowboy costume complete with sheriff's star, brown boots, silver spurs, and a twin set of shiny pistols. That had been two days before the "accident" that paralyzed his wife, killed his son, and ripped apart his family eleven years ago.

Much had changed.

"It'll be over in a day or so," he promised.

A monitor sitting next to his wife dinged and a message appeared. **Then, I die? Please.**

"Don't talk like that." Arthur wrapped his hands around the picture tucked into his wife's hands. He adjusted her fingers so they would have a better grip on the image.

So much pain.

"I know. I know. I'm sorry, but don't give up. We've waited so long for this!"

His mind flew back to the beginning. He'd joined the Shadow Council because of a lie, strung along by the promise of revenge in due time. At first, the Council simply used him for his many connections, but eventually, he worked his way up to a position of power. By the time he discovered that the Council—not the Club—had orchestrated the accident, it was too late to turn back.

Adjusting a few dials on a different machine, he let more morphine flow into Maria. Slowly, her eyes closed. Once certain sleep had full reign, Arthur placed the picture back on the end table and adjusted the blanket engulfing his wife. He considered taking the other picture out of the drawer but that one was even more painful for them, so he left well enough alone.

Psychological experts said the pain would fade in time.

They lied.

Arthur felt his losses anew every day when he looked into Maria's eyes and saw her repeated pleas for a peaceful end. The sentiment had been there since that terrible day. The thought reading program merely let her express that more clearly.

"Once we see this through, maybe we can join Leo in death."

The thought of ending this long journey made his eyes sting with tears. He had almost given up hope of the promised revenge. Then, about six months ago, a courier delivered five code names. His people had systematically tracked down almost every person listed and questioned them closely before bringing them to him for justice. The last two names were: Cassandra Mirren and Pedro Escalante. Both were Fixers no longer working for the Council.

Pedro was dead, at least according to the reports he'd been given.

That left Cassandra Mirren as his last hope for answers. She would be the key to his revenge one way or another. Rumors said she had gone soft, but Arthur had followed her career since it began. Her body count might not have reached the heights of some of her counterparts, but her nearly spotless track record couldn't be denied. If he could convince her to help, they could destroy the entire rotten Council from the inside out. If she refused, he would have to be content with her death.

Much as Arthur wanted to stay by Maria's side, many details for his revenge still needed to be worked out. He wished there had been some other way than involving the FBI woman, but every report on Cassandra said that Megan Luchek might be the only person the assassin counted as a friend. He questioned the wisdom of bringing the two women into his home, but no matter which scenario played out, it had to happen here. Maria couldn't be moved and needed to witness this. He had shown her videos of the other deaths, but since this would likely be the last, it had to be special. On the other hand, Leo's room and seeing Maria stood the best chance of convincing Cassandra to help him exact revenge.

Retreating to his office, Arthur signed into his secure laptop and opened the program that tracked the finances of the top twenty-five Freelancers, those known for accepting jobs from multiple employers. He wasn't naïve enough to think his people had tagged every relevant account, but given the scarcity of reliable talent, he stood a good chance of learning who the Club would hire on his behalf. He'd allowed the negotiating price to settle at $255,000 because it would be relatively easy to track. If the Club kept to the same sort of accounting as they had in place last year, the Freelancer's account should jump by $248,000. The rest would go to administrative costs.

He input the simple command to find figures in the appropriate range. While he waited, Arthur watched a slideshow of pictures featuring Leo and wondered what life would be like had things been different. Dr. Rieber initially encouraged such thinking, but his stance on the alternate scenarios had changed recently. It might be time to get a new psychiatrist. Without the Shadow Council, Arthur would be much poorer, but he might also be happier. Everything in him wished to go back and make that trade: money for family.

If Leo had lived, he'd be off to college by now. He would probably have a few more siblings too. The accident had stolen more than Maria's health. It had also ended an early pregnancy. Arthur's mind wandered to other painful what if's, but as usual, he threw them in a mental box and slammed the lid.

An alert made him sit up straighter. He squinted at the screen and murmured the name aloud.

"Curtis D'Angelo." He reached for the keyboard, navigated to a new program, and started typing. "What do we know about you?"

Soon, he had the limited profile for Mr. D'Angelo. Apparently, the man was a rising star in the Freelancer world. He'd completed two jobs for the Club with exemplary ratings and one for the Shadow Council with a rating of excellent. His skill set included assassination, but he specialized in retrieval of both inanimate objects and live specimens.

"If you do well, maybe I'll hire you for an extra day or two."

He opened his mouth to elaborate on the thought process, but then, he shut his mouth with a snap. Dr. Rieber said he should find more meaningful human interactions instead of talking to himself all day. Needing to move, Arthur loaded the new profile on to his phone and queued it up behind the other ones he'd been listening to on loop the last few days.

***

Jeffrey Gatton checked the ADAM report for the sixth time, just to be sure. He mentally followed the software logic paths taken by the Automated Danger Analysis Machine and agreed with the conclusion. He groaned. The knowledge he now possessed had a 77.43% chance of being accurate. Because it relied heavily on experimental technology and illegally obtained data, spreading the word in the hopes of preventing the outcome wasn't exactly an easy first option. Legally, it wasn't an option. Period. But morally, he should really sound the alarm. Hence his awkward position.

A shadow company run by the United States government had commissioned the research that made ADAM possible. Many moving parts and much of the machine's brains fell under Gatton Technology patents, but the government still technically owned the data. Jeffrey had signed so many nondisclosure documents to get this contract even his lawyer had complained about the excessive measures. Doing anything but turning the data over to the Central Intelligence Agency liaison could be considered treason. He'd lose his company and wind up in jail. He wasn't supposed to know the man who handled the contract worked for the CIA, but the machine had reported such during a standard calibration subroutine. That might give him some leverage, but knowing the government, they'd simply hang that particular agent out to dry and feign innocence.

Usually, the reports were useless, predicting car accidents in bad weather and terrorist attacks in major cities. This was something else entirely. Gatton had been monitoring ADAM's reports closer since it had accurately predicted three assassinations over the past year. He had only uncovered the predictions after the deaths, but this time, he wasn't too late. Worse, he actually liked the people being targeted: Special Agent Megan Luchek, FBI and Assassin, code name: Cassandra.

"Who'd you tick off this time, Luchek?" he mumbled, backtracking the data trail that pulled up her name.

The government monitored every large transfer of normal money and even some of the so-called untraceable digital currencies. They couldn't get into most accounts thanks to solid security walls created by companies like Gatton Technologies, but transfers became public knowledge for the few seconds to minutes they took to complete. Over time, analysts like the machine Gatton had programmed would follow those money trails and the surrounding events. The prediction side still needed a lot of testing, but Gatton was inclined to trust it this time.

Agent Luchek had been involved in several incidents with ties to shady organizations such as the Club and the Shadow Council. The government maintained detailed files on both organizations, keeping the amount of illegal activities in check when necessary. That's why the recent years had seen an uptick in tension between the two organizations. Gatton half-suspected the Shadow Council might be a government-sponsored entity. The last few rounds with the Club brought up Cassandra's name. Out of habit, Gatton had plugged both of the women's names into ADAM, so when a semi-obscure Freelancer thug with moderate computer skills started running their names, red flags started flying.

Gatton's mind raced through options. He could burn another identity and use it to deliver an anonymous tip or use one of his untraceable laptops to sow some discoverable seeds on the internet. Both methods seemed too slow to be of any use, but anything more direct would endanger everything he'd worked his whole life to build. Using Eagle Eyes to contact Agent Luchek would be the quickest option, but unless he wanted to do some serious coding to cover his tracks, that would also be the easiest way to nail his hide to a wall. Anything too complicated would declare his involvement because sophisticated methods limited the field of people capable of utilizing them.

Maybe he should consider simple options. Spy novel plots intruded on his thinking time. Gatton jerked upright so fast the chair tipped precariously, wrenching his back. Wincing, he leapt out of his chair and limped toward the attic. He needed an old school burner phone with a few minutes left. Once he made his call, he could smash the card and dispose of the phone. The government might be able to trace the phone call to this region of the country, but they would never be able to prove anything if he flushed the smashed pieces of the phone card.

Pulling down the attic stairs, Gatton hesitated as he gazed up into the black abyss. He hated attics. His back wasn't too thrilled about the prospect of a climb right now either.

"This better be worth it," he muttered, stepping onto the first rung.

He considered hopping into a car and driving to a store to pick up a simple phone, but the convenience of online stores had driven most regular retailers under. Besides, his general aversion to most people prompted him to live thirty-five miles from civilization's nearest mall. Even same-day shipping on the fastest online retailer would fail to arrive in time. That left the attic as his best hope.

Technology had always fascinated him. During his teen years, he'd dismantled, cannibalized, and rebuilt dozens of phones and computers. Most ended up in the attic.

Chilly air hit his bare arms as he reached the top. Being careful not to shove his hand into a pile of pink insulation, Gatton propped himself up and swung his left arm in the direction of the light. He groaned upon seeing the many rows of plastic containers. The sheer size of his junk collection used to impress him, but now, it annoyed him. Thinking hard, he vaguely recalled hauling most of the phone stuff to the back right corner. Despite the temperature, he started sweating. Megan and Cassandra had no idea what awaited them. Truth be told, Gatton had no real idea what awaited them, but they deserved a head's up that a known high-end thug had been doing some homework on them.

Chapter 3:
Life Lessons

Megan spent her morning tracking down the right flowers, circling a crowded lot for a parking spot, and navigating a maze of corridors to the private room assigned to Edith Shipley. The sympathetic gazes of the nurses providing her with directions didn't bode well. Megan's pace automatically slowed when she approached the room. Since her hands were full, she gently kicked at the semi-closed door.

The middle-aged woman answering the door quickly pulled Megan into a hug.

"Thank you for coming."

Returning the hug as best she could with two giant bouquets of flowers, Megan fumbled her way through the pleasantries.

"Dan called ahead." Fresh tears traveled well-worn tracks down Virginia Cooper's face.

Megan wanted to hand the woman the flowers but hesitated, not wanting to cause more tears. Instead, she clutched the flowers close, like an emotional shield.

"You must be the guardian angel sent to protect our Danny." The speaker's Southern drawl made the sentence ebb and flow and last a few beats longer than expected. "I'm so glad to meet you." Turning her eyes from Megan to Dan's mother, the woman continued, "Here now, Giney, it's high time ya took a break from all this depressin'ness. Go get yerself a nice hot breakfast and let me chat with the youngin'."

"But. What if—"

"I promise to not die in the next half-hour." Aunt Edith's pale blue eyes sparkled with amusement as she cut off Dan's mother.

Sniffling, Virginia nodded, squeezed the lady's hand fiercely, and fled the room.

Once certain the other woman was gone, Aunt Edith leaned back into the propped up pillows and closed her eyes.

Not sure what to say, Megan chose to stay silent.

"I just need a moment, child." The woman sounded tired. "Set those flowers down and come closer so I can get me a good look at ya." Aunt Edith's direct, guileless statements started to put Megan at ease.

"Where do you want them?" Megan asked, stepping up to the bedside.

"Oh, anywhere," said Aunt Edith with a casual wave. "How about that chair?" The question was accompanied by a gesture to an uncomfortable looking chair on the opposite side of the bed. "Giney can move them when she gets back. Thank you for deliverin' them. They'll look fabulous at my funeral."

Megan flinched like the lady had struck her.

"It's all right, honey. Death comes for everybody in good time. I've straightened my will and squared things up with the Good Lord. I'm ready to trade this world for the next one." She sighed and stared off into the space next to Megan's head. "But I don't think my family is ready to let go."

Again at a loss for words, Megan dragged out the process of arranging the flowers on the indicated chair. Her phone buzzed from her pocket, but she didn't want to be rude by checking it.

"Do you believe in God, child?"

"Yes, of course." Megan answered quickly in the hopes of keeping the conversation brief. She had attended several years of Catholic school, but she had also seen much of the world's dark side. That brought her to the conclusion that God took a very hands-off approach to running the world these days.

"Do you know Him well, as a friend?" Aunt Edith pressed.

"Not really," Megan admitted, mentally kicking herself for not picking up the phone before.

"Would you like to know what He thinks of you?" asked Aunt Edith. She held her right hand out to Megan, palm up.

Instinctively, Megan grasped the cool, leathery hand.

Closing her eyes, Aunt Edith smiled broadly. In fact, her whole face lit up.

A warm, inviting heat traveled up from Aunt Edith's palm to Megan's hand, radiating up her arm to her elbow. She could only stare at the woman, watching her expression morph several times, while her brain tried to figure out the heat source.

For a while, nothing was said, but Aunt Edith nodded a few times. Finally, she grinned again and spoke.

"I see a picture of a human heart. Part is darkened, but the rest glows so brightly it's hard to look at. You have great strength in your heart, despite the many scars you bear. I also see a cabin set deep in some woods surrounded by rose bushes and you as a child holding a rock and clutching a kitten. You guard your heart carefully but love others well and defend the weak whenever you can."

The heat stopped radiating up Megan's arm, but she clung to the old woman's hand anyway. Emotion closed her throat. Megan had never told anyone about the cabin in the woods. The mental image had been her safe place many times in her life, including that awful period where she had endured an abusive relationship with Derrick Belmont.

"You are a strong young warrior, child," said Aunt Edith.

"Thank you." Megan meant more than acknowledgement of the compliment. She carefully set the woman's hand down on the bed and peered at her with concern.

Aunt Edith appeared paler than before.

"Think I'll rest for a minute," said Aunt Edith.

"Do you need anything?" Megan asked. She hated feeling helpless.

"Just some company," replied Aunt Edith.

"That I can do," Megan said, speaking gently. She quickly moved the flowers to the large recliner tucked into the corner and scooted the other chair closer to the bed. Settling onto the cushion, she crossed her ankles and placed her right hand on the woman's arm to let her know she was present.

A short while later, her phone buzzed again. She planned to ignore it but decided to take a quick peek anyway. When she saw the name, Megan sat up straighter and stared at Aunt Edith. The lady looked like she really needed a short nap, but there might not be a later for this call.

"Would you like to see Dan?" Megan inquired.

Taking the faint smile as an affirmative answer, Megan accepted the FaceTime call from her partner.

"Hang on. She's still waking up," said Megan. She turned the phone so Dan could see his great-aunt.

"Wake up, sleepyhead. It's time to rise and shine," Dan said.

Megan couldn't see him, but she heard the strain of the forced cheer.

"Danny! It's so good to see you," Aunt Edith greeted.

"Why don't I leave the phone and let you two catch up?" asked Megan. Hearing no protest, Megan picked a castoff pillow from the floor and carefully laid it on Aunt Edith's stomach so she could place the phone against it. She cranked the volume up so they could hear each other over the low hum from the machines surrounding the bed. "Let me know when you're finished."

Retreating to the larger recliner, Megan relocated the flowers to the floor and curled up in a comfortable position and closed her eyes to give the illusion of privacy. The heat rumbled beside her, lulling her into a pleasant dozing state. Not wanting to fall asleep, Megan let her mind return to the cabin in the woods. She hadn't needed to visit it for ages, but this time, without the fear, she sort of enjoyed the journey.

The rosebushes were in full bloom. The outside appeared weathered, but the inside offered a comfortable couch by a large fire. The thick wood of the cabin door brimmed with many locks to keep everything evil out. Megan remembered that the cabin had no windows and thought perhaps it was time to add some. The dark braided rug in front of the fireplace also didn't fit anymore. She replaced the rug with a cheerful red and gold one with a complicated pattern and imagined the windows from her childhood room into place around the cabin.

She awoke to the smell of coffee and found Dan's mother standing next to the chair.

"You must have needed some rest," Virginia commented. She held one of the two cups out to Megan. "Daniel described how you like your coffee. It's not the world's best, but it's comforting."

Accepting the cup, Megan thanked the woman for thinking of her. Wondering about the time, Megan patted her pants pocket for her phone. A jolt of mild panic shot through her before she spotted her phone with Aunt Edith.

Virginia pulled the other chair over, and the two women sipped the coffee in companionable silence. Dan's mother kept stealing glances back at her aunt.

"Will you be all right?" Megan winced at the dumb question. The lady was literally watching a loved one in their final hours. Irrational fear of death tried to creep in, but she banished it.

"I'll miss her," whispered Virginia. "She has such a … peace and presence. She was always there for me as a kid and as an adult. What will

I do without her?"

"Live well," Megan answered, though she understood the question to be more than half rhetorical. She wanted to say more but figured she would end up butchering the point.

"Sounds like something she would say," Virginia observed, nodding approval. She looked at her aunt and sighed. "I just … don't want to be alone."

"How so?" Megan wondered.

"I'm retired. My husband left years ago. My kids are grown and scattered far and wide," Virginia explained.

"Have you considered moving closer to one of them?" Megan asked. She wasn't sure what Dan would say to that suggestion because she didn't know much about his relationship with his mother.

"Many times," Virginia admitted, "but my home is here, in Texas."

"What keeps you here?" Megan prompted, genuinely curious.

"Deep roots," said Virginia. "My great-great-great-grandfather bought the land our ranch house is built on. I'm hoping one day Daniel will settle down and revive the farm."

The Dan Megan knew would never give up law enforcement for farming, but she didn't want to burst the lady's fantasy.

"But who am I kidding? He's a fighter, not a farmer." Virginia's statement had a self-reflective quality to it. She leveled a long, measuring look at Megan. "I never got to truly thank you in person for saving my son and his family. He tried to downplay the danger, but I know how to interpret his stories. They never would have survived without you."

They probably wouldn't have been in danger without me either. Megan nodded to acknowledge the thanks, but she could tell the woman was thinking similar thoughts from the new kind of strain apparent on her face.

"He's a great agent," Megan commented. "I'm glad I get to work with him."

"Keep him safe," said Virginia.

"I'll do my best," Megan promised. "That's what partners are for."

She didn't say that more often than not it was Dan's job to keep her out of trouble. Even from Hawaii, he had participated in the coordinated efforts to help her battle some human traffickers. Even though the raid up in Reno went well, Megan felt like she had unfinished business with the Club.

Chapter 4:
Late Warning

Megan spent the better part of a half-hour weighing the idea of staying longer to offer support and letting the pair spend the last few hours together. When Dan's phone conversation with his great-aunt finally wound down, she recovered her phone and took her leave as gracefully as possible. It felt awkward because she knew for certain she'd never see one of the women alive again. After exiting the room, she practically ran to her rental car.

Once safely in the driver's seat with the doors locked, Megan paused. Thoughts of mortality didn't usually pursue her, but the hospital air must have made her particularly susceptible to such things this morning. It left her in a melancholy mood. She kind of wanted to return to her hotel room, order a bottle of wine, and spend the rest of the day in bed with the comforters wrapped around her.

Shaking off the feeling as best she could, Megan fiddled with the car's navigational system. It refused to show her more than a blue screen with the message *no signal* until she left the parking garage. She circled the block a few times while poking through the options to let the magic satellite in the sky tell her the best places to shop in Dallas.

The most tempting choices were located uptown. A brief detour would take Megan right past her hotel, so she decided to drop off her car and check out how well Dallas Area Rapid Transit worked. She enjoyed the challenge of learning a new transit system while shopping because it always helped her focus. Removing the convenience of the rental's trunk would force her to select only the very best items, since she would have to lug them around the city. Her mother had instilled the "you buy it, you carry it" policy in her life from an early age.

Megan considered calling her parents but decided to delay until after the shopping trip so she could report on the scores. Her mother would grill her on the clerks' looks and marriage status, and her father would ask her what she saved, since he was the bargain hunter in the family. For one split-second of insanity, she considered teasing her mother by saying she'd recently met an eligible bachelor who happened to be a billionaire. While true, Gatton evoked more *baby brother in need of protection—and the occasional beating* feelings than *possible suitor* material, even though the age gap between them probably didn't top seven years.

The next several hours flew while Megan hit up some department stores. Finally, she circled back to the first store she'd visited and splurged on a pair of black flower heel pumps that would impress her mother. Besides, she liked buying shoes that could knock the cheap socks off slimy lawyers when she entered a courtroom. The hazard pay bonus Jeffrey Gatton had insisted upon after Reno had been burning a hole in her bank account for at least three days.

As she passed a Tex-Mex diner, her stomach reminded her that many hours had passed since breakfast. Deciding to go with the pleasant impulse, Megan ducked inside. A healthy line almost deterred her, but she decided to ask about the wait anyway. As luck would have it, they had one opening at the bar. A booth or a table would have been more relaxing, but she didn't have anybody to entertain today. If lunch didn't take too long, she could squeeze in a second round of shopping and a nap. Her running sneakers could use an update.

The bartender gave her a menu then rushed to the other end to fix new drinks for the couple lingering over their meals. Scanning the whole menu, Megan focused on the taco selection. Everything sounded good. The mental debate featured fish tacos, traditional beef tacos, and the house special—a trio of tacos—until the bartender reappeared and mentioned the day's special: five-cheese cheesesteak. Megan needed to check out the hotel's gym later this evening anyway, so she might as well have proper motivation to show up.

After perusing the lengthy list of wines and beer, she also ordered sparkling water. She'd get a mixed drink later based on how the food looked and tasted. She would have ordered a soda if she didn't have a deep aversion to drinking soda served from a bar since that tended to be tainted with beer. Soda was good. Beer was good. A mixture of the two never ended well.

The pepper jack cheese dominated the others on the cheesesteak, but the overall effect still came out amazing. Midway through the meal, Megan's phone rang out with the standard random-person-calling theme. If it had been a quiet place, she might have fumbled with the cheesesteak, cleaned her hands quickly, and rushed to silence the phone. Since the noise blended decently with the lively music being played, she ignored it.

After several seconds, the incoming call music cut off and started again. Curious, Megan did the whole cleaning ritual and checked to see the caller's ID. The number came up blocked. Deciding she had the time to mess around with annoying sales people today, she accepted the call.

"Don't hang up!" cried Jeffrey Gatton. "Don't say my name either. Just listen. You're in danger. Don't ask me how I know. Just get to a very public place and stay there."

"I'm in a very public place," Megan replied, grateful he'd mentioned not addressing him. Otherwise she might have started out with something far different. "I was about to pay and leave. What's up?"

"You're in danger," Gatton repeated. The kid sounded frantic, and he spoke almost too quickly to follow.

"Yeah. I got that part," Megan said, trying for beast-taming tone. "Why do you think that? And why aren't you using our special connection to talk to me about this?" The second question came out a lot softer so nearby neighbors wouldn't think she'd lost her mind. Picking up her drink, Megan spun around on the stool and leaned back against the bar counter to scan the room. Valid or not, Jeff's warning had kicked her work-mode instincts into the *on* position.

"Long story. Can't explain much," Gatton said, practically panting. "Your name and a very dangerous mutual friend of ours got flagged in a search done by a competitor of the said mutual friend."

"That's not good," Megan muttered. To her knowledge, Cassandra Mirren was the only mutual acquaintance Gatton would be cagey about naming over a phone. Though the lady's current occupation was unknown, her former profession involved assassinating people for a powerful, shady organization with possible ties to the government.

"What do I do?" Gatton's voice jumped an octave. "I can't use—the thing because I'm not supposed to know. How do I warn our friend?"

In any other circumstance, Megan would find Gatton's discomfort with avoiding certain names and phrases amusing.

"Calm down," Megan urged. "Take deep breaths. Let me think."

Quickly constructing a profile for possible assassins, Megan renewed her people-scanning efforts. The lunch crowd had thinned enough to give her a clear view of most areas. She quickly sketched mental cordons, dividing the room into thirds and looked for parties that contained only one or two men or women of a certain type. Odds were more than good that any "competitor" of Cassandra's would be male, but in this day and age, she couldn't dismiss anybody without at least a quick evaluation.

The parties with very small children or multiple children were dismissed. That left roughly half the customers. Remaining parties that contained more than two people were also crossed off. Next, she evaluated all remaining pairings and discarded them for various reasons. Three were too old, one was too young, and another one wore a cast. Somebody who posed a threat would want to blend in, but they would also value mobility.

"Do you know anything about the possible threat?" Megan twisted her phone around so she could speak directly into it. "Think a moment while I do something."

"No—"

Megan missed the rest of Gatton's protest because she pulled her phone away from her ear, switched over to the camera, pretended to take a selfie, and then took a quick video of the crowd. For good measure, she took a selfie that happened to include the bartender in the background. Digging a pair of earbuds out of her purse, Megan put one in so she could continue to speak with Gatton and study the video.

"I'm going to send you some pictures and a video in case something happens," Megan said. "Oh, hello. I think I found something. Mid-thirties male. Sharp suit. Lousy taste in football teams."

"What?"

"I saw this guy this morning at the restaurant in the hotel I'm staying at," Megan explained. She isolated that part of the video, took a screen shot, and added it to the file she was emailing Gatton. "Should I have a chat with him?"

"No! Stay put. Let me handle him," Gatton begged. "If I have his picture, I can get an alert put out on him within minutes."

"Might not be an option," Megan warned. She had turned around on her barstool and found a piece of scrap paper tucked under her plate. A chill shot up and down her spine, but she refrained from whipping around to try and see who had left the note.

It read: **Need to talk. Right corner booth. If you tell someone, they die.**

"What do you mean?" asked Gatton.

"I'm going to have to call you back," said Megan. She kept her voice calm even as her heart rate picked up the pace.

"You don't even know this number," Gatton reminded her. "It's about to die anyway because it's ancient and the battery pack I rigged to it is pathetic."

"Can you use our special connection to track me passively?" Megan asked.

"You mean like without actually using the … thing?" Gatton's tone got calmer as more brain cells focused on the intellectual problem.

Megan's phone went dead, cutting the conversation with Gatton short.

Exclamations and curses told Megan the problem wasn't isolated to her phone.

The bartender cleared away her plate and dropped another note in front of her.

"You're a lucky lady," he said cheerfully.

"Why?" Megan wondered.

"Because that gentleman over there paid for your lunch and these drinks." The bartender pushed two bottles of a local beer toward her. He nodded and pointed somewhere over Megan's left shoulder. Picking up a nearby rag, he stepped away to wipe up a spill on the back counter.

Rotating on the stool, Megan saw the suited man smile and wave. Leaning back against the counter, she silently regarded the man and flipped through options. She could follow his script and go to him with the beers. The option didn't appeal for the simple reason of letting him set the tone of any future negotiations. She could wait, arguably the safest for her but the most dangerous option for bystanders. Always a fan of third options, Megan calculated the distance separating her from the exit and the distance to the restrooms. The public restrooms were closer, but Megan didn't like the idea of retreating to a place with only one entrance and exit.

As she decided to risk a mad dash to the door, the man got up and cut off that option. Fight or flight instincts made Megan's right hand clench around her phone. She wanted to spin around and snatch up one of the beer bottles, but she refused to turn her back to the creep. Instead, she gave him the death stare and silently dared him to approach.

He did so with hands raised in mock surrender.

Megan stood and prepared to smash her phone in his face if he tried anything.

"Susanne! How are you? It's been so long." The stranger shouted the greetings as he threw his arms around Megan and drew her into a bear hug.

Megan stiffened upon hearing the name.

When his lips were next to her left ear the man whispered, "Let's not make a scene or dear mommy dies."

Chapter 5:
Hard Bargain

Knocking her left shoulder into the stranger, Megan swept an arm out—hard—into his chest and gave him part two of the death stare.

"Come on, baby, let's talk about this," said the man. He winked at the bartender and leaned around Megan to grab the beers. "I got us a nice, quiet booth."

The tactic worked. People actively avoided looking at them.

Annoyed at people for being so easy to manipulate, Megan snapped up her purse and marched over to the indicated table. Her hand twitched to feel the handgun tucked in the purse. Slipping into the side facing the room, Megan observed the man as he walked over, still carrying the drinks.

Taking his place opposite her, the man slid her one of the beers and took a sip of the one he kept. His green eyes never left hers.

Never one to simply sit back and let somebody else call the shots, Megan leaned forward and placed both of her hands on the table. Her fingers itched to reach for the beer bottle and clobber the guy, but his smooth, even movements as he had walked over to the table told her he probably had stellar reflexes.

"I'm going to tell you this once, maybe twice if I think you're extra thick. Whatever this job is, it's not worth dying for," said Megan.

Surprise lit behind the man's eyes, but he recovered quickly.

"It's nice to meet you, Agent Luchek," said the man, obviously returning to his original script. He reached into the breast pocket of his suit, withdrew a phone, and navigated to the photos section. "Let's get right to it. Time is money. I was asked to escort you to a meeting with my employer. We're aware of your skills and reputation, so we've taken measures to ensure your cooperation." The phone slid toward her across the table.

Instinctively, she stopped it before it could slide off the table. The first picture showed her parents' house. A date and timestamp declared it only a few hours old. The second picture was of her leaving the hospital this morning. A third image must have been stolen from Dan's Facebook page because it featured his whole family last Christmas. Underneath, somebody had typed out his address. The fourth and last image showed Angela's son Jaden walking into the Grand Game Hotel in Las Vegas.

"You've done homework," Megan acknowledged, "but what have I done to deserve such special attention?"

"I'm not at liberty to say," said the man.

"You don't know," Megan concluded. "Of course, you don't." She leaned back from the evil phone. "Are you 'at liberty' to tell me where you're supposed to escort me to?"

"No, but the sooner we leave, the sooner you'll get your answer," replied the stranger.

"Do you have a name?"

"Bob." He flashed a bright smile her way.

"Great." Megan rolled her eyes. "All right, Bob. Let's imagine this little fantasy goes your way. What exactly happens next?"

"We get up, we exit, we get in the truck waiting around the block, you let me restrain you properly, and I take us to the final destination. Easy."

Megan winced at his use of the phrase "final destination," but the restraints could be a good sign that they intended to release her later.

Or maybe they want to make killing you easier on them. Get it together, girl. No means clock this guy with the beer bottle and scream bloody murder.

"The amount of trouble you give me determines how many random people die," said Bob. "Cause a scene here and I open fire."

"Are you nuts? This is Texas. You'll be dead in a minute."

"Not if I have a human shield," Bob replied. "Even if you escape, there are at least three hostages in easy reach, and if you make me chase you, everybody on that phone has a really rotten day."

"You're bluffing," Megan said. Nevertheless, she agreed with his assessment of how many ready hostages sat oblivious within striking distance. If she started something, most people would escape unscathed, but Bob could kill at least five people in a matter of seconds and not break a sweat grabbing a sixth person for a hostage.

"Would you like to speak to my colleague watching your parents' place?"

"I would," Megan answered, knowing he'd never let it happen.

"Fine, but it's going to cost you." Bob held his hand out for his phone.

Megan started to slide the phone over to him, but stopped when his words sank in.

"Wait. Explain that statement. What cost?"

"Blood, of course." Bob's eyes had a cruel, crazy glint to them. "Whoever he runs across first. But don't worry, he won't kill them yet. I simply need you to understand the delicacies of the situation."

"Can I get y'all anything else?" asked a cheerful voice to Megan's right.

"No thanks. We won't be long." Bob's pleasant tone contrasted with the warning look he shot Megan. When the waitress retreated, Bob continued, "Still want to make that call?"

"You know I don't." Megan sat back and crossed her arms to keep from touching the phone or reaching for her purse. "So, I guess we're stuck here. Maybe we should order another drink."

"If you make me wait too much longer, everybody on—"

"I get it," Megan interrupted. She held up a finger to prevent more words from Bob.

Her mind raced. If she stalled long enough, Gatton would probably whistle up some sort of rescue, but that wouldn't help her parents, Dan's family, or Angela's family. Unless whoever was truly behind this had endless pockets at least some of the threats must be bluffs, but that knowledge didn't help her distinguish amongst them. Most likely, Dan's mother faced the most danger.

Bob, despite his lousy taste in code names, had a professional air about him that likely meant he cost serious money to hire. That didn't bode well, but it did pique her curiosity.

The age-old question—*Who would bother and why?*—came to mind.

Drumming the fingers of her right hand on the table, Megan gave the matter her full attention. Conventional wisdom told her to sit tight. The likelihood of Bob wanting to physically carry her out of the restaurant caveman style was nil. But if any of his threats were real, people she cared about would come to harm very soon. FBI training also told her to stand her ground as mst threats were empty, but Bob and his ilk fell into that small percentage of filthy rich, entitled scumbags who operated in the Club and the Shadow Council.

"You drive a hard bargain, Bob," Megan noted, internally triple checking her sanity. Soul-searching revealed a tiny, bright spot of anger burning in her chest. She had serious issues with the way these people treated others, and she wanted to take them down. If Fate had marked her for death, she might as well take a few of them with her. "But before we go anywhere, get in contact with any and all goons and get them to back off."

"Agreed." Bob waved for the phone again.

This time, Megan slid it over to him. He quickly tapped out a text message and let her read it.

Subject acquired. Stand down. Await further instructions.

"That's not exactly comforting," Megan protested.

"It's the best you're going to get. Make a decision. We're on a tighter schedule now."

They locked gazes. The crazy glint had left his eyes, leaving a deadness that chilled her even more. His eyes practically begged her to defy him, releasing whatever constraints his employer had placed upon him. Beneath the pleasant, cool exterior, lurked a cold-hearted man who enjoyed the violent side of his job.

"Guess we should get some fresh air," Megan said. Moving slowly so he wouldn't overreact, she scooted to the edge and stood up. "Are you leading, or am I?"

"You are," Bob said. "Make a left when you exit. I'll tell you more when you need to know."

Clutching her purse, Megan wove between tables to head for the exit.

"Wait!" called the waitress. "Isn't that your bag?"

Megan froze. She wanted to bolt for the door. Leaving the shoes behind would at least leave some mark of her presence upon the world and give her colleagues a starting point.

"I'll get it." Bob's tone bounced with good cheer. He dashed to the barstool where Megan had left her new shoes, scooped them up, and rushed back. "Time to go, dear." He politely opened the door for her.

Managing a tight nod of thanks, Megan marched past Bob and turned left, as instructed. She slowed as she reached the end of the block, but since he said nothing, she waited for the light to turn in her favor and crossed. At the end of the next section, Bob instructed her to make a left.

The narrow street they'd turned into was lined with cars. A white bread delivery truck sat midway down the street, parked in front of a fire hydrant.

"Give me your purse," Bob demanded.

Megan considered arguing but getting shot here on the street wouldn't exactly be a productive development.

Once he had her purse in hand, Bob wasted no time finding and removing her borrowed handgun. For good measure, he dumped her purse into a nearby garbage can.

She could only shake her head at that. Some homeless person was going to have a field day. Megan had to remind herself that being kidnapped topped being robbed for things that should worry her.

"Open the back and climb in," said Bob, setting her new shoes by the back right wheel. "You'll find your seat behind the bread pallets." He tried to explain how to open the back, but finally, he made her sit down on the ground while he opened it himself. Once the back door was raised, he nimbly hopped up before ordering her to join him. "Step right up. Your chariot awaits."

Megan's entrance to the truck was far less elegant than Bob's, but she made it. She wanted to bring the shoes with her but left them in the small hopes he'd forget about them. Slipping past the bread pallets, she found a rolling office chair chained to the floor. That didn't disturb her as much as the roll of duct tape, the sleeping mask, and the capped syringe sitting in the chair. The ceiling light was bright enough to cast everything in an eerie glow.

"No drugs," Megan insisted, planting her feet. Her current position blocked Bob from reaching the chair.

"Not your call," said Bob.

A stiff shove sent Megan flying toward the chair. She grabbed the syringe and ripped off the cap, intending to depress the plunger and release the drug onto the floor.

"I have more."

The calm in Bob's tone made Megan turn and look at him. She wasn't surprised to see the gun in his hand. He nodded to a long, narrow shelf built into the truck. It held an entire box of capped syringes.

"Re-cap the sedative, put the tape and mask on the ground, and sit down," Bob instructed. "Once you're secured, I'll give you the sedative and you'll wake up at the meeting. Easy."

His habit of saying "easy" started to irk her, but Megan decided to let it go. Instead, she followed his instructions carefully. The only tense moment came when her hand clenched around the syringe and held it like a dagger.

"Hand it over nicely." Bob backed up the order with his gun. He held out his left palm for the drug.

Megan barely resisted the urge to stab his hand.

When it dropped onto his hand, he pocketed the syringe.

"Put your hands on the arms of the chair and don't move them," said Bob.

When she complied, he taped her arms to the chair. The next order involved keeping her ankles together so they could be secured. At that point, Bob delivered the unknown sedative.

"What is that?"

Bob didn't answer, but the drug worked fast. By the time the mask slipped over Megan's eyes, she felt extremely lightheaded and kept her eyes clenched shut by choice.

"The headache will fade in time," Bob promised.

Megan didn't even have the energy to think up a curse or a comeback. A sharp stabbing pain pierced her head and she blacked out.

Chapter 6:
Catch Phrase

Jeffrey Gatton held his head in his hands. Megan's last question before the phone died haunted him. He thought as he rigged up batteries for untraceable, ancient flip phones. No matter what happened, he would likely need them later. At the moment, he had no idea who to call, but the batteries would need several hours to counter a few decades of electrical neglect when it came to those phones.

Can Eagle Eyes be used passively as a tracking device?

The question ran through his head on loop. As is, the answer stood at a big fat no, but it might work if he sent the right script in the guise of an update or a patch to an update. The last update had happened a few weeks ago. If he tried anything, they'd have a lot of questions. The government oversight goons were stuffy about their precious update schedule, but this wasn't the first time he'd deviated from the pre-approved plan. His one huge advantage lay in the fact that most government people checking up on him had no clue what Eagle Eyes could really do.

Once finished with the phones, Gatton sprinted back to his office and selected one of the brand new laptops. Sitting in his comfortable chair and flexing his fingers, he settled in to work. Even writing a normal patch would take him several hours, let alone one he had to embed a virus in. For that matter, he had to write the virus itself. They were never his specialty, and since starting Gatton Technologies, he hadn't had much of a chance to play around with such things.

While the computer did its warmup exercises, Gatton mentally considered the types of programs he could write. He decided on a simple match phrase. It wouldn't be a useful addition to any commercial version of Eagle Eyes unless each module came with its own unique sequence, but that would be a headache for his development team if they wanted to add the tracking feature later. For now, he only needed to find one FBI agent with the bad habit of being kidnapped.

First, he set up the framework and wrote the commands that would get Eagle Eyes to accept the patch. He had to proof that part very well because his team had put the best anti-virus software they could dream up on there. Next, he checked the notes for things that needed fixing from the last update. There wasn't much, but any massive update had at least a few glitches and bugs. Gatton had never appreciated bugs more in his life. He might as well make it a useful patch.

Hours passed.

He had forgotten how much he enjoyed the what-if side of programming. If interrogated later, he could claim intellectual curiosity before they threw his butt in prison for treason.

I wouldn't do well in prison.

The thought motivated him to type faster. Soon, he was lost in the rhythm of the work. Programming of this sort required deep concentration and skill, but it also resembled an art. In the digital realm, Gatton could create literally anything as long as his fingers could tell the computer how to fashion it.

When his vision started to blur and his head pounded from dehydration, Gatton forced himself to take a break. His phone told him it was 4:53. Assuming Megan was still in Texas, that would make it 5:53 wherever they took her. He winced when he realized that assumed the kidnapper decided to travel by car or truck. If he had access to a plane, they could be anywhere.

The patch would need to include a local time stamp request. Eagle Eyes could tell him, of course, but he wanted the patch to work without activating all the bells and whistles that would alert the government of the unauthorized use. They had gotten away with previous uses because Gatton had passed them off as prototype exercises.

Luciana must have been through recently because the refrigerator held fresh fruit, milk, and a tray of cheese and crackers. Tucking two bottles of water under his arm, Gatton picked up the whole cheese tray. Hopefully, that would be enough food to sustain him through what promised to be a long night.

Before retreating to his office, he let Pudgy out for his evening potty excursion. The Pug could let himself back in when he desired, but for some reason, he insisted on being formally released each evening. The dog door had been installed after Gatton once forgot poor Pudgy outside all night last summer. It had taken a week for Mr. Pudges—as Luciana called him—and the maid to forgive him.

Gatton refreshed Pudgy's water and put a post-potty treat in his bowl before heading back to work. The task gave him the phrase he wanted to use in his patch program. A string of numbers and letters would tip off the anti-virus programs. Still, it had to be a sentence not yet formed in the history of recorded things, and it couldn't be something as blatant as "a way to save Agent Luchek's bacon again."

Mr. Pudges takes a pee near a fig tree as he pleases then waits for Luciana to pet him.

The sad part of that statement was its truth. The dog seemed fonder of the maid than Gatton. He'd give her the dog if it wasn't technically his mother's. She'd developed a mysterious allergy to Pudgy three years ago, hence his permanent resident status at Gatton's house.

The next pause consisted of five minutes inhaling food at the designated table in his office lair. Most days he didn't care what got where, but certain projects demanded a slightly higher standard of care when it came to the computer equipment.

At last, Gatton sat down and hashed out the rest of his patch program. He tucked the catch phrase in several places. Next, he wrote a program that would search for that phrase and let him know its location. That would be trickier because Eagle Eyes didn't have an IP address to track. Instead, the phrase would have to trigger a series of commands instructing nearby electronics to reach out to him with an echo. Smartphones would be the best because then it would be a simple matter of activating the internal GPS trackers. If he had more time, he could probably rig the program to reach out to satellites itself. His excitement for the possibilities got tempered by worry for Megan.

Gatton double and triple checked his work start to finish then checked it again to be sure. Several of his projects held inadvertent power over life and death, but somehow, the knowledge that this one life depended on his work being perfect, cranked up the pressure. As his finger moved to hit the send button, Gatton's hand spasmed and he wrenched it back. He'd almost made a huge mistake.

He hadn't saved the program or instructed it to try again if it couldn't get through the first time. A few more minutes of quick typing fixed both issues, but that could have been disastrous. Tweaking it to keep knocking if denied at first, Gatton backed up his new creation to several locations both cloud-based and USB drives.

In theory, as long as Megan was anywhere near a smartphone or an activated computer, she should receive the patch. Once the patch was situated, it would start blasting the catch phrase at five second intervals until it received an acknowledgement and further instructions from Gatton. He would then be able to pull GPS coordinates from any number of nearby devices. On the slim chance Megan's kidnappers took her to a place remote enough to be technology free, Eagle Eyes itself could become the contact device, but that would require a lot more work from Gatton's end. He really, really hoped it didn't come to that, but since karma seemed to be in a bad mood of late, he decided to plan accordingly. Besides, he hated waiting and the work would give him something to do.

Wishing to delay the tedious work a tad longer, Gatton checked on the phones. Most were still down in the dangerously low category, but one looked alive enough to give him a few minutes of airtime.

Who do I call?

The main options were Megan's partner—Daniel Cooper, Special Agent Ophelia Pitman, and Cassandra Mirren. Gatton dismissed the idea of calling Cassandra since he had already done so and reached a voicemail. That had been hours earlier, but if the former assassin wanted to contact him, she would have done so already. The decision had nothing to do with the fact that the lady also scared the crud out of him. Pitman could get him an entire SWAT team if he begged hard enough, but that would not qualify as subtle. Right now, Gatton really needed subtle. Dan Cooper would likely never arrive in time to be of any use, but he could help and stay under the radar.

Opting to call Cooper first, Gatton looked up the number on his phone and dialed on the flip phone. A man answered on the fourth ring.

"Agent Cooper speaking."

"Say 'yes' if you recognize my voice, but do not say my name over this line," Gatton instructed.

"Yes. I think. What can I do for you?" The agent's voice grew more confident by the time it voiced the question.

"You're needed in Texas." Gatton figured that even if Megan was taken elsewhere, Cooper would have to start the investigation in Dallas. "What are the chances of you getting time off to come here immediately?"

Uncomfortable silence answered him for several beats.

"What happened?" Cooper asked softly. "Is she all right?"

"I can't discuss that here, but if you agree to come, I'll send a clean phone and as many details as I can manage," Gatton promised.

"Why not go through proper channels?" Cooper asked.

"They're too slow," Gatton answered honestly. "Can you get the time off?" The question came out sharper than intended as Gatton's patience drained almost as fast as the phone's battery life.

"I can get the time. I can't afford the trip," Cooper said. His clipped tone also spoke of frustration.

Gatton nearly sagged with relief. Money problems he could deal with.

"I'll make the arrangements and include a bonus to compensate for the short notice."

"I'm not doing this for money," Cooper said. He hesitated a few seconds before adding, "But would you pay for tickets so my family could fly to Texas? My great-aunt is dying, and I can request bereavement time off. It would add to the authenticity of my claim if I could bring the family along."

"Sorry about your great-aunt, but do you really want to bring your family here, knowing the mission I intend to send you on?" The agent's logic made sense, but Gatton was still wary.

"I'll leave them at the hospital," Cooper said. "They should be safe enough there."

Megan should have been safe in public too, but I doubt that.

The phone beeped in Gatton's ear to warn him it would soon quit.

"I have to go, but I'll text you some account information shortly. Use what you need to make the arrangements. You'll have access to the account for twenty-four hours."

"Thank you. I'll—"

The phone went dead, cutting off whatever the agent had to say. Gatton stared at the phone and hoped the communication troubles would be at an end. Megan couldn't afford prolonged communication issues.

Gatton's knees cracked as he stood. He'd have to call his accountant to see which slush account to burn over this. If the government ever investigated, it wouldn't take them long to connect him to Daniel Cooper, but if he used a personal account, he could at least claim the money was a gift to help a friend reach his family. He fervently hoped that's all the money was needed for.

Chapter 7:
Fancy Prison

When Megan Luchek woke up, she wasn't quite sure if she'd stepped back into reality or was still riding the knockout drug. Aches and pains throughout her body helped convince her that this was no dream. At first, she thought something was wrong with her vision, but soon, she realized that the lights were dimmed. Cautiously, she moved her arms and legs. Both legs seemed fine, as did her left arm, but her right arm remained above her head.

A few panicked curses zipped through her mind as she craned her neck around and yanked her right arm more forcefully. The move earned her sharp pain in her wrist. Using her free limbs, Megan maneuvered to a sitting position where she could examine the metal handcuff and the bed itself. Both looked plenty sturdy. Her struggles knocked several white pillows to the floor.

The lights around the room brightened when she moved. Megan glanced about quickly to make sure she was alone. Relief coursed through her when she confirmed that the room held no masked surprises for her. Disappointment soon followed. The lack of people meant that answers too would have to wait.

Grateful for the better light, Megan took stock of her surroundings. Besides the comfortable bed she'd been left on, the room's furniture consisted of an ornate privacy screen, a large end table, a fancy floor lamp, and a giant vanity set. Clearly, the room had not begun its existence as a prison. Spotting several sets of doors around, Megan guessed the ones to her left went to a closet and a bathroom while the one to her right opened to the rest of the house. The large electronic lock above the normal door lock gave her the clue. Pity. The normal lock was one of those old-fashioned monstrosities that looked pickable with a hairpin and patience.

At least she had her clothes on. Apparently, whichever brand of kidnapper she'd attracted this time didn't fall too far over the creeper line. Spotting the video cameras mounted at several points around the room, Megan mentally adjusted her assessment of the kidnapper, moving him—or her—further along on the creeper line.

The posts on the Queen-size bed looked gorgeous and expensive. The one currently hosting the other end of the handcuff bore deep scars where her struggles had marked it. Guilt struck her, but she shook it off. She had been minding her own business in a popular lunch joint when the kidnapper-for-hire had paid for her meal and warned her against making a scene. She'd asked for none of this.

Her stomach reminded her that time had marched on while she slept. She didn't have a watch and her phone was nowhere in sight, so Megan had only her instincts to tell her the time. Then, she remembered Eagle Eyes. The contacts had become so much a part of her lately, she'd forgotten they existed. Gatton hadn't seemed eager to use the program, but one could hardly blame Megan for peeking at the time.

The program reported the time as 8:54 Central Standard Time, but every other request was met with a polite **administrator access required** message. Everything would be so much nicer if it reported her exact coordinates and called the police for her.

Feeling lightheaded, Megan propped one of the remaining pillows behind her and leaned back to think. She had two main body problems requiring her attention, and she couldn't address either while cuffed to the bed. Thinking would be so much easier if she had working brain cells, but most of them were on strike from lack of food.

Sometime later, a phone's cheerful ringtone ripped through Megan's pleasant, drowsy state. The surprise caused her to move her right wrist again. By the time she guessed that the phone was in the end table's drawer and twisted her body around so she could open the drawer, the phone ceased making noise. A ping a moment later told her she had a text message.

It read: **Key here. Food in medicine cabinet. You can't escape. Do not call for help or people die.**

Since she didn't have a great angle to see the whole drawer, Megan cautiously felt around until her fingers brushed a small key. In her haste to pull it out, she almost dropped it. As quickly as possible, she inserted the key and released her wrist. Then, she removed the cuff's other end from the post and threw the handcuffs into the drawer with the phone. Belatedly, she hoped she didn't damage the phone in the process. It was sort of her lifeline, even if she couldn't use it to summon help.

She leaned over and stared at the phone, longing to call 911. Instead, she shut the drawer firmly. If the evil people behind this plot could afford a place like this, their threats probably held some substance as well.

Her legs carried her unsteadily over to the bathroom. Even though she couldn't see a camera in here, Megan gave the place a thorough once-over before using the facilities. After washing up, she peeked in the medicine cabinet. As promised, she found two power bars and a bottle of water. It wasn't gourmet food, but it would satisfy her hunger for now. Midway through the first bar, she paused to wonder if it was poisoned. She continued eating, reassured by the massive efforts to bring her here. One did not spend thousands to have somebody kidnapped and then poison them.

She hoped.

The bar tasted kind of odd, but that could simply be her unfamiliarity with the brand and flavor. Blueberry was not her go-to choice when she had options. Since she did not have options, Megan ate the two blueberry power bars and drank half the bottle of water before returning to the main room.

Fueled by the food, Megan wandered her spacious prison. Behind the privacy screen, she found a bench with a towel, some jeans, and a long-sleeved T-shirt. Curious, she checked the sizes. They'd be big on her, but they were close enough to make her wonder. The thought of a shower was mighty tempting. On the other hand, stripping down for a shower would make her even more vulnerable than she was currently. Just because she couldn't see any cameras in the bathroom did not mean they were completely absent.

Thinking of the cameras made her visibly check out each one. If she leapt from the bed, she might be able to break two of them, but the other two were well out of reach. The vanity held dust, several jewelry boxes, and makeup stuff that hadn't been used in years. The closet revealed another mystery. Every outfit and pair of shoes had been vacuum sealed and preserved like museum pieces. Closer examination revealed that everything belonged to a tall woman with good taste and large feet.

Another ping pulled her away from the closet. She rushed to check the message.

Stay out of the closet!

It puzzled her. For a text message, it sounded emotional, but why would anybody lock her in an opulent room like this in the first place, let alone forbid her from exploring certain parts of it? That brought her right back to the *why kidnap me* question.

Aside from a bruised wrist and a lingering headache, Megan remained unharmed. So, either the kidnapper's boss wanted something from her or she was a means to an unknown end. Since Megan honestly doubted she had anything a person of such wealth could want, she leaned toward the idea that they weren't truly after her. During his ramblings, Gatton had mentioned Cassandra, so it followed that the boss sought her. Megan would be the first to admit Cassandra wasn't the easiest person to get ahold of, but kidnapping seemed an excessive step to take.

Because she was bored, Megan wanted to explore the things on the vanity, but she figured that would only get her yelled at again. Instead, she chose to shower. Despite the day's festivities, her clothes hadn't gotten too grimy. They could reasonably stretch to another day. Then again, the long-sleeved T-shirt would be easier to sleep in. She compromised, settling on the shirt left for her and her own jeans.

The shower felt glorious. Megan kept the water as hot as her body could stand, hoping the heat would wash away the last of the drug-induced headache. Paranoid that there might be hidden cameras, she dried off with a towel and dressed in record time. Residual heat from the shower kept her warm. She found a hair dryer and brush in the cabinet below the sink. Strands of blond hair still clung to the brush.

Did it belong to a former prisoner?

Megan rejected the idea almost as soon as it formed. The room wasn't designed to be a prison, crazy-complicated electronic lock notwithstanding. The things she'd seen in the closet had been lovingly preserved. The brush probably belonged to somebody important to the kidnapper's boss. The text message's tone indicated strong feelings.

Still pondering the mystery, Megan pulled out as much of the blond hair as she could before using the brush and drying her hair. Drying her long, brown hair took a while, but the droning noise helped relax her.

She took a moment to stretch and gather her scattered wits. Anger and fear simmered in her, but the many questions surrounding her presence in this place distracted her. She evaluated everything she touched for its potential as a weapon. Unfortunately, aside from the hair dryer, nothing she came across had any heft to it. If she could unscrew one of the posts, she might be able to defend herself.

Yeah. If you had that and a horse, you could joust with the next jerk to stroll through the door.

Frustrated, Megan stood in the bathroom listening to the hair dryer. When it started to smoke, she shut it off. After putting the hair dryer away, she rinsed out her mouth. She drew the line at using a stranger's toothbrush, especially one that was well-used and falling apart with age.

Another check of the time told her a couple of hours had passed. In the dark, she felt the handcuff key brush her fingers. She picked it up and hid it in her palm, holding it in place with one finger. She intended to keep the thing close because if she needed to bust out of here, having use of her hands would definitely help. Deciding she might as well try to sleep, Megan pocketed the key. She'd think about a better hiding spot tomorrow. Sleep might not come easily since she'd spent quite a few hours unconscious. Driving off the headache had given her mind an excuse to race.

Megan retrieved the pillows she'd knocked to the floor earlier and arranged them around her, cordoning off the unoccupied section of the bed. Force of habit had her reaching for the phone to set an alarm. The urge to call for help hit her strongly, but thoughts of people she cared about made her slam the door shut with the phone inside. She rolled to face away from the drawer. Even if she managed to call 911, this wasn't a landline, and she had no idea where to tell rescuers to go. If luck favored her, the center that fielded her call could triangulate her position if she left the line open long enough. Given the day she'd just had, she wouldn't bet on a horse race featuring one horse.

As predicted, sleep eluded her, giving Megan plenty of time to think. The guy—she had no doubts about his gender now—who owned this place had serious money and emotional baggage. That made him dangerous.

Did the hired kidnapper stick around?

Megan wasn't sure which way to wish in this situation. The less unhinged people she had to deal with at one time, the better, but she still owed that guy at least a solid punch for the knockout drug that came with a hangover style headache.

Whose bed am I in?

The more she saw of the place, the more she wondered about

the woman who owned the clothes, shoes, makeup, and hairbrush. The sheets hadn't smelled musty, so somebody must have taken care of the room in the last few years. Yet everything else might as well have come from a time capsule.

What happened to her?

The thought lingered in Megan's mind. She felt a void left by the woman's absence. Something terrible had happened to this household.

Tomorrow would probably hold some answers, but Megan wasn't sure she'd like them.

Chapter 8:
The Summons

Someone shook Megan awake. Normally, she greeted a new day slowly, but the stress hormones snapped her to full consciousness instantly. Rolling away from the touch, she snatched up a large pillow and clutched it defensively, crouched on the bed ready to fight. The pillow would do squat against any other weapon, but it brought her some comfort.

Two men, her kidnapper from yesterday and a middle-aged man, stood before her. Both wore expensive suits. The creases on the kidnapper's suit told her it might be the same one he had on yesterday, but she didn't have time to dwell on it.

"Stay there." A handgun gave the kidnapper's order some weight. He stood to the left from her perspective.

The other man presented an odd picture. He carried himself like someone used to being obeyed, yet his hands were splayed in a gesture that begged for patience. Steel gray hair made him distinguished, but his brown eyes held deep sadness. The lines on his face looked equally carved from prolonged worry and sustained anger.

"I apologize for the discomfort," said the older man. "That was never my intent. Please eat something, dress, and join me in my study in half an hour. I will explain further then." He waved toward a tray table holding a steaming cup of coffee and a plate of scrambled eggs and toast. "Mr. D'Angelo will stay with you for the time being."

Megan's gaze flicked over to kidnapper Bob. His expression didn't show whether the revelation of his name bothered him.

"Before you try anything, please consider the whole situation." The boss man's voice drew her attention back to him. "I am asking for your cooperation, but I will force it if I have to. Should the day go well, I have a contract for you to sign before your release."

The notion of release elated Megan, but everything before that confused her. She had half a mind to take her chances smacking Mr. D'Angelo with the pillow.

Probably reading the intent in her eyes, Mr. D'Angelo backed up a step and adjusted his grip on his handgun.

"Please don't be late." With that last request, the man left the room swiftly.

Time passed while Megan considered her options again. Not much about the situation had changed, except she had a more concrete idea of Bob's real working name. Like it or not, cooperation seemed the path of least resistance. The idea rankled, but the food smelled great. The possibility of being poisoned reared its ugly head again, but she brushed it off as she had before.

The eggs were a tad rubbery and definitely needed salt, but the coffee tasted fantastic. The toast was limp with too much butter, but Megan forced that down as well since she honestly couldn't predict when or if another meal would come. If a fight broke out later, she wanted enough energy to do her part.

I should write a guide to being kidnapped.

She asked for and received permission to wash up before dressing. They had a brief debate over whether the boss intended for D'Angelo to follow her into the bathroom, but Megan won by slamming the door in his face. She reminded him that he stood in front of the sole exit. The morning activities provided a bit of relief from prying eyes, but they didn't last forever. She had a half-hour deadline to abide by anyway.

As soon as she opened the door, Mr. D'Angelo once again watched her like a hawk tracking prey. His gaze made her uncomfortable until she ducked behind the privacy screen to put on the blouse she'd worn yesterday. Though the long-sleeved T-shirt had been comfortable, Megan felt much better once wearing her original shirt. Even after she finished changing, she paused to carefully fold the other shirt, dragging out the precious time without an audience.

"Hurry up," said Mr. D'Angelo.

Megan counted out another thirty seconds before emerging from the privacy screen. A pair of handcuffs flew her way. Catching them instinctively, Megan frowned down at them.

"Put them on," ordered D'Angelo.

"Why?" Her tone implied: *What's the point?*

"Because I have a gun and I said so," D'Angelo replied.

"You can't use the gun without permission," Megan pointed out. Nevertheless, she made a show of snapping the cuff into place around her left wrist. Getting the right one on required putting down the clothes and working at it. She had to stabilize the metal cuff against her waist while her left hand cinched it closed. "Now what?"

The unhelpful, but delightful, image of her choking Mr. D'Angelo with the cuffs brought a feral smile to her face. He lacked the bulk of Jabba the Hutt, and she lacked the hair and bikini of slave Princess Leia. Still, it could work.

"Now, you take the lead again, like you did yesterday," said D'Angelo. "Go left out the door."

Walking with as much dignity as she could muster, Megan followed the quiet directions. At least he hadn't insisted on a blindfold. Every long hallway contained several decorative tables, and they descended two full flights of stairs. As they approached a large set of double doors at the end, a ping announced somebody was receiving a text message. Since Megan had left her new phone up in the luxury prison cell, she guessed it was D'Angelo.

"Stop," he called.

She turned to see him staring at his phone.

"This way." He led her back up a flight of stairs they had just descended and part way down another corridor. They passed numerous closed doors. Finally, he stopped in front of one. "He wants you to meet someone." D'Angelo's tone softened as he ushered her inside.

The room possessed the same opulence that dripped from everywhere in the mansion, but the atmosphere in here was different. Medical equipment hummed and hissed in regular rhythms, yet that only added to a somber stillness filling the place. A large hospital cot occupied the room's center, surrounded by monitoring machines. The woman sleeping on the cot answered some of the mysteries for Megan. Her well-dressed captor stood next to the bed, staring at the patient.

"Megan Luchek, meet my wife, Maria. She's paralyzed from the neck down." The man's gaze never left his wife's face. Her condition must be the reason for each worry line marking him.

"I'm sorry." The response came through reflex, but Megan genuinely pitied the woman. She couldn't imagine how awful it must be to require that many machines simply to live. "What happened to her?" She stopped at the end of the bed.

"There was a car accident, but it was no accident," the man

whispered. "You're here to help me right that wrong."

"Who are you?" That wasn't the question she'd intended to ask, but it couldn't hurt. Her mind scrambled to place either of their faces. To her knowledge, she'd never met these people.

"You don't know me, and it's safer for you if it stays that way," said the man. "In a few minutes, we're going to receive a call from your friend, Cassandra. Speak to her briefly. Let her know you're alive and well and urge her to cooperate. Mr. D'Angelo can then provide her with instructions. If she follows them, you'll be returned to your hotel tonight."

"And if she doesn't?" Megan didn't like her odds for a happy ending.

A dog-eared picture on the end table caught her eye. It featured a boy beaming at the camera.

In the best of circumstances, Cassandra Mirren could be unpredictable. In recent dealings, she'd proven herself surprisingly loyal, but their friendship defied convention, logic, and good sense. The known facts of Cassandra's life numbered less than the fingers on Megan's right hand, including her real name.

"That would be ... disappointing," the man admitted, "but you'd have to die in her place. For Leo and Maria and—"

"What? Why?" A horrible thought struck her so hard she gasped. "Did she—Was the accident ... her work?"

Thoughts continued flooding Megan. Leo must be the boy. She also did some mental math. The picture looked at least a decade old, given the style of clothes worn by the boy. Age had never come up in conversation with Cassandra, but given how hard she punched, she couldn't be too much past forty. If forced to guess, Megan would say mid-thirties. People in the assassin's line of work tended not to live to ripe old ages. She had a difficult time picturing a mid-twenties woman masterminding an accident that killed a little boy and paralyzed his mother. The few dealings Megan had with the assassin told her the woman stuck to a strict moral code. Even if that code allowed for certain people to be killed, a boy and a random wealthy woman seemed strange targets.

"Several people were involved," said the man.

"How do you know?" Megan fired the question like it was any normal interrogation.

The man turned and looked at her.

"Because I belong to the Shadow Council now, and it was

members of this same group that forced me to join by destroying my family."

"That doesn't make sense," Megan remarked. "Why would you join the group that destroyed your family?"

"I didn't know it was them at the time," the man said. "They promised revenge if I obeyed." He hesitated, looking eager to unburden his soul further. After another long look at his wife, he met Megan's gaze. "They also promised to help me find my daughter."

"I'm so lost." Megan raised her bound hands to her head. "Start at the beginning. What happened to your family? How does it involve the Shadow Council? What do you want from Cassandra? And why do you think I have any influence over her?"

"You don't have to understand," said the man, "just do your part."

"I can do my part better if I understand," Megan argued.

"Her last question could be important if you want to control the assassin." The unexpected help came from Mr. D'Angelo.

After some more coaxing, the man started to tell his tale.

"I have two jobs. One gives me money and the other gives me influence. Over a decade ago, the Shadow Council approached me with an offer to join them. I turned them down. They said they could protect me, arranged for the accident that killed my son, paralyzed my wife, and lost my daughter, framed a rival group, and promised me revenge in due time."

Silence fell, but Megan knew he had more to say. D'Angelo must have picked up the same vibe, for he too waited patiently.

"I joined out of grief, but over the years, the lies came to light. Lia, my daughter, was never lost. She was taken. A few months after the accident, I started receiving pictures of her growing up. They thought that would control me, but it made me angrier. Six months ago, I received a list of names, my promised revenge. Cassandra's is the last name on that list. She's going to help me locate my daughter to atone for her part, or she's going to die."

As if on cue, the call from Cassandra came through to D'Angelo's phone.

He answered it, spoke briefly, and then shoved the phone into Megan's hands. The speaker button was already highlighted.

The boss nodded for Megan to speak first. D'Angelo moved to the side so she could see the handgun he'd drawn. The casual stance he assumed didn't fool her, and the threat came through loud and clear.

"Assassin? Are you there?" asked Megan.

"Agent," the other woman greeted.

"I'm in a delicate position here," Megan said.

"So I gather. Tell Senator Carmichael I'm on my way."

Alarm stabbed into Megan. Carmichael tensed, as did D'Angelo. His tension worried her more since he now pointed the handgun directly at her.

"That's a really bad idea," Megan blurted. She wondered how Cassandra knew Carmichael's name, and the assassin's confidence implied she also knew where to find them. Even for her extensive contacts, that seemed a stretch.

While Megan was distracted with questions, Carmichael came over and snatched the phone out of her hands.

"You know where to go. Come alone." Without waiting for a response, he ended the call.

Chapter 9:
You're Offline

"Take her to the Vault," said Carmichael.

That sounded ominous. D'Angelo came close and placed a hand on her right elbow. Megan worked hard to quash the instinct to shake off his touch and smash her elbow into his nose.

"I don't care what you think Cassandra can do for you. She's not somebody you want to mess with," Megan warned. "Your best bet is to let me go and tell her none of this ever happened."

"Come along," D'Angelo urged. He prodded her with the gun to reinforce the order.

Not having much of a choice, Megan let him tug her back toward the door. At the threshold, he turned her around and pushed her toward the stairs. As they re-entered the maze of corridors and staircases, Megan pumped D'Angelo for information.

"What's he paying you?"

The question earned a chuckle and a small shove.

"Thinking of trying to outbid him?" asked D'Angelo. "I know your net worth, Agent Luchek. You can't afford me."

"Wouldn't dream of it," Megan replied, "but I think you're thick enough to require a second warning. Whatever the amount, it's probably not worth dying for. Cassandra—"

"Is my problem, but I appreciate the concern."

The confidence in his voice disturbed her enough to make her stop walking.

"You knew she'd come here." The statement was mostly whispered to herself. Megan's mind grappled with this new angle.

Thus far, she'd had D'Angelo pegged for the hired thug role, but if he was cut from the same cloth as Cassandra, that automatically made him more dangerous and unpredictable.

"I knew she would come here," he confirmed. A hand at the small of her back urged forward progress.

"How?" Megan demanded.

"I'm just that good," he boasted.

"Nobody's that good," she countered. "You know something you're not telling me."

He grinned.

"I know a lot I'm not telling you. Keep moving."

The rest of the trip down to the vault passed in silence. Megan dragged her feet the closer they got to their goal. She had a vague idea about what kind of vault she'd be locked in and wanted no part of even a luxury panic room.

"What's wrong with the room I was in before?" Megan wondered, upon seeing the tiny room.

"This one is more secure," replied D'Angelo.

That's what she was afraid of.

His next words chilled her further.

"And if the air vents are turned off, it functions as a built-in timer."

A strong shove sent her sprawling into the center of the vault. By the time she recovered her feet, the electronic locks on the door chimed success at being reengaged. Futilely, she tried the handle. It didn't budge. Anger gave her enough strength to bloody a few knuckles pounding on the thick door.

When rational thought reasserted itself, Megan dug the handcuff key out of her pocket and freed her wrists. Next, she stumbled to the sink and rinsed off. Finally, she took stock of her new prison. This one paled in comparison to the other room. For one thing, it was about twelve feet by twelve feet. The small size meant it didn't take Megan long to explore the space. She found more power bars.

"You're offline." The cheerful male voice spoke within Megan's head.

"Gatton?"

"And by offline, I mean really offline. Like middle of nowhere, back in the Stone Age, offline, but fret not. I'm here to help," the voice continued. It was Jeffrey Gatton's voice, but definitely prerecorded. *"Let's start by figuring out where you are. Describe*

your location, please."

"I'm locked in a storm shelter," Megan replied.

"Storm shelter. Excellent. We at Gatton Technologies make many components for those. Find the manufacturer and model number. I'll wait while you look for these."

"Look for them where?" Megan asked.

"The location for the manufacturer and model number differs based on manufacturer, but most put some information on the inside panel of the sliding compartment housing the sink."

After digging a flashlight out of the First Aid Kit, Megan opened drawers and panels until she found the necessary information. She started reading it aloud, but Gatton's voice spoke even before she finished.

"You're in luck. This model has three backup options for re-establishing communication with the outside world. There's a battery-operated phone wired into the electrical components. There's the emergency beacon stored in the wall, and there's a backup power source that should kick in if the original lock is compromised. Good luck. If you need any of this information repeated, say 'repeat emergency backup options.'"

Megan wasn't certain the information would be useful, but she made the recording repeat itself five times anyway. She sat on the only available seat—the toilet—to think. She couldn't wait around for Cassandra to walk into whatever trap D'Angelo was setting. The vibe he'd given her before locking her in the vault said Carmichael wasn't in control.

"I need to get out. I need to get out." Megan chanted the phrase to motivate herself.

To her surprise, Gatton's voice spoke again.

"If waiting for rescue's not your thing and you really want to see what a mess the world outside is, press or say 'three' to review release options."

"Three," Megan said, probably louder than necessary.

Careful questioning and a lot of talking in circles revealed several options. Basically, the storm shelter was designed to disable the electronic locks if any of the internal wiring were to be damaged. One would still have to manually push free the fifty-pound door, but that problem could be dealt with in sequence. As long as the locks remained intact, Megan was going nowhere.

"Disrupt the wiring," Megan muttered. "What could go wrong?"

The First Aid Kit held a rudimentary hatchet and a pair of medical scissors.

Thirty minutes later, the shelter looked like the aftermath of an ax murder. Megan's cheeks and hands bore numerous small cuts from flying wood and plastic, but thankfully, nothing had lodged in her eyes yet. Her woodshop teacher would have been horrified at the destruction and her lack of goggles. But it had been worth it. A small hole near the bottom right corner revealed several brightly colored wires. The rest of the vault consisted of concrete, but the area immediately surrounding the door had been modified to accommodate the electrical wires.

As she moved the scissors toward the wires, the voice spoke again.

"Whoa. Looks like you want to cut some wires. Are you sure that's a good idea? Have you double checked the safety standards here?"

"I'm trapped and I need to get out right now. If you have a better idea, let's hear it," Megan said, losing patience with the emergency program. "Otherwise, I'll take my chances with snipping these wires."

"Let me have a closer look at the wires," suggested the program. After a few moments, it repeated the request.

Feeling like an idiot, Megan dropped down to the floor and shone a flashlight beam directly onto the wires while peering as close as she could. If she ever got to speak to the real Gatton again, she needed to tell him how weird his emergency program could be.

"Excellent. These wires were not made by Gatton Technologies. They look like Kuiza Industries. Your best bet is to pull the yellow one up until it's exposed and gently melt it."

"'Gently melt it?'" Megan repeated.

Taking that as a request for more information, the program happily provided her with a detailed description of how to accomplish the technique. Thankfully, the First Aid Kit was also a survival kit, so it came complete with a book of matches. With the program coaching her, Megan exposed the yellow wire, lit a match, blew it out and quickly touched the smoldering end to the wire.

Something hissed, and Megan's heart nearly exited her chest. But the door remained locked.

"If at first you don't succeed, try, try again," encouraged the program.

"Shut up," Megan said.

"Shutting up. Say 'resume' when you're ready for more sage

advice."

She tried two more matches with the same disappointing results. Questions to the program went unanswered until she remembered to reactivate it.

"Why didn't this work?" she demanded.

"Failure can have many meanings," replied the program.

"Less philosophy, more problem-solving," said Megan.

"Let me see the problem again," requested the program.

Megan repeated the flashlight and close look thing and got the same advice as before. As she pushed herself off the ground, it occurred to her that the wires went up the wall. She probably couldn't reach the highest one without a step stool, but there had to be another cluster near the locking mechanism itself.

Forty minutes and two blisters on her right hand later, Megan had hacked a second hole in the wall, exposing a set of wires. Next to the wires sat a small box. A quick inquiry confirmed Megan's guess that this was a smoke detector. Smiling to herself, Megan lit the entire book of matches and held it beneath the sensor. Belatedly, she hoped it didn't cause an alarm Carmichael or D'Angelo could detect.

To her dismay, an ear-shattering alarm wailed.

But she didn't care. More importantly, the lights monitoring power to the door faded to black. Holding her breath, Megan said a silent prayer and tried the door handle.

It turned.

Throwing her whole body into the task, Megan leaned on the door. It creaked and groaned in protest, but slowly, it opened an inch, then two, then three. Panting, she rested a short while and renewed her efforts. When the gap stood wide enough, she picked up the hatchet, pocketed a few power bars, gathered up the handcuffs and key, and slipped out.

Once free, she froze. For the past hour or so, every ounce of effort and ingenuity had been spent on breaking free. There hadn't been time to dwell on what came next. Escape would be the wisest option, but that would leave her with the same problem she'd had before. People she cared about had been threatened. The only way to win back their safety and her peace of mind was to take the fight to the bad guys and triumph.

If she waited long enough, they'd come back for her, but waiting seemed like a bad idea, especially since her enemies clearly had better weapons.

Hiding in the basement could work but hiding wasn't her style either.

She needed to go hunting.

D'Angelo was a wild card, but Carmichael would likely be up in his wife's room. A mansion like this probably contained dozens of hidden passages to allow servants to slip unobtrusively from place to place.

She also needed a phone. No matter how the next few hours played out, she needed help. If Cassandra showed up, this place could turn into a warzone in a heartbeat. Megan hadn't seen any other thugs lurking about, but that didn't mean much. Dan, her parents, and her Vegas friends also deserved fair warnings that danger might be headed their way.

Text appeared in the lower left corner of her vision.

You're online. Welcome back to Eagle Eyes. How can I help you today?

"Show me the layout of this place," Megan ordered. "And try to contact Gatton. I need to speak with him."

Seconds later, her mind filled with information from original architecture drawings to thermal imaging options. As predicted, the mansion held many more people. Using the program to find a safe hiding spot was simple enough, but it took some serious studying to determine which orange blobs represented D'Angelo and Carmichael.

Mr. Gatton is unavailable. Shall I leave a message?

"Tell him to find me ASAP."

Acknowledged.

Knowing she had some time to kill before Cassandra would show, Megan started mapping out the mansion. The architectural drawings were only accurate to a point. Carmichael must have done some renovations over the years. The spatial awareness protocols for Eagle Eyes alerted her every time it suspected a hidden passage. She didn't always find the passage and a few times it was boarded up, but she left mental markers in place on the usable ones.

Gatton could be a pain, but he had a touch of genius in him. Megan hoped his program could pull off a few more miracles today.

Chapter 10:
You Know Me

Once she had the house well mapped out, Megan stole some real food from the kitchen and slipped into one of the fifteen bathrooms to hide out. She would have chosen one of the back passages if she hadn't spent much of her morning locked in a storm shelter vault. At least this bathroom featured a giant skylight and large windows, letting her feel less trapped.

The bed in the spacious room outside this bathroom looked inviting, but she spent her time monitoring the ebb and flow of people throughout the rest of the mansion. As time marched past noon, the number of bodies in the house almost doubled. Carmichael must have called in reinforcements. When it looked like the two-man patrols were venturing higher and farther, Megan took that as her cue to hide out for real.

As the secret door clicked shut behind her, Megan noted that every orange blob started moving at a much faster pace.

Something's up. Or they found out I'm missing.

You were discovered missing eight minutes and fifty-two seconds ago.

Why didn't you tell me?

You did not ask.

Annoyed with herself and the stupid program, Megan instructed Eagle Eyes to scan for the radio frequency used by the bad guys. If she could hear them, maybe this mess would start making sense. She plotted a path to get to Carmichael's study. The two locations he was likely to meet Cassandra in were the study and his wife's bedroom. His main office wasn't really equipped to receive guests, and most other rooms offered too many possible exits. Besides, an unusual number of orange blobs congregated in rooms near the study.

She flinched when her head filled with random radio chatter of patrols checking in. Silencing that, Megan asked to be patched into the security feeds. She got a feel for how tedious and boring normal security work could be while staring at grainy black and white video feeds. Since having multiple windows working side by side gave her a headache, she took to scanning one for a few seconds before moving on to the next in line.

Suddenly, multiple orange blobs raced this way and that again. Pulling up the security cameras for those zones, Megan soon had a bird's eye view of the commotion. She let the image fill her vision. A figure in black moved through the room like a tornado, toppling security men like bowling pins. Several men had drawn tranquilizer pistols and fired wildly at the figure. The figure spun aside as gracefully as a ballet dancer, wrapped an arm around a random security guy, and shoved him into the line of fire. He caught one dart in his neck and another on his bulletproof vest. The one on his vest did nothing. The one to the neck made him loopy. The figure's grip on his neck tightened until he collapsed.

Megan silently cheered.

Then, everything went wrong.

One of the men managed to grab the figure's facemask, yanking it partway around. The figure stumbled, grabbing for the mask. Sensing victory, multiple security men pounced. Two knocked into each other. A third took an elbow to his throat and went down. The fourth and fifth each grabbed an arm and forced the figure to its knees. A sixth plucked away the facemask, releasing a cascade of hair.

Proximity alert. Danger!

An arm wrapped around Megan's neck and a hand covered her mouth, forcing her head up and back. That left her arms in a useless position for fighting. Panic took over until a quiet, steady whisper broke through.

"Just relax! Don't fight me. I'm going to release you shortly, but you have to keep calm and quiet."

The sound of Cassandra Mirren's voice made Megan simultaneously want to weep with relief and scream a dozen questions. When the other woman finally let go, Megan whirled and squinted hard. She couldn't see much in the dim shadows of the secret passage. The nearest emergency light, little more than a night light, glowed several feet away.

"If you're here, who's out there getting captured?" Megan demanded.

"My apprentice." Cassandra's answer caught Megan off guard.

"I thought you were retired," said Megan.

"So did I," Cassandra said wearily, "but that's a lot harder said than done in my line of work. Besides, she needs this meeting almost as much as he does."

"You … lost me," Megan admitted.

"Just watch," Cassandra urged. Touching a spot on the wall, she brushed something aside. Soon, a thin beam of light flooded the space.

"How did you know that was there?" Megan hissed the question warily.

"Because I drilled it several years ago," Cassandra answered. "Now hush. Listen."

Pressing her eye to the peephole, Megan watched in horror as six security men dragged a thin, dazed figure into the room and dropped her to the floor. Now that she had a good look, she realized the form was too slight to belong to Cassandra. Prying her gaze away from the unfortunate girl, Megan forced herself to locate the other people in the room. Since she couldn't see every angle from the peephole, she supplemented her knowledge with security camera footage through Eagle Eyes.

Carmichael stood behind his desk glaring down at the still form. D'Angelo stood out of the peephole's line of sight, roughly two paces left of the secret passage entrance. The six security guys fanned out in a semi-circle behind their prisoner.

"Get her up," Carmichael ordered. "Why isn't she bound? I told you she's dangerous."

"It's not her, sir," said the lead security man. His expression managed to be both defiant and apologetic. He gestured for two others to pick up the prisoner.

"What do you mean?" Carmichael demanded.

"I've met the assassin once. This isn't her," the security man repeated.

Two of the men dragged the prisoner upright and put her in a chair facing Carmichael's desk. The rough welcome and the ski mask had made a mess of the girl's hair, so it obscured much of her features.

"Wake her," Carmichael said impatiently.

One man retrieved a glass of water while another rubbed her

wrists and a third gently slapped her cheeks. When the water arrived, the leader splashed some on the girl's face. He used more water to smooth out her hair and brush it off her face. While all this went on, his body blocked Megan's view, so she relied on Eagle Eyes to keep track of everything.

When the man stepped aside, Carmichael stiffened and sank into his throne-like office chair.

"What's wrong?" D'Angelo inquired.

"Sir?" said the head security guy.

"Get out." Carmichael's order was soft but potent.

The security team responded immediately, filing out without a word, but D'Angelo didn't move.

"Get out!" Carmichael shouted.

"Who is she?" D'Angelo asked.

Megan bid the computer program to isolate one of the security frames that had captured the girl's face. She then ran it through a few enhancement programs and algorithms that would age it forward and backwards fifteen years. At the same time, she searched for every article that mentioned Carmichael or his family, particularly focusing on the years when the accident could have occurred. The answer to each query arrived about the same time things in the room came to head.

"You know me," said the young woman.

"Lia!" Carmichael looked faint. "What are you doing here? Where is Cassandra?"

"Eleven years and that's the best you've got?" Anger crackled through the woman's question. "My name and a demand to see someone else. Did you even look for me? Did anybody?"

"I was *ordered* not to." Carmichael's voice hardened with frustration. "We held a funeral for you. Nobody knew, not even your mother. Where have you been?"

Shock and sadness battled across the young woman's expression. Sadness won.

"I was raised by the Council, Father."

"Touching," D'Angelo muttered. Drawing his gun, he leveled it at the young woman. "Where's the assassin?"

"Put that gun away," barked Carmichael.

"Stay out of it, Senator," said D'Angelo. Closing the distance between them, he pressed the gun to the side of the girl's head. "It's a simple question," he added, speaking to the girl even as his eyes rested on Carmichael.

"She didn't come with me," said the girl.

"Lia, please. Tell him," Carmichael begged. "She's one of them. They destroyed us. They killed your brother."

"She had nothing to do with that," Lia argued.

"But th-the list—" Carmichael sputtered.

"Is a lie," Lia finished. "She was an apprentice at the time."

"How do you know?" D'Angelo asked.

"Because we were held in the same dorm for a year before she aged out and took on jobs for herself," Lia answered calmly.

"Who were the others on the list?" Carmichael looked physically ill.

"Forget that, Senator," said D'Angelo. "We need to find the assassin and the agent quickly."

"The others were people the Council couldn't abide any longer," said Lia. Something softened in her gaze. "People like me. You've been duped into doing their dirty work, Father."

Carmichael groaned.

"Pull yourself together," D'Angelo ordered. "Get the men back in here and have them cuff her. Then, go wait with your wife. I'll handle the assassin."

"No," said Carmichael.

"It wasn't a suggestion," D'Angelo said darkly. "If there's even a scrap in you that values your daughter's life, do it."

"Do as he says. Help is coming." Lia addressed the promise to her father with her eyes.

At Carmichael's order, the security men returned and took custody of Lia.

"Where should we take her, sir?" asked the head security man, looking to Carmichael.

The senator looked at D'Angelo.

"Is there a room with a single entrance and exit?" D'Angelo inquired.

"Some of the bathrooms might fit the bill," offered the security leader. He looked curiously between D'Angelo and Carmichael.

D'Angelo rejected the idea with a shake of his head.

"We'll make do here. Get me a chair she can be secured to and station men in every room on the first floor."

Megan sensed movement behind her. When she looked up to check, Cassandra leaned around her and closed the peephole.

"Go home, Agent. This isn't your fight," Cassandra whispered.

Megan snorted softly.

"I have no idea where I am, and I'm not about to let that suited son of a monkey kill that kid. Do you have a plan?"

"Even the score. Top down," said Cassandra.

"You'll need my help," Megan insisted. "I'm still connected to Gatton's fancy toy."

"So am I."

An irrational stab of jealousy hit Megan, but she shoved it aside. Eagle Eyes would be especially dangerous in Cassandra's hands, and if they wanted to survive the next few hours, they would need every advantage they could muster.

"Should we stay together or split up?" Megan wondered.

"Divide and conquer," Cassandra replied.

"I was afraid you'd say that," Megan muttered. "Was the kid right? Is more help coming?"

"Maybe. Gatton was being awfully cagey when I spoke with him."

Ladies, your window for movement is closing. If you'll pardon the intrusion, I have a suggested path for each of you.

"This isn't a video game," Megan protested, even as she silently thanked Gatton for the blue dotted line now flowing in front of her.

A red line flowed from Cassandra.

It sort of is.

"Try not to get us killed," said Cassandra. "And get the agent a better weapon soon." She slipped out of the secret passage and sprinted away, following Gatton's red line.

One weapon coming up. There's a two-man patrol three rooms over I think you can get the drop on. Get moving, Agent.

Megan paused and stared down at the hatchet that had made such a mess of the vault this morning. She shuddered to think what it would do to a man.

Use the blunt end like a hammer and swing like you mean it. If either guy gets away, you're toast, extra crispy toast.

Thanks for the pep talk, Gatton.

Despite her sarcasm, the warning focused her.

Chapter 11:
Pick Your Battles

Abort mission!

Not really an option, Jeffrey.

No, seriously. STOP! I mean go left now. Freeze. Let them pass.

Megan followed the halting instructions as best she could, following the blue line into an empty room. It led her over to a shadowy corner. Crouching by a bookcase, she tried to get her breathing under control. Her heart pounded so hard her head hurt.

Geez. You're worse than my GPS. Make up your mind. I still need a weapons upgrade pronto.

Yeah, I get that. But not from that pair.

What's the problem?

Tell Eagle Eyes to update the biometrics algorithms and you'll see.

Not really understanding what Gatton was babbling about, Megan followed the advice. The orange infrared blobs suddenly had a bunch of numbers over them. Focusing on one, Megan glanced at the numbers. Height, weight, body temperature, body mass index, and a dozen other facts bombarded her.

Narrow the scope to height and weight.

When she did so, she finally understood his panic.

I see. Good call.

The pair that had passed by had both topped six feet, three inches in height and weighed over two hundred and twenty pounds. She would practically have to leap off a step stool to even reach their heads, let alone muster enough bashing power to knock them out.

Eureka! Okay, so a fair fight's going to get you killed.

Nobody says that anymore, and thanks for the vote of confidence.

Let's fight dirty.

Get to the point.

The next two minutes consisted of Megan speed reading Gatton's convoluted plan. Since she couldn't hide forever and had no better plan, she chose to trust him.

It's like any video game. If you can't use brute force, you use trickery.

Can we stop likening this to a video game?

Sorry. I know you hate it, but it's how Eagle Eyes was designed.

Fine. Show me the objective.

A dashed golden line spread out from her feet, leading to one of the secret passages. Over the next fifteen minutes, Megan painstakingly picked her way across the mansion. At times, she had to change direction, stop and hide, or sprint past a patrol. Finally, she arrived at the out-of-the-way section reserved for staff that lived on the premises. The golden line disappeared beneath the third door on her right. Cautiously, Megan crept in that direction.

Eagle Eyes informed her that the tiny room held one occupant, a person four feet ten inches and one hundred and thirty-three pounds. A little welcome sign on the door read: Rosa.

Do I bust right in?

Try knocking. When she answers, then bust in.

The plan worked swell. Megan knocked urgently several times until she heard movement within.

"Yes, how may I—"

Without giving the woman time to finish, Megan thrust out her right arm and wedged her right foot against the door so it couldn't be closed. The short woman stumbled backwards with a startled cry. Moving like her life depended on it, Megan lunged forward, clamped her hand over the woman's mouth, and pushed right until the lady's back met the wall. Thinking the hatchet tucked close to the lady's chin gave the wrong impression, Megan slipped the handle into the back left pocket of her jeans.

Kicking the door shut, Megan prayed the woman spoke decent English because her high school Spanish skills were sadly out of date.

"I don't want to hurt you, but I need the master key," Megan explained. "Please. Just tell me where to find the key, and I'll be leaving. I promise."

She slowly moved her hand so her prisoner could speak. The woman rattled off something in Spanish so fast that Megan doubted she would have understood if she was fluent. The cry was accompanied by fluttering hand movements Megan recognized as the sign of the cross.

She said, "Dear God, deliver me from this crazy lady."

Thanks, Gatton. I got the gist.

"Calm down," Megan soothed. She deliberately took a few deep breaths, hoping the woman would mimic the movements. "My friend's in trouble and I need to help her. You would help your friend, right?"

Tears pooled in the woman's eyes, and she released another torrent of rapid-fire Spanish.

She thinks you're going to kill Lady Maria.

Shaking her head vigorously, Megan worked hard not to shake the woman in her frustration.

How do I convince her that's not my intent?

That's not your objective. You need to get the key. You can take the menacing approach, the kind approach, or the persuasive approach. Since you lack the language skills and Google Translate's not quite up to the task, I say go kind approach.

What the heck are you talking about?

Hit her, bribe her, or talk her down, but do it quickly. Your friend's in trouble.

"I'm not hitting her, I'm fresh out of twenties, and how bad is it?"

Ooo. Or you could try searching the room for metal. That module's in beta testing, but it should work.

Practically growling, Megan bid the program to highlight everything metal and peered into the small room. Everything glowed. The twin bed was outlined. The drawer knobs and the lamp fixtures stood out. Coins sitting in a bowl on the end table sparkled. Looking back at the woman, Megan also saw the places she glowed, most notably, her earrings and neckline.

Ask it to isolate key shapes. The program's only as good as the parameters you give it.

Most of the room stopped glowing, but the spot beneath the woman's flower printed blouse still glowed. This time, the necklace formed the shape of a large key. With trembling fingers, Megan pulled the necklace free from the woman's shirt.

Cold fingers wrapped around Megan's right hand. Another wave of frantic words flowed. Since the same phrase kept being repeated, Megan gathered the meaning before Gatton translated.

She says, "Please don't kill me. It's my job. I protect the family."

Covering the lady's left hand with hers, Megan stared deep into her black eyes.

"I think the family's in trouble. You've done your part. Now, let me help. I can protect them. Not all of the security men are loyal. I need your key to save the family."

The woman weighed Megan's words, but her grip on the key never wavered.

Tell her about Lia.

"Lia's here too. They're going to hurt her if I can't stop them."

The woman's eyes closed as if to pray, but she also reached up and pulled the necklace over her head. She spoke again as she folded the large, ornate key into Megan's hand.

That too needed no translation.

"I promise."

Clutching the prize, Megan left the room. The old-fashioned thing spanned the whole length of her palm.

You should lock her in, just in case she has second thoughts.

I'm not about to burn the only goodwill I've got going. Where do I go?

Fair point. Back the way you came. If you hurry, you might be able to catch a pair checking out the East Library.

Feeling like she'd been dropped into a sadistic game of live action Clue, Megan jogged where the new golden line pointed. As she reached the correct door, the bright line shot past and kept going.

Gatton! You're doing it again. Give clear, decisive directions.

Sorry. It's going to get more intense as soon as you trap the first pair. There's a locker room a little beyond the kitchen. You'll have to take a roundabout route, but you can make it. There should be better weapons there.

The promise of better weapons mollified her slightly. The trip to the locker room proved more nerve-wracking than the quest for the key. Megan felt like she was backtracking more than moving forward. Eagle Eyes helped her monitor where patrols might be, but things changed so fast, she often had to make split-second decisions about running and hiding.

Most lockers had personal combination locks on them, but that didn't matter because in their haste, several security guards had left the boxes of spare tranquilizers strewn about the room. A glass case in the corner held several kinds of guns, including additional tranquilizer guns.

How hard do you think that glass is?

More than a match for that hatchet, but there's probably a key to it in the manager's office.

Spoilsport.

Despite the sentiment she sent Gatton, pure relief flooded Megan when she found a small key labeled "armory" in the top center desk drawer. She selected and loaded a Glock 23 as well as a pair of tranquilizer guns. Since her jeans wouldn't hold the new weapons well, Megan donned a tactical belt. After a brief hesitation, she traded the power bars for a pair of spare gun magazines.

Feeling whole, Megan picked up a third tranquilizer gun and checked that the dart was properly loaded.

I suggest strapping two tranq guns together for the first pair. You can't afford to miss because you won't have time to reload. Steal the guns from the guys you take out. Rinse and repeat. Aim for their necks. Most are wearing tactical vests.

The reminder made Megan look around for a vest that would fit. She debated herself over whether she had time to climb into one of the vests.

Got time to get shot?

Rolling her eyes, Megan stripped off the tactical belt, dove into the smallest bulletproof vest she could find, and rearmed.

With Gatton's help, she soon found her first set of security guys. They reacted swiftly to her presence, but not quickly enough. Her first dart struck the taller man in his left cheek. She winced but fired her second dart at the shorter man's neck. Both men yelped and clutched at the wounds, giving her time to smack them with the flat side of the hatchet. They slumped to the ground. She proceeded as best she could, but only managed to neutralize one more set when Gatton declared their progress too slow.

You're not going to like this plan, but we need to speed things up. Will you hear me out?

Do I have a choice?

Up ahead several rooms are connected. They're holding upwards of ten to twelve guys each. Lock them in then get rid of the key.

How do I get rid of the key? I can't exactly swallow it. I'd choke to death.

Flush it.

You're right. I hate this plan.

It gets worse.

Oh. Goody.

I need you to run around like a maniac firing your gun. You need to lead any stragglers away from Cassandra and Lia.

Where are they?

The tiny map in the corner of Megan's vision got bigger and showed her two green dots. The stationary one down this hall had to be Lia. The one bouncing around somewhere on the second floor, slamming into orange blobs had to be Cassandra.

And where exactly am I leading the merry men to?

There's a hedge maze out back.

Sometimes, I hate you.

That's the stress talking. Get moving. Cassandra can't keep up her end much longer.

Where's the nearest bathroom?

Together, they plotted a path for Megan to follow. Things went off without a hitch until she locked the fourth door. By then, the radios squawked with confusing shouts. A security guy stuck his head out the fifth door as Megan approached.

"What the—"

He didn't get any further than that because Megan smashed his face with a tranquilizer gun. Several men tried to push their comrade out of the way so they could rush Megan. Taking this as her signal to leave, she fired the tranquilizer gun blindly, dropped it, whirled, and sprinted away.

Go left and draw the real gun. Shoot the window out and exit. Use the lamp.

Megan didn't even have time to question the crazy. Unlike the movies, shooting while running was devilishly difficult so it took the entire magazine to hit the glass several times. Thankfully, the glass was not up to the rigors of multiple bullet impacts. The lamp in question happened to be in her way anyway, so she scooped it up as she mounted the desk and used the lamp as a battering ram of sorts to clear out some of the glass.

A bullet hitting the wall above her head motivated her to move faster. Dropping the lamp, Megan scrambled through and sprinted for the fountain, running in a zigzag pattern to lower the chances of being shot in the back.

You better have a backup plan.

You won't like that one either.

Chapter 12:
Hedge Maze

The sight of Dallas off in the distance surprised Megan. With everything that had happened in the last twenty-four hours, she felt certain she should be hundreds, if not thousands, of miles away from where she started. She ran all-out, holding nothing back, because fight or flight instincts fully controlled her body. Her grip on the handgun remained sure, and her arms and legs pumped in that familiar sprinter's rhythm. Beyond exhausted from sustained adrenaline, she ran on anyway, covering the few hundred yards to the maze quickly.

Heck of a vacation. If I live through this, I'm asking for eight months of stakeouts and paperwork.

The wishful thinking distracted her from the terror of waiting for gunshots to ring out behind her.

Let's make sure that happens. The maze entrance is dead ahead. Make a right when you get inside.

Won't that lead me into a trap?

Sort of, but hey, you have me. Your pursuers don't, so you can dodge them.

For how long?

Much as she didn't want to admit it, Megan was grateful Gatton never answered that question. The next several minutes passed tensely. She crept as quietly as she could, but the dry path between the hedges crunched with each footfall.

Gatton directed her through a convoluted path around the maze, roughly in a circle. Megan didn't have to patch into the security frequency to hear her pursuers' frustration. She learned to categorize their shouts by tone. The barked commands from multiple directions meant the chain of command wasn't quite clear. She gathered that two different security companies had been tapped for manpower. The long, sustained cries usually meant a dead end. Short-lived ones typically resulted from someone blundering into a hedge. Megan understood how easy that could be and bore a few bloody scratches from close encounters with the rough walls. The caretakers had slacked off on their trimming duties during the winter months, so a few odd branches jutted into the paths.

Make two lefts and a right. Then go six steps and push on the hedge wall. There should be a hidden door there. It covers a small area with a maintenance shed and backs up to the central gazebo.

Heart pounding in her ears, Megan searched for the door described. It was so well-hidden that she stepped right past it the first time and had to loop around again to avoid one of the security men. Once through, she had no trouble finding her way to the shed and ducking into the crawl space beneath the gazebo.

Footsteps clomped across the wood a few feet above Megan's head. The security guys had made the gazebo a staging ground for conducting their search.

Closing her eyes, she concentrated on controlling her breathing. She doubted they would hear her with the fine racket they were making, but she didn't want a stray gasp to betray her location.

Congratulations. You're safe. Sit tight and wait it out.
What's going on inside?
Megan waited through a ten-count before repeating the query.
Gatton. I need to know. What's going on inside?
You're safe. That's what counts. We both think so.
Hot anger flared through Megan's chest.
You don't get to make that decision for me!
Let it go. It's a lost cause. Carmichael hired two dozen security guards and D'Angelo tripled the order last night. Not even Cassandra and Lia stand a chance against that many.
Don't you dare give up on them. There must be something you can do. Trip the fire alarm. Recall the guards. Send the cops. Do something!
The cops can't face a mercenary army without a bloodbath, and my teams are at least an hour away. Calling the fire department is going to get a lot of people killed. The Council's not after you, not really. If you wait it out, the guards will go away, and

I can direct you to the nearest neighbor's house to get help.

Running away, even for good reason, had never been Megan's style. On a fundamental level, she needed to face this thing, but she didn't want to charge in blindly.

What do they want? Who's on what side?

Don't know for sure. Carmichael's practically a prisoner at this point. D'Angelo was supposedly hired by him to get to Cassandra so he could have his revenge.

"But he was tricked," Megan whispered.

Agreed. D'Angelo's probably been sent to clean house. That means that the three inside and the lady of the house are goners as soon as they catch Cassandra.

Who's really after Cassandra and why?

Does it matter?

Every motive matters. Take the guards for example. Are they loyal to Carmichael or their companies or only money?

Probably their companies. They'd get fired if they weren't at least partly loyal to their employers.

We need to thin their numbers.

How?

Are they all connected to the same communications network?

Hang on. Let me check.

While waiting for Gatton to get back to her, Megan pondered the baby plan forming. If she could speak with Dan or Special Agent Ophelia Pitman, she could summon real help. Either of them would have the right contacts to get through to the security companies, but Pitman also had a reputation for fiercely defending the Honolulu federal agents no matter which badge they wore. She'd move Heaven and Earth to save one of her "children."

Everybody's on the same frequency.

Call for help. Go through Ophelia Pitman and Dan Cooper. They can get you people from the FBI's Dallas Field Office. Then call the police and file a missing person's report on me. Next, call both security firms and tell them what you've done. Get them to make their people back off. That should even the score some. If that doesn't work immediately, put me on their frequency and let me speak to them directly.

That could work …

I know. Get moving, Gatton. You've got some serious sweet talking to do.

It felt really good to fling that at him.

If we had more time.

Make the time. Let me speak with them.

Sorry. This is for your own good.

Megan's heart lurched when parts of the Eagle Eyes program started shutting down. Gatton was re-asserting administrator controls. The orange blobs of the security men disappeared first followed quickly by the bars monitoring her vital signs and anything to do with communications. The sense of loss struck her hard, but she had no time to dwell on it.

Slowly reloading the handgun with a magazine she'd stored on the tactical belt, Megan pondered her next move. Gatton's sudden withdraw severely limited her abilities and options, but if she thought about it, the essence of the situation remained unchanged. Lia and Cassandra needed her help immediately.

Now that she had a plan, she simply needed a way to enact it. Moving back through the shed to the hidden door that opened into the maze, Megan listened closely. She didn't have long to wait. Soon, the steady crunch of boots on hard-packed soil alerted her to company. As soon as the figure passed the hiding spot, Megan swung the door open and leveled her gun at the guard.

"Hands up! Fingers off the radio," Megan ordered.

The man spun to face her, hands dropping to rest on a gun holstered at his waist. The intensity in his eyes spoke of experience.

"You don't want to do that," Megan said. "Step in here and close the door. I need your phone."

As the man stepped forward, Megan retreated to maintain a decent distance from him. He moved reluctantly, probably dragging out the process in the hopes that a friend would come save him.

"Quickly, now. I don't have much time," Megan urged. "If I run out of time, you run out of time. I've got nothing to lose." The last part was a lie, but he didn't know that.

"I shout and you're as good as dead," said the guard. His voice betrayed no nervousness.

"You shout and you're dead. Who do you think has the better odds?" Megan asked. "Put your phone on the ground and step back into that corner. Neither of us has to die today."

The man silently considered her words for three long seconds before slowly retrieving his phone from his pocket and tossing it to the ground at her feet.

"What's your name?" Megan inquired as she knelt to pick up the phone.

"Why do you want to know?" he countered.

Mostly, she wanted him focusing on something besides tackling her the second she made the phone call.

"It's a lot harder to kill somebody once you know their name," she replied.

"Axel Garvel."

Something about the name rang false, but she couldn't spare the brainpower to riddle through the feeling.

"All right, Axel. I'm Megan. Stay calm and let me make a phone call."

Barely glancing at the phone, Megan hit the home button then touched the bottom left corner where it said: Emergency. When the keypad came up, she dialed 911. When the call connected to a dispatcher, Megan waited through the customary question.

"911. What is your emergency?" asked a cool female voice.

"This is FBI Special Agent Megan Luchek. I was kidnapped yesterday in Dallas. I don't know my exact location, but you might be able to get the location from the phone. I'm also going to give you a name. You can look up the address attached to the name."

"All right, Megan. My name is Kayla. I'm here to help. What's the name I can look up to find you?"

"Senator Carmichael."

Silence fell.

"This is not a joke. I'm going to give you a phone number to reach Special Agent Daniel Cooper, also FBI. He can coordinate with the Dallas office to get my people out here. I also need a number from you."

"For what?"

"Karok Security," she answered, reading the name off a patch on Axel's uniform. "If you can, please connect me to them directly." She rattled off Dan's cell phone number.

"Ma'am, I'm going to need you to stay on the line," said the dispatcher.

"That's not going to be possible soon," Megan said.

"Are you in a safe place?" asked Kayla.

"For the moment," Megan answered, "but I have two friends up in that house, and they're running out of time."

"If you're in a safe place, stay there," said Kayla.

"No place is truly safe." Megan disconnected the call. She had to hope the senator's name would be enough to get them an address because her other call was vital, and Kayla sounded like a dead end.

Tossing the phone back to Axel, Megan said, "Call your bosses and give the phone back."

"Why?" The man stared at her steadily. His expression wavered between uncertainty and suspicion.

"I need to explain the deal to them, so fewer people get caught up in the fallout," she explained.

He shrugged.

"I'll call, but you're not going to get anywhere with them."

Unfortunately, his prediction proved accurate. The call went straight to a machine with a long menu of options.

Megan's head dipped as she absorbed this new roadblock. Her mind churned with possibilities and partial plans. She needed more time.

Axel tensed, ready to spring the moment her attention slipped.

Reaching a decision, Megan released the ammunition magazine and ejected the bullet from the chamber.

"What are you doing?" Axel asked, dumbfounded.

"I'm surrendering," Megan replied. "Get me back up to that house."

Chapter 13:
Dangerous Deals

Jeffrey Gatton disliked lying to Agent Luchek. He also hated abandoning her, but he wasn't fond of thoughts of prison either. Something about Curtis D'Angelo's neat little profile had prompted him to do some digging. The actual hacking part had been both thrilling and challenging, but now, he really wished he could rewind a few hours. Grandma always said "ignorance is bliss," but the phrase had new meaning today.

He expected a call any minute now, and he needed at least a week to think his way out of this one. Once upon a time, Gatton believed the government existed to serve the people. Now, he knew the truth. Protecting the nation as a whole meant individuals were exploitable and expendable. He was still relatively safe since they needed him and his company to keep Eagle Eyes running smoothly. Although he didn't have many close friends, he still had plenty of family for them to threaten.

His black cell phone rang. Sighing heavily, he picked it up.

"Gatton," he said.

"Jeffrey. Jeffrey." The way the man said his name made it both condescending and menacing. "You've been busy. How's our special project?"

"The program works fine," Gatton said curtly. "The patch I put in place today made the target tracking module sixteen percent more efficient."

"Excellent. I see from the readouts you've put two prototypes into play in the same situation. How was the interaction between the carriers?"

"They didn't interact through the system," Gatton admitted,

feeling defensive. "There wasn't enough time to work out the problems that would arise from unexpected interference."

The man made a low, disappointed noise.

"A missed opportunity, but let's move past that. You know why I'm calling."

Gatton locked his jaw, concentrating on not confessing anything over this line. His handler often went on verbal fishing expeditions like this.

"I won't apologize."

"Nor should you," said the man smoothly. "Your skills are impeccable as usual. If we didn't keep such a close eye on some of your signature moves, you would have slipped in and out unnoticed."

Pain shot from Gatton's jaw up through the rest of his head from clenching his teeth so hard.

"But alas, here we are with you in possession of some rather … inconvenient information."

Yeah, proof the CIA operates here at home. Inconvenient.

"The nondisclosure clauses are still in place," Gatton said.

"I know. I know. I'm simply calling to leave a friendly reminder to refrain from doing something self-destructive." The man's tone shifted from patronizing to serious. "You've proven the product works well. We're ready to move into the next phase. I'll have my men scrub the situation and get back to you with firm figures of how many units we need."

Alarm shot through every nerve.

"You can't do that," Gatton argued.

"They're ghosts. You know I can."

"Luchek's not a ghost. She's FBI," Gatton blurted. "It was in my report."

Harsh silence fell.

"Can she be recruited?" asked the man, after a very long pause.

The question wasn't really aimed at Gatton, but he answered anyway.

"I doubt it. I think there was a failed pitch somewhere in her past already." Internally, Gatton added, *Fat chance.*

"Don't worry about it. I'll speak with her," said the man.

"You can't kill her," Gatton babbled. "Too many people know where she is. Too many people know *who* she is."

How do I get through to him?

"I said, don't worry about it." The man's tone had stilled to a deadly calm.

"She's also one of the few people in the world who has worked with the program and excelled at it. You'd be wasting an asset."

The brief silence was less frightening than the previous one.

"I'll think about it," the man promised.

That could go either way. Megan's life still hung by a weak thread of the man's goodwill.

Inspiration struck Gatton.

"She's also mine." He flushed even though nobody could see him through the phone. "I-I mean she works for me."

"You hired her?" The man's tone dripped suspicion.

"Yes. After the first round of tests, I even paid her a bonus from the program's main account. There's a record of that."

The man cursed softly then chuckled.

"Well played, boy. You make some good points. Get your people in gear to make the first dozen units. I will speak with the agent."

This time, that sounded less threatening.

Sinking deeper into his chair with relief, Gatton gave a neutral, noncommittal answer. The man wouldn't like his real answer to the order of a dozen Eagle Eyes units. The training runs with Agent Luchek had convinced him each unit needed an experienced, dedicated handler. That limited the number of units that could be effectively put into the field because that person would have to train with Gatton for months. But he could break that news to the man another day. For now, he would take the small win.

***

It took Megan most of a minute to convince Axel Garvel her surrender was genuine. After reporting their position, he asked for orders and received confirmation to take her up to the house. He seemed skittish throughout the process of securing her wrists behind her back with handcuffs. But his confidence bounced back during the long walk up to the house.

They re-entered through a door two rooms over from the one that featured Megan's daring escape.

She thought her capture might calm things down.

She was very wrong.

Security men ran back and forth, closing doors, righting fallen objects, and heading for the front and side doors. The chatter coming through Axel's radio convinced her that a full-scale retreat was in the works, though she couldn't fathom why.

Something changed in Axel's gait as he escorted her through the chaos to Senator Carmichael's study. Before each step rose and fell with nervous energy, but as they approached the office, he started placing his feet more cautiously, like someone used to sneaking around.

Megan thought the tension in the house high until she crossed the threshold into the study and found a situation ready to explode.

D'Angelo stood in front of Carmichael's massive desk holding a cell phone in one hand and a gun in the other. The gun pointed at Lia who had been tied to a thin wooden chair. The regular chairs had been shoved into the far corner. To D'Angelo's right and Megan's left, stood Carmichael being physically restrained by two security men. Across from him, next to the gaping secret passage entrance, stood Cassandra, aiming a gun at D'Angelo. Another pair of security goons had their weapons fixed on her. Megan didn't have to look. She sensed Axel retreat a step and saw him shift to a shooting stance.

His gun would soon center on her.

Hanging up the phone, D'Angelo slipped it into his suit jacket and used his free hand to steady the one with the gun.

"Two to one, Cassandra. I win," said D'Angelo. "Put the gun down, and they get to live a few extra minutes."

"That's not a very good incentive. You'll have to do better than that, Curt," replied Cassandra.

D'Angelo's eyes narrowed with annoyance. He nodded briefly at Axel then strode over to the chair holding Lia. Spinning the chair around to face Cassandra, D'Angelo pressed the gun to the base of the girl's neck.

A kick from Axel sent Megan to her knees. A hand on her left shoulder steadied her before cold metal settled against her neck.

"What happens beyond that is up to the agent," D'Angelo said. "Whether she gets to hear the offer is up to you. My current orders involve you alone. The kid's a ghost. She can be retrained or spend her life buried in a black gate prison. Either fate's out of reach if she dies now."

"This is outrageous!" declared Carmichael. "I demand—"

One of the security men restraining Carmichael shoved a tranquilizer gun under his ribs and fired. For good measure, the other man clobbered the senator over the head with his gun. Carmichael collapsed in a heap. Lia tried to turn her head to see what was happening, but D'Angelo braced her neck so she continued facing Cassandra.

"You have three seconds to comply," D'Angelo said.

Unshed tears glittering in Cassandra's eyes were the last thing Megan saw before clenching her eyes shut.

Her whole body tensed.

Her mind strained to imagine what death would feel like.

A dull thunk touched her ears instead of the expected roar of a gunshot.

Her eyes flew open in time to see both security men approach Cassandra cautiously. They moved like soldiers.

Even without a gun, the assassin looked ready to clear the room with her wrath.

"Gently now," urged D'Angelo.

Megan wasn't sure if he meant the comment for Cassandra or the security guys.

"Don't do it," whispered Lia. "You can still leave. Live. They won't—"

"Shhh shhh shh." D'Angelo's left hand clamped across the girl's mouth. "None of that. I went through a lot of trouble to get to this moment."

Cassandra bristled but submitted to handcuffs that attached her wrists to a chain linked to her ankles. One guard knocked the assassin to her knees while the other fit a black ski mask over her head.

"What are you doing?" Megan's question came out shakier than she liked. Her knees burned, but she couldn't pry her attention away from Cassandra. She'd always thought the assassin invincible, so the chains were an odd sight.

The assassin strained against the bonds, methodically twisting her wrists in subtle motions. Megan doubted it would do much good, but she needed to believe Cassandra had a plan.

"Telling a story, Agent Luchek," said D'Angelo. He released Lia's mouth and moved left so he could face Megan. "The exact tale that's told depends on you."

The words caused Megan to refocus on D'Angelo.

"Meaning?"

"You could be a hero and slay the unwanted intruder, or you could perish in a tragic misunderstanding," D'Angelo explained. "Or both. My boss would actually prefer both."

"I don't get it," Megan admitted.

At another nod from D'Angelo, Axel pulled Megan up to her feet.

"He wants you to join the CIA, Megan," said Cassandra. "That would involve faking your death."

The news slammed into Megan with near physical force.

"The Shadow Council's CIA?" Disbelief rang through each word.

"In part," D'Angelo confirmed.

"Then what's going on? Why would the CIA want Cassandra dead?" Both questions burst out of Megan on waves of anger.

D'Angelo shrugged and tucked his gun away.

"She's a threat. I don't question my orders. Her fate's a foregone conclusion. It's your fate we're discussing."

"So what, join or die? You people stink at recruiting pitches," Megan spat. "And the answer's still no."

"It's not a bad life, Agent," said Cassandra. Her voice held a soul-deep weariness.

"You wouldn't be a normal recruit," D'Angelo assured Megan. "You'd continue to work with Gatton Technologies to train agents to handle Eagle Eyes."

"Gatton." The way Megan said it turned the name into a curse.

It's not what you think but take the out and walk away. You can't fight this.

I can always fight it.

"Still no." Megan flung the answer at both Gatton and D'Angelo.

While everybody's attention rested on Megan, Lia moved. Heaving her body sideways, she knocked into D'Angelo, pinning him against the desk with the chair. Somehow, she had wriggled her right hand free of the ropes. Snatching D'Angelo's gun, she pressed the weapon under his chin.

"Are your orders worth dying for?" asked Lia. "That question goes for everybody."

D'Angelo twitched his head left and right briefly in answer.

"Good." Lia raised her voice to address the security men. "Release them both then get out of here."

The guards obediently dropped their weapons before exiting. One man gave Cassandra a handcuff key on his way out. She used it to good effect on her bonds before sweeping off the hood and moving to free Megan. Soon, only D'Angelo and the unconscious senator remained. Picking up one of the discarded weapons, Megan covered D'Angelo while Cassandra finished freeing Lia.

"You defied the Council. I won't be the last with these orders," D'Angelo declared. His eyes locked on Cassandra.

Faint sirens could be heard in the distance.

"Give me the gun," Megan said to Lia. "You two need to leave right now."

The girl hesitated. Confusion and suspicion marked her expression.

"The agent's right," Cassandra said. "We can't be here when help comes." Picking up one of the tranquilizer guns, she calmly shot D'Angelo. "That will take a moment to fully kick in. She'll need the weapon in the meantime."

The handover went smoothly. Cassandra promised to be in touch and ushered her young apprentice out through the secret passage.

"You're making … a mistake." D'Angelo's head lolled to the side and his statement had a dreamy quality to it.

"I have a habit of that, but who's keeping score?" asked Megan.

Chapter 14:
Leave the Demons

Attending a funeral wasn't exactly what Megan had planned to do the last day of her vacation, but she wanted to support Daniel Cooper and his family during their time of sorrow. His great-aunt, Edith Shipley, had passed away the same night Megan had been kidnapped. Apparently, Edith had made quite an impact during her long life and throughout her career as an elementary school teacher.

The program format was unlike any funeral Megan had ever attended. The graveside service had taken place earlier in the morning with only family and a few close friends present. This service functioned as a celebration of life. It started off with a short, powerful sermon on appreciating every moment of life then moved into a time of sharing by family members. After that, the pastor opened the mike to anyone who wanted to share memories and anecdotes about the lady. Megan thought that might be awkward, but a line immediately formed and didn't slow down for forty minutes. Dozens of people stood up to share how Ms. Shipley had shaped their lives.

After a time, the stories started blending together, but Megan appreciated getting to vicariously know this vibrant soul she had only met briefly. Through their stories, she got a clear picture of a woman both fearless and outspoken yet also humble and kind. She'd loved to "make joyful noise" even though God had not blessed her with the ability to carry a tune. She visited sick people and brought them tubs of homemade chicken soup. No event was too big or too small for her to grace with her presence even if the connection was tenuous.

"I think Ms. Shipley attended graduation at Parkside High for thirty-five years straight," said one young woman. Her voice caught as she fought off sobs. "Mine was the last she attended. See, I'm an orphan raised by my grandma. Ms. Shipley sought me out to ask for one of my graduation tickets because she knew I didn't have any other family to give it to, besides Grandma. She said she wanted to 'cheer me on as I moved out into the wider world.'"

"I became a dentist because of Ms. Shipley's career day project," said a middle-aged man. "All the other kids wanted to be soldiers, cops, and firefighters, but not me. They started to make fun of my choice, but Ms. Shipley supported it. In fact, she asked about it every year until I entered grad school. And yes, she came to my graduation too, even though it was a three-hour drive away."

When the last person who wanted to speak had their chance, the pastor closed out that section with a prayer.

"Holy Father, we come before you today to celebrate our sister and your daughter. Edith sure loved Jesus, and He loved her more. Thank you for every moment we had with her and for every blessing she's delivered into our lives. Give us peace through our grief. Help us not to dwell on what's missing but to daily renew our commitment to honor her memory by living each day to the fullest. Amen."

The crowd echoed the last word and stood when the pastor motioned for them to rise. He led them in two hymns to give the family time to move to the back of the church. Megan particularly liked the one titled "What Wondrous Love is This" as it seemed to capture the strange mixture of sorrow and joy permeating the air.

"On behalf of the family, I'd like to thank you all for coming," said the pastor. "Please join us downstairs for a time of fellowship and refreshment before departing."

The promise of food caused every child to make a mad dash for the stairs. Megan sat down to wait out the rush. The three sets of doors at the back of the sanctuary were open, but most people headed for the middle set to give the family final condolences. She needed the time to compose some thoughts anyway.

Gentle piano music still floated throughout the air, lending to the somber atmosphere.

A woman wearing a decorative headscarf sat down next to her.

"Agent," said the woman.

Megan stiffened instinctively but forced herself to relax. Knocking her program to the floor, she leaned over to pick it up.

"What are you doing here?" she hissed, casting a sideways look at Cassandra Mirren.

The bits of hair sticking out from under the scarf were jet black. A small mole decorated the bottom left side of her chin.

"That's some makeover," Megan commented, forcing herself to stare at the program.

"What does anyone do at a funeral? I'm saying goodbye," said Cassandra, "but I figured you needed one more chance to unload some questions first. I owe you that much."

Fiddling with the program, Megan nodded absently. She could fill three hours with the questions crowding her head, and she had minutes at the most to voice them.

"Do you know the fate of our misguided friend?" asked Megan. She almost didn't want to know. The last she saw of D'Angelo involved an officer helping him into the back of a cruiser.

"He's been hired by my former employer," replied Cassandra.

"Should I be worried about that?" inquired Megan.

"Not particularly," assured Cassandra. "Official status means he'll be on a much tighter leash. Besides, they'll want to keep him far away from anything having to do with you for at least a few years. I think things should work out all right with him."

"Will *you* be all right?" The question surprised Megan. She really wanted to ask: *Where will you go? What will you do? How will you live? How long will you be gone this time?*

Cassandra must have sensed the other questions lurking.

"I tend to land on my feet, same as you, but leaving the past behind has been harder than anticipated."

"What happens to the kid and her family?" Megan couldn't imagine the emotional fallout Lia must be experiencing.

"She's taking them to a safe place," Cassandra answered. "They have some catching up to do, and it's time the good senator retired."

"You're ... okay with what happened?" Megan wondered. Tricked or not, she wasn't sure she could forgive and forget somebody for trying to kill her. She glanced around to make sure nobody was close enough to eavesdrop.

"I'm *not* okay with you being dragged into this," said Cassandra. "That's why I'm not leaving you a card this time. I'm going to take my demons with me."

Megan wasn't surprised at the conversation's turn, but it frustrated her all the same.

"Leave the demons. We can fight them together."

"What do you want from me, Megan?" Cassandra's quiet question finally betrayed some emotion.

"I want you to admit that you can't protect somebody by running away," Megan said, "And I want you be safe and happy, and running forever doesn't sound conducive to either."

"As soon as I can arrange some things, I plan on a quiet retirement, but I'll be watching your career." Cassandra's tone fell back into its usual cool, confident stride. "Somehow, I doubt you're capable of laying low. I might not be able to help directly, but I have a good number of friends who owe me favors."

"Don't worry about me," said Megan. "I have a badge, a gun, and a stubborn streak the size of this state. I'll be fine. You're the one with disgruntled former bosses sending hitmen."

"Gatton has agreed to help me deal with them," Cassandra assured Megan. "You don't need the details, but he's in a position to require my assistance. They won't be a threat much longer."

"Will you let me help?" asked Megan.

Cassandra hesitated before replying.

"I appreciate the offer. It really means a lot, but no."

"Why?"

Surprisingly, Cassandra reached over and placed her left hand on Megan's right one.

"Because of the three of us, you alone have the chance at a normal life. Gatton's got his company and billions of dollars to balance, and I'm a ghost. We just heard how precious each moment can be and how powerful normal human interactions can be. Since you have that chance, take it. Leave these demons to us. You'll find new ones to play with, I'm sure."

Cassandra rose.

Swallowing hard, Megan looked directly into Cassandra's eyes, noticing the vibrant green color for the first time.

Contacts.

That reminded her she still had the Eagle Eyes contacts in.

"Wait a moment," said Megan. Patting her suit pocket, she found the fluid-filled case meant to hold the contacts. Carefully removing each, Megan tucked them into their homes, twisted the lids on securely, and held the package out to Cassandra. "Will you deliver these to the boy wonder for me? I think I'm done with them."

"He said you could keep them as his gift, but given the amount of strings they come with, it's probably for the best." Cassandra accepted the proffered case. "Be safe, Agent."

"You too, Assassin."

The brief touch of their hands let Megan glimpse the bruises on Cassandra's wrist. Folding the program, Megan dropped it into her purse, which had somehow survived its stint in a Dallas garbage can. She also let her gaze linger on the shoes. They'd been found abandoned in the same truck that had delivered Megan to Carmichael's mansion.

When she looked up, Cassandra was gone.

"Aunt Maggie!" The exclamation came in the loudest stage whisper possible.

A small, blond figure slammed into Megan.

"Daddy said to give you this!"

A pile of crumbs dropped into Megan's lap followed by a greasy napkin.

"They have chocolate chips!" Giggles shouted, forgetting to whisper. Ashley Ann Cooper beamed up at Megan. The chocolate outline to her lips said she'd sampled them during the delivery.

"Thank you. They look delicious," said Megan.

"I ate two!" The girl followed the declaration with her signature round of giggles.

"I think you're wearing two," said Dan Cooper, gently tugging his daughter away from Megan so he could clean the kid's face.

Megan used the time to brush the pile of crumbs back into the napkin, fold it into a little pouch, and slip the whole thing into her pocket.

Ashley whined and made a face until Dan suggested she see if there was a cookie left for her mother and sister. They watched her sprint through the main aisle, intent on her errand. The sanctuary suddenly felt empty, though several stragglers still lingered about.

"Thanks for coming," Dan murmured.

"That's what partners—and friends—are for," said Megan.

"We should head down and make sure Giggles leaves some cookies for the guests," said Dan. "Are you flying back tomorrow?"

"Yes, sir," Megan answered. "It'll be a full day of travel from Dallas back to Vegas then on to Honolulu. I think this vacation requires at least three weeks of normal work to recover from."

THE END

Thank You for Reading!

I sincerely hope you've enjoyed Megan Luchek's Eagle Eyes adventures. If you'd like to read more about this agent, reach out and let me know.

I try to keep several of my books permanently free. Visit my website: juliecgilbert.com to find a link to the current free works. If it's down for some reason, please email your interest to **devyaschildren@gmail.com,** and I will get you entered as soon as possible.

Join "Julie C. Gilbert's Special Agents" on Facebook for monthly book discussions and additional giveaways.

Sincerely,

Julie C. Gilbert

Other Contacts:
Facebook: **https://www.facebook.com/JulieCGilbert2013**
Instagram: **https://www.instagram.com/juliecgilbert_writer/**
Twitter: **https://twitter.com/authorgilbert**
Bookbub Partner link: **https://www.bookbub.com/authors/julie-c-gilbert**